A Dancer's Guide to Africa

Also by Terez Mertes Rose

Off Balance
Outside the Limelight

A Dancer's Guide to Africa is set in Gabon, Central Africa. A map, glossary, pronunciation guide and further information about the country can be found, courtesy of The Classical Girl, via the following link: http://www.theclassicalgirl.com/zee-africa-page/

A Dancer's Guide to Africa

A Novel

Terez Mertes Rose

Published in the United States
Classical Girl Press - www.theclassicalgirl.com
Cover design by James T. Egan, BookFly Design, LLC
Formatting by Polgarus Studio

ISBN (ebook) 978-0-9860934-4-9
ISBN (print) 978-0-9860934-5-6

Library of Congress Control Number: 2018905819

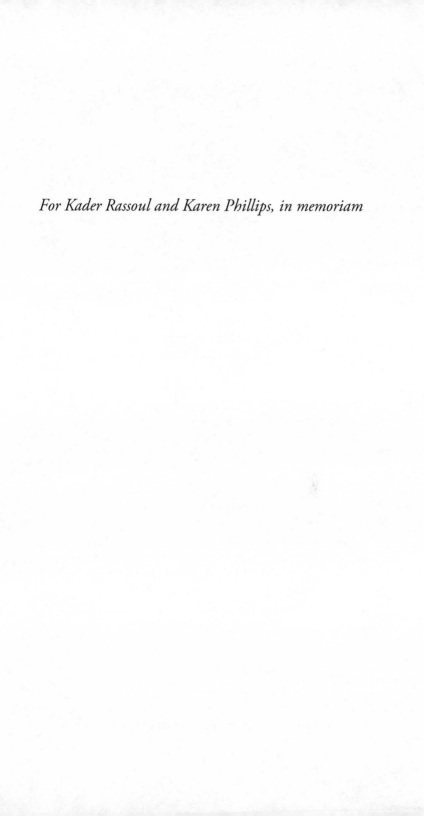

For Kader Rassoul and Karen Phillips, in memoriam

And those who were seen dancing were thought to be insane by those who could not hear the music.

— Friedrich Wilhelm Nietzsche

1990 K Street, N.W.
Washington, D.C. 20526
March 17, 1988

Dear Fiona Garvey,

Congratulations! You have been selected to join the Peace Corps 1988 Training Group for Gabon. Enclosed are reporting instructions for your Staging and Departure from Washington D.C. to Gabon, Central Africa.

You have been assigned to the English Teaching program. Upon your arrival in Gabon, you will take part in an intensive eight-week training program, which will include pedagogical training, French language instruction and cross-cultural training.

Your host country, Gabon, is a sparsely populated, politically stable country of just over one million, independent since 1960. Straddling the equator on the west coast of Africa, it is approximately the size of Colorado, mostly covered by rainforest. Gabon's climate is warm, humid and overcast in the dry seasons (May – September, December – January) and hot and humid in the rainy seasons the rest of the year. The country receives about 99 inches of rain a year.

Gabon is a relatively wealthy African country, rich in natural resources, including petroleum, manganese, uranium and wood; however, rural communities benefit little from its wealth. Gabon's largest city and capital, Libreville, is home to approximately one-third of the total population. More than half of the people live in rural towns and villages and practice subsistence slash-and-burn agriculture.

Please complete all your forms and read the Peace Corps handbook included. We look forward to meeting with you in person in Washington D.C. in June, prior to your departure for Gabon.

Sincerely,

Evie

Evie Kavanaugh
Staging Coordinator, Gabon Training Group

Part One
The Trainee

Chapter 1

The first thing I noticed was the AK-47, cradled in the arms of the Gabonese military checkpoint guard. That, and the fact that the man looked angry. He sprang to attention as our dust-caked van rolled to a stop, clutching his rifle close, arms at rigid angles. A steel bar, supported by two rusting oil drums, stretched across the unpaved road, preventing us from passing without his permission. Since my arrival in Gabon seventy-two hours prior, part of a group of twenty-six trainees, I'd discovered military checkpoints were common in Africa. At the first one, outside the Gabonese capital of Libreville, the guard had waved us through without rising from his seat. At the second, a soldier was sleeping in a chair tipped against a cinder-block building. Only the noise of our honking had awakened him. But this third official took his job seriously.

Inside the Peace Corps van, I glanced around to see if anyone else noticed the danger we were in. No one was looking. Animated chatter filled the overheated van. "Um, excuse me?" I called out over the din, my voice abnormally high. "Someone with a big gun out there looks very angry." My seatmate and fellow English-teaching trainee, Carmen, leaned over me to peer out.

"Whoa," she murmured, "he kind of does. Cool!"

Her fascination shouldn't have surprised me. Carmen seemed to embrace the gritty, the provocative, evidenced by her multiple piercings, dark spikey hair, heavy eyeliner and combat boots. Although we were the same age, twenty-two, I would have given her a wide berth back home. Here, she'd become my closest friend.

Together we watched the guard draw closer. His eyes glowed with a fanatic's fervor, as if he were drunk on his own power. Or simply drunk. The authorities here bore little resemblance to the clean-cut police officers back in Omaha who patrolled the suburban neighborhoods, stopping me in my dented Ford Pinto to politely inquire whether I was aware of how fast I'd been driving. That world seemed very far away.

Our van driver, a short, wiry Gabonese man, stepped out of the vehicle and waved official-looking papers at the guard. By the determined shake of the guard's head after he'd perused them, it clearly wasn't enough.

The two began a heated discussion. When the driver held up a finger and disappeared back into the van, the guard scowled, tightening his grip on his weapon. Restlessly he scanned the van windows and caught my worried gaze. And held it.

I am going to die. The thought rose in me, pure and clairvoyant.

I pulled away from the window in terror. "He's staring at me!"

"What are you talking about?" Carmen peered closer out the window.

"No, stop." I yanked her arm. "I don't want him to look this way."

"Fiona. He wasn't looking at you. He was looking at the group of us."

"No, he wasn't," I insisted. "He was looking for someone to single out."

Someone to pull from the bus and shoot. The thought, however irrational, made my gut clench in fear.

Carmen studied me quizzically. "You know, they say taking your weekly dose of Aralen gives you weird-assed dreams. Even violent dreams. You didn't just take your Aralen, did you?"

4

"No! And are you saying you don't find this angry military guy with a gun more than a little scary?"

"I do not. I mean, I would if it were just him and me on an empty road at night. But we're a van full of Peace Corps volunteers and trainees. How sweetly innocent is *that?* This is Gabon, not Angola. And besides, do you see anyone else in this van getting anxious?"

I glanced around to see if anyone else was bothered by the danger. Conversations had continued without pause. Aside from the occasional idle glance out the window, no one was paying the drama any attention.

"No, I don't," I admitted.

Our van driver returned to the checkpoint guard. He said something that made the guard relax his grip on the rifle. He opened one hand and accepted the two packs of cigarettes our driver offered him. Pocketing them, he gestured to a structure adjacent to his building, and the two of them strolled toward it.

"You know, I'm not sure who won," Carmen said.

I released the breath I'd been holding. "At least he didn't shoot off his gun."

Another uniformed guard crunched over to our van. "*Descendez, descendez,*" he called out in a bored voice.

Carmen and I exchanged worried glances. The volunteers in the van rose, grumbling and stretching.

"What's going on?" Daniel, another English-teaching trainee, asked, frozen halfway between sitting and standing.

One of the volunteers shrugged. "Checkpoints...."

This wasn't part of the plan and that concerned me. We were supposed to arrive at our training site in Lambaréné by mid-afternoon. We'd already stopped once for a flat tire and another time for a steamy, bug-infested half-hour, the reason never made clear. No one else seemed bothered by all these delays. Or worried. I could only fret to myself as we descended from the Peace Corps van into the staggering humidity, squinting at the overhead sunlight. Away from the city, deep inside the country's interior, the whine of insects was a noisy symphony of clicks, buzzes and drones. Jungly trees crowded the landscape, broken only by the red-dirt road and clearing. A group of children, wearing an assortment of ragged thrift-store castoffs, shrieked at our sudden appearance and ran from us. The rifle-toting soldier and our driver had disappeared.

"But what's the problem?" I quavered, trudging behind the others over to a mud-and-wattle shack set up next to the checkpoint station. "How long will we be here?"

"Who knows?" a volunteer named Rich replied. "Long enough to have a Regab." He entered the shack and we followed like ducks. In the dim room, lit by sunlight filtering through cracks, Rich pointed to a table where our driver was sitting, relaxed in conversation with the guard. Both clutched wine-sized green bottles of beer. Regab.

"There's malaria, of course," Rich was telling us after we'd grouped around a back table, armed with our own tepid Regabs. "Then filaria, hepatitis, typhoid…." He ticked off the diseases on his fingers, undistracted by the whispers and giggles of the children who'd returned. Through gaps in the wall, I could see them outside: a half-dozen pairs of eyes watching our every move.

"Don't forget giardia," a woman sitting next to me on the bench sang out. "Purple burps and green farts," she added for explanation.

"These are diseases a person might theoretically get here?" I asked.

"They're diseases the volunteers have right now," Rich replied.

"You're telling me someone's walking around with malaria?"

"That would be me," he stated with obvious pride.

I scrutinized him. Tangled blond curls framed his gaunt, stubbled face, but there he sat across from me in a poncho-like shirt with wild swirls of color, swigging his Regab and chuckling as if having malaria were great fun.

"Aren't you, like, supposed to be delirious and burning with fever?" Carmen asked.

He shrugged. "The fever and chills come and go. I feel like shit at the moment, but hey, might as well drink and have a reason to feel that way."

I stared at him, uneasy. "I thought taking Aralen kept us from getting malaria."

"In principle, yes. But it's chloroquine-based and the mosquitoes are becoming chloroquine-resistant." He wagged a finger at all the trainees. "You're not safe from *anything* here." At his pronouncement, the contents of my stomach—an earlier lunch of mystery meat in fiery sauce over rice—leapt around.

"Oh, don't go scaring them," the purple-burps woman told Rich, her pale, sweaty face earnest. "It's been years since a volunteer in Gabon has died, and it's usually from car accidents anyway. Aside from intestinal parasites and skin fungi, I've never gotten sick. If it weren't for the stares that make you feel like a circus freak, and problem students in the classroom, life here would be a breeze. Well," she added after a moment's reflection, "except for those packages from home that keep getting torn into at the post office and arriving to me empty. Oh, and the loneliness, of course. That's a killer. But hey, there's Regab." She raised her bottle and paused to regard it with something akin to reverence.

"Have you talked to Christophe about the post office business?" Rich asked her.

"No. Think I should?"

"Definitely. He might know someone there."

"This guy, Christophe," Carmen said. "I heard someone else mention his name. Is he Peace Corps staff?"

"Only as a trainer for you English teachers. But his father's the Gabonese Minister of Tourism, so he knows a lot of people."

Regab seemed exotic, heavier and darker than the Coors Light I drank back home, but very drinkable, in the end. It began to soothe my jangled nerves, numb my overstimulated brain. Sitting in a dark shack in the sultry equatorial African interior almost became the grand adventure it was supposed to be. Pinging foreign music blared from a battery-operated cassette player. Two chickens crooned and wove their way around our ankles, pecking at the dirt floor. Inconceivable to think that only five days prior, I'd been in Washington, D.C. with the other twenty-five Peace Corps Gabon trainees, beginning preparation for our two-year assignment.

The delay extended into another twenty-four-ounce beer. Apparently our driver didn't have all the correct papers qualifying him to drive a group of us in the Peace Corps van. Chuck Martin, Peace Corps Gabon's country director, also en route to the Lambaréné training, could solve the problem with a signature. When he showed up. I drank more Regab and pressed the bottle to my sweaty face. Carmen fanned herself with her *Welcome to Gabon!* leaflet. "I need to use a bathroom," I mumbled to her. "Where do you suppose it is?"

"Got me." She shrugged and grinned. "I think you need to go ask those friendly guys at the checkpoint next door."

Instead I asked the bar owner, in careful textbook French, the next time she brought beers to our table. "*Là-bas,*" she told me, pursing her lips in the direction of the back door. Over there. "Follow the path," she added in French.

"Want company?" Carmen asked.

"No thanks." I teetered through the bar and stumbled outside where the brightness momentarily blinded me. The Regab, heat and jet lag had made me queasy and disoriented as well. But I found the path and started down it.

The forest directly behind the checkpoint station appeared scraggly, commonplace. The thin trees and spindly brush were like something I might have found in rural Nebraska. The number of flies, however, was remarkable, as was their tenacity. Waving them away from my ears, nose and mouth, I wandered down the foot-worn path, in search of the latrine. Past the clearing, weedy scrub rose on either side of the path, up to my waist. I began to wonder if my translation for *là-bas* as "over there" was way off. Because I'd gone pretty *là-bas* and I was nowhere. The marching cadence, however, relaxed me. In the past week, through the Peace Corps stateside training and the group's transatlantic flight to Gabon, I'd rarely been alone. And I craved solitude the way I craved dance.

Dance. My ballet practice.

The thought made me stumble. To deflect my attention from the sadness that billowed up like a storm cloud, I focused on my sister, Alison. Alison and her boyfriend. The rage kicked in, clearing my head, making me feel strong again.

Okay, so maybe the Peace Corps business had been a mistake. At least it had offered me an escape. Nine months ago, back in September, Dad had given me an ultimatum. I'd just commenced my fifth year of undergraduate studies—the cost of changing degree programs twice—performing with a local dance company, enjoying life precisely as it was.

"Time to wrap it up, Fiona," Dad told me. "Get that psychology degree—"

"—Sociology degree," I corrected.

"Fine. Get your bachelor's degree and go find work. A real job, not just dancing."

Dutifully I dropped by the university placement center the next day, where I scanned the listings of job offers and recruiting interviews tacked up on the bulletin board. My heart sank further with each one I read. Actuary. Oscar Meyer sales rep. Claims adjuster. UPS supervisor. No, no and no. They all seemed to want to crush something unnamed and precious within my soul, that only dance brought me.

Then I spied a Peace Corps brochure. Teaching English in Africa sounded responsible and yet romantic. To placate Dad and my own anxiety over leaving dance, I started up the application process. The CARE commercials on television, after all, had always touched me, with their drama and beautiful background music. I visualized myself, noble and selfless, helping rid the world of poverty. Africa would be real life, a true adventure, yet something with soul.

The acceptance letter six months later, after a series of interviews, made me want to run the other way. Somehow my grand idea, viewed up close, had lost all its charm. I told my family about the letter, more for show than because I was going to do it. But while Mom and Dad congratulated me, I saw my two siblings exchange glances.

"You're still playing with that idea?" Russell, the eldest and the family's academic super-achiever, asked.

Alison, the family's beauty queen—literally: she'd been Miss Nebraska four years earlier, in 1984—didn't speak at first. Her expression creased in bemusement before she shook her head and began to chuckle. "Oh, Fiona," was all she said.

I knew what that shake of my older sister's head meant. I'd seen it constantly through my bumpy, awkward, adolescent and university years. It was the pained look you gave someone who'd just stepped in dog shit. This, on top of the most recent humiliation and grief she'd caused me. I had to get away from her. The Peace Corps was my ticket out.

"Yes, I'm still 'playing' with that idea." I glared at them. "In fact, I've decided to accept."

And so I did it. Except now I was stuck in Africa for two years, thanks to my sister—and, admittedly, my pride. But I was going to stick it out, even if it killed me. Which, evidently, it might.

It dawned on me that I'd walked for a long time without seeing the latrine. "Screw this," I muttered. Stepping away from the path, I squatted down to pee. Afterward, smoothing my skirt back into place, I turned around and headed back. But the return began to confuse me, after the path forked. I stopped and looked around. Had that grove of banana trees been there before? After another minute of walking, my heart began to pound against my ribs. I retraced my steps back to the fork and went the other way. It was worse—I recognized nothing. Five minutes later, I turned around again. This time, I could find no fork at all. Dizzy and nauseous, I began to trot, stumbling on a gnarled vine half-buried beneath the path. I followed the path until I came to a new fork. Or had I taken this fork? The overhead equatorial sun offered no directional clues. It sank in that I was hopelessly lost.

I dropped to my haunches, covering my face with my hands, my breath coming in short, panicked gasps.

"*Eh… Ntang, wa ka ve?*"

I dropped my hands and looked up. Like a mirage, a tiny, dusty African woman had appeared out of nowhere. She stood in front of me in bare feet, bent from the wicker basket load on her back. A twig poked out of her matted hair. She wore a sheet of fabric, the print faded with age, wrapped around her body like a bath towel. As I stood up, her face broke into a wide grin, revealing gaps from missing teeth. Her milky-brown eyes lit up in pleasure as she reached out with both hands to clasp mine in greeting.

"*Ntang, wa ka ve?*" she repeated, pumping my hand. She smelled smoky.

"Uh … *bonjour.*" I pasted a bright smile on my face.

"Ah, *madame.*" She beamed at me. In French, I explained I was lost, and could she help me find the checkpoint station? She bobbed her head and cackled. It dawned on me that she didn't understand French. I imitated an AK-47 with my arms, putting a fierce look on my face. She nodded and patted me. She began talking, a patter of incomprehensible language in a soothing, hypnotic voice. Her face was serious, eyes riveted to mine as if this would make me understand her language better.

"I'm sorry," I interrupted in English, my voice breaking. "I don't understand a word you're saying and I'm lost and I'm starting to freak out here. That stupid Regab…"

At this, her eyes lit up. "Regab, *oye!*"

"Regab, yes? Regab—to buy, to drink!" I mimed gulping down a big bottle, tossing my head back and making glugging actions. "Where—" I placed my hand over my eyes and with sweeping theatrical gestures, pretended to scope out the scenery, "—is Regab? With guns?"

This time she understood my rifle imitation. Taking me by the hand, she led me back the way I'd come. For a few minutes, I heard only the hushed rustle of the grass as we passed. Even the bugs seemed to be holding their breath.

We arrived at the fork. "Regab," she said, and pointed to the right.

I paused. I'd tried this way already. She sensed my hesitation and made a little "eh" noise and nudged me down the trail. After a few steps, I turned around.

"Please, *mama*, this isn't the right…" I started.

No one was in sight. The woman had disappeared into the grasses as silently as she'd come. A chill crept over me, in spite of the sweat pouring down my back. She'd been there and now she wasn't. But I had no time to ponder the woman's disappearance. Pushing down my panic, I hurried past the trees until I heard the sound of voices and laughter. The trail rounded a bend to reveal the clearing, the two buildings, the Peace Corps van, which, in my absence, had become two, with my fellow trainees and volunteers milling around.

Chuck, the Peace Corps country director, a burly, vibrant man with a buzz-cut, had arrived. "There you are, Fiona," he said. "We were wondering what happened to you."

"I don't know where that latrine was that they were talking about. I went forever and got lost."

He glanced to his right. My gaze followed his down a better traveled path, at the end of which stood a wooden outhouse.

"Oh," I said. "Okay."

As we walked together to where the others were starting to board the vans, I caught sight of the checkpoint guard. "Peace Corpse, *oye!*" he called out to everyone as they boarded. A broad grin now covered his face. He waved his arms, benevolent as a mother seeing her first-grader off to school, the image marred only by the presence of the rifle in one hand.

It was all too weird. I slowed down.

Chuck glanced over at me. "What's wrong?"

It took me a moment to decipher my uneasy feeling. First, the rabid guard who was now our buddy. Malaria Rich and his stories. Getting lost. The old woman. My intestines began to grumble, in tandem with my pounding head. I didn't know what I'd seen out there or how I'd gotten un-lost or what had happened. Gabon was feeling a little like The Twilight Zone.

"It's just that…things here don't make sense."

Chuck's face widened into a smile.

"Welcome to Africa. You'll be saying that a lot."

Chapter 2

Twelve Gabonese students regarded me as I approached the front of the classroom. Through the latticed walls that doubled as windows, I could see across the dusty courtyard into another classroom, where a fellow English-teaching trainee was performing the same show. I turned to face my students, adolescents in blue and white uniforms. They sat at their desks, eager and expectant, their hands folded on the wooden desktops. Aside from the shrieks of nearby roosters and the rattle of trucks over potholed roads, silence reigned. The girls' dark eyes, fixed on me, seemed both innocent and worldly. The boys looked younger, painfully shy. Whenever they stood to speak, their hands swooped down to cup their genitals.

It was the first day of practice school, after three weeks of preparing with trainers. My voice shook with nervousness. Sweat dampened my cotton blouse. The students, all here voluntarily, repeated the five new English vocabulary words after me. By the end of the hour, they were turning to each other and asking, "What's this?"

"It's a pen."

"A pencil?"

"No, it's a pen."

"Oh. Thank you for the pen!"

And like that, they were chatting in English, these kids who'd never spoken a word of the language before setting foot in this classroom. They could greet me, confirm whether a pen or pencil was in my hand, thank me and say goodbye. It felt like a small miracle.

Beaming, I looked to the back of the room to see if Christophe, my trainer, could appreciate how well I'd done. He stood there, arms folded, his expression cool, assessing.

I'd blown it when I first met him, but in my defense, I'd had other things on my mind. Like survival. Acclimating to this strange new place I lived. Absorbing impressions that had flashed by too fast since our arrival: the complexity of French; the rickety dorm beds; the communal bathroom with its stand-up toilets and the sour, bitter smell of a zoo on a hot afternoon; the names of my African and American trainers. The morning of our first teacher training session, I'd still felt rattled and disoriented. But I'd tried to be helpful, moving surplus boxes out of our classroom for Meg, the training coordinator and education volunteer leader. Unable to see around an oversized stack, I bumped into someone when I approached the door. The boxes tumbled to the floor as both of us recoiled with murmurs of annoyance. When we straightened, we met at the same height of five-foot-eight. I hadn't seen this guy before. I would have remembered. The other African trainers were vibrant, well-dressed and confident, but still friendly and accessible. This stranger seemed as polished and unapproachable as a movie star in his starched button-down shirt and tailored trousers. His skin was the color of melted Hershey's chocolate. Startling green eyes punctuated his regal, fine-boned face.

"You're tall." He spoke the words with disdain, easily pronouncing the "r" that plagued the other African French speakers on the compound.

I was accustomed to exceptionally attractive people, having shared a home with one for many years. I'd learned not to feed their egos. Furthermore, this guy had knocked down my boxes but frowned at me as though it had been all my fault.

"No," I matched his tone, "it's just that you're short."

Silence followed. Shocked outrage swept over his smooth face, as if I'd pulled up my shirt and flashed my breasts at him. Before either of us could apologize or introduce ourselves, however, Meg breezed in and surveyed the scattered boxes. "Whoops," she said, "Christophe, how about giving Fiona a hand here?"

"I'd be happy to help Fiona." He glanced at me again, his expression now unreadable.

So this was *the* Christophe, the government minister's son. I'd just insulted one of the most important Gabonese in the Peace Corps community. I wanted to cry. Instead, I grabbed half the boxes, deposited them where they belonged, and made a beeline to the courtyard, framed by a cluster of low, whitewashed buildings, where I hovered out of view until our session started.

But Christophe was all composure and decorum in the classroom thereafter. He was, I had to admit, a highly qualified trainer. He'd taught English in Gabon for four years and spoke perfect, idiomatic English from his years of living in Washington, D.C., where his father had been a high-ranking diplomat. I disliked the style he advocated, though: overly structured and unsmiling. I thought teaching English should be more like a show. I'd spent years performing onstage; I knew you had to smile and act lively in order to engage your audience. His method made no sense. When I complained in a training session, he asked me who the trainer was. I whispered to Carmen that he must have forgotten who the native English speakers were. This elicited a snort of laughter from her, but glares from Christophe and Keisha, another one of the trainers.

After the first practice class, Christophe met with me to discuss my teaching. He wore cologne, an expensive-smelling citrus blend that made me want to lean in closer to sniff his neck, a prospect so idiotic and alarming, I felt even more uncomfortable around him.

"You see your 'entertainment method' working here," he said, tapping his pencil on the critique form for emphasis, "but you had twelve students, all of whom wanted to be here. At your post, you will have anywhere between thirty and eighty students in a room the same size. Once the novelty of having a pretty American teacher wears off, they will grow bored, undisciplined."

The determined set of his face left no room for further discussion. But that wasn't going to stop me. I raised my hand timidly.

He frowned. "There's no need to raise your hand. What is it?"

"If they grow bored, aren't you, as the teacher, responsible for presenting something more interesting?"

His face remained composed, but he took a long time to breathe in and out before replying. "The teacher's job is to teach. That is the role for which I am training you. Please endeavor to focus on that."

I offered him a bright smile. "Thanks for the feedback! I'll be sure and keep it in mind."

He didn't smile back. "I hope you do."

French class and cultural awareness sessions followed practice school. Afterwards, I escaped to the dorm room Carmen and I shared, a cramped space that held a desk, plastic chairs and two rickety metal-framed cots. I dropped onto my mattress, a pad with the thickness of sandwich bread. Carmen found me there ten minutes later, reading.

"You spend too much time in here," she said. "Robert and I are going into town for a beer. You should join us." She and Robert, another English-teaching trainee, had become close friends, hitting it off when he admired her combat boots. Carmen ran her hand through her hair to freshen her spikes before nudging my cot.

"C'mon, I won't take no for an answer."

Lambaréné was one of Gabon's main cities, a large inland island that bisected the Ogooué River. The smell of waterlogged foliage battled with the diesel fumes of rumbling trucks and overripe odors from the market, a noisy place choked with people, dust, chickens and produce. Robert led us through the crowds to his favorite bar, the backyard of a bright blue house on the periphery of the action. We found seats under the protection of a giant coconut palm, at a picnic table. Inside the house, pots clanged in dinner preparation. Outside, hens clucked, children giggled and shouted. A goat snuffled through nearby weeds. This was my favorite time of the day in Gabon. As the afternoon light grew soft, the golden rays mingled with wood smoke that curled up from neighborhood cooking fires. The air smelled sweet and comforting.

"Perfect," Robert announced. He struck me as a person who knew these kinds of things. During our training in Washington, D.C, he'd smoked Gitanes and drunk Pernod, items as exotic to me as caviar and hashish. He was a native New Yorker and always wore black tee shirts, particularly ones advertising obscure rock bands. Today it was Cantankerous Wallababies. Yesterday, it had been The Zodiac Debriefers. The only rule was it had to be black. "It's a New York thing," he told me, pushing his floppy brown hair from his face.

A woman sailed past, basket on her head, baby on her back and toddler clutching her hand. She turned without losing balance of her load and shooed away a group of loitering kids. They scattered, only to regroup around the bar, staring at us. One boy, older than the rest, took a few steps closer. He wore torn gym shorts and a grayish tee shirt displaying a fading, improbable *Los Angeles Yankees* logo. "*Bonsoir,*" he said.

"*Bonsoir,*" the three of us replied.

The boy stayed. "If you please," he began in halting English. "The hair on madame. Is this the true hair?" He pointed to my hair, which I'd freed from its ponytail. Robert and Carmen swiveled around to scrutinize it too.

I hated my hair. There was too much, it was unruly, and the color defied categorizing. Strangers would approach me back in Nebraska and demand, "Just what color *is* your hair?" The answer was usually expressed in the negative: not brown, not blond, not auburn, but an odd combination of everything. "Like sunlight filtering through autumn leaves," Mom would tell me.

"Like dirty pennies," Alison would scoff. Another thing it wasn't: a duplicate of her honey-blond tresses, groomed religiously to create a sleek curtain against her face. My sister got the enviable color, I got the scraps. Like our eyes. Hers were the intense blue of a cloudless winter sky, while mine were the palest blue possible, as if Alison had used up the pigment when she was born, eleven months before me.

"Yes," I told the boy, "this is my true hair."

He took a step closer, followed by the other children, who reached out to touch it. African hair, a stateside trainer had informed me, didn't grow much at all. My long hair would draw attention. The kids oohed and aahed before skittering away. The boy with the *Los Angeles Yankees* shirt flashed us a thumbs-up before joining the others.

"I'm already hungry," Carmen announced. "I hate those fish head and rice lunches."

"Better to have the fish heads served at lunch than dinner," Robert said. "That means they'll have something better tonight."

Fish heads still freaked me out. The first time I'd seen a serving pan of them, three dozen heads all staring with glassy eyes, I'd thought it was a practical joke, and that the real main course would be out once everyone had had a good laugh at Fiona's reaction. But the Gabonese server had only regarded me expectantly, repeating his question of whether I wanted one head or two.

"The thing that annoys me," Carmen said, "is how you have to pick and dig at that spot between their eyes—do fish have foreheads?—to get any decent meat."

"Yes, but they say the eyeballs are a delicacy," Robert said. "I tried one today."

I stared at him. "What was it like?"

"Crunchy. Piquant." He seemed pleased by my reaction.

"I remember the time my parents tried to force caviar on me," Carmen said. "It seemed very important to them that a child of theirs enjoy it. What snobs. I told them not a chance, I'd rather starve. It became a battle of wills. My father said no other food until I tried at least a bite of it. I said fine. And so I went thirty-six hours without food."

"Who won?"

"I did." Carmen grinned. "My mom couldn't handle the stress of it."

"You were a devil child," Robert said, chuckling.

"I was. My dad liked to tell me that their original plan had been to have multiple kids, but after I came along, they didn't think they could manage more."

"I would've loved to have been an only child," I said wistfully.

"Don't be so sure. It can get lonely."

"Better to be lonely than to always be arguing with them."

"Do you miss them?" she asked.

I paused to fortify my response with a gulp of Regab. "I'm not sure."

"Fiona… That's an unusual name for a Midwesterner," Robert said.

"My mom loves musical theater. She was going through her *Brigadoon* phase."

"I heard you say you used to perform."

"Yes. Ballet."

"Did you know the training compound has an auditorium with a stage?"

"You're kidding!"

Robert grinned at my open-mouthed reaction. "Nope. It's behind the other buildings, near the grove of palm trees. Nothing dramatic, just a big room with a stage."

"Can anyone use it?"

"I don't see why not. It's not locked or anything. The only time I've seen it in use is on Wednesday afternoons for the staff meeting."

"So you think I could slip in there and use it on Saturday afternoons?"

"Give it a try."

On Saturday afternoon, I changed into a leotard and sweatpants, and grabbed my ballet slippers and cassette player. I'd brought none of my pointe shoes to Africa. They had short life spans under the best of circumstances, and within a dozen sessions in this hot, humid environment, they would have been as soft as my infinitely more comfortable leather slippers. I hurried through the courtyard, dried leaves scudding in my wake, until I found the auditorium. The door was indeed unlocked. I trembled with excitement. Once inside, I opened a few of the shutters that doubled as windows, letting light pour in. I surveyed the room, the size of an elementary school assembly hall. The stage, a narrow wooden platform rising three feet high, was hopeless. The floor, however, once cleared of chairs, made a perfect dance space.

Using the backs of three folding chairs as my barre, I placed my leg on one and stretched over, hand around my calf, face against my shin. As the tightness in my hamstrings eased, a sense of unexpected happiness welled up in me. My chattering thoughts slowed. To the lilting strains of Chopin, I began barre with pliés, tendus and dégagés, just like back home, in every ballet class I'd ever taken. Right side first, swiveling around to repeat the exercise on the left. I could almost hear the teacher's soothing voice, leading me onward, through ronds de jamb, frappés, développés. Muscles I hadn't used in six weeks reawakened. The burn in my quads, my calves, felt good. I even welcomed the cramping in my feet as I arched and pointed, pausing afterward to massage the knot, flex and re-arch the toes, holding the position in a relevé balance.

Once I'd completed barre, I switched out cassettes. I'd made a compilation tape of favorite ballets and pieces I'd performed over the past few years. I would start, I decided, with *Interludes,* a ballet set to symphonic music by Saint-Saëns, with a mix of both energetic and lushly romantic variations.

The moment I heard the opening notes, the hard shell inside me dissolved, and I slipped right back into performing mode. Two counts of eight, near stillness, except for a pulse of the arms. Another, bigger pulse. Then movement, a sauté-chassé run, sweeping the perimeter of the performing space, heading to its center for a lunge with a full port de bras for my arms. Deprived of my practice for so many weeks, the energy poured out of me. The moves flowed, one into the other, polished and precise. My développé and arabesque extensions were absurdly high for someone who hadn't danced for six weeks. Pirouettes were rock-solid, doubles and triples, with clean landings, another unexpected gift from the dance gods.

I'm home again. I'm safe.

For the next several minutes I danced, utterly absorbed, spirits rising ever higher. The brisk first movement ended and the second movement, the adagio, began. The music here was heart-stoppingly beautiful, the melody supported by the low, sonorous chords of an organ played so softly, you could feel more than hear it. The choreography was equally sublime: a romantic pas de trois, myself the lone female interacting with two males, who supported me in promenades, turns and lifts, even as I remained elusive. I could almost feel my partners' presence, the brooding drama, the longing and desire the adagio and its music stirred up. Dancing it alone didn't feel wrong. Instead, the mood it created became even more dreamy and haunting. Almost like a sacred experience, one touched with mysticism, as I moved alone-but-not, practically fibrillating with the power a good performance always produced.

The movement ended with another deep lunge that gradually brought me down to sitting, legs at right angles. To the adagio's final notes, I shut my eyes, arched back and slowly lifted my arms to the sky.

Pure magic. My throat tightened. Prickles passed over my arms, my back, like a shimmering wave of heat. Power, indeed. But as the music wafted away, so did the safety. The mystical feeling hovered in the air for a moment longer, just out of reach, before disappearing.

The third movement commenced, brisk and propulsive, relentlessly forward.

My hands dropped down to my side. Gone, that other world. Replaced by sweaty, magic-less, inescapable reality. I shifted, pulled my legs close, rested my forehead on my knees and began to cry, choked sobs that shook my body.

The music played on. I didn't move. But when a creak by the door drew my attention, it dawned on me I had a visitor in the back of the room. Someone well dressed, regal in his posture, in his authority. A hint of expensive-smelling citrus cologne dispelled any doubts as to his identity.

I couldn't believe my bad luck. Then anger replaced disbelief. This was *my* space. Here, Christophe was the foreigner, the intruder.

And even though the magic had disappeared, the power still hovered in the air. It was my power, and he knew it.

I rose and strode over to the cassette player, which had moved on to the cheery finale. I snapped off the music and in the newfound silence, I turned and regarded him, unsmiling.

He, too, was unsmiling. He looked almost stricken.

"I'm sorry." He gestured to the door. "But it was unlocked…"

"Yes," I conceded.

He began to walk toward me. "How long have you danced?" he asked. His voice held a note of respect that, I would have argued, was impossible for someone like him to produce.

"Since I was seven."

"Why did you stop?"

"To come here."

"Were you a professional dancer?"

I shook my head. "Just a college student, performing in a local company."

"You're very good."

It felt odd to hear him compliment me. "Thank you," I said, searching for my towel to mop my sweaty face. "How long were you watching?"

"When I heard the Saint-Saëns from the courtyard, I came over here."

At this, I regarded him with surprise. "How did you know that was Saint-Saëns?"

He frowned. "Do you mean, oh, how could an African possibly be familiar with classical music?" He relaxed, waved away my stuttered defense. "An educated guess, in truth. I'm thinking his Symphony No. 3? The Organ Symphony?"

Impressive. I nodded.

"It's quite distinctive," he said.

"It is."

"My mother taught me to enjoy classical music," he said. "She's half French. She grew up in Paris and had a lot of exposure to it. During the years we lived there, we attended the symphony, but it's the Paris Opera Ballet, of course, that's the big draw there."

He was right; the Paris Opera Ballet was as big as it got, right up next to the Kirov, the Bolshoi, The Royal Ballet.

"It's nothing I expected to see in the Peace Corps," Christophe said.

"No. Me neither. They don't blend too well, do they?"

"Maybe not. But I see you didn't let that stop you." He smiled, which transformed his face, his whole persona, into something dazzling. A mock-stern expression followed. "This certainly explains that habit you have of performing in the classroom."

This time, I could only laugh. As I tried to wipe the sweat off my face with my arm, he pulled a neatly folded, monogrammed handkerchief from his pocket and tossed it to me. I caught it with a grin. I knew at that moment—the way you know about a good pair of pointe shoes—that a friendship had just begun.

Chapter 3

Henry, a construction trainee, carefully balanced an empty Regab bottle on the two beneath it. The ten of us watching held our breath as Henry released his hold and slowly stepped back. "Done!" he crowed. "The third row of my pyramid creation is now complete. Gimme a beer to celebrate."

"Another empty or a full one?" asked Buzz, a construction trainee and Henry's assistant.

"A full one, of course! Actually, give me an empty, too, for row four."

It was Friday night, six weeks into our training, and all the action centered here, in the *refectoire*, the compound's enormous dining area. In addition to our group, others were doing their own thing: playing cards, gossiping, flirting. With the lights partially dimmed and African music playing from somebody's boom box, the atmosphere in the refectoire felt like a cross between a nightclub and a junior-high dance.

We all sized up Henry's efforts. He'd used two dozen bottles, and another half-dozen empties were clustered adjacent to the pyramid on the cafeteria table. "Dude, stop while you're ahead," one of the other trainees told Henry.

"Shhh." Henry unsteadily approached the pyramid again, a full beer in one hand, an empty in the other. "I need silence for my art."

Henry was the unofficial leader of the construction trainees. He looked just like what I'd expect a guy from Minnesota to look like— a burly, blond lumberjack, like the man on the Brawny paper towel packaging. He roared more than talked, his speech liberally sprinkled with obscenities. I had a hunch his gruffness was an act.

The construction trainees comprised over a third of our group of trainees, but they seemed like a different breed, filling a room with their boisterous energy. Although everyone ate meals together in the refectoire, the constructors trained for their jobs off-site. From the English-teaching classroom, I'd hear them laughing and shouting as they hopped in and out of the dusty Peace Corps Toyota pickups.

Buzz eyed my bottle. "You're almost empty," he said. He popped open two beers and handed one to me. As Henry began on the fourth row, Buzz bumped the cafeteria table. The pyramid trembled and an instant later, all the bottles came tumbling down. "Oops," Buzz said.

"You bum," Henry shouted, and gave the downed empties a swipe with his arm. A dozen of them fell to the floor where they clattered and rolled. Buzz dropped to the floor and began crawling around, retrieving the bottles and arranging them like bowling pins. Someone found an unhusked coconut to use as a bowling ball. Another construction trainee burst into song, a boozy country number, but his efforts were cut short when Henry grabbed a sweatshirt and threw it at his face.

"Hey, careful, that's my best sweatshirt," Buzz complained. He nudged a trainee named William, who was sitting in the corner. "William, we need more beer."

William, whose thick golden hair always seemed to defy gravity, was the quiet one of the group. He had a medium build, a neutral, even-featured face, and was tall in that "perfect size for partnering me" way that every tall female ballet dancer notices in men. Clearly

William wasn't a ballet guy or a performing arts guy. You looked at him and thought, "exceptionally serious and intelligent guy." He reminded me of those university students who would stand with a clipboard in front of the Student Union all day long, soliciting signatures for a petition to help save the whales. He didn't smile much, certainly not in the easy way Henry did. He was the only one in our training group who'd worn African attire prior to leaving the U.S.

"Buzz," William said without moving, "go get that beer."

"But you're drinking the most."

"I don't think so."

"Oh hell, I'll get more beer," the singing trainee said, struggling to his feet.

Carmen and I exchanged grins. "Now, isn't this better than hiding in your room, reading?" she asked. "Aren't you glad I dragged you out?"

"I am." I took a sip of beer and glanced around until my eyes settled on the trainers, congregating across the room. Keisha, a perpetually frowning, heavyset, African-American volunteer, was talking with Christophe and several of the French-language teachers. I studied the Africans' animated faces, the way their tapering fingers fluttered to illustrate their stories and how their bodies moved and swayed as if involved in a never-ending dance. Christophe's skin, I decided, wasn't the color of milk chocolate at all, but more like coffee with a dollop of heavy cream added, giving it a luscious toffee hue. In contrast, Toussaint, from Senegal, had ebony-colored skin. When later I returned from a trip to the bathroom, I took a detour in order to pass by them. Toussaint had just put on new dance music and beckoned to me.

"*Viens*, Fiona. Come dance with us."

"*Merci, non*," I replied with a laugh. "I don't dance African."

"But she does dance," Christophe offered with a lazy smile, and for a moment, it was as if we were sharing some delicious secret. When I looked away, I noticed Keisha scrutinizing me with a greater frown than usual.

Christophe and I had established a routine. He knew I'd be in the auditorium on Saturday afternoons, practicing ballet, performing various vignettes or choreographing my own. He'd show up, feigning surprise, and stay to watch, offer his opinion on the new choreography, or inquire about ballet terms or etiquette he didn't understand. What was meant by a dancer's "lines," and was a second cast equivalent to an understudy? How long did a pair of pointe shoes last, and why didn't they make them stronger? Why did dancers wish each other *merde*—French for shit—before a performance? Did all ballet classes worldwide use the French terminology? He was always polite, deferential, which was like catnip to me.

Sometimes, as if to test this unexpected slant to our relationship, I'd switch the conversation to more personal, potentially controversial fodder. In some odd way, I still felt the need to argue with him, disagree, elicit a reaction. I sensed too few people challenged him in that way. "Tell me, how does it feel to be rich and privileged in a poor country?" I asked him the day after the Regab pyramid party.

His chin jutted forward, a sure sign that my provocation had hit its mark. But he kept his tone light. "I could ask you the same question."

"My family is far from rich," I protested. "Middle class, at best."

"Did you grow up in a home with electricity and running water? New clothes every year? Shoes? Food? Did your family have a car, a television, a washing machine?"

"Well, yes."

"And so your argument seems to be that because I was born in this country, it is wrong for me to have the same things." Scorn crept into his voice. "And as for you—you have no idea of the privilege your white skin and your Western status grant you, do you?"

As he railed on me, I analyzed him in an attempt to decipher what made African men seem so different from American men. Was it the vibrancy that seemed to lurk just beneath their skin? Or was it the graceful way they moved, making them appear so at ease in their bodies? And Christophe's eyes—who would have thought an African could have green eyes?

When he noticed I wasn't paying attention, he stopped speaking. Flustered, I fumbled for a diversion.

"Okay, I apologize for bringing it up. Clearly I didn't anticipate how defensive you'd get."

His face grew tight, his lips compressed, before his irritation dissolved into a relaxed, practiced smile. "Tell me, do you always speak this way to men?"

"No. Sometimes I'm rude."

His smile widened and he burst out laughing, an infectious sound that made me join in. "You are an unusual woman, Fiona Garvey," he said, and we grinned at each other. The moment lasted longer than it should have. Something in his eyes changed, making a bolt of heat flash through my body and settle deep in my pelvis.

Oh no. Not this. I scrambled up and busied myself, turning off the tape player and slipping my sandals back on. Christophe stayed where he was. I could feel him watching me. Finally, he spoke.

"Why are you afraid of me?"

I turned and forced myself to meet his gaze. "I'm not afraid of you. I'm just a private person. And I'm not a chatty, flirty type. Sorry to disappoint you."

He ignored my words. "You're afraid of men. You challenge them even as you run from them. The only one you trust is that clown, Robert." His tone grew softer, infinitely more dangerous. "Are you a virgin, Fiona?"

Was this acceptable African conversation, I wondered, or his attempt to challenge my composure? Heat crept up my neck and flooded my face. "No, of course I'm not," I sputtered, furious at how easily he'd flustered me.

Lane.

The memory shot through me, unbidden, unwelcome.

Lane Chatham, my one and only love. No, not a grand love, but the only person for whom I would have been willing to change, even give up ballet. A fraternity guy, more my sister Alison's social group than mine. I'd met him on campus through a chance encounter at the Student Union. He and his frat buddies, all of them good-looking jock types, had stopped to study a poster nearby, advertising my company's fall concert. Featured was my photographed self, in makeup and costume, en pointe, holding a dramatic pose. Lane and his friends had been divided on whether the elegant creature was me. I recreated the pose, right there in the Student Union, and watched Lane's eyes go soft with infatuation.

He was the most impressive guy I'd ever gone out with, classic good looks with glossy black hair and sexy, heavy-lidded brown eyes. He drove a Jaguar, wore oxford button-down shirts to class, and had the silken voice of a radio announcer, with just a hint of Savannah, Georgia in his accent. Against reason, he remained intrigued by me even after our awkward (to me) first date. He told his friends he thought I was gorgeous, exotic. I couldn't reconcile this information with my high school loser past. I was still gawky, taller than Alison, with frizzy hair that went everywhere. But Lane continued to pursue me, especially once I'd admitted I was still a virgin.

Fifteen wonderful weeks together. Or at least the first six weeks had been wonderful, roughly the time it took him to deflower me. It made me ache with shame now to consider how long I'd hung on after his interest waned. I'd have done anything for him. I *did* do anything for him. That I'd found no personal gratification from our hurried, almost distracted sexual couplings, hadn't even bothered me at the time. As for the rest, really, I should have seen it coming.

Christophe seemed to be enjoying my discomfort. "It's not easy to be a private person here. You're going to have to accept the fact that you'll be the center of intense scrutiny. People will ask you if you're married, if you would marry *them*, if you'll sleep with them. They see a single white woman, they assume she is looking for a partner. Your desire for privacy will be ignored."

"Maybe I'll just be the person I am."

"It won't work."

In irritation, I stepped to the window and looked out. The trees in the courtyard had dropped their leaves, giving the impression of an Indian summer afternoon back home. Two boys raced each other through the dead leaves, while a trio of others ran alongside a rolling tire, propelling it with a stick. "I am not about to change who I am," I called over my shoulder. "In fact, I don't think it's truly possible to change who we are, deep down."

He considered this before speaking again.

"Where have you lived, in your life?"

I kept my gaze on the scenery. "Nebraska."

"Where else?"

"Nowhere," I admitted.

A Peace Corps van rumbled up the drive. When it stopped, cries of greeting arose from a half-dozen people who spilled out of the refectoire and hurried over to the van. Christophe drew closer. I could feel him standing behind me. Dangerously close.

"And yet you feel so confident, preemptively judging your experience here," he said.

I tried to keep my voice as casual as his. "All right, point taken. I don't know how living here might change me."

"Indeed, you don't." I felt the gossamer touch of his finger against my neck, as he caressed a strand of hair that had escaped my ponytail. I couldn't breathe. My knees shook. Outside, the van doors swung open and a few strangers in jeans and sneakers hopped out. Americans, no doubt. One was a pretty woman with long, shiny black hair, who threw her arms around Keisha and hugged her. "Ah," he said. "Diana." His finger skimmed a path down my neck, my shoulder and arm, before dropping away.

"Who's Diana?" I asked, my voice barely above a whisper.

He stepped away and turned to me, his demeanor once again cool. "My girlfriend."

That evening I had no appetite for dinner. The buzz of animated conversation filling the brightly lit refectoire seemed to bounce off the plaster walls and redirect itself toward my pounding head. While Robert and Carmen chattered, I prodded my plate of rice and turkey wings with my fork. I glanced two tables over where Keisha, Christophe and Diana were sitting. When Diana reached out to caress Christophe's arm, I felt a stab of baffling possessiveness. Robert followed my gaze.

"Diana Theodorakis," he mumbled between bites of rice. "Poor little Greek-American rich girl from Boston. Math volunteer. Good looking—too bad she's taken."

I couldn't tell whether the last part was intended to serve as a taunt or as a warning. Robert wasn't stupid; he'd seen my private smiles the past few Saturday evenings. His expression, initially puzzled, had developed into a wounded "how could you?" look. He disliked Christophe and had assumed I was his ally there. It was too complicated to explain to Robert how I both liked Christophe and didn't, so I'd kept silent. Now Diana's arrival seemed to have cheered him inordinately. I ignored his comment and focused on plucking the few slim morsels of flesh from beneath the rubbery turkey skin. Diana, Robert continued, had just returned from a ten-day reunion with her parents in Crete, where the family had a vacation home. She'd come to Lambaréné for the weekend to see Christophe and Keisha, her best friend. She was said to be one of the nicest volunteers in the group.

"You sure know a lot about other people around here," Carmen commented.

"I make it my business to know," he replied. "You can never tell when it might help."

I looked up from my food to see Carmen scrutinizing me. By her concerned expression, I could tell she'd worked out the situation.

"Your spikes are sagging," I said in an attempt to change the subject. Which was true: with each passing week, she was losing her wild-girl appearance. Piercings had diminished to two per ear, the nose stud gone. As her supply of hair gel dwindled, her spikes sagged further and further downward.

"I could say the same for you and your spirits."

Meg, our training leader, approached our table, food tray in hand. "Anyone sitting here?" she asked, gesturing to the spot next to Robert.

"Go for it," Carmen said. "You can help me tell these two about our trip today."

Carmen liked to attend the Saturday daytrips, which usually involved helping a local volunteer on a project or visiting a nearby site of interest. Today had been ten miles inland, to a village where a Peace Corps school, built back in the sixties, needed a repair and repaint job. Meg and Carmen took turns recounting the experience.

"Was it work or was it fun?" asked Robert.

"I had a ball," Carmen said. "Henry and William were there. Henry's so funny. And I learned a lot more about William."

"I did too," Meg said. "A dual degree, in international development *and* civil engineering. Impressive, huh?"

"Well, not if it's from some obscure college," Robert said. "Anyone could do that."

"Um, UC Berkeley?"

"All right," Robert grumbled.

"He spent six weeks in an Ethiopian refugee camp one summer, and four weeks in Malawi the following one," Carmen added.

"Okay, I get it," Robert said. "He's super-qualified and amazing. But can he speak Amharic? Because I know how to ask for two beers in Amharic."

Carmen chuckled. "Let's go ask him." She gestured to where he and Henry were sitting.

"Fine, let's." He rose and Carmen followed him, still chuckling.

Meg and I ate in silence. "You seem a little down, Fiona," she commented.

"I'm fine," I lied.

"You should have joined us today. It was fun."

"Yeah, well, I sort of wanted to do my own thing."

"Carmen mentioned you like to practice ballet on Saturday afternoons."

"I do."

"Look. Can I be frank?" Her eyes behind her wire-framed glasses were serious.

Warily, I nodded.

"I'm going to say something you might not want to hear. You're making this little bubble for yourself, an oasis of comfortable things. Books, ballet, spending time alone, speaking only English when you can."

I didn't know how to reply. "I'm successfully learning my teaching job," I quavered.

"You are. You're a dynamic teacher and you've picked up the TEFL methodology admirably. You're a great asset to the program. But being a teacher isn't going to be your only job here in Gabon. You'll be an ambassador of sorts. A community resource for the locals."

I watched Christophe leave the refectoire with Keisha and Diana on either side of him. He and Diana were holding hands. I felt sick.

"I don't want to go scaring you or anything," Meg continued, "but there are education trainees, like Carmen, who are taking advantage of this training period to go out on daytrips and attend community health events. They're asking what we can go do together on Saturday afternoons that might help acclimate them to what life is going to be like out at post. For the community health trainees, all of this is super helpful. But the education trainees are profiting too. It never hurts to have an understanding of how one creates community projects, maybe to help promote literacy, sanitation, maternal and child health. These daytrips are a fun, relaxing way to gain exposure to this kind of thing."

"Ballet un-stresses me."

"I can see that's important to you. Have you ever asked yourself if, well... if this is the job you want to be doing right now? The place you want to be living?"

My heart began to hammer. "You're not going to fire me, are you?"

Her laughter made me breathe easier. "No. I was just curious."

"I want to be here," I said. "I'm sure of it."

"Good."

I drew in a shaky breath.

Meg dug her fork into her rice. "Next Saturday, I'll be taking a group to the Albert Schweitzer Hospital Museum. The compound is just a few miles away. It's a fun daytrip, with pirogue rides down the Ogooué River beforehand, and a picnic on the grounds afterward. I think you should consider going." She paused, fork midair. "In fact, I'll go so far as to say, I think you need to go."

I was screwing up here. Everything Meg had said made sense. I wanted to tuck myself into a little ball and cry.

"You've got two weeks left in training, Fiona," she said more gently. "It's enough time to turn things around. Apply yourself here, and you'll profit tenfold at your post."

"Okay."

"Albert Schweitzer with us, next Saturday afternoon?"

"Yes. Count me in."

Chapter 4

Rachel, Peace Corps Gabon's medical officer, carried a cardboard box into the classroom where the trainees had gathered. She plunked the box down on a table and pulled out one of the contents. Condoms. Hundreds.

"Take 'em and use 'em," she announced. She pushed a stray brown curl out of her face and regarded everyone expectantly, hands on her hips. "Well, go on," she demanded when no one moved. Laughter rippled from the room and everyone rose. "Take them, that is. Do the rest of what I suggested somewhere else."

It was our last group training session. Rachel had come from the Peace Corps office in Libreville to give us our final round of immunizations and lead a health discussion. She moved to stand beside Meg as we milled around the table and picked up supplies—insect repellant, Band-Aids, aspirin, anti-malaria pills, rehydration salts. "This should be enough for me," Henry called out, holding up the box of condoms. "How about the rest of you?"

Carmen grabbed a handful, stuffing them into her canvas shoulder bag. She eyed the three condoms I'd taken. "That'll last you the first night," she commented.

I shrugged. "I'm just not much of a wild girl, I guess." In fact, my seriousness had impressed even me. I'd become a model trainee since the talk with Meg. I'd applied myself to all my French and English-teaching lessons. At night, under the fluorescent glare of the refectoire lights, I studied and prepared for my practice-school presentations. On Saturday afternoons, I joined the daytrip group to wherever they went and learned what I could. Christophe, meeting my eye each Saturday upon our return, seemed perplexed, then privately annoyed. I ignored his reprimanding gaze. He was taken, anyway. That we could have continued any sort of special relationship was an illusion I needed to crush.

No ballet, no Christophe. No illusions.

Practice school had ended the previous day. We, as well as our students, had advanced on, in a ceremony commemorated by picture-taking, wide smiles and orange sodas. Today felt curiously flat—no English training, just French class and this final group session. Tomorrow the construction trainees would fly to Franceville, build a prototype school together and after that, be sworn in as volunteers. The community health trainees and education trainees would head to Libreville, the capital city, for one last week of training in their respective jobs. Then we'd break into small groups and go *au village*—to a village—for four days, before swearing in and awaiting our postings.

They called this the "Last Chance to Scare You Off" session. Rachel started it off with a Q and A on health issues. Carmen raised her hand. "This might just be a rumor," she said, glancing over at Robert, "but I heard that one of the volunteers came to you with a worm in his eye, and you had to pull it out."

Rachel nodded. "Yes, that would be Ron, who had an advanced stage of filaria, also called loiasis. You get it when a bite from an infected deerfly transmits a parasitic larva. For a while you can't tell you've been infected—the worm takes up to a year to mature. But then the adult worm starts moving around." Her eyes gleamed. "The most common complaint is swelling and aching in the joints, maybe the arm, leg or hand. When Ron came to me a few months ago, though, the worm was moving across his eye."

"Can people *see* the worm?" I asked Rachel uneasily.

She nodded. "Plain as day. Looks like a piece of dental floss that's stuck under the cornea. That's when you come to me in Libreville and have me extract it." Rachel frowned at us and wagged her finger. "No extractions between yourselves allowed, no matter how tempting it looks and how many Regabs you've had."

Next, we learned how to treat malaria, how to recognize typhoid or dengue fever, how to deal with the inevitable loneliness and isolation at post and what to do if a green mamba slithered through your window. Female education volunteers should wear dresses, skirts and blouses at school, saving the jeans—a tolerated American idiosyncrasy—for casual. Shorts and skimpy dresses were best set aside for Libreville, where, incidentally, you should always stock up on cheese and chocolate. Forget about finding fresh vegetables locally. And expect to be stared at, in your local store, in your neighborhood, as you walk, as you try to relax in your house. Your house might get broken into. That, and thefts, happened. Because you are American, people will assume you're rich. They will also assume you're CIA. Those speaking English will call you Peace Corpse; no need to worry that this is a threat, it is simply how they think Americans pronounce the word "corps."

By the end of the hour, uneasiness had filled the classroom. Rachel looked around and laughed. "Honest, we're not trying to make this sound awful. But if you found this training challenging, you should be aware that it's a piece of cake compared to the issues you'll confront at your posts. You may be the only American in your town, which will be a given for you constructors in the villages. Your post will be all Africa, all the time. Your volunteer leader will visit you annually at your post to check on things. Ditto someone from the administration team. You'll be flown to Libreville for a week-long conference in April. But that's it." She paused and her expression grew serious. "If you think you're not up to the task, do us a favor and come forward now."

Over lunch, she had a taker: one of the math trainees. "There you go," Robert said. "That makes four trainees who've quit. They say, on average, there's a fifty to sixty percent early-termination rate. Think about it. Another nine or ten from our group probably won't make it the full two years."

"Have either of you ever thought this might be too much for you?" I asked hesitantly.

Carmen and Robert both shook their heads. "What I'm sick of is this training business," Carmen said. "Time to do the job instead of talking about it."

I'd grown fond of the training site's insulated environment and was reluctant to say goodbye to everything. And everyone. A wave of melancholy swept over me. I made my excuses to Carmen and Robert and wandered over to the dorm room to rest. A boring novel, combined with the effects of the afternoon heat, made my eyes grow heavier, heavier.

It was the trip to Lambaréné again. The military guard who'd stopped us had pulled me from the Peace Corps van after all. He was going to shoot me, the way he'd just shot my beloved, who lay dead on the ground behind me. The violence simmering in the guard was overpowering, the darkest thing imaginable, except, no. Knowing my beloved was dead, that I'd never again hear his voice, see his face light up in a smile, was a death itself that echoed through my heart, my whole being. The guard drew closer, clutching his gun as I stood there, paralyzed with terror, trying to scream, only nothing came out.

Carmen, from inside the dust-caked Peace Corps van, knocked against the window. She knocked more vigorously a second time. But when she spoke, out came not her voice but my beloved's.

"Fiona? Are you in there?"

With a gasp, my eyes flew open. I was in my dorm bed and Christophe had entered the room Carmen and I shared.

He froze. Through my disorientation, I became aware of my sprawled limbs, my hiked-up skirt. I felt too drugged with sleep to react. Besides, it was Christophe. My beloved—which I hadn't realized until this very moment—wasn't dead. Euphoria exploded in me. I wanted to tell him how glad I was to see him, but I couldn't get my brain and mouth to work together.

"Forgive me," he said. "I knocked, but no one answered." He held up my notebook. "I thought you'd want this. You left it in the cafeteria."

"Thank you," I managed. He shut the door, set down the notebook and approached the bed. His face creased with concern.

"Are you all right?" he asked. Frowning, he reached over and rested his hand on my forehead.

In the moment I reached up to him, it was like reaching for life. Embracing it. Letting life swallow me whole. From monochromatic grey to dazzling Technicolor.

My hand slid up his arm and around his neck to pull him down on top of me. The feeling of his body against mine shocked me into awareness. "I'm so happy to see you," I gasped out before his mouth latched onto mine.

He was alive. I clutched at him, all but weeping to feel his skin, his weight on me, his vitality. His familiarity. As if by watching me dance for him, we'd already performed the most intimate act. I tugged at his shirt, sliding my hands beneath, around to the silky warmth of his back. He unbuttoned my cotton blouse in seconds.

His hands roamed my body as his mouth worked a trail from my neck to my exposed chest. The sight of his dark lips against my nipple sent me into a kind of erotic paralysis.

I was fully awake now, and yet I didn't push him off me and primly inform him I wasn't that kind of girl, the way I'd done with Lane. Instead here I was, clawing his back, tangling my legs around his, arching against him.

The door was unlocked. I could hear people conversing outside, in the courtyard, less than twenty feet away. Something about celebrating with a drink. It didn't matter. Nothing did. That is, until I heard my name. Robert's voice, saying, "Fiona should join us. Where *is* she?"

"I'll go check our room," I heard Carmen reply.

Christophe had heard, too. He half-rose as we regarded each other, frozen. Fury replaced the alarm on his face. I gave him a push and scrambled to my feet, where I buttoned my blouse with trembling fingers. I readjusted my skirt, smoothed back my hair, and hurried to the door. Glancing back at Christophe, I saw his clothes were all tucked in, his manner composed, leaving me to feel as if I'd dreamt the whole thing.

I eased open the door. The hallway, to my relief, was empty. Christophe came up behind me, but made no move to leave. "There's a post opening in Mouila, where I live," he murmured against my neck. "I can see that you get it."

A dozen arguments and caveats flooded my mind. The thought of seeing him, living close to him, filled me with dizzying euphoria. And yet, what about Diana? I turned and searched Christophe's face for clues, but found none.

"Think about it," he said as he stepped into the hallway. "I'll contact you in Libreville." Without another word, he strolled down the hall, casually greeting an approaching Carmen and leaving me to deal with the aftershocks.

Chapter 5

Darkness had fallen, an inky blackness studded with millions of stars. The music began: a percussive clatter of sticks, drums, rattling gourds and the high, strident voices of singing women. The blaze of the bonfire cast shadows behind the villagers as they danced around a man, a bwiti initiate who swayed in a daze. He wore a red *pagne*—a swathe of fabric—tied around his waist. Red paint had been smeared like a giant cross from his forehead down to his waist and across his shoulders. Two men, bwiti elders, stood close by for support, streaks of chalky white paint punctuating their faces. Around their necks and the necks of the other initiators, hung necklaces composed of feathers, shells and ominous-looking bones I couldn't categorize.

The bwiti ceremony mesmerized and baffled me in equal parts. It made me uneasy in ways I couldn't explain, even to myself, as if some energy I'd never before considered had been stirred and now swirled around me like smoke in an enclosed room.

My fellow trainee Joshua and I had spent the past three days in this village, hosted by the community health volunteer who lived here. The trip had been filled with hand-shaking and lots of confused smiling, wandering from house to house to shake more hands, sit and listen to the others talk, usually in Fang, the local tribal language here in the Woleu Ntem province. In addition to Regab, we'd drunk palm wine, a thin, sour, fermented beverage. Meals had been daunting: rice or *baton de manioc* topped with a fiery-hot red sauce, sometimes with meat, sometimes not. Manioc, an indigenous tuber, contained cyanide, which meant it had to be soaked in the river or a pond for several days before it was dried, peeled, washed again, then pounded to a pale mush. This was rolled in a banana leaf—the Handi-wrap of Gabon—to form a baton, which got boiled once again. When cut into slices, it looked (and tasted) like those translucent erasers I'd used in grade school. I ate it; it was amazing what you'd eat when you were hungry enough.

Tonight there was *feuille de manioc* too, the tuber's chopped leaves, mixed with palm oil, onion, chilies and bits of smoked fish. There was more palm wine, in abundance, during this, the culminating ceremony of our visit.

Bwiti, I'd gleaned, was a local animist religion that utilized the root bark of iboga, a local shrub, to aid in paranormal communication. Joshua, a slim, mild-mannered Seattle native, appeared to know a lot about the ceremony.

"It's a big deal, a multi-day event. The bwiti elders were probably up with the initiate all last night," he murmured to me. "I'll bet they started giving him doses of iboga at dawn, continuing on through the whole day. Look at the way the initiate's having trouble standing. He is so out of it. Any minute now, they'll take him into the hut where he'll lie on a mat and slip into his spiritual journey."

"Those sticks and roots there are really considered sacred wood?" I pointed to what looked like spring-cleanup yard clippings you'd find in any Omaha backyard.

"Very much so. The root bark is only a stimulant in small amounts, but a hallucinogen in bigger doses. You need a super-big dose for the spiritual journey. I read that the elders give the initiate near-toxic levels, to get him to that place where life hovers close to death."

I stared at his calm face. "God, that sounds too creepy. What's the point—why do people do this?"

"Lots of reasons. Communicate with the ancestors; address infertility issues; maybe discover the answer to some haunting question. Or some of us are just spiritual seekers at heart."

A man approached and ceremoniously offered us flakes of the iboga. Following Joshua's lead, I took a piece. It tasted awful, like a wood shaving sprayed with something you might use to kill roaches. I gagged at the terrible bitterness. When no one was looking, I spit it back into my hand.

A sharp sting on my back made me bolt upright. One of my many bug bites was bothering me again. I had over two dozen of the itchy welts on my body. Nor had I been able to shower for three days. Being au village was a lot like camping. "Ready to head back to Libreville?" I asked Joshua.

"I guess so. But actually, I like this environment a lot more than I'd expected. I think I might request a more isolated post."

Most education volunteers were posted in large towns or provincial capitals, which meant running water, electricity and populations over 4000. That sounded good to me: a provincial capital post. Like Mouila.

By late the following afternoon, Joshua and I were back in Libreville. My initial impression of the city when we'd flown into Gabon, eleven weeks previous, had been of a scraggly backwater capital with an excess of dirt, cars, people and dated architecture. After two months in Lambaréné and our trip au village, however, it was the uplifting energy of a cosmopolitan, multi-cultural metropolis I noticed. French and Belgian expatriates and Africans from all over the continent mingled on the crowded sidewalks. On paved, four-lane highways, Peugeot sedans, battered Renault taxis and BMWs shared the road with dusty pickups. The city was a hodgepodge of affluence, growth and tropical decay. Glossy skyscrapers, shanties of makeshift housing and government palaces all stood within blocks of each other. At the half-built hotel that housed the trainees, on the cusp of swearing in as volunteers, guests entered a reception area decorated with glass, polished wood counters and marble floors. A few steps down the hall, however, the amenities disappeared, replaced by roofless cinder-block walls and poured concrete floors. Ladders, paint cans and bags of cement lined the corridor. The guestroom doors were flimsy particle board, but once inside, luxury reappeared: solid beds, plush bedding, the muted hiss of air-conditioning, tiled bathrooms with hot running water and sit-down toilets.

Libreville had one more great perk: the Atlantic Ocean bordered the city. Through the window of the Peace Corps van that had brought us in from Lambaréné twelve days earlier, I'd watched the azure waves sparkle and crash against a long stretch of palm-fringed beach, with a landlocked Midwesterner's reverence. "This feels more like Southern California than Africa," Daniel, a fellow trainee who'd come from Los Angeles, had commented. I'd needed no further incentive. Within two hours, I'd found my way to a beach. I'd swum daily until we went out to our site visits.

The morning following Joshua's and my return, I headed right back. Tossing my towel onto the sand, I splashed into the warm water, ducking under the waves until I was out past the breakers. As I dove and darted through the salty water, my tight muscles loosened and my buoyant spirits rose even higher. Swimming, I decided, was like dancing, but without the constraints of gravity. My slow-motion leaps produced the feeling of suspension every dancer craved, that magic moment of being airborne and ethereal. In the water, I could be the ballerina of my dreams. I swam, bobbed and leapt until my muscles burned. I lay on my towel afterwards, spent but happy, soaking in the warm sun. It felt like a Hawaiian vacation.

"You've been swimming again, haven't you?" Carmen greeted me with a hug at the Peace Corps office an hour later. She shook her head. "Didn't I warn you that raw sewage is pumped straight into the estuary?"

"I always use the beach north of town. It's ocean, not estuary."

Carmen and Daniel, whose friendship had recently budded into romance, had just returned from their village visit, twelve hours later than expected. They took turns recounting the adventure. "...So, after our driver decided he couldn't fix the van," Carmen finished, "we had to spend the night literally on the road until someone could help us the next morning." She and Daniel laughed and exchanged long, meaningful glances, signaling the end of our three-way discussion. I turned and leafed through the basket reserved for incoming mail. When Daniel went to greet Robert, Carmen hoisted herself onto the counter next to me.

"No new letters here," I announced. "Does this mean the postal strike is still going on?"

"It does, and it is."

"Damn."

It had been over two weeks since I'd received a letter from home. Letters, I'd quickly learned, were a marvelously diplomatic way of sharing my life here. I picked the right time to write them and kept them full of positive news. My parents, and even Alison, had responded with comforting frequency. Except during postal strikes.

"Here's something to cheer you up." Carmen grinned at me. "A certain Gabonese man came in fifteen minutes ago and gave me a message for you."

My heart gave a wild leap. "Who?"

She ran her fingers through her hair by habit, but the spikey hairstyle had been replaced by domesticated chestnut waves. "Oh, who do you think? Christophe, of course."

"What did he say?"

"He told me to tell you 'it was all arranged'."

"What was all arranged?" Robert called out as he and Daniel walked back over.

"Man, are you nosy," Carmen gave him a lazy nudge with her foot. "None of your business."

But Robert wasn't done with the issue. After a trainee meeting, we all headed to Mont Bouet, Libreville's main market. It was a city in itself with its blocks of bustling crowds. Car horns, conversations and stereos kept noise at a blaring constant. Every nook of space, from stalls, covered tents and shops to card tables and spread-out blankets, was used to sell. Cheap perfume emanating from hundreds of sweating bodies did little to disguise the pervasive body odor, which competed with the stench of trash, decaying produce and unrefrigerated meat. It was a smell I'd learned to accept, an unmistakable characteristic of urban Africa.

Robert and I stopped at a cramped stall that sold music recordings. "Man, I sure miss listening to my albums," Robert said. "Had hundreds of 'em. It was quite the hobby of mine." I nodded as I riffled through cassettes on display. So, how about you?" he asked. "Keeping up with hobbies?" His voice sounded too casual.

"What, like ballet?"

"Sure. You seemed to really enjoy that back in Lambaréné. Every Saturday for a while, wasn't it?"

I looked over at him and sighed. "Glad to know someone was keeping tabs on me."

"Look, no offense, but you strike me as a little naïve."

"Oh please. I can handle things on my own."

"That's good to hear. Which means you've discovered Christophe's true nature."

"Of course." Something inside me clenched.

"So it won't shock you to learn that he's a notorious womanizer. American, Gabonese, French, Scandinavian—he's a regular cross-cultural Romeo. But you knew all this."

"You got it." I congratulated myself on my calm voice, even as my thoughts darted around like seagulls behind a barge.

"You want to know what else I heard?"

"Not particularly."

"That he's living with Diana in Mouila."

Robert wanted a reaction. I wasn't going to give him one. "Thanks for that information," I sang out, pushing his words away. What Robert was saying was impossible, of course. Christophe would have told me, back in Lambaréné. No one would fail to mention that important detail.

Would they?

The bug bites on my back, shoulders and arms were agony. Needle-like stabs of pain kept shooting through me during the day. Back at the hotel, I peered closer at them in the bathroom mirror. They didn't look like mosquito bites after all, I decided, but more like pimples. I squeezed one on my forearm tentatively and then harder as I saw something pushing out of my skin. It popped out onto my finger and I recoiled in horror at the sight of a small white maggot that squirmed to escape.

"Ooh, Tumbu fly maggots," Rachel, at the medical office, exclaimed when I went in to show them to her.

"How did I get these?" I asked.

She prodded a welt on the back of my arm. "Usually the female flies lay their eggs on damp fabric. Like clothes drying out in the fresh air, which is why it's best to iron your clothes before wearing them."

"How about fabric—like beach towels—that never quite gets dry?"

"That'll do it. The larvae hatch after a few days and if they make contact with human skin, they'll burrow in. After several weeks of growing, they come out on their own."

I slumped in misery on her examining table. This, on top of the Christophe issue. I hadn't been able to get Robert's words out of my head.

"How many are there?"

She scanned my backside and counted. "Twenty-nine," she announced. "A new record."

I winced. "Can you get them out?"

"I can try to remove the bigger ones, but the smaller ones will just burrow deeper. We'll have to give them a few more days."

The following afternoon, Carmen, Robert and I took a taxi to a posh district to buy art supplies at a stationery shop. As we left with our purchases, Robert looked around at the French women in their silky dresses who passed on the sidewalks with a click-click of high heels, leaving us in a cloud of expensive perfume. "These French expatriates," he sneered, "they only contribute to the uneven distribution of wealth here. Like that." He pointed to a black Mercedes sedan that glided past. As he tried to flag a taxi to take us back to our hotel, another glossy Mercedes rolled to a silent halt just past us. Parking by the curb, the driver got out of the car and looked back at us. My next comment seized up in my throat. Christophe.

"Look," I managed, and Robert and Carmen peered over to where I was pointing.

"Would you like a ride?" Christophe called out.

"Heck, yeah," Carmen said, and hurried over. Robert and I

followed more slowly behind. Carmen opened the back passenger door and stared pointedly at Robert. The front seat, clearly, was reserved for me.

Entering Christophe's car was like returning to a long-forgotten world. Air-conditioning cooled the plush leather interior. The car smelled like money, security, privilege. When I shut my door, the noisy, stinky Africa disappeared. I studied Christophe out of the corner of my eye as he pulled back into traffic. If possible, he'd become even more attractive. I'd forgotten the creamy perfection of his face, his aura of glamour and the way his clothes—a crisp linen shirt and sleek navy trousers—fit him perfectly. His full lips were curled up in a smile.

The ten-minute ride to our hotel went by far too quickly. When Christophe pulled into the hotel's parking lot, I stayed in my seat. Robert frowned at me.

"Remember, we're meeting the others for dinner in forty-five minutes," he said.

Christophe's smile at Robert grew more forced as Carmen yanked Robert out of the car. I watched them disappear inside.

I'd dreamed about seeing Christophe again, touching him again. It was my last thought every night before drifting off to sleep. Now, however, I couldn't think of a thing to say.

"I don't recognize this Fiona." His words broke the silence first. "She hasn't insulted me yet."

This drew a chuckle from me. I raised my eyes to meet his. Christophe reached out and planted a warm hand on the back of my neck, stroking softly. "It's good to see you again," he murmured. A jolt of desire slammed into me.

I had to act fast before I got myself into trouble. I licked my lips. "I need to ask you something."

"Speak."

The words didn't want to come out. Drawing a second breath, I plunged in. "I need to know if you're living with Diana."

Christophe's hand stopped. "Who told you that?"

"It doesn't matter. Is it true?"

He sighed. His hand dropped. "Yes, I'm living with Diana."

There it was. The news settled in with a thud of sickening finality. I slid my hands under my legs to keep them from shaking. It was a moment before I could speak again. "And yet you're suggesting I move out to Mouila. Why would you do that to me?" My words were slow and deliberate, outrage building beneath them. "To make me watch the two of you in your domestic bliss—did you ever stop to think how that might make me feel?"

Christophe hadn't replied. When I looked over, he was shaking his head. "You Americans… you're so obsessed with analyzing everything in advance. You'd rather think it than experience it, live your whole lives through your heads and not your bodies."

This wasn't the argument I'd expected. I didn't know how to respond. Through the window I watched two men pass by, holding hands, the way adult males did here. How innocent the Gabonese could seem sometimes. How foolish of me to assume that made them easier to understand. Christophe was talking again, idly tracing an outline on my skirt with his finger.

"I've never tried to hide from you that I'm seeing someone else. But I'm not bound by a contract. Diana and I are both free to make choices."

"But you're living together."

He laughed, but it was a sound devoid of mirth. "Oh, so it's the living together that was the deciding factor here. If we'd just been dating, you're saying you would have happily joined me in Mouila? Isn't that a bit hypocritical?"

Frantically I searched for a retort. "There *is* a difference. You're an established couple. I'm the odd one out. You have no idea what it feels like to be the person on the outside, looking in. It's the worst feeling in the world."

Christophe sighed. "You know, if you stopped dramatizing, Fiona, you'd see that you're creating your own problem here."

His words, so like something my siblings would have said, made my blood race. I clawed at the door and scrabbled out of the car. He got out at the same time. We both slammed our doors and faced each other. "Thanks for the ride," I spat. "And I think it's safe to say I have no interest in living in Mouila."

"What if I told you it was arranged?"

"Then un-arrange it."

He scowled. "It was to help you, Fiona."

"Oh, right."

"I could have minimized your problems."

"Thank you. But I won't be needing your help."

"Don't be so sure." He came around the back of the car and strode toward me. Uneasy, I took a step back and promptly bumped into the side-view mirror poking out.

"Is that a warning?" My voice squeaked.

He stopped just before me. "No. It's simply that I know this country and how it works. And I know you, and how you work."

I had no answer to that. In the silence that followed, he took a step closer, hands falling to my hips. Another step. Our pelvises met.

Desire sank through my rage, muzzling it. He was so close I could feel his breath warm against my cheek. From his neck, I caught a whiff of the cologne that haunted my nighttime fantasies of him. Here was the real thing—mine for the taking if I could play by his rules.

I couldn't.

"I'll take my chances," I said. "No Mouila."

"All right. Fine."

Like that, he became all business. He pulled me away from the car and reached over to brush a speck of dust off my skirt. "I'll walk you to the door," he said.

We walked down the path in silence. At the hotel entrance, he stopped and turned toward me. His face was cool and impersonal, that of a tutor sending off a pupil of whom he'd grown bored.

"Good luck. I'll be thinking of you," he said.

When Robert appeared, arms folded, Christophe turned and left.

That evening, I was in one of those moods my family knew well, one that told them to keep clear, or else. Carmen took one look at my face and swallowed her comment. Robert, however, wasn't so smart. Over dinner, he bragged to Joshua and Daniel about the river rat he'd tried for lunch the previous day. "Fiona wouldn't go near it. I keep telling her these things are an acquired taste." He chuckled and shook his head as if to admonish me.

I'd just about had it with meddling, overconfident men. I searched my forearm and found a ripe twin bump. "Acquired tastes, Robert?" My voice, after an hour of stony silence, seemed to startle him from his reverie. "Yeah, well, acquire *this*." With a practiced pinch of my skin, out popped two maggots. I rose, extended them over Robert's chicken and rice and dropped them with a flourish. "Care for some grated manioc with that?" I cooed.

When Robert saw the maggots wiggling around in his food, he let out a yelp. He scrambled up, but caught his legs on his bench. Both bench and Robert went crashing back. Carmen and Daniel laughed so hard tears began to run out of their eyes as Joshua helped Robert up.

"Oh Fiona, you bad girl," Carmen gasped. "Who'd have thought the prissy ballet dancer we met in training would turn out to be such an animal?"

It was one of the best compliments I'd ever received.

Part Two

The First-Year Volunteer

Chapter 6

"On your mark, get set....*go!*"

My cry set off a scene of pandemonium. Two students raced to the front of the classroom and scribbled an English word on the blackboard. Their teammates began to shriek and encourage them as they hurried back to home base, sandals slapping against the concrete floor. After a handover of chalk, the next student was off. The girls played to win, hiking up their navy uniform skirts in order to run better. Their braids, poking up all over their heads, waved like antennae as they scurried. I watched the words accrue on the blackboard and congratulated myself. Another successful Fiona-style lesson.

Vocabulary: to run, to write, to teach, to learn. Grammar point: present progressive. The student is running. The boys are laughing. Miss Fiona is cracking up. I loved teaching them that phrase. The students had loved it too. When one student called out, "Miss Fiona, this English class is cracking me up," we'd all laughed.

"What's going on here?" A harsh voice broke our game. A tiny man with a bushy moustache, the *surveillant*—the school disciplinarian—stood at the door, his angry voice compensating for his size. The students stopped in their tracks. The excitement and happiness drained from their faces. Silent now, they slunk back to their seats with their eyes cast down.

"It's all right," I assured him in French. "The students were practicing new vocabulary." When he directed his frown upon me, I straightened to my full height, inches above him, and launched into my speech about the value of incorporating activity into the learning experience. "You see, Monsieur Auguste, these students can speak English. Michel," I called out to one of my better students, "tell the surveillant what you learned from today's lesson."

"The students are running to the blackboard in the classroom," Michel, a lanky teenaged boy, announced in careful English. "They are learning to speak English. The game is cracking them up." This last part produced a flurry of giggles that made the surveillant glare at them. But he couldn't deny Michel's proficiency, nor the fact that every student in the classroom had understood what Michel had just said. This, after only two weeks. Judging from the defensive look on the surveillant's face, he clearly hadn't been able to translate what "cracking up" meant. Probably because he'd had an English teacher who'd taught by the more traditional rote method: lecturing to silent, note-taking students who, at the end of class, would parrot back the phrases.

The surveillant gave me a curt but respectful nod. "I'll leave you to your teaching." His gaze swept back over the class. *I am watching you,* his narrowed eyes told them. The students kept their expressions carefully blank. After the surveillant had left the room, I exchanged grins with my co-conspirators.

"All right," I called out, "please write these words from the blackboard in your notebooks."

As the students settled to work, I thought back to the scene I'd encountered on the first day of school. I'd walked into the classroom, under the scrutiny of fifty Gabonese teenagers, and wished them a good morning in English. From some of the students, the academic equivalent of ninth graders, a hesitant "good morning" in reply. From others, a bored mumble. I'd halted midway to the desk. In spite of my hammering heart, I'd managed to keep my voice light as I informed them in French that I needed everyone to wish me good morning. I'd walked right back out. When I popped back in a moment later and sang out "good morning" again, they laughed and replied correctly. By the time I left the classroom an hour later, the students were sitting up straighter, alert with interest. By the second week, everyone was participating.

Teaching English was a lot like a dance performance, I decided, with the audience's rapt attention on me, and the way my actions could produce a palpable energy in the room. I watched my students' eyes come alive. I could almost hear them thinking, *This can't be learning because it's fun*. It galvanized me. Ideas for class events and projects filled my head: a trip to the market, where we'd bargain in English with my money; maybe an after-school ballet class for the girls. A pen pal program with American students. The possibilities were endless.

The *lycée*, the French equivalent of junior and senior high where I taught, was a collection of whitewashed buildings in a clearing dug out of the rainforest, forming an L-shape around a courtyard. As I was leaving at the end of the "race for English" day, I overheard one of my students boast to his friend, "Miss Fiona is the most interesting teacher here."

"It's not fair," his friend grumbled back. "You have the American while I'm stuck with Monsieur Assame."

I hid my smile as I sailed past the students with a queenly nod. They liked my style. They were learning. It was just as I'd visualized.

The euphoria of successfully teaching energized me during my walk home and through town. Makokou, provincial capital of the Ogooué

Ivindo, was a pretty place, I decided. Tucked into the northeastern section of the country, it had forested hills that tapered off at the banks of the Ivindo River, which snaked and sparkled in the afternoon sun. The air smelled fresh and sweet, like potting soil laced with honeysuckle. I strolled along Makokou's main drag, a haphazard collection of buildings and coconut palms lining the town's lone paved road. While I had no American colleagues at the lycée, Malaria Rich and Keisha both lived in Makokou, on the other side of town, and taught math and English, respectively, at the Catholic mission near them. Their close-but-not-too-close presence helped me feel less alone here.

In the general store, I bought a baguette and a can of lentils, exchanging greetings with the owner. A bright, can-do smile stayed on my face as I headed home, until the moment I caught sight of my house.

I'd envisioned many things, back in Libreville, when dreaming of my future home. A sturdy yellow house with a modest verandah; a cottage with a walkway and flower tubs in front. Perhaps a bungalow on a hill with a sweeping view of the river and surrounding forested hills. I was, after all, a teacher, a respected profession here in Gabon. I'd seen the pictures of other volunteers' houses. One was cream-colored with giant blue shutters that swung open to expose screened windows, like Switzerland meets *Out of Africa*. But within a neighborhood of tidy, whitewashed houses, my house, a squat, poorly painted wooden structure, stood out like a wart.

I walked down the weed-strewn path that had resisted my efforts at clearing and went inside. A permanent musty odor emanated from the bedroom, which featured a sagging bed crowned with mosquito netting. In the living room, a single light bulb dangled from the water-stained ceiling. A set of rodent feet scampered above me, somewhere between the ceiling and the corrugated tin roof. I sighed and headed into the galley-sized kitchen. Time for lunch.

After *la sieste*, the lunchtime break where everything in the country shut down for three hours, I headed to the post office. The strike had been resolved the previous Wednesday. On Thursday, the building had remained dark inside. Friday, there'd been workers but apparently no mail to distribute. Today, Monday, there was mail, and lots: six bulging bags. "It is from Libreville," one of the clerks confirmed. My heart leapt. I probably had over a dozen letters there, forwarded by the Peace Corps office to my new address.

"How soon will it be distributed?" I asked.

The worker shrugged. "Toward the end of the week."

"The end of the week?!"

"Maybe longer."

Deflated, I shuffled over to the row of metal post office boxes. Empty, for several more days. I wanted to cry. I pulled out my key and fit it into the lock of my box, as if doing so would produce a letter. And to my stunned surprise, inside I found a thin blue international aerogramme. From my sister. Sent to my new Makokou address and dated only ten days earlier.

"How is this possible?" I asked a worker who strolled by. He took the aerogramme and studied it.

"Ah. This letter is not from Libreville."

"But surely it went through Libreville?"

The man shrugged, the catch-all response to most of my queries in Makokou. He explained that, most likely, because it was international, it had circumvented the bottleneck of the accumulated mail. Regardless, there it was: my first letter from home in six weeks.

I tore into the letter as I walked home, scanning the contents. *Hi, Fiona!* Alison had written. *Mom got your letter with the news of your new posting yesterday. She read it to me, and I thought I'd try the address right out. Hope you're doing well there. We're fine. Last night, as you might have guessed by looking at the calendar, was The Show. Of course a group of my girlfriends and I came over to watch it with Mom, like we've always done.*

The Miss America Pageant. I'd forgotten the pageant this year. I laughed out loud, a mad cackle laced with increasing hysteria that I curbed only when I realized the locals were staring more than usual.

As predicted, there'd been no escaping the attention my presence drew. I was one of a handful of white faces in a town of six thousand Africans. Conversations always halted when I passed, as male and female alike sized me up. Only the older women, barefoot and bent from a load of wood on their backs, trudged past without curiosity. Small children, spying me, would hesitate, turn and run the other direction. One time, a naked toddler, unable to keep up with the others, had looked over his shoulder at me as I drew closer. He stumbled and panicked, squalling in terror until his sister raced back, swooped him up and carried him to safety.

The Show, indeed. What had Alison been thinking, that I'd still be caught up in that? But this was new territory we found ourselves in, communicating pleasantly through letters. I sensed we were both tentative, awkward, striving to find common ground.

The letter went on to detail the cold spell Omaha had been caught in, news of our brother Russell's big promotion at work. But it was the third paragraph that most caught my interest.

I saw April Manning the other day. She was in town visiting family and stopped by the house to say hi. Wow, she looks glamorous, quite the star ballerina. She said she's a soloist now, with the American Ballet Theatre, but you probably already knew that. She asked about you and I gave her your address in Africa. She promised to write.

April Manning, my first ballet buddy. My steps slowed as I walked the last blocks in a reflective reverie.

I had Alison to thank for my friendship with April. And, in truth, the Miss America Pageant, for igniting Alison's interest in ballet. The year she was eight and I was seven, we'd stayed up, like always, to watch the annual broadcast. The next morning, Alison announced that she'd decided on her talent for her own future run at Miss America. A classmate of hers named April took ballet classes. "Dance will so be easy," Alison told the family at the breakfast table. "I mean, what does it take to spin around, flap your arms and smile for the audience?" Even easier, the dance studio was walking distance from our house, which Mom liked. She agreed to pay for ballet lessons, provided Alison could convince me to do it too. Initially, I balked. I was a bookworm, a dreamer, far less ambitious than my older brother and sister. Alison alternately cajoled, threatened and sweet-talked me. When she tossed her new strawberry delite lip gloss into the bargain, I agreed.

The following Monday afternoon, we walked to the studio, stowed our street clothes in the dressing room, and took a place at the barre with the other congregating girls. Alison immediately made friends with the prettiest ones and decided aloud that she liked ballet class. But fifteen minutes into class, I could tell by Alison's expression that she didn't like it. The teacher's strictness, the complex and foreign movements set to classical music—none of this suited her. Meanwhile I was instantly engrossed, not frustrated by what I couldn't do so much as intensely curious. I watched the best girl in the class, which turned out to be Alison's classmate, April. She had thin arms and long legs like mine that easily turned out from the hip, so our toes, in first position, pointed in opposite directions. I strove to mimic April's smooth, fluid movements, the way she held her head high, letting her legs do all the work, while her arms remained calm, beautifully curved. I tried pointing my toes like she did, arching my foot into a banana shape, and once again, it came naturally. The teacher, observing, gave a murmur of pleasure.

The class practiced a turn called a pirouette, where the teacher kept her focus riveted on April. "You're not quite straight enough, dear," she said. "Act like there's a string running through you and holding you up. Like a marionette. And the instant you take off from your preparation, *shoot* that supporting leg right up to passé."

April paused to consider this, demi-pliéd in preparation, and spun, executing a perfect double turn. Dazzled, I burst into applause. April swiveled around to regard me. No one else had clapped. The other girls, in truth, looked much like Alison did: irritated about being overlooked and outclassed.

"That was really good," I murmured to April, abashed.

"Thank you," she said shyly. Our eyes met and I knew I'd found a friend.

For that, I thought as I walked up my path and unlocked my front door, I owed Alison an eternal debt of gratitude.

For that, alone.

Inside, the urge to practice ballet overpowered me. I changed into my dance clothes and put on my leather ballet slippers. I pulled out the cassette player and adjusted the living room shutters for privacy.

I found immediate comfort in the familiar music, familiar barre routine. My feet cramped in tendus as I pointed my toes; it happened when I didn't practice regularly enough. My extensions, too, were lower than they used to be. But still the love, the swept-away feeling.

Until my audience arrived.

This had occurred the last time, too. It was as though, each time, I'd set up a loudspeaker on my rooftop, blasting out classical music, as much of an oddity here as I was. In no time, the house had drawn a crowd of spectators. I heard them now, neighborhood children, their murmurs, their jostling to get the best view. I paused the cassette player and firmly shut all my shutters, which acted as both windows and blinds. I turned on the overhead light, which felt wrong in the afternoon, but gave me privacy. But the children didn't leave. As I continued my barre, I could sense their presence, their sharp exhales of breath, their whispers, the occasional thump of a hand or a forehead against the shutters, two of which, I realized, had a chunk missing that the kids could peer through.

I told myself I had to learn to ignore them. Otherwise there could be no ballet in my life here. I deepened my focus through développés and grand battement. I overheard an adult male voice call out for the kids to scat, go away, which most of them appeared to obey. My neighbor, I surmised. I didn't hear his footsteps crunch away on the gravel path and I sensed that he, too, had paused to watch, through the broken shutter.

After a distracted adagio in the center of my living room, I called it quits. I slipped on shorts and flung open my front door, expecting to see my neighbor nearby. But to my surprise it was someone else, a young man who seemed vaguely familiar. One of my colleagues at the school? No, surely too young. I'd seen him at the general store— was he one of their employees? He had a bullish jut to his chin and wide shoulders that strained against his faded tee shirt. He was taller than the average Gabonese. He looked surprised to have been caught there in my yard, but he only smiled at me, in a way that seemed both polite and sinister.

"Good afternoon," he said in French. "It is good to see you again." Which confirmed that he knew me and thought I remembered him.

"Good afternoon," I replied in French, my brain whirring, trying to place him.

He approached, and I wondered in dismay if he expected me to invite him in, the way people did here. Provincial Africa had a very sociable, connected culture, and adults and colleagues paid each other visits. Since no households had phones, no one could call to say "is this a good time to stop by?" and instead, simply showed up. I'd always hated inane, cocktail chitchat, and these days all conversations had to be conducted in French.

As the non-invitation issue hung in the air between us, I saw him take in my attire. I'd put on shorts but hadn't bothered to cover the pale, thin-strap leotard, which had become old and stretched. Back home, dancing and/or rehearsing for hours daily, I'd been lean. I'd gained weight here, and it all showed up in my breasts, a deeply unwelcome sight to any ballet dancer. My visitor, it seemed, couldn't take his eyes off my chest.

"You'll excuse me if I'm not free to invite you in," I said. "I've just finished my exercise and I need to change my clothing."

"I can wait while you change," he said.

As if. Knowing he was outside my door as I shucked my leotard and peeled back sweaty tights, exposing my nude body with just a wall separating us? After the way he'd just eyed my chest? Distaste curled in my gut.

"No, thank you."

He nodded as if he'd been expecting the rebuff. "Before I go, I wish to offer my services."

"Which are?" I asked suspiciously.

"Monsieur Shawn," he said, referring to the volunteer I'd replaced. "I helped him in his house. This house. I cut his grass. I came over after school. I can help you." His eyes traveled up and down my body. "I can make sure you do not feel...alone."

This was precisely the kind of thing Christophe had warned the men would propose.

"No, thank you," I replied coldly. "I do not need your help. I can take care of myself."

"But—"

"I said, no thank you."

He scowled at me, and for a moment I regretted my harsh tone.

It was too early to make enemies in this town.

"Thank you, though," I added, and smiled. "I appreciate that you stopped by."

This softened his scowl. In fact, I saw the glimmer of something else in his eyes when he smiled at me, which told me I'd overplayed my friendliness.

This was going to take some learning.

"Goodbye," I said, in a tone I hoped was firm yet cordial. I began to shut the door.

"Goodbye," he called out. "I'll see you at the school."

Once I'd shut the door and locked it, I puzzled over his words. No, not a fellow teacher, I was certain. But someone who knew me at the school.

A prickle of horror came over me, as recognition filled my mind.

His name was Calixte. He was a student. He was *my* student. One who'd seen my sweaty, overexposed body. One I'd almost invited in. One I'd spoken to, respectfully, even smiled at, as though we were equals.

I didn't need Christophe to tell me that I'd just made a big, big mistake.

Chapter 7

The fever came around sunset one day in November. At first I thought my muscles were aching from the previous night's dance workout, a punishing two-hour session to make up for the half-dozen aborted daytime efforts of the last month.

The aches intensified and my face grew warmer, but even that was no great sign. As the short rainy season edged in, the air had become hotter and more humid, which I wouldn't have thought possible back when I arrived in Gabon five months earlier. But when the chills set in, waves of them, like a giant rotating fan hitting me every few minutes, I knew I was in trouble. It took tremendous effort to rise from the couch and stagger to the bedroom. I lay slumped on the bed and listened to my teeth chatter, which I'd always assumed was just a cliché. It wasn't. It reminded me of rosary beads clacking together, like when I'd jiggled them in my pocket as a kid, bored and restless during Mass.

Malaria.

I knew the drill: five tablets of Mefloquine—five times the normal malaria prophylaxis dosage—with a glass of water. Expect several hours of fever, chills and strange dreams. And the dreams didn't disappoint. In one, I was flying on the back of some giant bird over a lemon-yellow river that sparkled and undulated beneath me.

Ancient okoumé and ficus trees, tangled with overgrown liana, lined the banks. The trees reached out to snag me, but I eluded their grasp, rising above the emerald canopy. It terrified me to be so high, only I didn't know how to get down.

Suddenly I was in a plane instead, that crash-landed with a violent, noisy *whump* in a clearing. I scrabbled through the wreckage and stumbled down a path that led to a group of villagers who were dancing and singing with rattling gourds and pounding drums. The people drew me into the circle with cries of greeting. They all had blue eyes that matched the blue bonfire crackling and spitting in the center of the circle. They wanted me to dance for them. When I told them I didn't know how to dance like them, they laughed and nudged me toward a bent, withered woman. She was neither black nor white, but a rusty gold, like the color of the earth. Bright red feathered tufts sprouted from her shoulders. I tried to run away from her but she was faster. Taking me by the hand, she led me to a great, gaping chasm in the earth. She motioned that I needed to fly over the abyss to get to the other side. My gut contracted in fear. I tried to tell her I couldn't fly, and that I would die if I tried, but the words stayed lodged in my throat. When I leaned over to contemplate the black depths, she chuckled and pushed me.

I awakened with a jolt in the darkness of my room, my heart slamming against my chest. It felt like the night had been going on forever. I looked at the time. It was nine o'clock. I'd been asleep for less than an hour.

Thus began a long hallucinogenic night where I'd wake with the bedsheets drenched, my body alternately wracked with fever and shaking with chills. Lying half-awake in the darkness, trembling from the nightmares, I contemplated my isolation. I was on my own here in Africa, more alone than I'd ever been. I'd always thought I couldn't get enough of solitude. Now the truth hit me like a blast from a fire hose: I didn't want to be alone. It terrified me. I wanted to go home. I wanted my mom, her baked chicken and cheesy mashed potatoes, her hugs, her cool hand on my burning forehead. I wanted to turn back the clock and be a kid again, trusting that everything would work out all right. But I couldn't.

The intensity of my fever compounded my sense of isolation. I'd never been this hot before. Could you die of a fever? Could you die of loneliness? Maybe tonight I'd find out the answers.

I woke much later in a fog of disorientation. Light filtered through the cracks in my shuttered windows. A sunbeam illuminated the dust swirling in the air and stretched down to the floor where it created a puddle of sunshine. I stared at the puddle blankly. Morning. The demons that had whispered in my ear all night were gone. And absurdly, so was the fever. I felt as wasted as I had the weekend I'd danced back-to-back *Nutcracker* performances, but I was able to stand and get dressed. Afterward I walked on unsteady legs over to my neighbors' house.

My neighbors had remained a bit of a mystery to me. There were several children, a man and two older females. One of them, a plump woman with a baby tied to her back, had come over a few days after my arrival. I'd been working in my yard, hacking at weeds. Without much introduction, she'd handed me a set of keys her husband had been safekeeping, one for my post-office box, the other for a bicycle shed. Her husband, a silent, shiny-faced Gabonese man who always seemed to be wearing the same light-blue, short-sleeved, polyester suit, worked in the lycée's administrative office. He was neither attractive nor ugly, young nor old, friendly nor unfriendly. After our first encounter, I'd felt a stab of disappointment. I'd been hoping for some personal connection, a fatherly type with a jolly smile who would dispense advice for me on how to cope here. It wasn't to be.

The rest of the household disappointed me as well. Everyone greeted me politely, but attempts at anything beyond routine exchanges always fell flat. Neither of the women became my confidant, my tour guide, my best friend, like they always seemed to do in the movies and Peace Corps recruitment videos. Instead, a glass wall seemed to eternally separate us.

Today it was the younger of the two women, diminutive and solemn with short hair poking up in yarn-laced tufts, who answered my knock. "I have malaria," I told her. Her only reaction was a grunt of assent. Not exactly the soft-eyed sympathy I'd been seeking. Instead it was the same resigned expression she wore much of the time, whether sobbing children were clinging to her legs or the man of the house was shouting at her. "Can your father inform the lycée administration that I won't be teaching today?"

Her impassive face broke into a smile. "My husband?"

I'd forgotten about the polygamy business. "He's the one who works at the lycée?"

She nodded.

"Yes, him."

Business finished, I thanked her, staggered back to my house, hit the bed and slept.

Malaria Rich was more sympathetic, when I went to his house for dinner several days later. Since my arrival, he'd been friendly but cautious, as if having a new, potentially clingy American around might taint his African experience. With the malaria, however, I seemed to have passed some sort of initiation. In his kitchen, we compared experiences. "Did you do the Aralen treatment or the Mefloquine?" he asked.

"Mefloquine. How about you?"

"I tried Aralen first. Hate the way Mefloquine messes with you. The problem is that the chloroquine-resistant mosquitoes like the Aralen treatment better too. The malaria kept coming back, every third day, for two weeks. Finally I gave in and hit the hard stuff."

"Did you get weird dreams?" I asked.

"Yeah, and I was dizzy for weeks afterwards."

"I had a second bout two nights later, but that seemed to be it for the fevers."

"If you got over it within a week, it probably wasn't the plasmodium falciparum type," Rich said. "Probably plasmodium ovale or vivax. The good news is you didn't die, which can happen with plasmodium falciparum. Within *a day* of the symptoms appearing." Rich's eyes burned into mine. "The bad news is that if you had the vivax, it will probably come back. I've had it three times already."

He turned to his stove, jiggling the pan that held frying onions. He was making his dinner specialty: corned beef and tomato sauce à la Rich, served over rice. It was salty, processed and oddly comforting, like something Mom might have made for us on nights Dad wasn't around. Rich had been happy to provide me with the recipe the first night we met for dinner. "Fry up some onion and garlic in oil, toss in the corned beef, the tomato paste, some water. And voila, thirty minutes later, you're set. Now if you add more tomato sauce and water, throw in a little dried oregano, you have a killer spaghetti sauce. And if you take out the tomato paste and mix everything else with eggs, you get a great corned beef scramble. Add cheese, crust, it's a quiche."

He had a total of seven corned beef recipes ("one for each day of the week!"), most of them liberally dosed with *piment*, a fiery local chili. He pried the corned beef out of the newest can and dumped the gooey rose-colored mass into the frying pan. "You know," he mused, "they said it would be hard to eat well here, but I don't know what they were talking about."

A knock at the door saved me from replying. Keisha had arrived. As Rich finished his food preparations, Keisha and I wandered into the living room.

"How's school?" she asked.

"Pretty good. The kids can get a little wild, but the lessons seem to really be sinking in."

"Don't let them get too wild," she warned.

Keisha didn't like me. We'd established that early on, back in Lambaréné, the first time I'd mouthed off to Christophe during a training session. To her credit, she was making an effort here, which was crucial because I needed her. She was a fellow volunteer; she had a year's worth of English teaching under her belt. Our American-ness, as well, bound us. She knew where Omaha was and that Hollywood wasn't bigger than New York. She knew who the Brady Bunch were; she'd eaten Oreo cookies and Snickers bars. In more ways than one, we spoke the same language.

I told Keisha about my idea, American pen pals for my students.

"What about the cost of mailing?" she asked. "And are you going to do that for every class? How would you choose without causing the others to mutiny?"

"I don't know," I replied, flustered. "I haven't worked out the details. It's just that I thought it would be fun."

"Fun," she echoed distastefully.

"Well, work too. They'd have to produce a letter on their own. In English."

"Have you made contact with someone in the U.S. willing to participate with you?"

"Of course. My former high school French teacher." I made a mental note to mail her a request the very next day.

"That's a good start," she admitted.

Rich joined us in the living room. "What do you think of our students so far this year?" he asked Keisha.

"Not bad. My third hour has some troublemaking *redoublants*, though. They're starting to act up."

Rich nodded. "I know which class you're talking about."

Redoublants were students forced to repeat or "redouble" the previous grade. Here in Gabon, repeating grades was not uncommon. Academic standards, based on the French learning system, were high, while parental guidance and support were low. The redoublants tended to be older and more confident than the others. Like Calixte. Sometimes this worked in a less-accomplished student's favor. But other times, the redoublant became potential trouble. Like Calixte.

He and I hadn't spoken of our encounter on my porch. It almost seemed like a dream, except for the knowing look he gave me, from time to time, when our eyes met. Which was infrequent. He was a poor student and rarely knew the answer and thus avoided my gaze in the classroom. But that didn't deter him from watching me outside the classroom. I'd feel his gaze on me as I passed him during break or after class, both of us aware that I'd mistaken him for a man, smiled at him, and all but invited him in.

I opted to not share this with Keisha.

As I was preparing to leave Rich's house that evening, Keisha held up a finger. "I almost forgot to give you something," she told me. She reached into her backpack and withdrew a cream-colored envelope. "This is yours. They put it in my post office box by mistake."

I looked down at the envelope. It was not the pale blue of the international aerogramme or Mom's white American stationery, but an elegant envelope with a Libreville postmark. I glanced at the sender. Essono Christophe. A wave of dizziness passed over me. I covered it up with a polite smile as I thanked Keisha.

I could feel the presence of the letter in my backpack as I bicycled home, as if the letter were giving off its own heat. Back in the house, I savored the anticipation, neatening up and getting ready for bed. I slipped under the bed's mosquito netting with the envelope. I held it, afraid to open it. Finally I slit it open and pulled out a matching cream card with the gold letters EC embossed on top.

Ma belle Fiona, he'd written. *I am with my parents in Libreville this week. Last night, my mother played a recording of Saint-Saens' "Rondo Capriccioso." The music, so intriguing and full of passion—it is you. You've been in my thoughts ever since.*

Further below his scrawled signature, he'd added a P.S. *I'll be in Libreville again over the Christmas holidays.*

I read the note again, more slowly. He'd called me his belle Fiona. Beautiful Fiona. I caressed the words with my thumb, as if that might somehow help them sink in. He thought I was beautiful. He'd been thinking about me. I read the note a third and fourth time. His mention of being in Libreville over the Christmas holidays was surely no casual aside. Robert, Carmen, Daniel and I were meeting in Oyem, in the north, for Christmas break. We'd have plenty of time to travel to Libreville afterwards. There'd surely be a Peace Corps party, a chance to issue in the New Year properly, maybe even with a stolen kiss.

I reached through the netting and turned off the light. I lay in the bed, awake, for a long time. Smiling.

Chapter 8

It didn't take long to decide the driver of the beer truck delivering me to Oyem was a madman. He raced the lumbering vehicle down the narrow, unpaved roads, swerving wildly to avoid crater-sized potholes that punctuated the washboard ruts. Chickens fluttered and goats scattered in panic as we thundered through villages. Ascending hills, the weight of the truck slowed to a crawl. The driver made up time on our descent, giving the term "breakneck speed" new significance. He glanced over at me after an hour.

"The last white woman who traveled with me begged to be let out," he commented. No surprises there. I unclenched my jaw long enough to tell him I could handle it. "Peace Corpse?" he asked in English. When I told him yes, he nodded as if that explained it all.

Rich had recommended taking the beer truck to my Christmas reunion in Oyem. "It's one thing here you can count on," he'd said. "No crisis, strike or bureaucratic drama is big enough to stop Regab from being delivered. And besides," he'd added, "from Makokou, it's either that or hitchhike." In Makokou's general store that morning, I'd negotiated a ride on a Regab truck that was leaving, the clerk promised, *immédiatement*. But "immédiatement" was a relative term in Africa. My five-minute wait turned into thirty minutes. One hour became two. Now, however, we were on our way. All I had to do was survive the trip.

We crested one particularly steep hill and began rocketing downward in the center of the road, where it was the smoothest. I glanced sidelong at the driver's face. He was smiling, his expression filled with the kind of rapt glee you see on the faces of ten-year-old boys playing arcade games, the type with steering wheels and virtual roads displayed on the screen. The difference, of course, was that with the game, when you made a bad turn and your vehicle rolled and exploded into a churning inferno, you simply shrugged and put in a few more quarters. But the constraints of the real world and the laws of physics didn't seem to deter my driver. Nor any other driver, judging from the trucks that came barreling toward us from the other direction, also in the center of the road, veering off to their respective sides only at the last moment to avoid head-on collisions. It was then I decided that Gabonese truck drivers were indeed mad as hatters.

When we arrived in Oyem at the end of the day, I couldn't decide whether to throttle the driver or kiss him. Instead I asked him to drop me off at the high school where Carmen taught. I followed her directions from there, and found her home just as the sun was setting. It was another one of those "why couldn't this have been mine?" kind of houses, an elegant cream cottage framed by palm trees and hibiscus. It was big; she shared the house with a second-year community health volunteer, who, according to Carmen, spent most of her time in Libreville, officially due to chronic tropical-related health problems and, unofficially, because she had a French boyfriend there.

Carmen flung open her door and greeted me with a hug and a cry of welcome. I studied her afterwards. "Something's different with you," I said. Her hair was getting longer, prettier. I looked down at her feet. Sandals. "Where are your boots?" I screamed.

She shrugged and grinned. "Hey, my feet were getting hot. I got this gross foot fungus and Rachel told me to give them some air."

"Damn, you're looking so feminine."

"I know, I know, isn't it awful? Anyway, come on in—everyone else has arrived." We wandered into the kitchen where Daniel was at work peeling green papayas. "He uses them for a pie that's a dead ringer for pumpkin pie," Carmen said, reaching out to stroke his arm. "Wait till you try it."

"You said everyone's here. Who's everyone?"

"Henry and William," Daniel replied. "They're out buying a truck part."

Carmen handed me a Regab and raised her own bottle. "Here's to no teaching for two weeks."

The three of us clinked bottles. "Wait…" I looked around. "If everyone's here, where's Robert?"

"Not here, of course," Carmen said.

"What's that supposed to mean?" I asked.

Daniel and Carmen glances. "You mean you haven't heard?" Daniel asked.

"Heard what?"

"Robert quit."

I stared at them. "No way. He friggin' quit? After all those little know-it-all speeches and *he* was the one to quit? Why? What happened?"

"I got a letter a few days back," Carmen said. "It was this tirade about how he hated teaching, hated speaking French all day long, felt lonely and alienated, etcetera."

"No shit! Was he expecting to have fun here?" I flung my duffel bag to the floor.

Carmen regarded me curiously. "You mean you're not? Not at all? Your letters have all sounded pretty upbeat."

My outburst had taken me by surprise as well. I'd told myself I liked my job, reciting the phrase like a mantra to keep my spirits up.

But I could be honest with Carmen. No, I suddenly realized, I didn't like my life in Makokou. I was always sweaty and lonely, I missed my ballet world and I'd made no local friends.

"I can tell the students enjoy my class," I said, "but it's become so tiring to teach. They're not even meeting me halfway anymore. It's like they just want to sit there and be entertained. On top of it, I had this weird occurrence last week."

"Do tell." Carmen gestured to the living room and we wandered to the couch.

"You got any problem students, the big, hulky redoublant kind?" I asked as we sat.

"Sure."

"So this kid, Calixte, was getting disruptive last week, as per normal. I marched over to his desk and, in a loud voice, asked in English if he was too busy for me. All the students went wild."

"Busy," Carmen repeated. "Oh, you didn't." She squeezed her eyes shut. "Oh no. I know what's coming next."

Her amused reaction annoyed me. "Okay, the joke's on me, and clearly everyone gets it but me. Do you mind telling me where the grand faux pas is?"

"*Baiser*," she replied.

"No, busy."

"Yes, but it sounds like the French word, '*baiser*.'"

"Which means?"

"In the old literary sense, it means to kiss. But in current slang, basically…" Here, even Carmen looked abashed.

"Basically what?"

"It means 'to fuck'."

Great. I couldn't have picked a worse student to humiliate myself in front of.

"How did your students react?" she asked.

"Oh, they just screamed with delight. Or shock. I don't know." I buried my face in my hands.

As for Calixte, he'd been gape-mouthed with astonishment and silent the rest of the class. I'd assumed I'd chastised him good, but Carmen's words explained why he'd strutted, not slunk out of the classroom when the bell rang. Furthermore, he'd been smiling.

Carmen began to chuckle. I scowled at her. "It's not funny," I said.

"Yes it is. It's hysterical. And you're probably the hundredth English-speaking teacher to make the same mistake. It's almost a rite of passage."

"You're saying you did it?"

"No, but the volunteer before me did. I got the scoop from the other English teacher at my school. But I did try to explain to all my colleagues that I was a happy person. I described myself as *une fille de joie*."

"A girl of joy? They had a problem with that?"

"Ah, but *une fille de joie* means something different in French slang. I pretty much announced to the entire lycée staff that I was a prostitute."

The beer I'd just sipped sprayed out of my mouth. This set Carmen laughing harder, which got me started as well. "Have to tell you," Carmen wheezed a minute later, "I've had no trouble making friends here since then." We sat there and howled with laughter till my sides ached.

On Christmas Eve day, all of us piled into Henry's truck and headed to the city center to shop. Oyem was Gabon's third largest city, a bustling metropolis more reminiscent of Libreville than Makokou. For the first time in over three months, I encountered heavy traffic, stoplights and taxis. Some of the streets—all paved, of course—even had four lanes. Business professionals and shoppers, both African and European, thronged the sidewalks. I drew no stares here; instead, I was the gawker, like the rural Nebraska hayseeds I used to snicker over, who would stumble through downtown Omaha, wide-eyed and gape-jawed. I'd forgotten how sophisticated the well-dressed Africans looked, how cosmopolitan the city dwellers seemed. It was as if a giant vacuum had sucked up the glossy, attractive people throughout Gabon and deposited them in the big cities. I half-expected to see Christophe pop out of a shop here. I decided I liked Oyem. A lot.

While Henry and William visited the hardware store, Daniel and Carmen brought me to Score, a supermarket that catered to the French expatriate community. I discovered caviar, *foie gras,* cheeses by the dozen and produce I hadn't seen since leaving Nebraska. The prices shocked me, such as the equivalent of twenty dollars for a stalk of limp broccoli, but it was broccoli, nonetheless. Chocolate filled an entire row. Wine comprised another. I wandered the aisles in a happy reverie.

Holiday music played through the overhead speakers, as out of place as a dusty village mama at an English tea party. Bing Crosby should be dreaming of a "White Christmas" on another continent, I mused, wiping the sweat off my face. I was perusing the spice rack when, to my shocked surprise, Tchaikovsky's "Waltz of the Flowers" from *The Nutcracker* played next. The music invaded my senses like a drug injected into my bloodstream. Something in my body leapt to life, while another part froze in dismay. It was like seeing an old boyfriend I wasn't yet over.

I'd performed in *The Nutcracker*—or Nutz, as we dancers called it—every year for the past ten Christmas seasons. I'd purposely avoided playing the cassette recording Mom had recently mailed me, to keep from feeling the nostalgia that now swept over me. But like an alcoholic being handed a drink, I had little choice but to succumb to its seductive power. I shut my eyes and I was there, lights blazing down as I leapt across the stage, every muscle and nerve in my body tuned in, focused on the dance, the other dancers, the backstage crew in the wings, the audience's captivated silence. Listening to the store's muffled music, I could almost feel the high of dancing it again, that surge of power coursing through my limbs. That intoxicating, otherworldly feeling—it was why I danced.

"Fiona?"

My eyes flew open. Carmen had reappeared with the shopping cart. "We're ready to check out. Are you okay?" she asked.

I tried to shake myself free from the music's spell, which now seemed to mock me, rubbing in what I'd lost. "I'm fine. I just need a little fresh air. Could you pay for my stuff?" I dumped my purchases into Carmen's cart and thrust a handful of CFA currency bills at her. "Thanks, I'll wait for you outside."

Home, the place I'd successfully avoided thinking about, until the Nutz music brought it back. Following dinner that night, I stepped outside Carmen's house to look up at the stars. The memories, along with the rage, slid back into place.

Christmas Eve, last year. The family had, like always, gathered at the house. A Christmas tree filled one corner of the living room, bloated with decorations, gifts spilling out from underneath. I'd come home from college two days earlier, having just finished a run of eight Nutz performances. By the last one, I'd felt unutterably drained, both physically and emotionally, yet paradoxically missing it all terribly. In Omaha, once again just crabby, difficult, little-sister Fiona, I felt like Cinderella the morning after the ball. Except that Prince Charming was heading the wrong direction.

Things weren't going well with Lane Chatham. We'd been dating for twelve weeks, which was eight weeks longer than any other relationship I'd had. It was love, or so I'd thought. But something had gone off. I could see it in the way he seemed to be seeking out things to disagree about, or the way he recoiled in annoyance when I spoke too philosophically ("stop showing off your vocabulary") or reacted emotionally to something ("stop overreacting"). I'd tried to modify my moods, my words, to accommodate his preferences. I tried to be lighthearted and stick to cocktail party chitchat. Nothing worked; it only grew worse. He started avoiding me, making excuses. At opening night of Nutz, he thrust flowers in my hands (cheap, wilting ones) and told me we needed to talk. I looked at his handsome, smooth face, his now-unreadable eyes, and told him I couldn't possibly discuss anything during *Nutcracker* season. He looked relieved. Which made me feel relieved. It wasn't a breakup if the guy looked relieved about not discussing things.

Was it?

He went home to Kentucky for the holidays while I completed the Nutz run. I told myself we'd talk about things after the New Year, back at school. No New Year's Eve together? No problem. These things happened.

But here in Omaha, in the house, it was family business as usual. Russell had flown in earlier from Palo Alto, California, where he had a new job in research and development for Xerox, something baffling to do with computers. My brother and I shared the same pale-blue eye color, the only thing to mark us as siblings. He'd been a short, bespectacled math geek growing up, five years my senior, but puberty had treated him kindly. He'd become tall and attractive, which, in turn, made him more intolerable to be around.

Alison lived locally, but I didn't see her until the family gathering on Christmas Eve. I prayed she wouldn't ask how things were going with Lane. I wanted to sustain the illusion of having a successful romantic relationship, like my glamorous sister did so effortlessly, for a little bit longer. And magically, she cooperated. After she asked about the Nutz run, the conversation shifted to neutral, family-related banter, and what was going on in her world of public relations and the social and civic committees she'd remained involved in, since her Miss Nebraska reign.

Tonight, Russell seemed to have designated himself as my tormentor. "Graduation will be here before you know it, Fiona," he boomed, jiggling the ice in his highball glass. It made a musical sound, like the silvery, delicate celesta in the Nutz Sugar Plum Fairy solo. A role I would never dance again. I pushed away the grief before it could engulf me.

"Yes," I told Russell.

"What kind of jobs are you considering? Just what does one *do* with an undergrad sociology degree? That is your major this year, right? Or did it change again?"

"No, it didn't change." *Asshole,* I wanted to add, but I bit my lip. Alison, I noticed, didn't seem to be relishing Russell's harassment of me as much as usual. Instead, the flickered look she cast me seemed sympathetic. Even apologetic. Which made no sense, but I appreciated the quasi-support. I squared my shoulders and met Russell's eyes without fear, the way you were supposed to do when a snarling dog confronted you.

"Not too many jobs in the sociology field, I'm thinking." He jiggled his ice again.

"As it turns out, last month I had an interview with the Peace Corps."

"The Peace Corps?! Why?"

"Well, *duh.* For a job. In Africa, or something like that."

He looked skeptical. "And just what were you planning to do in the Peace Corps?"

"Teach English."

He studied me, still acting so baffled, you'd think I'd asked him to compare and contrast the trademark choreographic differences between Balanchine and Marius Petipa and their impact on twentieth-century ballet. He gave a slow shake of his head. "Little sister, where do you come up with these half-baked ideas?"

"Russell," Alison protested, even as she began laughing.

Tonight, it was all more than I could handle. I looked wildly from Russell to Alison.

"I'm so sorry I'm not some miracle of intelligence like you, Russell, with job recruiters clamoring to represent me," I screeched. "I'm so sorry I'm not a carbon copy of the two of you perfect people."

A hush fell over the room. My aunts, standing nearby, took two cautious steps back toward Mom, who was shaking her head.

"Oh Fiona, let's not start this again and ruin another holiday gathering," she said. "Why do you let your siblings get under your skin? Come on, it's Christmas Eve. Let's enjoy ourselves."

The party continued, faces growing flushed with wine and good cheer. No one noticed when I grabbed my jacket and escaped outside.

Silent night, black night. The frigid winter air hurt my lungs when I breathed in. Frozen puffs of rage rose and dissipated. The stars glittered above me, distant and aloof. Inside, Mom began playing "Oh Little Town of Bethlehem" on the piano and the others joined in singing. My chest heaved as if I'd just finished dancing "Waltz of the Flowers."

"I'm getting out of here," I said out loud. "To hell with all of you."

And so I'd gotten out of there. Problem was, I was the one to suffer for it. Back home, they'd be having the same Christmas Eve ceremony without me, probably commenting on how much calmer it seemed. Tears stung my eyes as I looked up at the night sky above

Carmen's house. Even the starry constellations were foreign, reminding me how very far from home I was.

The back door creaked open and I hastily wiped the tears from my face. Henry joined me. He was silent for a moment, hands tucked into pockets as he glanced up at the studded sky. "So Minneapolis is fucking freezing as always," he said. "I hear they had thirty days below zero and for seven days straight it didn't get above fifteen below. Mom probably has ice on the brain, so I'll forgive her, but you know what she sent me for Christmas?"

He looked over at me and I shook my head.

"A scarf, she sent me a goddamned scarf."

It was impossible to be in a gloomy mood around Henry. A snort of laughter escaped me and then we were exchanging "can't beat this one" Midwestern winter stories. By the time we joined the others in the living room, I felt better. Homesickness had its advantages, I reflected. I was away from my family and I missed them. It was easier than being with them and hating them.

By midnight we were all still going strong. Coffee cups and Regab empties littered the dining table. Daniel had brought out the bottle of Cognac he'd bought earlier. We drank it from a mismatched assortment of glasses as we played Gabopoly, a Monopoly board game the previous volunteer had Africanized. We'd been at it for hours, shrieking over Gabonese property, railroad lines (only one, half-built) and utilities (corrupt and thus highly profitable), with Gabon's CFA franc as currency. In between rolls, we debated the existence of reincarnation, the merits of corned beef versus canned mackerel, the current Reagan Administration and the pitfalls of Western policy and aid in Africa.

William remained mostly quiet, only contributing to the conversation when he had a strong opinion on an issue. With his shaggy golden hair, he reminded me of a lion, relaxed to the observer except for the feline eyes—in this case blue-green and fringed by thick lashes—that watched everything, waiting for the perfect moment to leap up and attack. He came to life in the discussion on Western aid to the famine-ravaged regions in Africa.

"Refugee camps create their own problems," he argued. "My sister sent me this article summarizing the Ethiopian government's attempts to resettle a half-million refugees. Did you hear about this? We all shook our heads. "It ended up claiming the lives of 100,000 of them. I worked there for six weeks—I believe it. So, you can argue that our efforts to help them killed them."

Carmen didn't like this. "Oh, so you would advocate just standing there and watching them die?"

William regarded her impassively. "Yes. You watch them die. And then you go have lunch."

His words produced a cowed silence around the table. William intimidated me—I wasn't sure if I liked him or not. Carmen rolled the dice and moved her piece before speaking. "I never would have thought you could be so cold, William." Her voice trembled with hurt reproof.

William relaxed. He reached out and stroked Carmen's clenched hand. When he spoke, his voice was gentle. "I said it that way to prove a point, Carmencita."

Carmencita? My eyes darted to her face, over to Daniel's and back to William's, whose hand still covered Carmen's. I looked for heated glances, jealous or otherwise, but found none.

William was still talking. "You know, I didn't just show up on day one at the camp and act that way. God, the first time a kid died, I went to my tent and cried. I thought of how his family must be feeling, of what a waste of a life it was, of the enormity of the crisis. I was a mess for the rest of the day. I went and ruined three dozen blood cultures because I wasn't paying attention."

"Did they yell at you?" Carmen asked.

William shook his head. "I suppose they were used to that kind of behavior from the new arrivals. But I remember a few days later, someone received Hershey's Kisses in the mail and everyone was laughing and eating them like it was a holiday. We'd lost four people that day. I'd watched two of them die. And there the other workers were, partying over melted Kisses."

The room grew silent again. William's eyes were fierce, concentrating on the Regab label he was prying off a bottle.

"You have to learn to put your feelings aside and focus instead on what can be done, which isn't necessarily what you *want* done. If your goal is to save everyone's life, you've set yourself up to fail. Maybe not immediately, but eventually. All you can do is try, then let go of your personal agenda."

It was his turn to roll the dice. He moved his piece, still lost in his musings. "You learn to offer sympathy without empathy. Nonattachment is essential."

"I hope you feel that way about your cash, buddy," Henry said, "because I'm about to kick your ass. You just landed on my top-priced *Bord de la Mer* property and it's got a hotel."

William, jolted from his reverie, stared in dismay at the board. "Wait, that can't be. I just landed on your hotel last time."

Henry grinned. "Yup. I've got hotels on every block, now, don't I?"

"This is ridiculous. How did you get so far ahead? I've only got one house."

"Henry got one of those palm-greasing cards," Daniel offered. "The bank slips him the CFA equivalent of a hundred bucks every time he rolls."

And like that, we switched back into game mode. We argued more, laughed over Gabonese property crises and forgot about the serious stuff lurking outside all around us. Early on Christmas morning, 7000 miles from home, it seemed like the wisest thing to do.

Chapter 9

Carmen had agreed that New Year's Eve in Libreville was a great idea, so a few days after Christmas, she and I set off. Oyem had its own bustling taxi station, offering commercial transportation north toward the Cameroon border and Bitam, where Daniel lived, or south toward Libreville. We hopped in the back of an open-bed southbound truck, equipped with two stubby picnic benches in back for seating. Portly, middle-aged Gabonese women, younger ones with children, and older men dressed in fraying, thrift-store-reject clothing piled on after us. With each person added on, our shoulder space became more limited until we were snugly pressed, one against the other. The sharp tang of body odor was inescapable. And still more people squeezed in. A mother with a baby strapped to her back hoisted a struggling goat over the side of the truck. It spilled, bleating, into the center and scrambled to upright itself. Another woman got on, carrying a rooster by its legs upside-down, that craned its neck around in confusion.

The passenger truck, a makeshift bush-taxi—a *taxi-brousse*—took off. in a cloud of dust. Being crammed in, I discovered, had its advantages. Our shoulders and thighs, wedged closely together, acted as a cushion and shock absorber for the inevitable bumps and potholes of the road. When we hit a large pothole, we all bounced as one unit. No one spoke as emerald rainforest flashed past and the sun rose in the sky, but there was a relaxed intimacy to the silence. Carmen nudged me a while later and gestured to where a man had dozed off, face lolling against the shoulder of the woman sitting next to him. With each snore, his face slid further down toward her ample chest. Carmen and I exchanged grins. "So, excited about going to Libreville?" she asked.

"Oh, definitely. How about you—are you bummed that Daniel didn't join us?"

She shook her head. "Nah, I'm fine. He's not much for cities. He'd rather stay put in Bitam."

"I can't imagine wanting to stay at my post."

"Bitam's a great little town—he lucked out. His house is on the grounds of the Catholic mission where he teaches. Gorgeous place, and the nuns who run the school spoil him."

"He's going to miss out. Rich told me Chuck throws a great New Year's Eve party at his house each year."

"Cool. You'll be my date? I promise to give you a big smacking kiss at midnight."

"I'd be happy to be your date, *Carmencita*." I let the emphasis hang heavy in the words.

She looked at me and grinned. "Now what's wrong with Carmencita? It's what my Mom used to call me."

"And others as well, it would seem." I studied her casual expression. "So, are you going to tell me what's up?"

"Nothing's up."

"Fine, you just sleep with Daniel by night and let William caress your hand and murmur endearments by day."

She waved away my words. "William and I look so friendly because we *are* friendly. He's just that way. Back when I arrived at my post, I had a tough few weeks. One Friday afternoon when I was feeling particularly lonely, William showed up in town. I got all dopey and cried on his shoulder and he took me to his village. We hung out, took a hike along a river trail, and I made pizza in his propane oven. We played cards all evening." The truck hit a particularly large pothole that made us all shoot up three inches and slam back down. After Carmen regained the breath knocked out of her, she continued. "It reminded me of going home for the weekend during college years. Someone else is in charge, it feels safe and cozy, and it's there for you when you need the comfort."

"And how does Daniel feel about all this?"

"Daniel's cool. He spends more time with William than I do—Bitam is less than an hour from William's village. They eat bachelor food together and William tells him about his girlfriend back in California."

"You mean all this time William and this woman have been *dating*?"

"Yes, or whatever you call it when you do it in letters instead of in person. They're meeting in Paris over the summer, though."

"That's insane."

Carmen laughed. "I know. Long-distance relationships are suicide. I mean, what if you really, really need to get laid?"

I thought of Lane Chatham and his hurried groping. This scenario didn't strike me as too dire, but Carmen sat, mulling over this as if it were the worst thing imaginable.

Before I could reply, the taxi-brousse came to an abrupt halt on an empty stretch of road between villages. I peeked over the truck's cab to discover the road blocked by a huge Okoumé tree, ten feet in diameter, twisted from its base and lying in our way. The road, flanked by steep hill on one side and a vine-choked ravine on the other, meant the obstruction was impassable. The driver got out and studied the problem, rubbing his chin. He slapped at the tree and paced the length of it. Then he shook his head and returned to the cab and cut the engine.

The high whine of insects from the surrounding rainforest immediately filled the silence. Carmen and I looked at each other in dismay. "Can't we take a detour?" I called out in French.

"There are no other roads," another passenger replied.

We sat. And sat. "What are we going to do?" I grumbled to Carmen as I swatted at flies.

"Sit a little longer, I guess." She pulled out a paperback and began to read.

The heat grew suffocating. Two pickup trucks stopped behind us. The drivers descended, examined the tree and stopped to converse with our driver in rapid Fang. The drivers all shrugged, returned to their trucks and sat.

My fellow passengers' patience both awed and frustrated me. No one griped. I wanted someone to take charge, to leap up and say, "C'mon, are we going to let this situation get the best of us?"

"*NO!*" people would retort, sitting up straighter, hope growing in their eyes.

"Are we gonna solve this problem?"

"*YES!*" the galvanized crowd would shout.

"Then let's do it!" And with a war cry, we would all attack the problem. Someone would pull out a rope, another would mention a tow on their rear bumper, things would happen and a great feeling of camaraderie would sweep through the crowd. Kids would cheer, babies would gurgle and wave their fists, and we'd make it happen— this impossible task everyone said couldn't be done.

But this wasn't the United States, it was Gabon, where people had long ago learned to accept the hardships that befell them. After the wait stretched into an hour, people began to move around and pull food from sacks—baton de manioc, a baguette, cooked fish that had been neatly stored inside a banana leaf, the stem serving as a tie around the folded leaf's top. Cups of water and palm wine were passed around. Young mothers whipped out their breasts for infants to nurse, others clambered out of the truck and headed over to the edge of the road to relieve themselves. No one complained about the delay. Except me.

Two hours became three. Eventually, a bright orange government truck pulled up and two Gabonese men in uniformed vests got out. I sat up expectantly. But the inspection of the tree produced only head scratching and shrugs. After a babble of conversation between the officials and the gathered drivers, everyone nodded and returned to their trucks. Our driver came around to the back, making his announcement in both Fang and French. He was turning back to Oyem. The road would not reopen again until tomorrow. This elicited a reaction from the Gabonese—cries of protest, clicks of disgust and pursing of lips. Then the resignation kicked back in.

I freaked.

"Look," Carmen interrupted, "we really need to reconsider this plan. This puts us a day behind schedule. We're doing all this driving to spend three days in Libreville, only to turn right back around and take the same trip again. It was stupid to think we could drive there in a day with no problems. And I'm sure we'd only hit more delays."

I stared at her. "Are you suggesting we not go to Libreville at all?"

"I think we should seriously reconsider. We're not far from Henry's village—he invited us to their New Years *fête*. We should just do that instead."

"But I *have* to go to Libreville."

"Why? Don't tell me it's just about going to Chuck's party."

I was silent.

"Aha," she said. "Because 'someone' is going to be there."

When I didn't reply, Carmen sighed. "Why put yourself through this, Fiona? He would be there with his girlfriend."

My inner toddler wanted to scream and rail at this latest problem.

Instead I shoved my bag back under the bench in a stony silence.

"C'mon, let's just have our own fun," Carmen said. "Henry's great. Hanging out with him will be much less stressful. Screw Christophe. I mean, don't screw Christophe."

Changing our plans proved easy. At the junction village where the Oyem and Makokou roads met, we descended and hitched a ride with the next truck that passed by. Less than an hour later, we arrived in Henry's village, a roadside clearing of mud-and-wattle huts with rusting corrugated tin roofs, surrounded by dusty, open yards. Henry came out of the *corps de garde,* an open-sided, thatched structure in the center of the village, shouting in surprise. He introduced us to the village chief and some of the elders. We joined them in the corps de garde and sat back to drink Regab.

The sweet smell of wood smoke permeated the air as we listened to the men talk. Children banded together and raced around in yards kept free of foliage and thus the threat of snakes. Hens pecked at the dirt. The peaceful silence was periodically broken by a burst of scolding coming from one of the *cuisines*, a separate structure from the house that served as its kitchen. The children skittered away from the women and resumed their play. They crept up closer to the corps de garde and when I twisted around to look at them, they ran away shrieking. When I turned my back, they repeated the exercise. Clearly it was a game to see who could get the closest to the *ntang*, the scary white people. One kid finally became brave enough to touch my hair. As a reward, I yanked out a few strands and presented them to him. He skipped back to the others, who clustered around his prize, chattering in Fang.

Henry showed us his home after we'd finished our beers. Inside the dim living room, a young woman swept the dirt floor, nodding her greeting. "Living room, bedroom," Henry called out, pointing to the sparsely furnished rooms with crumbling walls that allowed light to peek in through cracks. "Cuisine to the right of the house, latrine out back."

The women of the village appeared to have adopted Henry. Several hovered nearby, in village attire of a pagne wrapped around the waist, accompanied by a blouse or tee shirt. "*S'il vous plait, monsieur Henri,*" a woman behind us said. "Will your women sleep in the bed with you?"

Carmen and I broke into snorts of laughter as Henry told her no, he would sleep on the floor in the living room while we used his bed.

Next we walked into the smoky cuisine to meet the woman who was preparing Henry's dinner. She was small, Pygmy-sized, neither young nor old. When she stood, I saw that one of her legs was hideously twisted in a way that made her limp when walking. She beamed and shook our hands with a surprisingly strong grip. She paused after shaking mine. Peering closer into my face, she crowed and said something in Fang. The other women exclaimed and nodded. One of them propelled me toward the door where the daylight spilled in. They all studied my face.

"It's your eyes," a woman explained to me in French. "She says you have spirit eyes."

If it wasn't my hair or my height—too tall for a female here—it was my pale eyes drawing attention. I nodded at everyone and smiled. "*Merci,*" I said to the lame woman, unsure of what I was thanking her for, but clueless how to otherwise reply. "*Merci,*" I kept repeating until the women returned to the cooking fire, chattering among themselves.

The darkness that falls in a region with no electricity seems that much more dramatic. The inky blackness on New Year's Eve however, did nothing to dispel the festive air in the village.

The food for the celebration, set out on a table inside Henry's house, varied little in color and texture. Bowls of rice sat next to dishes of pangolin, river rat and monkey, all cooked in a fiery tomato sauce. *Piment,* the local fiery pepper, helped disguise the gamey flavor of the river rat, which, I was assured, lived in the jungle, not in a sewer or latrine. *Feuille de manioc* was the dish of chopped manioc leaves I'd had on my site visit, that tasted a bit like spicy creamed spinach, with smoky, earthy undertones.

"Not bad," I said to Carmen as we sat on benches set up outside. "Except that I just pulled this thing out of my mouth." I pointed to a grayish curl of skin on the edge of my tin plate. "It was furry against my tongue—I think it's monkey skin."

Henry held up his plate of stewed pangolin. "Tastes just like chicken, doesn't it?"

Music blared from Henry's battery-operated cassette player. Someone lit an enormous bonfire. When food had been cleared, there was dancing—a slow, lazy shuffle in the dirt, but not necessarily between the sexes. "Young men and women don't mingle much at the parties here," Henry told us. "In public, at least. You never see couples holding hands here in the village. Guess that would be too shocking." He had a Gabonese girlfriend, we discovered, the first woman we'd seen in his house. "The village chief kept throwing these women at me," he said, "and I finally gave up on turning them down." His girlfriend paid him little attention while we were around. "But she'll slip in to visit tonight," Henry said with a grin.

Everyone drank Regab and palm wine until late into the night. "So, it's not Libreville," Carmen said, "but it's fun, isn't it?"

I pondered her question. "Oh, sure. Just not the kind of fun I'd anticipated."

"I won't even ask," Carmen said. Before I could reply, she spoke again. "His family's originally from Oyem, did you know that?"

"Christophe's?!"

Carmen nodded. "I saw him last month, in fact. With a woman who wasn't Diana."

"A relative?"

"Uh, I hope not."

Two of Henry's workers came over and started talking to Carmen. I was content to sit, dream about Christophe and stare into the bonfire, letting the others do the talking and dancing. The leaping flames lulled me into a trance. Sparks rose up from the crackling fire and disappeared into the sky like reverse shooting stars. I leaned my head back and watched their journey. The dark sky seemed endless and omnipotent, an upside-down ocean that soon made me feel dizzy. When I straightened up, I saw the woman again. Watching me.

The lame woman from Henry's cuisine had been tracking me since our meeting. Whenever I glanced around, the woman was there, studying me. Even from across a yard, she would find a way to catch my eye. Seeing she had my attention, she approached. She was wearing a red dress that looked like it belonged in a 1950s ballroom. From its faded condition, I was willing to bet it had been manufactured around then as well.

She clasped my hand again, but didn't seem to want to let go. Nodding and beaming, she began to speak in fractured French. "Those who are not here. You call them, with your spirit eyes. They will come to you."

Was the woman drunk? Crazy? Her unflinching gaze made me increasingly uneasy. Although I'd grown used to stares, they weren't like this—the appraising scrutiny of a juror who knows far more about the defendant than the court does. This, I decided, was why village settings made me uneasy. There was too much mystery lurking in the shadows, the trees.

"You dance," the woman was now saying. "That is how they will know you. And they will join you." She leaned closer. "Protect you."

Protect me? What the hell? And how did she know I danced?

"You will dance tonight?" Her question sounded more like a mandate.

My smile was starting to ache from the effort. My head had begun to pound. "*Merci, non,*" I told her. "I don't dance African."

Carmen turned her attention back to us and mercifully, the woman stopped badgering me. After giving Carmen a friendly nod, she limped away.

"What was that all about?" Carmen asked.

"I don't have a clue. Maybe Henry told her I used to be a dancer. She said I would dance. Also some weird shit about spirits and my spirit eyes, and how they'll come to me."

"Who is 'they'?"

"You tell me. Ghosts? Gendarmes? The dance police?"

"So, you're going to join them in dancing? That'll be fun to watch."

"Hell, no!"

My reply came out louder and more snappish than I'd intended.

Carmen regarded me curiously. "Okay, no biggie."

"Sorry. Didn't mean to bark. It's just... I don't know. That was creepy, somehow."

"It's all right, Miss Spirit Eyes." She snickered. "That'll have to be your nickname now."

"I think not. God." I winced and drove my fingers into my hair. "Why can't normal stuff happen to me?"

"Because you were meant for weird things, Fiona. The eyes and hair just sort of beg for it."

"Thanks. I knew some day I'd find my calling."

"Spirit dancing," Carmen said. "Next best thing to ballet."

My tension began to ease. "Sure. Maybe I'll make that next year's secondary project."

Carmen lifted her cup. "Anyway, here's to a very interesting new year ahead of us."

"'Interesting.' I'm sure that will prove to be the understatement of the year." I knocked my cup against hers and we both took a big, sloppy gulp.

The entire village seemed to have a hangover on New Year's Day. Only the roosters were up early. Even after everyone rose, the sleepy feeling never dissipated. "That's village life for you," Henry said, yawning over his cup of Nescafé. "No one rushes. The work will always be there, so why hurry?" Greeting people, he informed us, could take several minutes per interaction. "There's an etiquette to it all," Henry explained, "shaking everyone's hand, inquiring about health, about family, about family's health, commenting on the weather. Waiting while someone fetches Regab or palm wine. Making toasts before the first sip. The second one. The third. Only then will they talk about business. It's exhausting."

I found I could better appreciate the village's slower pace that afternoon when Henry pulled out a joint. As the marijuana sedated my body into a good-natured stupor, a part of my brain awoke. All the answers, I felt, now lay within my grasp. I tried to explain to Carmen and Henry once he'd returned with a bowl of popcorn.

"I understand what that woman was trying to tell me last night. And how she acted like she knew me. Because don't we all recognize ourselves somehow in the eyes of another? We all serve as a mirror to the other person's soul. Maybe every white person represents to them some shadowy reflection of what they've always known." I began to stuff popcorn into my mouth. I'd never tasted such good popcorn in my entire life. I chomped through another handful and another while continuing with my theory.

"How easy it must be to figure out each foreigner who comes here, instituting their own agenda into the serenity that is Gabonese village life. I can just see the conflicts within the psyche of each Gabonese— the side that resents us for still acting like colonials, but then the other part that looks at the vines in the forest and just *grows*, you know? Like, I feel a part of this growth. If I sit here really quiet, I can feel it happening."

It dawned on me that Henry and Carmen were laughing. "What's up?" I asked. "What's so funny?"

"Fiona," Henry asked, "have you ever gotten stoned before?"

Flustered, I tried to regain control over my thoughts, my words. "I had my art to think of first, you know. It's not something you'd do before dancing—it would be a real downer. No wait." I rose from my wicker chair. "It might not be bad at all." My ears perked up to the tinny sound of an African pop tune playing on someone's radio. "Especially because I hear the message within the music and it tells me what to do."

Sure enough, my hips began to swing on their own accord as I wafted around the dusty yard. An approving jury of inner critics assured me I had never danced better. Further away, a chicken in the yard pecked at the dirt to the beat of the music and I squatted down to watch, entranced. I'd never squat-danced before—I found it very sensuous and liberating. Carmen had not stopped laughing for ten minutes. Or at least it felt like ten minutes. Maybe even an hour.

"This song has been going on for a really long time," I told Henry.

"Actually, it's been less than three minutes. But keep dancing with the chicken—you're doing a great job."

Carmen finally stopped laughing. "And here you thought you were missing out on something by not going to Libreville." As we all started laughing again, I decided village life had some advantages, after all.

Chapter 10

Christophe broke up with Diana.

It happened in Libreville on New Year's Day, probably around the time I'd been dancing with the chicken. Rich, who'd spent the holidays in Libreville, gave me the news back in Makokou when I stopped by his house.

"Oh, no, poor Diana." My voice came out abnormally high. I paused to modulate it. "Was she upset about it?"

"Looked like it. Keisha took a few extra days to return with her to Mouila. Christophe had taken off already—moved into an apartment in Libreville the very next day." Rich shook his head. "Man, was Keisha hot about everything. Not a pleasant time to be around her and Diana. But, hey, the New Year's Eve party was great. Of course, others might have felt differently. You know Norman, a math teacher in your group? He quit the next day. I don't think it was because of the party, though."

He continued on about events in Libreville. I nodded, struggling to pay attention amid the clamor inside my head. *Christophe is free.* The news reverberated in my head and distracted me all evening. I bade Rich good night a few hours later and stumbled down the dirt road in a daze. Christophe was available. I would no longer be pursuing another woman's man. I'd be in Libreville in April, for the education volunteers' conference; we'd find a way to spend time together. I knew this, with a certainty I couldn't explain even to myself.

I returned to the classroom the following Monday, strengthened by the news, feeling it blanket me like a warm cloak on a chilly night. Whenever the students got too noisy, I drew the comforting feeling in closer. Through the course of the week, when I realized I really, really didn't like my job and that Makokou was lonely and depressing, the thought was there, sustaining me. This difficult year of teaching was just a way station, I decided. A trial before I changed posts and began my *real* experience in Gabon. With him.

I avoided Keisha for two weeks. I didn't want her wrath falling on me, the woman who'd caught Christophe's eye during training, maybe even the reason he'd broken up with Diana. But in the end, hunger for the company of other Americans drove me to Rich and Keisha's side of town late on Sunday afternoon. They were at Rich's house, sitting on his verandah in wicker chairs, drinking beer, catching the soft breeze that rose from the river. Keisha, to my relief, didn't treat me any differently. She inquired after my holiday trip to Oyem and sympathized about the roadblock and forced change in plans.

"How's life on your side of town these days?" she asked.

"Fine, I suppose. Except for the fact that someone broke into my house while I was gone."

"Again? How many times does this make?"

"Three."

"Shawn had the same problems last year. They weren't even supposed to put a woman in that house, or at that lycée post." She frowned at me as if both had been my doing.

"I don't know what to do about it. I keep wondering if it's the same person or a group of them. And why? Is it because they resent me?"

"Don't take it personally," Rich said. "It happens here. Especially to Americans and Europeans, for the obvious reason that we *have* valuables, and most people here don't. You ladies just need to toughen up a little." When Keisha turned on him in a fury, he ducked and grabbed her hand before she could hit him.

It had taken me a while to figure out they were sleeping together. Their relationship seemed to hover somewhere between close friends and an old married couple, with little of the groping and heated glances Carmen and Daniel were constantly exchanging. Occasionally, however, Rich would squeeze her knee or grab her by the waist and nuzzle her neck. At times, I profited from their togetherness—there was a settled, secure feeling in their homes. But other times, their intimacy made me feel all the lonelier here.

As it grew dark, the mosquitoes drove us inside. "Let me make dinner for you lovely ladies," Rich proposed. "That will prove I'm a nice guy, right?" He plopped down on the couch next to Keisha and gave her a kiss. "Do I pass?"

She sized him up before patting his thigh. "You do better than some."

He mock-cringed. "You treat us men so harshly."

"Only those who think they can get anything they want." Her last words were laced with hostility.

I knew who she was talking about: Christophe.

I bent my head to inspect the dirt under my fingernails, dreading a glare from her that would indict me as the Other Woman. When I looked up and caught her eye, however, her expression seemed oddly conspiratorial. "No kidding," I said, to test the waters.

This seemed to satisfy Keisha, acting as a sort of password that unleashed a torrent of words. "African men. Honest to God, they act like children who never had to grow up. Apparently some of them don't have to. Think they can treat women any way they want." Her angry gaze returned to me. "Asshole. He'd been acting so charming up to New Year's Eve, I even commented to Diana about that. She agreed. And then *she* shows up at the party. He'd invited her, can you believe it? And for her to actually come. The nerve…." She snorted in contempt.

I had no idea to whom she was referring. When Keisha caught my baffled expression, her eyes darted to Rich. "You told me you told her."

"I did."

"Then why is she staring at me like I have two heads?"

"I didn't mention that part."

"You're telling me you didn't tell her."

"Um. No. I mean yes, I didn't."

"You idiot."

"Why?"

"God, men are clueless."

My chest constricted. I didn't want to hear this. I wanted to walk out Rich's door right then and return to my crummy house and my life raft of dreams.

She scowled at him and turned back to me. "The other woman." She spat out each word. "The one he left Diana for."

I'd had years of experience in performing. If your toes had been rubbed raw by your pointe shoes after six hours of rehearsal and began to bleed, too bad. If they didn't heal before the performance, you taped them up, took a few Advil, gritted your teeth and went and performed. Image was everything in ballet. No matter how much your feet or hamstrings or pulled groin hurt, you went out there and smiled. My training kicked into place at Rich's house. *Ah, so the other woman lives in Libreville and that's why he decided to stay? How very interesting. So, a Gabonese woman, this time. She's gorgeous, you say? Imagine her showing up at the party like that! Oh, that Christophe, he'll never learn, will he?*

Keisha warmed to her task. "So here's the worst part. There was already a teaching replacement for him in Mouila. Apparently Christophe had told his lycée director in December that he wouldn't be returning the following semester. He *knew* he was going to leave Diana, but never gave her the slightest hint until New Year's Day. What a snake."

I stayed another fifteen minutes before making a great display of consulting my watch. Exclaiming over the time, I turned down Rich's offer of corned beef pizza. Finally I was free to make my way home, where I set the shattered bits of my heart on the kitchen table, right next to the crushed illusions. I pulled down my bottle of Cognac and a spare roll of toilet paper (no Kleenex sold here), and headed off to the bedroom to either get drunk or cry myself to sleep.

I did both.

The next day I was in a foul mood at the lycée. The students picked up on it and responded with gleeful unruliness. I was exhausted, my head hurt and I wasn't prepared for the day's lesson. By the third hour, Calixte's class, I was ready to explode at the slightest provocation.

In Calixte's class, no one wanted to give me the right answers. It was as though the entire class had taken a vote the previous Friday before leaving school that no one would do the homework or know the answers. Even my best students could only offer me sheepish smiles.

"Can not one person give me a complete sentence, using words we've already learned?" I asked in exasperation.

Calixte raised his hand. "Please, Miss. I practice English on the holiday. I speak very English now."

I studied him suspiciously. "All right," I said.

He rose to standing. He was huge; the desk was comically small for him. He cleared his throat theatrically. "Today I am busy with Miss Fiona in the classroom."

The students all screamed in unison and went on to shriek with laughter.

Calixte raised his hands for silence. "I love to busy with Miss Fiona," he continued. "I busy every day in the school. We busy together."

Through the continued shrieks of laughter, which now sounded jeering—toward me—I met Calixte's gaze. The irony was that he'd never before been so engaged in English class. Under any other circumstance, I could have found a silver lining in that. But this was intolerable.

Something in me snapped. "Screw you, you little shits," I screamed. "Screw every last one of you." A silence descended over the room as I continued, not caring that they couldn't understand my rapid English. "Do you think I left my family and my comfortable life behind to stand here and take this crap? Do you care? Do you ever stop to think this might be a little *difficult* for me?"

All eyes were riveted on me, round with shock.

"Open your fucking notebooks," I spat. This the students understood. Notebooks had never been opened so quickly. "Write down these goddamned words." I grabbed a piece of chalk from the blackboard sill and slapped the day's vocabulary words on the board, the chalk squeaking in protest. "Copy page seventy-three from your books." I wrote the page number on the blackboard and made slashes under the word "copy."

My fury had made me enormous. "Questions?" I barked and they all jumped in their seats, shook their heads no, and began to work.

All except Calixte, who sat back, arms folded, and regarded me with a proud smile.

The game had begun.

February signaled the onset of the long rainy season, where the morning clouds dissipated daily to expose blue sky, a burning sun and suffocating heat. In the afternoons, spectacular thunderheads piled up in the distance. A few hours later, the rumble of thunder would announce the imminent arrival of another storm. Torrents of rain would clatter on the corrugated tin roofs only to abruptly halt thirty minutes to an hour later. Energy spent, the clouds would break up, with the sun bursting out for one last encore before sunset.

The neighbor family's three-year-old daughter died. It had been a swift illness, I gleaned, something with high fever, and within forty-eight hours, she was gone. Their loss was devastating to consider, impossible to find the right words to offer in condolence. Grief saturated the air, heavier than the humidity. But it was African-style grief. After five days and nights of endless activity at their compound, with visitors, rattling gourds, wailing, singing, celebrating, it all abruptly stopped and the household returned, eerily, to precisely the same scene and hub of activity as before.

Chuck, Rachel and Anna, the education volunteer leader who'd replaced Meg, braved the muddy roads and came through town to check on the volunteers. "Great to see you're doing so well!" Rachel exclaimed, which I found curious—the mirror affirmed each day how awful I looked and felt. But it made more sense once I learned she'd med-evaced two volunteers in the last ten days. One had lost a dramatic amount of weight on an already thin frame, and looked like a walking skeleton, while the other had turned yellow, jaundiced with hepatitis. Next to these, my malaise seemed so minor that I didn't bother to complain. What could I say, anyway?

Instead, I turned to Chuck. "My house keeps getting broken into," I told him.

Chuck looked genuinely regretful. "This is an at-risk house."

"Any chance I could find a different place to live?"

"Speak to your school administrators. House assignments, and any changes, have to be made through them."

"I'm struggling in the classroom," I admitted later to Anna, who seemed less empathetic than Meg. I found I missed Meg. I missed Lambaréné. I missed American-tasting food. I missed my dance company. I missed hot baths and sweet-smelling lotions. I missed pretty much everything from my past life. Even my family. Especially my family. I would have added Christophe to the list, but I'd banished him from my mind. It hurt too much, otherwise.

Anna gave my shoulder a consoling pat. "All the volunteers feel that way this time of the year. Hang in there, through this month and next. In April you get to attend the education volunteers' conference in Libreville and see your friends again. It'll be great. It will rejuvenate you."

She beamed at me as though six weeks would fly past in no time.

It wouldn't. Not here in this house, this post, this place inside my head.

And there wasn't a thing I could do about it. Not this time. There was literally no place left for me to run away to.

Chapter 11

The *proviseur*, the director of the lycée, was a busy man, perhaps the only busy man in slow-paced provincial Gabon. There was always something going wrong at the lycée. Stolen books, no chalk. Teachers not showing up for class. Roosters wandering into the classroom. Pregnant students going into labor during class. The second week of March found me in his office, a nook of the main administrative building with particle-board walls that stopped two feet short of the ceiling. I sat waiting for him to finish his phone call. Telephones weren't a highly effective form of communication in Gabon. Calls from Makokou within Africa were hit and miss. Transatlantic calls were not even attempted. Inside the country, quality of the connection varied according to the day's weather. Today, a great deal of shouting seemed to be required to get the message across.

Five minutes later, the proviseur had finished his call. "Good morning, Garvey," he said with a distracted smile. "This is about your classes, yes?"

"No, it's about my house. The break-ins." I bunched and un-bunched the fabric of my skirt.

This was the third time I'd come in here complaining about break-ins. "Ah, yes. Regrettable," he said, shuffling through the papers on his desk in search of something more interesting than yet another gloomy story from me.

A bit more than regrettable, I wanted to shout. With the latest development, it had become more along the lines of nightmarish. "They broke in again last night." I tried to keep my voice from trembling. "While I was there. In my bedroom, sleeping."

This got the proviseur's attention. He stopped his paper ruffling and leaned forward, his face creased in alarm. "But this is terrible. They entered your home while you were in there? Did they attempt to harm you?" When I shook my head, he relaxed and waved his hand at me. "This is good news." He saw my expression and hastened to add, "Nonetheless, it must have given you a great fright."

"Yes. Or this morning, at least, when I discovered my back door was wide open. I didn't hear them at the time."

The proviseur looked confused. "You heard nothing? Then how can you be sure someone came in? Perhaps you'd simply forgotten to shut your door last night." His face brightened at this explanation. I wanted to argue that it would take a moron to leave a door open in this mosquito-infested country, saying nothing for my rabid need for privacy, but I didn't know the word for moron and rabid in French, so I stuck to facts.

"There are muddy footprints in my living room that came from a shoe larger than mine."

The proviseur's face fell. Before he could reply, the surveillant rushed into the office to claim his attention. Apparently a trio of goats had wandered into the *salle des professeurs*—the teachers' room— eating through a stack of the science teacher's graded but unrecorded tests. The issue seemed to be whether to give all the students credit or make them take the test again. The surveillant finally noticed me. He nodded and beamed.

"At last, you have come, seeking my assistance in disciplining your classes."

The proviseur explained my latest dilemma. As always, the news was followed by tsks of disapproval and a murmured, "Oh that house... it has always been a problem," as if we'd been discussing bug infestation and not thieves. But I could understand their lack of concern. In a culture where just getting by and raising a family beyond childhood was a triumph over the odds, my household thefts were inconsequential to the point of being absurd. A box of American stationery; the equivalent of eighteen dollars; a Mickey Mouse salt shaker; a frozen chicken.

The surveillant frowned when he heard about the previous night's nocturnal visitors. "Did they cause problems?" he demanded, rapping his stick against his palm.

The proviseur responded for me. "No. She only discovered the intrusion this morning, when she found her back door open." They exchanged complicit looks. I hated the way I was alternately treated as a fragile creature and a tiresome liability. The American. The single woman. The one who wouldn't let the surveillant punish the students, but who riled them instead.

In the end, the proviseur and surveillant agreed that my housing situation required change. Security bars on the window, or another home, or a room at the hotel. The proviseur promised to look into it. But after nine months in Gabon, I knew what that meant. It was one of those lines like "soon," or "we'll see tomorrow," or "perhaps," or how the director of the post office or school board or local ministry of education was always au village, but was expected back "very soon, very soon." Until then, you couldn't get your signature, your oversized package from America, your paycheck. That was how it went here.

The proviseur walked me to the door. "Perhaps by next year we will find you a safer home," he said in an encouraging voice.

Three more months in an open home. The thought made me feel sick with despair.

I pushed through my first two hours mechanically, grateful that I'd planned the lesson before bed. After the morning break, I numbly made my way to Calixte's class. Where, lo and behold, on the desk stood Mickey Mouse.

My salt shaker, from an earlier theft, back to visit. How kind. Judging by the expectant silence, the students wanted a reaction. My spirit leapt back to life. I'd give them a reaction, all right. Exaggerating my surprise, I wagged a finger at the salt shaker. "Mickey, you are late, late, late! Where have you been all semester? You must go to the surveillant and receive a punishment." I spoke in slow, deliberate English that all the students could understand. As they laughed in delight, I thought fast. My lesson plan for the day included the presentation of "if" and "could." Instead of using the vocabulary words and visual aids I'd prepared—a cut-out of a guy named Jack and his trip to a local market—I could use Mickey and his trip to Disneyland.

The revised class was a huge success. The students were enchanted with the concept of Disneyland. They needed little more besides their imagination to act it out. An eraser became a roller coaster, a duster became cotton candy. I pulled coins out of my backpack and passed them around. "If Mickey had some money," a student called out, "he could buy some cotton candy." Off they went, clamoring to hold Mickey the salt shaker and wave the duster high in the air, pretending to take bites out of it. The menacing teenagers of the past few months became excited children, cute and innocent beyond words. Except for the fact that two of the girls were pregnant and one of these boys had probably broken into my house and stolen Mickey.

Who was behind all these break-ins? Easy to accuse Calixte first, but he was not the only one grinning in a conspiratorial fashion. Joseph, another troublesome redoublant, looked alternately pleased and guilty when I met his eye. My instincts told me he'd been the one to place Mickey on my desk, whether or not he'd been the one to steal it from my house.

Last night's thief had taken nothing. That they'd been in my house while I was sleeping chilled me beyond measure. Had they lost courage and fled upon hearing me move around in my sleep? Had the intention been more ominous? Who was it?

In the end, I would never know. No student would betray a classmate. It was truly me against them, with the smirking Calixte as their ringleader. And they were winning.

Two days before Easter Break and my trip to Libreville, I came home in the afternoon to find my back door once again hanging open. Nothing appeared to have been stolen. Drawing a slow breath, I grabbed a broom in order to transfer my helplessness and anger into something productive. While sweeping, I noticed my ballet shoes weren't in their usual spot on the shelf in the corner. A hunt for them produced one by the back door. The other one, I concluded after an extensive search, was gone.

They'd stolen my ballet shoe. A battered, smelly, pink leather slipper with a hole where my big toe had poked through, important only to me. I sat on the couch, numb, letting the loss and its implications play through my head over and over.

My long-simmering unease and fear exploded into rage.

Fuck this. I quit.

I leapt from the couch, stomped out the door and down the road to the general store to get boxes. I'd pack my things and get out. I'd leave. I whispered this to myself like a mantra. Finally, I was going to do *something*. Anything to reestablish control. Inside the store, I commanded the clerk to bring me any empty boxes the store might have. He stared at me in fear. I saw myself through his eyes: the wild look on my face, the dark shadows under my eyes that came from a month of sleeping in a climate of fear and insecurity, the way my body was shaking. But he only nodded and slipped away.

My siblings had accused me of being a quitter in the past. I'd spent ten months resisting that. Now I felt the jittery triumph of an alcoholic stomping out of a bad AA meeting to hit a bar. It was all I could do not to burst into peals of mad laughter. An older woman nearby, arms full of purchases, edged further away from me. I swung around to face her.

"I'm getting the fuck out of here," I announced in English with a bright smile. She nodded, uncomprehending, and ducked her head.

The store clerk returned and handed over four boxes. I thanked him and marched out with them, trying unsuccessfully to balance them. Silence fell over the half-dozen men who were congregating around the entrance. I ignored them. But I couldn't ignore the group occupying the base of the steps. My students. Not just my students, but the "let's give the teacher the hardest time we can" kids. Calixte and all the usual suspects were there, from three different classes of mine. Instead of skulking away, like any self-respecting troublemaking kids would do back in the U.S., their faces brightened when they saw me.

"Hello, Miss Fiona, how are you today?" one of the students shouted in English. "It is a beautiful day and zee sun is shining and I am verrr happy." The other students laughed at his speech.

"What are you doing?" Another one pointed to the boxes.

I hesitated. It was not uncommon to speak with students outside the classroom, but a certain etiquette was involved. The teacher could appear more relaxed and jocular, yet at the same time, he or she needed to maintain decorum. I thought briefly about lying and trying to turn this into an entertaining charade, but decided I no longer had the energy. Besides, I was going to quit. How my students perceived me no longer mattered.

"I'm packing up," I told him.

"Why?"

"Because I'm leaving."

I expected gloats of triumph. Instead I got looks of incomprehension.

"Leaving for Libreville, yes?" one of them asked.

"Leaving for America."

Silence fell over the group. Jaws dropped, which would have been comical if I hadn't gone beyond finding amusement in anything here.

Joseph from Calixte's class recovered first. He switched to French. "Why are you leaving?"

I let the unsteady boxes topple. "It would appear that someone wants me to." I didn't look at Calixte. I focused on Joseph, who, although troublesome, was still a decent student. "My home is not safe from thieves who want to frighten me and steal from me."

They all proclaimed outrage at the thought, even as some of them looked guilty at the same time. From the corner of my eye I glanced at Calixte. He seemed calm, neither shrinking in shame nor rising to my defense like the others. I told the boys it had grown too difficult to teach as well. They protested, claiming they'd learned more in my class than in any other.

"You must continue here," one of them pleaded. "It is for you that I study."

"Thank you. I'll keep that in mind."

"May we help you bring these boxes to your home?" Joseph asked.

Sure, go on ahead, I felt like telling him. *I imagine many of you know the way in.* "No, thank you." My voice had regained a crispness that pleased me. The teacher was back. "I'll be fine. But thank you for offering."

"*Alors…* good luck, Miss Fiona." Joseph thrust his hand out and I gave it a firm shake. They all wanted to shake my hand after that, wishing me well on my upcoming trip to Libreville, from which they all declared I must return. Even the ones who plainly didn't like me appeared more respectful than they ever had in the classroom.

Calixte came forward as well, expression neutral except for a stealthy look behind his eyes. "Goodbye, Miss Fiona," he said in the chatty tone the others had used. "I hope to see you again soon. I would be very sad if you didn't come back." But when he withdrew his hand, he allowed his middle finger to slide along the base of my palm. It felt blatantly erotic, and shocked me speechless. I turned away from him abruptly and picked up my boxes. As I left, the students called out cheery goodbyes in English.

"Don't fall," I whispered to myself as I walked away from them. "Just don't fall."

Chapter 12

While I'd been suffering break-ins, Carmen had been fending off marriage proposals. Her lack of goats, she informed a group of us in Libreville, had saved her each time. Day three of our week-long conference, a breezy forum designed to help the education volunteers decompress and realign, had ended. We women, united by our unique problems, now sat in the faded blue living room of the *case de passage*—the Peace Corps transit house—and exchanged war stories. "The last proposal came about after I marched over to my problem student's house, about a month ago," Carmen told us. "I gave this long, impassioned speech to his father. I was so proud of myself, the way the father was really listening to me. He clung to every word and afterwards, shook my hand for a long time. I thought I was making a real impact. The next day the father shows up at my door and asks me, right there on the porch, if I'd like to become his third wife. And he was *serious,*" she added over our laughter. "The only thing that saved me was the line about no goats to offer as a bride-price. He next asked if my father had any goats. When I told him no, he nodded, almost in pity. Finally he left and never brought it up again. Goats…" She wagged her finger at all of us. "Don't ever buy them. Foolish mistake."

Being back in Libreville was a jolt, a largely pleasant one. Back to highways lined with palms alongside the vast blue of the Atlantic Ocean. We could take taxis, go to movies and buy ice cream again. In the company of the other volunteers, I didn't have to struggle with my French or speak slow, careful English. I could wear shorts and go swimming. The city still had its ugly side—its traffic, fumes and chaos; its lepers and cripples hobbling alongside the bustling crowds; rotting trash piled on the sidewalks. But it didn't detract from the capital's relentless energy. Libreville hummed with every aspect and flavor of life. It hid nothing. Urban Africa, I decided, slapped you in the face, seized you by the shoulders and gave you a good shake. You might hate it or love it, but you couldn't overlook it.

"The thing I resent," Sharon, a first-year English teacher, told the group in the living room, "is the way the male students don't want to give you the same respect they give your male colleagues."

Everyone nodded. I'd been surprised and relieved to discover in the past few days how many others were struggling with the same issues as I. Almost half the volunteers had suffered break-ins. That said, no one had complained of a student toying with her, using the break-ins as part of his elaborate game of intimidation. Terror flared up in me, yet again, over knowing Calixte might have been in my house, while I lay in the bedroom, vulnerable and sleeping. Who else would have had the nerve to do such a thing? No one. Stealing a salt shaker was one thing. Robbing a person of their security was another thing entirely. I hadn't had a decent night of sleep in that house since. The trauma of it was like an extra bag I carried around with me everywhere I went. A bag loaded with bricks, that no one else saw. It was killing me. I'd stopped doing ballet in my house; I simply couldn't summon the muse anymore. The ballet shoe theft had clinched its demise.

"One reason our colleagues get that respect," Carmen was saying, "is that the African males have no qualms about sending students out to be punished. Our surveillant's favorite method is whipping. I've got a Gabonese male colleague who kicks out two or three students per class session. Anyone who whispers or giggles is out. And whipped." She shook her head. "They're all convinced absolute silence and passive students are the best way to go."

"I remember Christophe pushing that style during training," Sharon said. "I've always felt guilty I couldn't teach more that way."

Christophe. Even hearing his name hurt. I reminded myself that it had to be even harder for Diana.

But Diana didn't seem to be hurting. "I think Christophe is a little too set in his ways," she said. "It annoys him when we Americans can't see the world through his eyes."

If Diana could rise above the situation, so could I. "Glad to hear I wasn't the only one who felt intimidated by his advice." I kept my voice light. "He was always foretelling gloom and doom if I taught my own way." I didn't bother to share just how gloomy and doomed my classes had become.

Keisha snorted. "Don't go thinking Christophe was the best teacher in the world, anyway. I mean, he's not even teaching anymore. What does that tell you? He's always been more interested in networking and deal-making."

"Yes, and it helps having the influence of Dad, the Minister of Tourism, in his back pocket." This time Diana didn't sound quite as gentle.

"He's a spoiled little boy," Keisha added. "All the men have it so much easier than the women here." And then we were off, complaining about African men, American men, and how we American woman could do just fine without them, thank you very much, but it helped to have them around to lug heavy crates of Regab back to the case de passage.

Carmen saw him first, as we were debating whether or not to go out for a beer. "Uh oh," she murmured, "looks like we've got a visitor." Her warning tone made us all look up.

The front screen door squeaked as it opened, and Christophe walked in.

It was like a mirage. A dream. I had trouble drawing a full breath. *He's come back for me.*

Keisha's expression grew hard. Diana swiveled to face him. She didn't say a word.

The silence in the room was electric. "*Bonsoir, tout le monde,*" he addressed us all with a smile, but his eyes returned to Diana.

I felt sick. *Of course Diana. You idiot. You fool.*

"How are you?" he asked Diana.

"Why are you here, Christophe?" Keisha interrupted.

Christophe frowned at her. "I'm here to see Diana."

"Dropping in on her just like that?" Keisha snapped.

"It's not as if I could have called in advance. There's no phone here."

Keisha glared in response but Diana waved her down. Christophe turned back to her. "I was hoping we'd get the chance to visit while you're in town. Are you free to go for a drink?"

Diana studied him, her expression cool. "I've got plans the next two nights."

"What about right now?"

I'd never had the opportunity to watch him like this, so focused on another woman. Christophe had no eyes for anyone but Diana. Maybe he'd broken up with the Other Woman already. Maybe he wanted to get back with Diana.

She paused to consider his question before flicking her curtain of glossy black hair over one shoulder.

"Sure, why not?" She rose to get her bag, leaving Christophe with six unfriendly females staring him down.

But Christophe wasn't the type to get intimidated, especially around women. He smiled easily at us before turning to Sharon. "Did my phone call to your proviseur make things better?"

Sharon blushed and stammered. "It did. It did help me out. Thank you for talking to them."

"Glad to be of assistance." His gaze continued around the room until he caught my eye.

I wanted to hit him. I wanted to touch him. I settled for a frosty stare.

He returned my gaze unflinchingly. Then he looked away. My heart gave a vicious twist. I struggled to keep the breath moving in, out, in, out, as he focused next on Keisha.

"Keisha," he crooned, advancing toward her with a teasing smile.

Her lips were compressed into a tight line. "Stop it. I'm still very angry at you."

He ignored her words and repeated her name in a singsong fashion until he was close enough to grab her. He lifted her to her feet.

"Stop it," she shrieked again, but began to laugh and bat at him as he hugged her.

Carmen caught my eye. By the pity and concern on her face, I knew how bad I looked. Pretty much as bad as I felt.

Which turned out to be precisely how I felt late that evening, as I lay on a couch in the darkened living room, sleepless, forced to listen to Diana and Christophe when they returned. Her melodic voice, outside, and Christophe's deeper chuckle were followed by a long silence, painfully easy to interpret. Afterward they both laughed softly and exchanged murmured goodbyes before she came inside, tiptoeing past those of us who hadn't grabbed a bunk bed fast enough, all sleeping peacefully except for myself.

Yet another bad night's sleep.

On Easter Sunday, the volunteers were invited to join the American expatriate community at the American ambassador's residence for a party. It threw me back into another world, one with trimmed lawns, white picket fences and prosperous-looking, chatty Americans. Hungry for exercise, even if it couldn't be ballet anymore, I headed for the swimming pool. The other volunteers stampeded over to the buffet table, which was crammed with trays of Virginia ham, smoked salmon and roast beef. Bowls of potato salad, cole slaw and fruit salad sweated over ice. No canned corned beef or manioc anywhere. Further down, a big pink cake was beginning to ooze at the edges from the heat. There was Budweiser in addition to Regab, but no Peace Corps people touched the former, so pale and insipid next to Regab. The volunteers crammed potato chips into their mouths as they piled their plates high. They acted as if they'd been fasting for months, which, in a way, was true. From the pool, I observed the pained expressions on the carefully made-up faces of the American expatriate wives. In their pressed khaki slacks and tailored white blouses, they had the uneasy demeanors of zoo visitors watching lions feed on raw meat.

I swam, hoping to quell the uneasiness bubbling inside me. Not only was it Easter, a major holiday for my Catholic family, but I'd just called home for only the second time since leaving Omaha. The conversation had felt rushed and distracting, with a transatlantic hiccup whenever both parties tried to talk at the same time. Russell had been surprisingly warm. Mom had cried. Alison, too, had sounded choked up.

"Fi, you're so far away! I miss you so much."

Her easy affection, the way it felt both familiar and foreign, threw me. I stuttered a reply. A few minutes into our conversation, she paused.

"Hello?" I called out. "Still there?"

"Fi, I'm getting married."

I'd seen this coming for a long time, but sensing it was different from hearing it. I took a deep breath. "Wow. Congratulations to you."

"Thanks. Do you… does it bother you?"

"No." I tried to brighten my voice. "I'm happy for you. The two of you seem well suited."

"It'll be next spring. Any chance that you'd come home for it?"

I chose my reply carefully. "I think that would be too much of a challenge."

"All right. I understand. I love you."

"I love you too."

She turned the phone over to Dad for one last exchange and that was it, my family time for the year, until the next difficult transatlantic call.

Now, as my arms and legs churned through the water, I tried to push the loneliness away. A few minutes into my efforts, I noticed someone else had joined me in the pool. He didn't linger; after a few laps, he hoisted himself up to sitting on the pool's edge. As I came to his end each time, I'd see his pale legs dangling in the water, feet wiggling. It made me feel like a shark. When I finally popped out of the water, he was looking straight at me, as if reading my thoughts. I grinned back. He introduced himself as Brad. His accent immediately identified him as American.

"Can I interest you in a beer?" he asked when we both rose from the pool's edge. I nodded and two minutes later he was back with two dripping Budweisers. We sat on lounge chairs and chatted. I learned Brad was twenty-nine, had been in Libreville for a year and worked as an information management specialist in the embassy's information program center. He was blond, well-built and decidedly attractive. He launched into a lengthy description of what the job entailed. I lost interest in what he was saying and instead watched his face, marveling at the lack of scruff, the smoothness of his skin and his even tan, as if he'd been plucked from a Southern California beach, hermetically sealed and popped open just for the ambassador's party. Brad didn't seem terribly interested in Libreville. For entertainment, he informed me, he went out to French restaurants with his colleagues. He had an extensive collection of videos at his apartment, shipped to him monthly via diplomatic pouch.

We ran out of interesting things to talk about, but that didn't stop him from talking. Interaction with him was like a dose of Midwestern food: predictable and on the bland side, but safe. And safe was precisely what I needed right then.

I thought of Christophe, gave myself a mental shake, accepted Brad's offer of another Budweiser and later, a lunch date for the following day. Although I disliked first dates, I clung to the notion of this one. It was the only way to move on.

For lunch the next day, Brad had chosen a French restaurant near the ocean, a hushed, elegant place with linen tablecloths and gilt-framed artwork adorning the walls. The clientele, both Gabonese and French, murmured in Parisian-accented French, punctuated by the clink of forks against china. In my tee shirt, faded cotton skirt and dusty sandals, I was clearly underdressed. But my self-consciousness didn't keep me from thoroughly enjoying my meal—poached fish in lemon cream sauce, flanked by tiny steamed potatoes and asparagus spears. Brad had ordered a bottle of wine, a Muscadet that slid down my throat like liquid velvet. Over lunch he droned on about his job, the inconveniences of living in Gabon.

Today, I had less patience for Brad. *Oh, the heartbreak of a broken VCR, when you have to wait until the next day to pick up a new one at the embassy store,* I wanted to say. *Or when your monthly shipment of Hostess Ding Dongs doesn't arrive on time. And when they serve your Muscadet at room temperature. The bastards! How can you bear it? Hey, Brad, ever had tumbu fly maggots plucked from your skin?* I looked at his unblemished face, sipped the exquisite wine and finished my lunch, recognizing with regret that the best part of the date was over. Whatever comfort I'd thought I could find by spending time with him had long since disappeared.

It dawned on me how like Lane Chatham he was: attractive and self-satisfied, ruled by the comforts of his life, unwilling to delve beneath the surface of things. Back when I was dating Lane, any time I'd try to direct the conversation deeper, he'd chuckle and say, "There you go again, sounding like a philosophy major." It was good-natured ribbing, but it would always annoy me. He was much like my siblings in that way. Like everyone I knew in Omaha, in fact. Sitting in the Libreville restaurant, it came to me with a flash of understanding that I would never run back to Omaha, no matter how bad things got here. I wasn't ready to surround myself with such people again so soon. Leaving Africa after ten months, I'd be caught between two worlds, having admitted defeat in both.

I had to stay.

I wanted to stay.

The restaurant's front doors swung open and Christophe walked in. I stared, afraid my eyes were playing tricks on me. But he was decidedly real, flanked by two men whose auras of power and privilege told me they were used to getting what they wanted. Their arrival caused a stir in the room. The restaurant owner hurried forward to greet them and show them to a table by the window. As they followed the owner, Christophe surveyed the room and caught my eye. He blinked twice before bringing a hand to his heart and pretending to stagger. The unaccustomed whimsy made me smile. Brad noticed my animation and turned around to look for the source.

"Oh, it's Christophe Essono." He said Christophe's name in a way no African would—placing the family name last, American style.

"You know him?" I asked, watching as Christophe and his two companions settled at their table.

"Oh sure, he's a good one to know. He's lived in the U.S., so he understands us a lot better than the others. Speaks great English. And his father is the Minister of Tourism, so he's got powerful connections. He's really a great guy, for an African."

For a moment I wondered if I'd misheard him. "Brad," I asked carefully, "does your work require any interaction with the local population?"

"Me? No, not really. That's more in the executive office."

A curl of disgust settled in my stomach. "That's maybe a good thing."

I watched as Christophe excused himself from his lunch partners and walked toward our table. From across the room we exchanged lazy grins, rich with private mirth. Euphoria exploded inside me. Christophe was here; nothing else mattered, not even the way he'd ignored me earlier.

Brad looked up as Christophe approached. "Hey Christophe, how's it going?" he asked in English, pumping Christophe's hand. "I guess you've met Fiona—um, sorry Fiona," he said, turning back to me. "I don't know your last name."

"Garvey," Christophe and I supplied at the same time. I laughed and motioned for Christophe to continue. "We know each other through Peace Corps Gabon," Christophe said.

"Okay." Brad didn't seem particularly interested. "Hey, did you know Bob is transferring to the American embassy in Dakar?"

"No, I didn't," Christophe said.

"There's going to be a farewell party Friday afternoon at the embassy. You should come."

"Thanks for letting me know. I'll consider it."

Brad glanced at his watch. "Well, nice of you to stop by." He balled up his napkin, dropped it onto his plate and looked around for the waiter.

Panic filled me. Brad was going to drag me away from Christophe, only to drone in the car about how he hated the traffic, the humidity, those sweaty Africans. "Are you ready to go?" he asked me.

I looked at my unfinished glass of wine and felt like telling him to go without me. Christophe caught my eye and seemed to instantly understand.

"Oh, but you haven't had dessert," he told us. "Their crème brulée is the best I've had outside of Paris."

"Unfortunately I have to be back at work," Brad said.

This was good news.

"I have a suggestion, if Fiona is interested." Christophe turned to me. "If Brad doesn't mind, why don't you join my friends and me at our table. You could enjoy some crème brulée while we have lunch and I can drop you off afterwards."

"Oh no, surely that's an imposition," Brad said.

Shut up, you moron. I smiled at the two of them politely. "That does sound appealing."

"Then it's decided," Christophe said.

Brad didn't seem heartbroken about ending our date in the restaurant. After the usual platitudes about nice meeting you and let's do it again (as if), I strolled over to Christophe's table, trying to appear casual. He introduced me to the other two men, who made a great display of standing respectfully and shaking my hand. As I settled next to Christophe, I decided this had been the kind of first date I could handle.

Chapter 13

I was finally alone with Christophe after lunch as we drove down the *Bord de la Mer*, the coastal highway, toward Libreville's city center. I was so happy to be with him, I forgot all about feeling hurt or antagonistic toward him. "Your French is coming along quite well," he told me. "Your face has filled out too—you've gained weight."

I ducked my head. "I know, I hate it."

He stopped for a light. "You're wrong in thinking it looks bad. You Americans always want to be thin. Here, gaining weight is a sign of health, of beauty."

"So I'm more beautiful than ever, huh?"

The light turned green and Christophe resumed driving. "I remember the first time I saw you. It was in Lambaréné, the night you trainees arrived," he said softly. "You looked so bristly and skinny and scared." He glanced over at me. "Yes. You are more beautiful than ever."

My heart sprang into fluttering mode. This kind of reaction, I decided irritably, shouldn't be allowed to happen still. "So tell me about your new love." My voice came out loud, accusing.

His manner, in turn, grew more curt. "She's a Gabonese woman who works at the Ministry of Education, where I'm currently employed."

"And…?"

"And what?"

"When did you meet her?" I hated my interrogating tone.

"November."

"Before or after you mailed me that note?"

He looked puzzled. "After, but I would have sent it had I been dating her already. That was between you and me, no one else."

I didn't know whether this made me feel better or worse. "Well, that's… great. I'm sure you'll both be very happy here in Libreville."

He sighed. "You're making too much out of this."

"Right. Out with the old, in with the new, no need to worry about hurt feelings, or anything silly like that."

He was angry now. He turned off at the next exit and drove down a dusty lane that ended near a beach. He cut the engine as a cloud of dust settled around the car.

"What is your problem?" he demanded. "Why are you attacking me?"

"Forget it. I don't understand you Africans and you can't figure out American women, can you?"

"You're right, I can't. Frankly, I think you're all a little spoiled."

I thought of my life back in Makokou, 7000 miles from home, the loneliness, discouragement and fear. I felt like I was six years old again and my father had just yelled at me. I dug my fingernails into my palms to keep from crying.

"I'm sorry," he said. "Let's start again." He drew in a deep breath. When he spoke again, it was in his hearty trainer voice. "Tell me how your classes are going."

"Why?" I turned on him in a fury. "Because you want to know how I've screwed up? How I've got discipline problems and it's all because I didn't follow your advice? Fine, you were absolutely right and I was absolutely wrong. I suppose that's why you offered to drive me back today. To gloat in your victory."

"No. That's not what I had in mind."

"It's not going well. So you won."

When he didn't reply, I glanced over at him. He'd managed to look wounded. "No, Fiona. I wanted to drive you back so we could spend time together. I've missed your company."

I tucked the comment away to replay over and over later. "You sure had a funny way of showing me that the other day, when you stopped by the case de passage."

He rubbed his temples ruefully. "You have to admit, I was facing the firing squad that afternoon."

"You deserved it."

"I realize that. I'm sorry if any of my actions have hurt you."

The apology and his genuine attitude disarmed me. Soon I found myself blurting out the truth about my situation. With the admissions came the warmth of our old companionship. I brought up the break-ins. "They're awful. They make me feel so vulnerable. But everyone's telling me they're no big deal."

"It does seem to be an unfortunate facet of life here for Americans."

"The last one hurt. They took a ballet shoe." My voice cracked.

"Oh, baby." His tone was soft. Of course he understood.

"But it gets more complicated," I said, and hesitated.

Christophe frowned. "What? Speak," he commanded.

"Someone broke in one night. They were in the living room while I was in the bedroom, sleeping. They stole nothing. It almost seemed to be a gesture, to prove that I was unsafe there."

Christophe had grown very still. Nervously I continued.

"I suspect a problem student, a redoublant I initially took for an adult, back in September, when he came by my house. Which he now uses to his advantage. He's got a game of intimidation going with me. He's making me nervous, and he likes my reaction."

The furrows over his brows deepened. "Tell me more about this student."

"In the classroom, even when he's not the one making the disruption, he always seems to be behind it, watching how I react. If he's not the one who's been breaking in, I still get a sense he's involved somehow. He knows my house. A little too well."

"Has this student threatened you in any other way?"

"Nothing I could report to my proviseur. He's clever about it."

"Has he ever laid a hand on you?"

"No. Except…" I found it hard to continue.

"Tell me." His voice sounded harsh.

I focused on a clump of sand that had made its way into the otherwise spotless car. "It's just that when he shook my hand farewell, just before I left Makokou to come here, he let his middle finger… stray or something."

"Are you telling me he brushed it against your palm? Like this?" He took my hand and did it, holding my gaze. Coming from Christophe, the warm, firm pressure of his finger against the tender vulnerability of my inner palm became undeniably erotic, like lips against a neck. It sent a bolt of sexual electricity ripping through me.

I managed to find my voice. "That's it exactly."

Calixte was trying to hit on me. The gesture had been a threat. A promise.

Christophe seemed to come to this conclusion at the same time. Rage built in his eyes as he took my hands and squeezed. "We're getting you out of that house."

Tears rose up from nowhere and settled in the back of my throat. My next words sounded thick and muffled. "That would make me feel better."

We drove to the Ministry of Education offices, housed in an anonymous, three-story building painted an industrial grey. Inside his office, he asked me specific questions and jotted down the replies on a pad of paper. I warned him what my administration kept telling me: there were no available houses, no vacancies for teachers at the hotel, no money in the Ministry budget for security bars on the windows. Christophe made a few phone calls and stepped out to talk with someone in a nearby office. I spied an oversized upholstered armchair in the corner of the room and went to sit in it. The chair was the perfect size to curl up in, with its two cushioned arms cradling me. It made me sleepy, more so when rain began to patter against the windowpane. How odd it was, I reflected, being here, so relaxed, in Christophe's office. This guy I'd thought was out of my life was very much back in it. I rose and went to the chair behind his desk and took his suit jacket to warm my bare skin against the air-conditioning. Tucking myself back in the armchair, I listened to the rain drum, inhaled the citrus of his cologne from within the folds of his jacket, and let my increasingly heavy eyelids droop shut.

A while later I heard a rustle. I opened one eye to see him standing there, hands on his hips, his head cocked to one side, smiling at me. "I borrowed your jacket," I mumbled.

"So I see. No, don't get up. I'll be another twenty minutes, at least."

I settled deeper into the comfortable chair. "Okay. I'll just keep your jacket company."

"You do that." His voice was soft, warm with affection. A giddy feeling of happiness welled up in me. It was as if every awful thing leading up to this moment had been worth it, to see him standing there, regarding me with such tenderness. I smiled back at him and shut my eyes again.

"Stop staring," I murmured a few seconds later. He laughed. A swish-swish of his trousers signified his departure and a moment later I heard his footsteps recede down the hall.

On the way back to the case de passage, we stopped for drinks at a café, where we chatted and swapped stories like old friends. His behavior was exemplary—solicitous and caring but not flirtatious in the least. Afterward he drove me back to the case. When he parked, I waited an extra beat to see if his hand would fall onto my knee or behind my neck. It didn't. Reluctantly, I slid out of the car. He came around to my side.

"Feel any better?" he asked.

"Yes. Thank you."

His arms slid around me for a hug. I sagged against him and realized how tired I was, how desperately lonely for contact. He released me all too soon and brushed an errant strand of hair from my face. I could feel him studying me, maybe debating whether or not to kiss me.

"You don't look good," he said. "You need more rest."

I couldn't help but laugh. The seducer had turned into the big brother. Nonetheless, it was an improvement over the cool stranger of a few days earlier. "A safer home will help," he said, and I nodded. "I'll try to have some answers for you before you fly out. Be sure and check at the Peace Corps office for messages tomorrow morning."

"Okay. Thank you. For everything."

"It was my pleasure," he said. He planted a light kiss on my forehead and gave my shoulders one last squeeze. "Off you go," he said. "Tell the firing squad inside that I said hello." He returned to his car and departed with a wave.

I flew back to Makokou the following afternoon. As Christophe had promised in his message, a representative of the hotel was waiting for me at the Makokou airport. He drove me to the hotel where I met the manager, a fussy, well-dressed Gabonese man, who showed me to one of their adjacent bungalows. It was a two-room unit, neat and clean, with a kitchenette, freshly painted walls, screens and bars on the windows and crisp cotton sheets on the bed. The bungalows, the manager informed me primly, were normally reserved for visiting officials. However, thanks to Christophe's influence, this one was mine to use until the end of the term. I moved in an hour later.

Sleeping well in a secure home with double locks and security bars on the windows did wonders. It got me through the first day back in the classroom; it protected me from the flotsam and jetsam of the students' restlessness, and it held strong before Calixte. I gauged his menace for a few days, knowing that the power lay in my hands. Christophe had wanted to make a phone call to the proviseur about Calixte, along with a strong suggestion to send him back to his village should he act up one more time. I'd said no, but promised him I'd start using administration as backup. When Calixte finally struck, a week later, by hurling a piece of chalk at me while I was facing the blackboard, writing, I felt no fear, no uncertainty. Once I confirmed it was him, I walked out of the classroom.

The ensuing cheers and laughter from my students abruptly halted when I returned a few seconds later with the surveillant. How absurd, I realized, to have had this resource at my fingertips and have been too stubborn, too idealistic to use it. Silly first-year Peace Corps volunteer.

"Ondo Calixte," the surveillant shouted, "come with me, this instant."

Calixte strode to the front and paused beside me, his eyes pouring out rage. This was my cue to shrink. I didn't. I had friends now. I had someone who could kick his ass. His eyes flickered with insecurity. A fatal mistake and we both knew it.

Game over. The teacher had won. The surveillant grabbed his arm and shoved him out the door.

I turned to the other students. "I will not hesitate to throw out any other student who disrupts my class." My words, spoken in precise, correct French, sliced through the silence. "I do not want this. But do not provoke me. I will spend the rest of the year lecturing you from your textbooks unless you can prove to me you are capable of a more lively class."

I hated the threat-method of teaching. But it worked, that day and the rest of the week. Calixte came back and promptly got kicked out again the following week. *Whatever it takes*, my eyes told him, and although he glowered, he could do nothing.

Next year, I vowed, it wouldn't be like this.

Next year.

I realized, with a growing sense of relief that stayed with me through the week, the month, that I was going to make it. Not gracefully. Nothing much to be proud of.

Except I'd done it. And that was enough.

Part Three
Second Year

Chapter 14

At the Lomé International Airport in Togo, a crowd of over a hundred shouting Africans surrounded a lone ticket agent behind the Air Gabon desk. It was chaos, like some incomprehensible contact sport. I pushed in and got a smelly armpit in my face and trod on another person's toe. It hardly registered. Like everyone else, I focused on wading through the sea of irritated people to reach my goal: ten seconds of the ticket agent's time. I made it to the desk and waved my plane ticket to Libreville in her face. The Togolese agent, trim and immaculate in her Air Gabon uniform, glanced at it and sniffed. "There are no seats," she told me.

"No seats? What does that mean?"

"You are not confirmed on this flight."

I looked at the ticket and pushed it back at her. "What does this big 'C' mean, then?"

She scrutinized the ticket again and shrugged. "All right, you are confirmed. But there are no seats available."

I tried to protest more, but the angry horde swallowed me. A heavy man and his two portly wives pushed in front of me to plead their case next, also to no avail. I stood in the heaving, jostling crowd, anxiety coursing through me like a fever. I'd spent almost all my money, keeping just enough for a taxi ride back to the case de passage in Libreville. The next flight to Libreville was twenty-four hours later.

Up to then, my trip had been a great success. Togo struck me as intensely African, crowded with industrious people, vivid colors, cheap food and tangy millet beer drunk out of gourds. Transformed into an extravert by necessity, I'd gone out and met people, spent time in their villages, sleeping in funky cylindrical mud huts with peaked thatch roofs, digging fingers into *fufu* and sauce with local families for meals. Two weeks of this, however, had proved exhausting, especially since the plan had been for Carmen, Daniel and me to go together. But Daniel's med-evac in May had changed that. Months of persistent low-grade fever and joint inflammation had worried Rachel enough to send him to Washington DC for observation. Forty-five days into treatment, the Peace Corps doctors there, having found no answers, refused to clear him for return. Which, according to regulation, meant medical separation from the Peace Corps. Like that, Daniel was out. Carmen and I had been working as teacher trainers at the Lambaréné training when Rachel arrived with the bad news. I'd never before seen Carmen break down and cry. When her parents wired her a round-trip ticket for her to spend two weeks stateside with Daniel and them both, she dropped the Togo plans. I couldn't blame her.

Back at the Togolese airport, I swayed with the mob several minutes more, stunned into inaction, until a Frenchman grabbed my arm and pulled me to the sidelines. My gender and white skin had aroused his sympathy. Fair or not, within five minutes, I held a seat assignment card in my hand. That was how it worked here. The crowd howled in protest. Soon, however, they were distracted by a richly attired Togolese man who also seemed to be receiving preferential treatment. As their glares and cries descended on him, I slipped out, leaving the bedlam behind. In relative calm, I boarded my plane to Libreville and two hours later found myself back on familiar land.

That evening, back in Libreville, I stepped into the case de passage and stopped short. I didn't recognize any of the people splayed on the couches. It was late, my head was pounding and I wanted nothing more than to collapse into one of the bunk beds. But a familiar face would have been nice, too.

"Hey there," a guy with shaggy hair and a half-grown beard called out. "Come join the party." His accent defined him as American, his worn, faded clothing the reassuring attire of a Peace Corps volunteer.

"So, this *is* the Peace Corps house?" I asked hesitantly.

He laughed. "Course it is. Don't mind us." He introduced himself and the others as I stood, listing with fatigue. The strangers were, for the most part, second-year construction volunteers. It seemed like an entirely different Peace Corps Gabon from the one I knew. I nodded after each new name and tried to keep a polite, engaged smile on my face.

"Have a seat and join us for a beer," the shaggy-haired guy—Ned? Ted? Fred?—said.

"I'd love that," I lied. "Maybe in a little bit."

Their loud voices followed me down the hallway as I went to claim a bunk in the farthest bedroom. To my relief, I found Joshua, my fellow English teacher, on the floor between the two sets of bunk beds. He was sitting cross-legged in meditation. He opened one eye and peered at me. "Hi there, Fiona."

"Whoops, sorry, I'm interrupting you."

"No, that's fine." He unfolded his pretzeled legs. "I'm done here."

"How on earth do you manage to meditate with all that noise going on?"

"It's because of the noise that I'm meditating."

I set down my bag, perched on a vacant bunk and we chatted about what was new. Two of the new trainees had already quit and gone home. Daniel was still in Washington DC, resigned to his fate, but happier with Carmen there, visiting him.

"Any idea when she'll be back?" I asked.

"Sounds like she extended her stay for one more week."

I shook my head. "Terrible luck for Daniel, huh? He was really enjoying his post."

"Yeah. Wonder if someone put a curse on him?"

I glanced over at him to see if he was joking. He looked serious, lost in contemplation.

"So, hey," I said. "Been to any bwiti ceremonies lately?"

That got his attention. He stared at me. "Why do you ask?"

Bemused by his reaction, I fumbled for words. "I don't know… it's just that it was about a year ago that we went on that site visit together and watched the ceremony."

"Oh. Well, it's interesting that you should ask, because I'm leaving to go to one tomorrow."

"What a crazy coincidence."

"Not really. I've gone to six or seven of them in the past year."

Joshua had one of the most isolated posts of the education volunteers: far from Libreville; no electricity; more a village than a town. "Boy, sounds like you've really gotten into it," I said.

He glanced over at the door and lowered his voice. "I have, but it's not something Peace Corps Gabon wants us to get involved in, so we'll leave it at that. And let's keep this conversation between us."

"Sure. Of course."

"What about you? I hear you might be changing posts."

I stretched out on the bunk and clasped my hands behind my neck. "Yeah, Carmen was pushing to get me Daniel's post."

She and I had discussed it in Lambaréné with Chuck, who'd

visited the training site after the bad news about Daniel. Chuck had been fretting over the fact that he'd have to tell Daniel's administration they'd lost their second-year volunteer, for the second time in a row. Carmen suggested I take his place. "That way they'll get their second-year volunteer and Fiona will have a safer place to live. Everyone's always saying a male volunteer's a better fit for that Makokou post, anyway." Chuck had eyed the two of us thoughtfully and told Carmen he'd think about it.

"Chuck said he'd have an answer for me this week," I told Joshua now.

"For what it's worth, I think it's settled," he said. "I overheard Chuck's phone call yesterday when I was in the Peace Corps office. He was talking to someone there at the Bitam mission school, and he mentioned your name."

Changing posts mid-service wasn't the challenging task I'd thought it might be. A meeting with Chuck the following day confirmed the news. Two days later I flew to Makokou and collected my belongings from the hotel storage. Henry, driving to Libreville on business, rerouted to stop in Makokou and pick me up. We rumbled into the capital the following afternoon after only one multi-hour delay. The case de passage was, if anything, even more noisy and crowded with strangers, mostly males. Henry fit in; I didn't. The next morning, I slipped out early, finding sanctuary at the Peace Corps office, where I attended to final details for the new post.

"My, aren't *we* busy?" I heard a familiar voice call out around noon. I looked up to see Christophe standing in the reception area. The world tilted crazily. I clutched the back of a chair to keep from moving with it. He looked impossibly glamorous in his pressed trousers and button-down shirt, like something out of an Yves Saint Laurent advertisement.

"They told me you were in Paris all summer," I told him, keeping my voice cool, while noting it seemed to have dropped an octave. They—the Peace Corps gossip circuit—had also informed me his girlfriend had joined him and his mother on their annual trip. The Other Woman was sounding rather permanent.

"I am back from Paris."

"And how was it?"

"It was very French." His smile was lazy, assured, focused on me, only me. Heat coursed through my body. Choirs of angels broke into song. "I don't suppose you have time in your schedule for lunch?"

I pretended to debate the idea. "I suppose I do need to eat."

"Correct."

"All right. Give me ten minutes."

We found a restaurant a block away, a casual, boisterous place with wooden tables and benches packed together. Over lunch, I told Christophe about my new post.

"That's wonderful." He looked pleased. "A much better post for you. When do you leave?"

"In four days' time."

"I'm glad I caught you before I left Libreville later this afternoon."

"Oh." I hoped my disappointment didn't show. "Where are you going?"

"Just to my parents' vacation home in Cap Estérias. A short drive from Libreville. Care to join me?"

My heart leapt at the thought. "Ha, ha, very funny," I said.

"I'm serious. It's a beautiful, relaxing place with plenty of rooms."

As if.

"No, thank you."

"Let me know if you change your mind."

I sought to change the subject. "So, tell me about Paris. I've never been."

"You've never been to Paris?! Oh, that's charming."

I bristled. "I'm from Nebraska. I hardly left the Midwest, much less the U.S. Not all of us can jet-set around the world, you know."

"I'm sorry, I didn't mean to laugh at you. It's just so refreshing to be around someone who isn't jaded about travel."

"Are you referring to your travel companion?" The Other Woman—I'd stepped into controversial territory.

"You mean Mireille?" He frowned thoughtfully. "Yes, I suppose you're right. She's grown up with the best of everything. Paris boarding school, vacations to Monte Carlo, Rome, New York. Her parents dote on her, give her all she asks for."

"Sounds like just another spoiled woman."

His eyes narrowed. I wanted to kick myself. Then he smiled. "Still the same Fiona."

"I'll never change."

"I hope you don't." He held my gaze, which, to my aggravation, had precisely the same power over me that it always had.

I took a steadying gulp of water, picked up my fork, and faked interest in my remaining rice. "So... where is this Mireille now?"

"She's still in Paris."

"Why did you come back early?"

"Paris in August doesn't interest me. I like my life here. Mireille prefers Paris, so she's staying with friends for two more weeks." His mother was still in Paris too, he informed me. His father was traveling abroad, as well. Christophe shook his head in mock sadness. "I'm all alone."

"Poor baby. But look on the bright side. You can go out and hit on women to your heart's content. In fact, what number am I on your list?"

I didn't like these comments that kept slipping from my mouth, one after the other, like soda cans from a 7-11 store dispenser. But neither did I like the way he was making me feel. This schoolgirl breathlessness—after surviving teaching, harassment, parasites, solo travel through West Africa—felt more than a little pathetic.

I'd forgotten one thing, however: Christophe was not one to passively withstand attacks. He sat there now, silent and grim-faced. The intensity of his look shrank me back down to the nervous, uncertain trainee of last year. "You know," he said finally, "sometimes I just want to shake you and make you listen to yourself. One minute you're taunting me and the next, you're playing the victim. You act as though you've been the one wronged, when the truth is, you never resist the opportunity to attack me."

I glared at him but said nothing.

"I always enjoy seeing you, Fiona. If you want to be just friends, fine. If you want to be lovers, that's more than fine. But don't paint me the villain just because you can't make up your mind."

I wanted to lash back and tell him this had nothing to do with sex. To my frustration, I was at a complete loss for words.

"And if you think I said all this because I don't care," he added, "you're wrong. I care deeply for you. Enough to tell you to stop playing games."

I sat there in a seething silence, refusing to meet his eyes, until he rose to pay the bill. Alone, the thoughts swarmed out of me, toxic and uncensored.

The bastard. How dare he scold me like I'm still his subordinate?

Can you believe his nerve? What a prince. Who does he think he is?

But then a less sympathetic voice chimed in.

Why, precisely, are you rejecting him?

The thought, annoying as it was, made me pause. Really, where *were* my virtues, my clinging to moral righteousness, getting me here? Was I more noble for denying him, not to mention myself, a sensual pleasure that had been missing from my life for well over a year? After

Lane, there'd been ballet to turn to. After ballet, there'd been…
pining.

Pining was, quite possibly, the most unproductive use of time and
energy ever. It was the kind of thing the Fiona of last year had
thought worth doing.

I didn't want to be that person anymore.

So, don't, the annoyingly pragmatic voice told me.

It was my choice. Just like the solo Togo trip, which I'd almost
canceled out of fear after Carmen had bailed. I could go with
Christophe to Cap Estérias. I could be that person I'd learned to be
in Togo, intrepid and, while still insecure and scared, not letting it
stop me from discovering new things. Places. People. Experiences.

When Christophe returned, temper cooled, he eyed me warily. I
watched his expression shift to shocked surprise when I told him,
through a roar of adrenaline that sent blood racing, pounding in my
ears, that if the offer still stood, I wanted to go away with him.

"You're saying you'll join me?" He looked incredulous.

"Yes. I'm in."

"So, if I swing by the case de passage in two hours' time, you'll be
there, ready and waiting," he said, in a way that suggested he didn't
believe a word I'd said.

"I'll be ready."

"You're serious."

"I am."

I wasn't sure I knew how to be a different, more evolved or
enlightened Fiona. But I sensed it was time to try.

Chapter 15

Cap Estérias was a scenic point twenty kilometers north of Libreville that jutted out into the Atlantic. When the main highway ended, Christophe steered the car down a dirt road framed by banana trees and lush, overgrown palms. The road changed to gravel as Christophe pulled up to a gated drive. He punched in a code, the iron gate swung open with a groan, and we drove in. The foliage cleared to expose an acre of manicured lawn. Set back on the grounds stood a cream-colored Mediterranean-style villa with bright pink bougainvillea growing in profusion against the side of the house. Rosebushes and hibiscus lined the pebbled walkway that led to the front door.

When I stepped out of the car, the perfume of frangipani and freshly mown grass swirled around me. The ocean rumbled a welcome. I couldn't believe this beauty and luxury belonged to just one family.

From there, my feelings split into two camps. There was my unspoiled Midwestern side, whose family didn't ever take fancy trips, and this was easily the most exquisite place I'd ever stayed at. The other side was the Peace Corps volunteer skeptic. This was Africa, the place I'd felt so compelled to help? Was this uneven distribution of wealth the source of the problem, or was this just how life was? It was yet a new chapter on the "Africa doesn't make sense" theme.

Too much thinking.

I looked at Christophe, who had come around with my bag, and decided to simply enjoy it all. He smiled at me, eyes still wary. When he reached out and took my hand, he seemed surprised that I didn't yank it back.

Inside the house, he led me through a marble foyer and down a hallway into a large, airy room with parquet floors and huge picture windows that overlooked the Atlantic. Sofas and matching tapestry chairs clustered around a glass coffee table scattered with French fashion magazines. On the walls hung French Impressionist paintings, interspersed with African batiks and masks. Christophe flipped a switch and a pair of ceiling fans began to rotate, stirring the flower-scented air.

"Have a seat," he said. "Kick off your shoes and relax. I'll be right back."

As Christophe disappeared into the kitchen, I perched myself gingerly on the sofa and examined the framed photographs on the end table. One was of Christophe and his parents, taken years earlier. His mother, beautiful and slender with long black hair and light brown skin, looked like a Brazilian fashion model. She stood next to a tall, imposing African man whose chin jutted out proudly. The young Christophe, with the addition of innocence in his wide eyes, was as beautiful as the adult.

"Would you like a glass of wine?" Christophe called out from the kitchen.

"Yes," I said in a voice that strove to be sophisticated, as if afternoons like this had happened all my life. "I'd like that."

I slipped off my sandals to better enjoy the soft, fleecy wool rug under my feet. We had scratchy, durable polyester carpets back home. This, in contrast, felt like standing on a cloud.

Christophe returned with two glasses of wine. "Your mother is half-French, right?" I asked. He nodded. "Tell me about that."

"Her mother—my grandmother—grew up here in Gabon," he said, handing me a glass. "She and my French grandfather met, got married a year later and moved to his estate in southern France. My mother and her two brothers spent most of their school years in France, summers and holidays in Gabon." He settled across from me and took a reflective sip of wine.

"Sounds like a nice life," I offered.

"True, but living like that has its disadvantages. In my mother's mind, she's French but not, Gabonese but not. For that reason, she's always encouraged me to see myself as fully Gabonese, and Gabon as my home, no matter how many years we lived abroad."

"She looks young enough to be your sister."

"She often felt like that, more of a playmate than a mother. She could have no other children, another thing always separating her from the other African women. My father traveled a lot and it would often be just the two of us."

His expression softened as he told me about the relocations to London, Madrid, Paris, Washington D.C. At times his father could stay only long enough to settle the family in, and then he'd be off on a month-long trip, leaving Christophe and his mother alone to acclimate. When the loneliness grew too much for either of them, she'd gather him close and sing to him, alternately in French and Fang, which soothed them both, even though her Fang was not as good as his, a native of Gabon's Woleu Ntem region, like his father. He told me about the ways she could counteract the isolation, the strangeness, turning it all into a sort of game, a grand adventure.

"Sometimes when she was feeling restless, we'd go on a 'date' to a restaurant. She used to tell me I was her boyfriend and I believed it. Once when I was six, my father returned from a particularly long trip. My mother swooped down on him and took him into their bedroom, locking the door. I was furious. I remember pounding on the door, demanding that she let me in. I felt so angry and betrayed, I wouldn't speak to either of them for two days."

He paused, abashed, and began to laugh. "I can't believe I'm telling you all this."

"Oh, please, don't stop. I like it."

He looked at the photo again and smiled. "She's a strong woman. You remind me of her, in many ways—stubborn, spirited, makes a definite impression on people."

"Thank you. I think." I rose from the couch and peered out the window at the ocean. A child's excitement arose in me to be out there in it. An hour remained before sunset. I turned to him. "Can we go swimming?"

"We can do anything you want."

He directed me to a chrome and marble bathroom where I changed into my swimsuit. Afterward we headed outside, down a narrow sandy pathway. We soon came upon a wide expanse of deserted beach, dotted with coconut palms and beached Okoumé logs. The air smelled briny yet sweet, like pineapple seaweed. We settled on beach chairs and watched the ocean recede and creep back. The sparkling waves, with a glint of afternoon gold, beckoned.

"I'm going in," I said. "Coming?"

He shook his head. "I'll stand watch."

I waded out into the Atlantic, diving into the breakers. The undertow tugged at me as I sliced through the warm water, stretching my muscles, freeing my body. It felt glorious, the closest thing to dance I'd come to in a long time. I swam back and forth for twenty minutes, releasing the surplus dancer energy I'd carried for weeks. Months. Finally I made my way, dripping, chest heaving, back to shore and the chairs.

"That was quite a workout," Christophe remarked as I collapsed into the seat next to him.

"I needed it. Bad."

"Are you dancing these days?"

I shook my head. "Got my ballet shoe stolen, remember?"

"We both know you could have obtained a replacement. In fact, give me the size and maker and I'll order you a pair. A gift."

I ignored the offer. "What would be the point, anyway?"

"Because you're a dancer."

"Ballet doesn't work here."

"Ballet is not the only form of dance."

"It's what I excel at. I'm not comfortable doing the other styles." I watched the ocean thunder onto the beach and whisper its retreat.

"Have you tried?"

"Of course I have. It would be hard to avoid."

Dance, I'd come to see, was everywhere in Africa. The Gabonese danced at clubs, bars, parties. They danced in church; they danced in rituals; they danced to honor the arrivals of politicians and luminaries. They danced any time someone put on the right music, which meant, any music with a beat.

"And how was it?" he prodded.

"I can't dance African."

"Can't, or won't?"

"Why are you pushing this issue? You've seen me dance. I'm classical. I'm Caucasian. I cannot move like an African."

And I didn't need Christophe to inform me why, that something in me was too rigid and had to loosen, not just physically but psychologically. I knew this. I'd watch the Gabonese move with a freedom within their bodies that I couldn't even imagine. Relaxed energy flowed from all parts of their body: the legs, the torso, the arms. Sometimes the movement would be so small, just this gentle, rhythmic shifting from one foot to another. There was an innate flexibility in their hips that I lacked. When I saw toddlers learning to dance in tandem with learning to walk, I understood the source of the intuitive movement. Even before that. Babies were tucked on their mother's backs, tied in place with a swathe of fabric. Every movement the mother made, and she went right along with her business, the child felt. Jiggling, swerving, dancing, striding, straining, from a child's earliest kinetic memory.

"You need to keep trying," Christophe said, and I twisted around in irritation.

"Can we just change the subject already?"

"Fair enough." I heard laughter in his voice. "Here's something less controversial. I propose I bring our wine out here."

"Yes. I think I can agree with you there."

Chuckling, he rose from his seat and leaned over me. His hands gripped my bare shoulders as he planted a kiss on my forehead. "My briny, difficult Fiona. I'm so glad you're here with me." He walked toward the house, still chuckling to himself.

My shoulders and forehead throbbed from the unexpected contact. I gazed out at the ocean and decided I was pretty glad too.

"Let's see," Christophe said an hour later, peering in the refrigerator. "There's a wedge of Pont-l'Evêque cheese, Moroccan olives, cornichons, grapes, some *pâté de foie gras* and a dozen eggs. I see our housekeeper bought two baguettes. Any of that sound appealing?"

I sat on the kitchen counter, wearing a gauzy shirt and shorts, munching on sliced guava as I watched him rummage around, shirtless. Track lighting shone down on us, making me feel like we were on stage. "It all sounds great," I said, "except I'm not sure what pâté de foie gras tastes like."

"Don't tell me you've never had it before."

I rolled my eyes. "Didn't we have a similar conversation earlier today? We don't eat foie gras in Nebraska and if you find olives, they're those chopped black circles that taste like wax." I finished my guava with a flourish. "And before you start on your worldly kick, let me educate you on a thing or two."

He stood back from the refrigerator, hands on his hips, regarding me in amusement. Gabonese men, I decided, were particularly suited for the bare-chested look, with their sleek, muscular bodies and smooth skin. I dragged my thoughts back to my tirade.

"Green bean casserole—bet you've never had that. With those canned french-fried onion things on top. Beans and hot dogs, tuna noodle casserole. You're not living till you've tried those." I found myself saying anything to keep him looking at me that way, his lips parted, his green eyes smoky. "Velveeta cheese. In a color you'll never find in nature. My mom used to wave the cheese cutter through the loaf as she was slicing it. She'd call it 'nervous cheese' because of the squiggle shape. That was a Saturday night special."

His approach sent a jittery thrill of anticipation through me. "How about dining out?" I continued. "Nebraska's finest, Pizza Hut, with plastic cups of Coors Light. Or for the final touch on that special cake, Betty Crocker canned frosting…" My voice faltered as he came up and rested his hands on the counter, on either side of my hips. He didn't say a word. He took one more step closer so that my open legs brushed against either side of his waist. The shock of the contact coursed through me like an electric current, leading straight to my pelvis.

"Keep educating me," he said. "It's fascinating."

My reply faded when he set his hand on my thigh. We both observed its progress, the chocolate skin sliding down my paler flesh. The hand took a detour around my knee, coming back up along the inside of my leg. My stomach contracted. Caveats flooded my mind:

he was a womanizer, he had a serious girlfriend. Then I thought of my earlier words. *I don't want to be this way anymore.*

And one last whisper: *get it out of your system once and for all.*

Best idea yet.

Christophe's other hand slid behind my neck, drawing my face closer to his. His lips brushed my ear. "Mademoiselle Garvey," he murmured, like a caress, before his lips moved to cover my mouth. His tongue slid into my mouth, tasting like red wine and danger. He nudged me off the counter and I slid slowly, deliciously against him on my way down. My hands, clamped like starfish against his chest, confirmed his skin was as hot and silky as I'd remembered from that long-ago Lambaréné afternoon. When my legs began to wobble, he lifted me, hoisting me around his hips, and carried me over to the couch, where we tumbled down.

His hands dove beneath my blouse and skimmed it off me in one swift gesture. As he kissed me, one hand moved over to my breast, while the other stroked and nudged me into a better position beneath him. It was intensely pleasurable and yet startling, unfamiliar. And that described everything: my writhing; the momentary sense of confusion when my fingers, seeking thick hair to plow through, encountered close-cropped curls instead. He felt foreign. But of course I was the foreigner here, bumbling and insecure about what came next. I was growing uncomfortable as well. He'd pushed my other hand down toward his crotch and the hand had gotten squashed en route, twisted at a bad angle.

Christophe rolled off me and pushed himself to standing. "You're coming to my bedroom," he told me, which produced a flicker of anxiety in me. I looked at the glazed stranger he'd become and nodded. He pulled me up and led me to his room, bumping against the door frame in his haste. An enormous bed with a plush white comforter dominated the room. With a swipe of his arm, the decorative pillows adorning the bed went flying. I took a deep breath and climbed aboard.

It had become a different game. I commanded myself to relax as he reached for me. He'd pulled off his shorts and I felt the shock of his nakedness and its intense heat. When he tugged off my shorts and underwear, nothing remained to protect me. His hands and mouth grew impatient, making my lips feel bruised and scratched. Leaning over me, he reached into the nightstand drawer to pull out condoms. He fumbled with them and then he was pushing inside me as I gritted my teeth, my head thumping on the headboard every time he thrust too deeply. I gave up on trying to enjoy myself and instead focused on just getting through it.

Afterward, when he'd finished and had slumped on top of me, a wave of terrible disappointment engulfed me. This event I'd anticipated, craved for a year, turned out to be the same animal coupling it had been with Lane. I'd been so sure someone as exotic and beautiful as Christophe would have transported me to the kind of ecstasy I'd read about in romance novels. At least, I comforted myself, it hadn't been furtive and guarded. Christophe had clearly enjoyed himself. He had rolled over onto his back where he lay, catching his breath, a smile on his face.

He inclined his head my way and laid a hand on my thigh. "Did you enjoy that?" he asked, his voice and expression telling me he was expecting only one answer.

"No." The reply slipped out before I could censor it. Then, to my horror, I promptly burst into tears, one of the most undignified, vulnerable responses I could have chosen. Christophe looked stricken, shocked. In different circumstances, I might have laughed at him. For a minute, neither of us spoke. He watched me sniffle and dab at my face.

"You were a virgin, after all. Weren't you?"

"I was *not*."

He sat up to study me better. I looked around for my clothes. They were scattered all over, from the living room couch to the bed. I reached down and grabbed a pillow from the floor instead, tucking it up against my body as I sat up. "I had a boyfriend, for your information. And we had sex." I could hear the distaste in the way my mouth formed the words. He heard it too. His smile returned, but at the same time, a stealthy look came into his eyes.

"How many times?"

"Plenty," I retorted. Christophe didn't need to know just how few times. It pained me to think of how little Lane had desired me, the last two months.

The ocean murmured and receded in the background before he spoke again.

"How many men?"

"One." I summoned as much dignity as possible into the word.

"Did you enjoy yourself?"

I didn't know how to answer this. I'd always liked the initial sensations, the kissing and gentle stroking. But things would ramp up, Lane would get frantic, and the wisps of growing pleasure would retreat, leaving me feeling tense and oddly cheated. I wasn't frigid; I'd had orgasms. Just not at the right time.

"Never mind," he said. "Your face answers my question." He reached over, yanked away the pillow I was clutching and tossed it. He lay on his side, propped up on one elbow, and tugged at me until I was resting alongside him. He began to stroke me again, calmer this time, until I began to relax.

"It's just that I always tense up," I said. "I can't enjoy myself."

His hand slid over my hip and waist in a soothing back-and-forth motion. "But you're such a natural sensualist."

"What's that even supposed to mean?"

"When you dance, for example, with all that passion. What are you thinking about?"

"I'm not thinking about anything. I'm just dancing."

"My point exactly." He began to nibble on my neck, little insistent bites. Goose bumps sprang up on my arms as something in me lurched back into action. "Maybe," he murmured against my skin, "what you need to do is make love the way you dance."

"Impossible." It was growing difficult to speak. "There's no music."

"Of course there is. You just haven't heard it yet."

With the initial sex business out of the way, my spirits bounced right back. I had two full days to watch him, touch him, feel his eyes on me as I crossed the room, not stopping until I was pressed up against him. After the disastrous first time, it became better. I relaxed and felt something in me give in to his persistence, becoming more pliant and succulent under his hands. It was all still too unfamiliar to be completely comfortable. Instead, however, it was exhilarating, daring. Why not grab his ass whenever he passed by? Why not reach over and rub his erection, or examine the frightening thing up close? I'd watch his face grow helpless whenever I touched him. He'd become instantly passive, almost slavish. I'd had no idea I could hold such power over him.

It was as if someone had flung open a door within a house I'd lived in all my life, only I'd never seen this room: full of pillows, sunlight streaming in and sensuous things like whipped cream, sultry music and slippery, cool, satin sheets. This room, this way of life, was something Christophe didn't seem to question. Sex just seemed to be a natural extension of who he was. I wasn't some furtive conquest, as I'd feared. I was simply another delicious dish from the cornucopia that seemed to comprise his personal life. I could get outraged about his casual attitude. Or I could leap in and enjoy the buffet myself.

I didn't waste my time on introspection. For the first time in my life outside of dance, I simply existed in the sensuality of the moment. Like eating mangoes. The stringy, juicy flesh and thick pit made them messy and difficult to eat gracefully. But the flavor was intoxicating, sweet, lush and complex, unlike any fruit I'd ever eaten in Nebraska. We'd take a basket of them down to the beach and I'd eat mango after mango, letting the juice dribble down my chin, neck and arms, until I'd have to run into the crashing surf and dive in the water to clean myself. Afterwards I'd lie in the sun and feel the salty water dry on my skin, tightening it, until Christophe bent over to make it moist again. There were other sensations as well, like the nubby comfort of thick cotton towels against my naked body, the jammy, silky taste of the red wine he poured, the soft rasp of his tongue on my abdomen, the sound of his breath catching when I did the same to him. Everything we did, from the profane to the mundane, seemed sensual. Had life always been like this, I wondered? Had the air in Gabon always been this heavy with fragrance and suggestion, the palms so intensely green and pliant, bowing and rustling in the soft breeze?

The getaway was a dream, like some exotic fantasy. And yet, it failed to quench some nameless yearning in me. Even with my lack of experience, I could tell Christophe was not a consummate lover. He didn't have to be—he'd always had the looks, wealth, privilege and charisma that guaranteed he was going to get laid. But I sensed there was more to great sex than proficiency and technique. I wanted to use the act of making love to deepen my understanding of him, to see behind the glossy exterior he put up to the world. Whether consciously or not, he resisted my efforts.

I wondered if all of this was characteristic of African men. The subject brought about our only argument of the trip. He'd mentioned his personal surprise at all he'd confided to me, and how normally he didn't let people, especially women, see this vulnerable, sentimental side of him.

"Why not?" I asked.

He looked at me, puzzled, as if I'd asked him why liquid felt wet.

"Because I am a man."

"Oh, please. Haven't you learned anything about American females? Beside the fact that we all seem a little spoiled, that is."

The mood shifted. "Why do you American women find it necessary to act as tough as men, anyway?" he asked.

"We don't. We believe women should be given the chance to rise to their full potential, that's all. I think it's appalling the way other cultures repress women."

"Oh, so the rest of the world is wrong and your country has all the answers? Here's what I observed when I last visited the States—American females emasculate men with their aggressive behavior."

I stared at him. "What a crock of shit," I said, eliciting a frown from him. "This may surprise you, but some men like women to be that way. They want women who challenge them."

"Like this former boyfriend of yours? Why did he leave?" His voice rang out, triumphant. "Where did he go?"

I tried to draw in the breath that his taunt had knocked out of me.

The anger left his face. "I'm sorry," he said. "That was impolite of me."

"Don't be sorry." My lips, like my heart, felt numb. "You proved your point."

"No, you proved yours." He moved closer and laid a hand on my thigh. "I was just fighting back. You're right, I like the challenge you offer. Even when I complain about it."

"At least you can't say our conversations are dull."

He met my eyes and smiled. "Dull is not a word that will ever describe you, Miss Garvey."

I might not have heard the music that weekend, but I certainly learned how to have a good time. On our last evening, in a charming reversal of roles, I found myself the center of attention amid three Frenchmen, friends of Christophe's, who'd joined us at our table at a nearby restaurant. Christophe retreated into a stony silence as the other men flirted outrageously with me. Back at the house, Christophe had to be coaxed out of his sulk.

"You're jealous," I exclaimed, secretly delighted.

"It's not that," he insisted, lower lip thrust out, like a petulant little boy. "It just that those men are the worst sort."

It didn't improve his temper when I informed him they'd said the exact same thing about him. But he couldn't stay angry for long. I'd learned the game too well, and how to manipulate his mood. The wine and attention of the evening had made me more assertive, and he responded in kind. When I climaxed, it felt more unhinged, uncontrolled, almost frantic, like the stomach-plunging sensation of falling off a cliff. I rocked against him and cried out, hardly recognizing my own voice. It was deeper, more infused with some feral element. I knew I was being loud, louder than I'd ever been, but even that was exciting, liberating.

Afterward we lay there, both of us panting, chests heaving, slick with perspiration. I began to laugh, my limbs still shaking. I propped myself up on my elbows and looked down at him. He reached up to smooth the tangled hair from my sweaty face, run his fingers over my cheeks, my bruised lips.

"*That* was you, baby." His eyes glowed. "That was the woman I always knew was there." He began to laugh with me, making us sound like two mad scientists who'd just come up with some spectacular theory destined to change the course of humankind.

Then again, maybe we had.

Chapter 16

What goes up, must come down. I may have failed my college physics class, but even I couldn't deny the irrefutable logic of this principle. And I came down with a vengeance after my Cap Estérias trip. Only the aerial view of Bitam, Gabon's northernmost town, close to the Cameroon border and site of my new post, roused me from my grief-induced torpor. William had told me I'd like the mission, but I'd ignored the comment, the way I'd ignored his presence during most of our flight from Libreville. Instead I'd angled my face to the plane's window and cried the whole way. I couldn't decide whether the getaway with Christophe had been the smartest or the stupidest thing I'd ever done, which, I realized, summed up my feelings about joining the Peace Corps as well.

William earned brownie points for knowing how to respond, interrupting me only to slip me Kleenex during the flight's descent into Bitam. He himself had only just returned from Paris, where he'd broken up with his longtime girlfriend. He was somber; I sensed he too was looking for a place to lick wounds and recover.

"Ready for this?" he murmured as he turned to me. His eyes with their thick fringe of dark lashes—oh, to have had those instead of false eyelashes for stage makeup—were serious, much like they'd been in training. This time though, instead of intimidating me, they reassured me.

"Here goes Part Two," I managed, and he smiled. He gestured out the window as we rolled up to the arrivals gate, where a trio of Belgian nuns dressed in white habits, an Africanized short-sleeved version with white headdresses, stood waiting.

"Your welcome party," William said, and for the first time in twenty-four hours, I felt the tiniest bit of optimism stir in me.

When I saw the mission thirty minutes later, a cluster of green-painted buildings located two miles from town, the optimism increased. The grounds were neat and manicured with an emerald lawn and a wide, palm-studded driveway. Flowers grew from windowsill planters. I stepped down from the mission's van and serenity enveloped me. But there was something more, a mysterious energy I could feel, if not name, carried in the wind like a distant whisper. It made the place comforting, yet unsettling. This was not the Catholic Church environment of my youth.

I followed William and the sisters down a cool, whitewashed corridor to their main room and dining area. Religious statuettes and books cluttered lace-covered end tables. A breeze puffed at diaphanous yellow curtains and stirred the warm air. In the center of the room stood an enormous Okoumé wood dining table surrounded by benches.

The sisters, *les soeurs*, were warm and friendly, speaking in slow, easy-to-understand French. They'd baked a coconut cake in honor of my arrival. It was like being in a roomful of aunts. On the wall, I noticed a portrait of Jesus, crouched in a mournful genuflection, hand on his bleeding heart, the very same picture that had hung in the foyer of my Catholic grade school. I explained this to the others. "You are Catholic?" asked Soeur Beatrice, the school directress, an engaging woman with rogue tendrils of red hair poking out from beneath her white linen headdress. When I nodded, all the sisters looked pleased.

"You and Guillaume both," Soeur Beatrice said, gesturing to William.

"Really?" I eyed William with interest.

"Yup. Big family and all."

"We're five," I told him. "Two girls and a boy."

"We're six. Three girls and me."

"Oh, boy."

He grinned. "You said it."

"Sit, sit." Soeur Beatrice gestured to the cake on the table. "Let's try Soeur Nathalie's creation, shall we?"

A Gabonese woman came to the door as we were eating our cake. William rose and greeted her with a kiss on both cheeks, French-style, before introducing her to me. Her name was Céleste and she owned a popular food stall in the heart of the town's marketplace. She had adolescent boys, who hung behind, clutching shallow boxes of brown eggs. They lived in an isolated neighborhood a quarter-mile past the mission, the last community before the dense rainforest took over. Céleste sold eggs weekly to the sisters.

After she shook my hand, she sized me up with luminous dark-brown eyes and asked William—apparently everyone here called him Guillaume, the French equivalent of William—a question. She'd switched over to Fang, the local tribal language here in the Woleu Ntem province. He laughed and his cheeks reddened. He shook his head and replied in Fang before turning to me.

"She thought maybe you were my, um, girlfriend." His cheeks burned redder. "Come to join me after our reunion."

"Oh. Whoops." I could feel my own face growing hot.

Soeur Beatrice explained in French that I was there to replace Daniel. Céleste pushed her two boys forward. "My boys, they are now your students," she said. "If they do not behave, you have my permission to beat them."

From their cowed expressions, I knew it wouldn't be necessary, but decided it couldn't hurt to establish myself. I rose to my full height, peered down at them and offered them a polite, professorial nod. This time I understood it had to start off formal. There would be plenty of time for smiles and fun later.

William excused himself to check up on his truck, which he'd stored at the mission while he was in Paris. Céleste collected her money from the eggs, then stayed to chat while the two boys gobbled down a piece of cake. Suddenly I heard a thud, followed by a blur of white. A bird had flown into the room, a snowy creature with huge wings that flapped about. Everyone shrieked and dodged the panicked bird, which couldn't find its way back out. It flew onto the table where it scrabbled around, planting a foot in the coconut cake. Soeur Nathalie, the cook, shrieked louder and covered her eyes.

It was like no bird I'd ever seen in Omaha. It looked a marsh bird, but stocky and short, closer to the size of a big chicken than a heron. When it spread its wings, however, they stretched out in an arc of dazzling white. The creature tried to fly across the room. Some of the sisters shrank back, while others, screeching with laughter, made ineffectual waving motions with their arms. Soeur Nathalie marched out and returned with a broom, which the bird kept eluding.

"Stop," Soeur Beatrice said. "We're only frightening him more. If we quiet down, maybe he will too." Céleste and her two sons huddled in the corner with wide, fearful eyes; they needed no further encouragement.

It worked. As the rest of us grew quiet, the bird stopped thrashing. He fluttered back over to the table. With deliberate steps on greenish-yellow legs, he approached the side where I stood. When he could get no closer to me, he stretched his wings out to their full span, as if to remind me he was no chicken. He tucked his wings back in and regarded me gravely for several moments with his odd yellow eyes.

The silence in the room was electric. Finally he turned and with regal dignity, hopped off the table, onto the grey concrete floor and stalked out of the room. Once outside, he took off with a great flapping of wings.

Everyone began talking at once.

"Did you see *that?* My heavens!"

"I've never seen one so close before."

"My cake! He stepped on my cake."

"Did you see how he studied Fiona?"

"He calmed right down then, didn't he?"

"With those wings, we're lucky he didn't break anything."

"He ruined my cake!"

"What was it?" I asked faintly.

"*Un pique-boeuf,*" Soeur Beatrice said. "A cattle egret," she added in accented English, observing my confusion.

"Are they common here?" I asked.

"They appear when the lawn gets mown each week." Soeur Beatrice leaned over to straighten a lamp shade the bird had knocked askew. "They forage for insects that the mower stirs up. But the lawn won't be mown until tomorrow."

"He must have come early to welcome Fiona to her new home," one of the other sisters said, and everyone laughed. All except Céleste, who gazed at me with the same wide, fearful look she'd given the egret.

Soeur Beatrice gave me a tour of the grounds. The school was a *collège,* similar to a lycée, but minus the final two academic grades. Like the lycée in Makokou, the buildings were grouped around a courtyard, but the resemblance stopped there. The courtyard here was green lawn instead of dirt. These schoolrooms were freshly painted, both inside and out. Pictures hung on the walls. Each room contained three long rows of two-seater desks, a blackboard and a teacher's desk. The rooms were smaller, consequently fewer students would be in each class. An air of optimism prevailed throughout the compound. A footpath led to an enormous sports field, where soccer was played and P.E. classes were held. Beyond that, the path continued on to Céleste's neighborhood a quarter mile away. I made a mental note to use the sports field to jog and stretch, the best ballet replacement I was likely to find in Gabon.

We strolled across a different lawn and down an incline toward the mission church. Here sat my new home, a snug, lemon-colored cottage with a porch and blue awnings. It was smaller than the house in Makokou, but more inviting inside, with cheery wicker furniture and fat, colorful pillows. The rooms were simply furnished.

"I hope this will all be sufficient," Soeur Beatrice said. "We live simply here."

"It's perfect."

Soeur Beatrice returned to her quarters once I'd assured her I'd come to them if I needed anything. Silence settled in the room and I gave a hiccupping sigh. The grief, the memory of my time with Christophe, was still there, hovering in the periphery, but under control in this new place that already felt like home. I pushed open curtains and windows throughout the house. Light flooded the rooms. I stepped out onto the porch overlooking the grounds and took a deep, cleansing breath.

I watched William approach from the direction of the church and a spasm of shyness came over me. He was more Carmen's friend than mine, after all. As he drew closer, he held up a dead bird.

"I brought you your dinner," he called out, and for a terrible moment, I thought it was the egret. William laughed when he saw my expression. "Chicken. It just needs to be plucked and have its head and feet cut off."

"I don't have a clue how to do any of that."

"I'll show you."

The dead chicken proved an excellent icebreaker. As we plucked, we talked about his trip to Paris, tactfully skirting around the break-up issue, and Peace Corps goings-on in Libreville. Once we'd finished prepping and cleaning the chicken, William reached into a bag and pulled out a few items, setting them on the counter. It was Americana galore: Dream Whip powdered whipping cream, something called pumpkin pie spice, oregano, mustard packets, dehydrated cheese sauce and chili powder. "My mom sent it all, six weeks ago," he said. "It was supposed to go to Daniel. He was a great cook. The rule was, if I procured the hard-to-find ingredients, he'd do the rest."

We regarded the items and William grew quiet, almost bewildered. "It never crossed my mind Daniel wouldn't be here this year. And when I left my village, I was thinking I might come back engaged to be married. Funny, isn't it? These plans and assumptions you make."

I imagined we were thinking the same thing: *And now it's difficult Fiona and an aching heart.* "I know," I mumbled, "I'm a pretty lousy trade."

"No, it's great that he was replaced with someone I know. This place is my closest contact with the outside world. My village is less than an hour away. I come into town every so often to pick up supplies—the sisters let me use a guest room here for overnight trips. That won't cramp your style, will it? Having another American around?"

"Not at all."

"Great." He smiled at me, finished unpacking the goods and folded up the bag.

"I remember Daniel's green papaya pie from last Christmas," I said. "If you want, I can try my hand at making it."

"Think you can do it?"

"I imagine I can get some sort of recipe from Carmen. All of his recipes. But I'll warn you, I'm not much of a cook. We'll probably end up with a Fiona special."

"It's a deal. These products are all yours."

He needed to get back to his village before sunset. I walked him outside to his truck. "Thanks for the chicken," I said. "And thanks for… being here for me this afternoon."

"No problem," William said. "See you soon." He got into the truck, which coughed and sputtered before roaring to life. And with a wave, he was off.

Classes didn't start for another week. I used the time to familiarize myself with the mission, explore Bitam's town center and get to know my colleagues. Oyem was less than two hours away so I was able to easily visit Carmen. She'd have changes this year too. Daniel's med-evac aside, she would be getting a new roommate, a newly sworn-in community health volunteer, within the month. She told me she didn't mind. It would take her mind off Daniel's absence.

"So how's everything going between you two?" I asked.

"Not bad, in truth." She handed me a cold Orangina. "I can make international phone calls from the big hotels in Oyem. We agreed to talk once a month. Aside from that, lots of letters. Maybe meet in Paris over Christmas break." She threw up her hands in mock protest. "I know, I know, basically the same thing I was giving William trouble about last year. Sheer lunacy." She grinned. "Won't be the first time anyone's accused me of that."

I told her about my getaway with Christophe.

"And now?" she asked. "How are you feeling?"

"I'm fine." I kept my voice firm. "It hurts, of course. But I think I got it all out of my system."

"Oh, right."

I scowled at her. "I am *not* going to spend my second year in a state of silly infatuation with a guy I can't have. I've wasted enough time as it is."

"Fine with me. We can be the celibacy sisters. How about a couple romantic dinners by candlelight?"

"Remember how eating by candlelight used to be the epitome of romantic? Now it just means it's another power outage or you're visiting au village."

We both laughed, good humor restored.

The next day, while Carmen took care of business at her school, I made a trip to Oyem's town center with its staggering abundance of stores and commerce. It was like a mini Libreville, I decided happily, looking around at the shops, the variety of items to buy. Furniture, glassware, French pharmaceuticals, a bookstore. The city catered to its many Europeans. Being white in Oyem wasn't the shocker it was in the provinces.

The anonymity made me relax my guard. When I saw a vaguely familiar figure, an African man, my first thought was, *hey, it's one of my new colleagues from Bitam.*

The man turned around.

Ondo Calixte. Not far away in Makokou, but here.

I froze. I could feel the blood drain from my face, all the triggers of fear and instability and everything bad about the previous year.

He was speaking harshly to a small, middle-aged women who wore a faded tee shirt, a pagne around her waist and a matching head-wrap. She nodded meekly over his words and bent to pick up her bags. He turned, as if sensing my presence.

His gaze met mine. I watched as the momentary fog of non-recognition cleared, replaced by shock, and finally calculation.

"*Alors*, hello, Miss Fiona," he called out as he made his way to me, eyes never leaving my face. "Is the beautiful day, no? The… sky is… shines very yes."

Having exhausted his ability to speak in English, he switched to French. "I am surprised to see you here in Oyem."

I hid my unease. "Yes, I sometimes visit Oyem. I have friends here." Self-preservation told me not to mention my new post.

He crossed his arms and relaxed against a signpost. He still had that way of forcing an unwanted intimacy into his body language. He knew what he was doing and that it bothered me.

"Why are you here?" I asked him.

"I have family living here, and in this province, as well as the Ogooué Ivindo." Little of the adolescent remained in him, I noted. It made him all the more ominous.

Yet he *was* still just a student, I reminded myself.

"You are returning to the lycée in Makokou?" I asked him, everything in me clenching in anticipation of hearing that he planned to attend school here. To my relief, he only nodded.

He didn't ask me the same question, and I didn't offer. Let him figure it out on his own, in a week's time. I offered up a silent prayer of thanks for the fact that he would no longer be my problem, and that this second year of mine showed every sign of being a good one.

"If you'll excuse me," I said. "Someone is expecting me."

"A man?" he asked. "One who eagerly awaits you?"

He sized me up and down, in the creepy, suggestive way he had, back in Makokou.

"That does not concern you," I spat, belatedly remembering my second-year vow to maintain a teacher's distance at all times. I drew myself an inch higher and injected frost into my tone. "It is discourse for adults and my fellow teachers alone. Goodbye, now." I switched to English. "I suspect you'll fuck up just as much this year as last, but

174

happily, it will not be my problem."

He stood there, uncomprehending.

I turned and strode back toward the grocery store, bastion of products and clientele European and beyond. He would not follow me in there.

Good riddance to him and all he stood for, I thought as I selected a half-dozen chocolate bars to take with me back to Bitam. That was so last year.

I had a more positive experience to move on to.

Chapter 17

Friday was bean sandwich day. It had become a ritual for my Gabonese colleague Lisette and me to meet Lance, the new English-teaching volunteer posted at the town's lycée, at the Bitam market after school. We'd wander past rows of Gabonese women who squatted over their wares—little piles of piment, avocados and mangoes, dried fish, coarse-looking manioc tubers—to Céleste's stall in the heart of the market. For the cost of roughly a dollar, Céleste would take a fresh, crusty baguette, split it and fill it with savory, freshly cooked pinto beans, topping it with a searing hot piment-oil blend. It was, inexplicably, the best sandwich I'd ever tasted.

September had flown and now it was October. Bitam and my new post suited me well. Although not a provincial capital like Makokou, Bitam felt livelier, with a market that buzzed with activity and commerce at all hours. The stimulus that had jarred me in my first weeks in Gabon energized me here. Honking taxis and trucks weaving through the crowds meant there was transportation available to go anywhere I wanted. The market odors, smoke from countless small fires mingled with cooking oil, the sour-sweet smell of baton de manioc and fermenting palm wine, and even the trash, told me food was available and plentiful. This felt like an Africa I could more easily embrace. Not impersonal and excessive like the big city, not stark and mystery-tinted like the villages.

Lance, Lisette and I took our sandwiches over to our favorite hangout bar. Over African pop music blasting from the bar's cassette player, Lance showed us his most recent acquisitions.

This, too, had become a weekly ritual. He had a habit of buying things he might or might not use, purchasing whatever suited his whimsy: a flowing African caftan; twin plastic ladles; a box of cigarette lighters; a crate of liquor bottles filled with peanuts. Today he'd bought a dozen rolls of chocolate-flavored digestive biscuits, the kind that sometimes got passed off as dessert and that no one would eat unless they were British or starving or had been subsisting on animal over manioc for too long.

"Why did you buy so many of those horrible biscuit cookie things?" I protested.

"I was haggling," he said proudly. "He gave me the twelfth pack free."

"Maybe because he just loaded twelve times the usual inventory off to you."

"I know a bargain when I see one, Fiona."

"What on earth are you going to do with so many?"

Lance grinned. "I don't know. Throw a party and serve them with the five kilos of guavas I bought on Tuesday?"

Lisette laughed; I sighed.

Mr. "Sure, whatever!" at his finest. Back during the recent Lambaréné training, that had been Carmen's and my nickname for him. With his easy, outgoing nature, bucktoothed grin and naïve curiosity, combined with admittedly sexy brown eyes, he was like a mix between Gomer Pyle and Tom Cruise. I couldn't decide if he was adorable or unbearable. Sometimes he managed to be both concurrently.

Lisette began to debate the merits of Coke versus Pepsi with Lance in her musical, French-accented English. I watched her round, animated face, the way her plum lips pursed in disagreement or amusement, the exotic tilt of her flashing dark-brown eyes. I adored her. Three years my senior, she was my closest neighbor at the mission and the Gabonese friend I'd never found last year. She claimed that her three years of university study in France had made her more bold and less traditional-minded, but I sensed she would have been a strong, spirited woman no matter what she'd done. Lance clearly entertained her. "You young American men," she said in English, "you are such the funny ones."

"I'll bet you I'm right," he told her.

Lisette's eyes sparkled. "A bet? Oh, my friend, you are on!"

Lance reached into his pocket for a CFA bill, but instead pulled out a wadded note. He stared at it, puzzled, until his eyes widened and his mouth formed an O. He looked up at me pleadingly.

"Forget your money again?" I asked him. "Don't worry, I can lend you some."

"No, it's not that. It's just, this is a message for you." He thrust the wadded note at me.

I held it but didn't open it. "What's wrong with this note that I should know about?"

"Nothing! I was just supposed to have given it to you already."

"Like when?"

"Like, Monday afternoon when you and I met up. Except I forgot, so I told myself Wednesday. But then I wasn't wearing these jeans when you stopped by."

I opened the note. It was from William. About Christophe. If I hadn't been sitting, I would have fallen over.

Hi Fiona, it read. *Was hoping to stop by on my way back from Oyem, but it was late and I had someone with me. Saw Christophe in Oyem and he asked about you. Told him I'd be in Bitam next wknd and he proposed a group meet-up for Sat pm. Told him sure. That ok? Send msg to me thru one of the bus drivers by Thurs if not. Otherwise, see you Sat pm!*

I looked back up at Lance, who had a hopeful smile on his face. "So, that night works, doesn't it?" he asked. "We were talking about doing dinner together this weekend anyway."

"Are you telling me you read my message?"

He nodded, unconcerned, and my voice rose accordingly.

"You knew I had to respond by Thursday and you *still* didn't remember to give it to me?"

"Fiona, please." Lisette laid a hand on my arm.

I showed her the note and watched her scan it. Lisette knew of Christophe; he was renowned in Gabonese social circles as being both a playboy and a prize catch. She'd been in Paris at the same time as him during university years, and a friend of hers had known him intimately. That had been the way Lisette had phrased it to me. I'd nodded and chuckled wryly, and there'd been no need for me to further elaborate on my own situation.

"This is not a problem," she said to me. "We can have it at my house." Her eyes brightened with enthusiasm.

I sputtered and searched for words.

"I love hosting dinner parties," she said. "And did you see? The grocery store had whole chickens today. Perfect for my menu."

"And hey," Lance added, "I've got all those chocolate biscuit things I bought today. And the five kilos of guavas. Here you were, thinking I'd made a mistake, Fiona. See? Somehow I know these things will come in handy."

"Maybe you knew because you read the friggin' *note.*" I glared at him.

Lisette and Lance ignored me as they chattered about the menu and who else might want to come and what time we should all meet. I'd been outnumbered. I stewed in silence and berated myself. I should have elaborated further, back during the "known him intimately" conversation. I should have explained to Lisette then how raw and vulnerable I still felt about Christophe. Instead I'd laughed it off as a long-ago fling, its intensity a thing of the past.

Lisette noticed my tension and patted my arm. "Don't you worry about this. You need only show up at my place. And introduce me to him, of course!"

"Yes." Dread filled my heart. "Of course."

Preparing myself late Saturday afternoon, I recited everything I had going for myself. I loved the mission and my snug home. I'd made friends. Teaching was going well. In short, life was as good as it had been since I'd arrived in Gabon, sixteen months prior.

I had no intention of continuing an affair with Christophe. I'd bawled the afternoon he'd driven William and me to the airport, as we said our goodbyes. He'd gently steered me to a quieter spot. "Baby," he'd said, with a note of confusion in his voice, "it doesn't have to be this way. I'm just a phone call away. I travel to Oyem regularly and I can easily meet you in Bitam."

But I hadn't wanted that either. Not after the way he'd talked about Mireille, how her father was a provincial governor and how her brother was counselor to the Minister of Education. "Their connections are going to be invaluable to us," he'd said, and the painful reality hit me. This was no fly-by-night relationship. I could hear it in his voice. Much like I'd foreseen Alison's plan to marry, I could tell Christophe was planning on a future with this woman. I had my own life to live.

And I'd found it, on my own. But the thought of his return made it all seem as stable as a house of cards.

Hold strong, Fi. Just hold strong.

When Christophe arrived, I put on my performance face, greeting him with a carefully rehearsed smile and a kiss on both cheeks. Together we strolled over to Lisette's house. Ignoring my hammering heart and the pained awareness that he looked so very good, I introduced Christophe to Lisette, who introduced her three other guests, all fellow teachers. Lance and William arrived minutes later. I'd never been so glad to see William; I latched onto him. By his side, I found it easier to look Christophe in the eye and treat him as the good friend I'd told him I hoped we could be.

"How is Mireille doing?" I asked Christophe from my seat, trying to sound casual. Code for, *is she still in your life, the other woman?*

On the other side of the coffee table, he smiled at me. "She's doing well, and thanks for asking." Code for, *yes, she's there, we're together, and are you sure you need that to matter?*

Before I could radio back a code response, Lisette joined us, making herself comfortable in the seat next to Christophe. "*Alors*, close friends, catching up?" she said, and we both nodded and smiled. "It's lovely to see. You are a good friend, Christophe, for driving all the way to Bitam."

"It's my pleasure. Thank you for hosting this gathering."

"You're most welcome." Her next words were directed to him alone. "Do you know, I believe we have friends in common."

"Oh?" He shifted her way. "Do tell."

"Ndinge Marie-Louise, from university days."

He considered this. "In 1982, perhaps? Paris, winter?"

"Yes, indeed." She beamed. "I was there, too."

"*Une étudiante à Paris?*"

"*Oui!*"

"*Au même temps?*" he exclaimed.

"*Oui, exactement le même temps!*"

"*C'est génial, ça!*"

"Oui, vraiement!"

They smiled broadly at each other. Their French grew quicker, more difficult to discern, the lower volume of personal conversation. Who had charmed whom first, I wondered? No matter. They'd become fast friends.

Fortunately there were other guests, equally charming: Moussa and Bintou, a Malian husband and wife who taught sciences at the mission, and Benoît, a Cameroonian and Lance's teaching colleague at the lycée. Like Lance, Benoît was friendly, outgoing, curious. He spoke excellent English. When he heard William had done undergrad fieldwork in eastern Africa, he wanted to hear all about William's impressions. William told him about the Ethiopian refugee camp and the four weeks he'd spent in Malawi. The latter had culminated with a memorable event, a festival, featuring something called the Gule Wamkulu.

Benoît's dark eyes widened in delight. "Excellent! You saw them perform?"

"I did."

"What is it?" Lance asked. "Or who is it?"

"A group of traditional dancers from that particular region," William said.

"The Chewa tribe," Benoît supplied.

William nodded and gestured for Benoît to continue.

Benoît explained. A male-only secret society of dancers called the Nyau brotherhood, around for centuries, they disguised themselves when performing, kept their identities secret, so the emphasis could remain not on the man but on the spirit presence they summoned forth. "Because, you see," he said, "the Chewa believe it is the spirit who dances, not the man."

"Oh, come on, that's not possible," Lance protested, but Benoît shook his head.

"But it is, my friend," he said, and the conviction, the reverence in his voice, stirred something in me.

Spirit dancers.

Benoît explained how the Gule Wamkulu performed at initiation ceremonies, weddings, funerals, the harvest festival and important local and national celebrations. Disguised in costumes and masks, or simply body paint and palm frond skirts, they embodied the spirits of the ancestors—the deceased being far and away the most powerful influencing factor of anything in Africa—in order to instruct, entertain, chastise or dispense wisdom. "Even the costumes, handmade with great care, are considered sacred and otherworldly," Benoît said, and I saw that he had the attention of everyone in the room.

"What was it like, watching them?" I asked William. "Did it feel... different?"

"It was like nothing I'd ever seen before," he replied. "It was theatrical, but something more. You really felt like you were watching something greater than the dancer. Their movement was so fast, their feet seemed to spend more time just above the surface than on the ground. They'd kick up dust as part of it. It made it look like they were hydroplaning. And, the way some of them moved their bodies—ways you normally don't see on humans. Cat-like. Boneless, between their knees and their chests. It was astonishing."

"I would have loved to have seen that," I said wistfully.

Christophe met my eye. "I don't know if you others know this, but Miss Garvey is a dancer of the highest caliber in the Western tradition."

"I'm not that good," I protested.

"Did you know Fiona was a dancer?" Christophe asked Lisette.

"No, I didn't!" She wagged a finger at me. "When we talked about going dancing last Saturday night in town, you expressed no interest."

"It's ballet, *la danse classique*, that I'm good at. The rest, I'm pretty white."

Which made everyone laugh.

Lisette rose and excused herself to check on her roasting chicken. Christophe continued to scrutinize me. "Does this mean you're *still* not dancing?" he asked.

"I'm not." I kept my tone light. "I jog on the mission's sports field, though. Three afternoons a week. It's great."

Jogging didn't interest him. "No dancing," he repeated, as if he couldn't believe it. "Not even since Cap Estérias?"

Code for, *not since we spent three days in a frenzy of sex and eroticism?*

It all came rushing back.

Worse was the way he kept his eyes on mine, hypnotizing me, pulling me back to that house, the getaway's reckless, careless euphoria.

"No," I managed. "Not even."

"Fiona," he said, playfully chastising. "You really should change that."

He turned to Moussa and Bintou and began chatting with them about Mali. His manner was cordial, relaxed, as if he hadn't given our conversation a second thought. I, meanwhile, felt bulldozed.

"I'll just go help Lisette," I mumbled to no one in particular as I rose and fled the room.

Over dinner, the wine, a velvety-smooth Bordeaux courtesy of Christophe, served to further chip away at my carefully laid defenses. At one point toward the end of the meal, I looked his way. He caught and held my gaze from across the table. A terrible jolt of desire ripped through me. I looked down quickly, seized my water glass and took several gulps. When I looked back up, Lisette, sitting next to him, had once again claimed his attention.

Lisette was a beautiful woman. Her full-figured body would have been considered heavy in the U.S., but when I looked at her proud bearing, the way she was so comfortable in her big frame, I could understand why African men found women like her so attractive. They liked her spirit, too, the way she returned their admiring glances with a flirtatious, speculative regard of her own.

Tonight, reassured by my fine performance of proving that Christophe and I were nothing more than friends, she grew livelier, more flirtatious with Christophe. Over dessert and coffee, she pointed out a speck of digestive biscuit that she claimed had landed on his arm, one she took great pains to brush away. I saw the way he shifted his attention toward her after that, attuned to her next move. Possessiveness slammed into my gut like a fist.

Unwilling to watch my friend flirt with my ex-lover, I rose and busied myself in the kitchen. My ears monitored the different conversations, particularly the one that mattered. I knew when it ended five minutes later and a chair scraped against the floor. *Please, please come to me,* a voice in me pleaded. The sound of his footsteps grew closer. I plunged my hands into the cold, soapy water, intent on cleaning plates, aware of the moment he joined me in the kitchen. I could see him without even looking. He would be leaning against the door frame, arms crossed, a smile on his face, his green eyes intent. I could sense, as well, the increased rising and falling of my chest, the feverish flush on my cheeks. The more sensible Fiona had somehow been consigned to the basement, where she hammered at the door with her fists and hollered to be let out so that she could knock some sense into this silly girl who stood washing the dishes, trembling, awaiting Christophe's touch.

When his hands found my hips, the plate slipped from my paralyzed fingers and sank back down into the dishpan with a soft clunk. "I was wondering," he murmured against my hair, "whether you might have interest in a private tutorial on African dancing. To help you get started back up with dance again." He took a step closer and spooned his body behind me. As if on cue, dance music sounded from the living room, coming from Lisette's stereo, amid cries of pleasure from the other guests. Christophe began to move his hips in that astonishing, fluid way African men did, and I wasn't sure which aroused me more—being with a male partner who really knew how to dance, or the eroticism of our tandem movements.

He didn't want Lisette, he wanted me.

My spirits soared. My body relaxed and I melted against him. Sensing acquiescence, he tucked his arm closer around my waist.

"Do you really think we should remain only good friends?" he murmured, his breath warm on my neck.

I could hear the strong Fiona, still downstairs, pounding at the door and shouting. I ignored her, choosing to listen instead to the soothing, dulcet tones of the weak Fiona. *Just one night. You deserve it. You know it would be wonderful. And besides, you know you can't resist him. And he knows it too.*

The last thought stopped me cold. It would seem the strong Fiona had found a back door and slipped upstairs to whisper in my other ear. In the course of a split second, she pointed out all that I stood to lose if I gave in here.

I pried myself free from him and forced the words out. "Yes, I think it's best we remain just friends."

Christophe waited till I'd turned to face him before he spoke. "That's your final decision?"

I nodded.

A flicker of surprise, almost disbelief, flashed across his face. "I hope you can respect that, given your decision, I'm going to go back out there"—he gestured to the living room—"and follow a less thorny, less challenging course of action. One that requires no cajoling on my part and, indeed, appears to be an invitation."

I marveled at his ability to send my spirits soaring, only to allow them to crash to the ground a second later.

"You do that," I said, mirroring his smooth voice. "My goodness, why brood about loyalty and morality at a time like this? Have your fun. Forget about Mireille or myself. After all, having fun is what matters."

Christophe's eyes glittered with anger. "I'm glad you feel so principled and self-righteous. Enjoy your judgments, all by your lonesome." He eyed me, his expression coolly dispassionate. "I believe I'll head back to the party and the hostess now, but perhaps you'd like to compose yourself further here. Your face is flushed. You look aroused. And that seems to be a problem for you."

"Thank you for the suggestion," I spat back. "Your consideration is exemplary."

"Yes. I know it is."

Rage made my hands shake. I left the kitchen to use the bathroom, where I splashed cold water on my face, counseling myself to not give him the satisfaction of seeing me reappear all upset. Returning to the kitchen, I took my time, knowing I did not want to see how Christophe would ultimately retaliate. I neatened, scrubbed two pots, and decided I couldn't delay it forever.

Cheery music blared from the speakers. Dancing was imminent. Christophe's hand rested on the table inches from Lisette's body as they chatted and laughed. Her swaying hips suggested a tacit encouragement that prophesized the hand's placement on her hip, if not her ass, within the next ten minutes. Her hand on his shoulder a moment later sent a knife thrust of hurt and jealousy through me. Lance began dancing with Bintou as Moussa and Benoît remained engaged in conversation.

William stood watching the others. He looked over and eyed me in concern.

I strode over to him and knocked my hand against his. He enveloped mine in his, a warm, reassuring grasp. He leaned in to catch my low, shaky words.

"Help me. I don't think I can stay here." To my horror, tears rushed up from nowhere and I knew I had to leave right then and there.

"Go," William said. "I'll explain."

"Okay. Thanks."

I fixed an unconcerned look on my face, pretending that the leaking eyes had more to do with dust particles in my eye than emotion, and bumped my way past the chatting, dancing people.

The moment I stepped outside, I knew I'd made the right decision. The cool night air cleared my head, loosened my shoulders. I took deep, cleansing breaths that gradually slowed down.

William came out of the house and joined me.

"Thank you," I said.

"No problem."

"Do you suppose I should I go back in there and tell Lisette thank you, and good night?"

To my relief, William shook his head. "I did the honors for us both. Christophe told me to tell you he'd come by tomorrow, later in the morning."

"Okay. Thank you."

We began walking in the direction of my house and the guest room the sisters offered him when he stayed overnight.

"I'm sorry I made you leave early," I said.

"I was ready to go anyway. I have to leave early tomorrow morning."

"I owe you. I seriously owe you."

"No, you don't. Lance told me what happened with the note. You didn't have the chance to say no."

"It needed to happen sooner or later, seeing him."

"I'm so sorry. I assumed you two were involved. You looked so close, there at the airport, when he drove us for our flight."

"We *are* close. Except when we're not. It's…complicated."

"I can believe it."

He said no more. The scene we'd left had required no translation.

We trudged in silence up the hill toward my house. The full moon had risen high in the sky. In the bluish light, the mission grounds had never seemed more beautiful, the enormous, shaggy palms like prehistoric creatures crouched in repose. The manicured lawn felt like an endless carpet. My spirits lifted.

"Oh this is so great," I said, circling around. "I can't believe how bright it is." I began to run.

I have to dance. There was no further thought process involved— I simply began dancing, grand jeté leaps across the endless lawn, chassé sautés into tour jetés. I danced down the length of the enormous lawn, feeling cleansed, safe again. It wasn't pure ballet; I broke the rules by mixing in cartwheels, running, hops and skips. I whooped as I leapt back to William, who laughed.

"You're like something out of *A Midsummer Night's Dream*," he called out.

"One of those fairy sprites—that's it exactly!" Impulsively I took off again and repeated the same quirky passage. And again. It felt great. Being winded, with burning calf muscles, felt great.

I returned to William's side. "Sorry about that," I said as I caught my breath. "It's a dancer's compulsion."

"It was fun to watch. I can't believe I didn't know you were a ballet dancer."

"Yeah, I've kept that part of my life pretty compartmentalized since arriving in Africa. Christophe was the only one to discover it, back in Lambaréné. He used to come watch me."

We're not going there, Fiona.

"Did you dance professionally?" William asked.

"No, I wasn't nearly good enough for that."

"Sure looked like it to me."

I seized the opportunity to think about ballet and not Christophe. "I know how good the real deal is, from watching a friend who went professional. Her name's April and she's a soloist with the American Ballet Theatre. I met her back in Omaha, when I was seven and brand new to ballet. She was amazing. You could see, even then, that she was destined for the big time."

"How so?"

"Let's see. Perfect turnout, arched feet, long legs, short torso, narrow chest, high extensions. Great musicality—she literally was like poetry in motion. Of course she was gone from Omaha in no time. By fourteen, she was living in New York, having been accepted on scholarship to the School of American Ballet."

"That's big, huh?"

"Huge. Every aspiring ballet dancer's dream school."

"Fourteen, wow. You have to be pretty ambitious and focused to make that all work."

"You do. She was like my sister, Alison, in that way. Alison was Miss Nebraska in 1984—did I ever tell you that?"

"Fi, no way!"

It showed how comfortable I'd grown around William, to have told him that. But he'd told me about his sisters—he was the only boy in a family with three sisters—so it seemed only fair. "April and Alison were in the same grade at school, too. But April was my friend, not Alison's." A chuckle slipped out. "I used to fantasize that they'd been switched at birth, and that April, not Alison, was my true sister."

He began to chuckle, too. "You remind me of my sister, Katie. All full of passion and strong opinions."

"Sounds like me, all right. It drives my family crazy."

"That's a big family for you. Everyone taking their turn driving the others crazy."

"You know, I think you're right. Why hadn't I thought of it that way before?"

"You needed my wisdom to show you the way."

We both laughed and slipped into a companionable silence as we trudged on.

At my doorstep, he wished me a good night. "I'm leaving super early tomorrow, so I'll say goodbye as well."

"Okay." I smiled at him. "Good to see you. When do you think you'll be back in town?"

"Next Saturday afternoon, probably. Wanna meet up?"

"Sure! Let's call it a plan."

My good spirits lasted until I was alone again, settling into my bedroom. Then I remembered Christophe nearby. And Lisette even closer to Christophe. I had a hunch it was going to be a long night for all of us.

Chapter 18

I lay awake half the night, sick with the knowledge that Christophe was quite possibly in bed with my friend. I couldn't believe I'd all but assured Lisette it wouldn't matter to me. The worst part, I knew, would be seeing Christophe the following morning, all relaxed and smiling. I didn't want to be around for it.

I had to get out of there.

I needed an accomplice. Not Lisette, certainly, since she was another one I was desperate to escape. Not William, who, although he could provide transportation when he left in the morning, would discourage any impulsive, hurtful behavior. The situation required someone who lacked moral righteousness, who didn't take anything too seriously. As dawn stained the eastern sky, I rose from my bed. Once I heard William's truck start up and drive away, I mounted my bicycle and headed into town, passport and cash tucked into my backpack.

Lance's house was an anonymous, peeling white structure four blocks from the market. Goats rummaged around the door, grunting and snuffling through the overgrown weeds. They skittered away as I approached and pounded on the door. Lance showed up, bleary eyed and confused.

"Good morning," I said, pushing past him into the house.

"Fiona, are you crazy? It's not even seven o'clock. It's a Sunday."

"Get dressed. And grab your passport."

He perked up. "Where are we going?"

"Cameroon."

Most of the Bitam market still lay asleep in the aftermath of Saturday night, but the taxi-brousses were running. Lance and I hopped in the back of one headed north and within thirty minutes, we were moving.

I escaped, I thought, with the jittery glee of a kid playing hide and seek. I'd forgotten how intoxicating it felt to run away. I knew Christophe was going to be furious with me and I didn't care. Right then, I longed to hurt him as much as he was hurting me. *Why did you have to come back?* I wanted to scream at him. *I was happy, I was finally getting over you.*

Lance's company was the perfect antidote to my mood. He made friends with all the people sharing the back of the taxi-brousse and soon had them singing rounds of "Row, Row, Row Your Boat." The words after "boat" came out as gibberish, but everyone got the melody and the rounds down perfectly. As rainforest flashed past, the scruffy papas and tiny mamas sang their hearts out, eyes riveted on Lance. I couldn't stop laughing.

The border patrol was a breeze and like that, we were in Ambam, Cameroon, less than fifty kilometers from Bitam, but a country away from Christophe. "You know, leaving the country without notifying Libreville is probably against Peace Corps rules," I told Lance, whose eyes brightened.

"Cool, we're AWOL. What should we do first?"

Ambam was a bustling market town, smaller than Bitam, but full of animated people dressed in colorful, traditional attire who milled around the stalls and shops, chattering in Fang and French. We got a cup of instant coffee and a buttered baguette in a restaurant-bar and afterward wandered among the rows. The newfound foreignness exhilarated me. The air smelled different—sharper, earthy and tinged with optimism. Even the surrounding rainforest seemed more exotic somehow. At the market stalls, we bought things we could easily find in Bitam, but which seemed so much more intriguing here: music cassettes, bars of soap, pads of paper. In a tremendous coup, we found a stall that sold, curiously, Betty Crocker devil's food cake mix and 100-pack Dixie paper cups. I bought three of the former; Lance seemed convinced he'd make good use of a pair of the latter.

On impulse, Lance decided to purchase a mattress for his bed from a merchant nearby. After watching him bump around ineffectually for a while with it, I proposed a lunch break at a nearby bar-restaurant with outdoor seating. The mattress, we discovered, made a comfortable back rest, propped between the restaurant's exterior wall and our bench beneath an awning. From our spot, we could watch the comings and goings of the market crowd.

I scored a coup in the beverage department. In addition to the ubiquitous orange soda one found in every restaurant and bar in Gabon, often the only alternative to Regab, this place sold Top *Ananas*, Cameroonian pineapple soda. I ordered two. Lance studied the beer bottles on display. "They don't have Regab," he said.

"This isn't Gabon, what do you expect? Ever wonder why it's called Re-*gab?*

Lance's eyebrows arched high with astonishment. "*Gab* for Gabon. I never thought of that before. So, what do I drink here?"

"I have a hunch they'll have something similar."

The answer was "33" Export, which wasn't an export at all, but Cameroon-brewed, a brown-bottled equivalent of Regab. Lance was so impressed with the smooth flavor, he decided we should keep our seats after lunch so he could have another.

"We really should get up and explore, you know," I said when he'd finished his second and was considering a third. "Take advantage of being in Cameroon."

"We *are* taking advantage of it." He gestured to my depleted pineapple sodas and his beer bottles. "Cultural appreciation."

"The non-liquid kind of cultural appreciation."

Lance made no effort to rise. "Know who you remind me of? Jenny, the new community health volunteer in Oyem."

"Carmen's new roommate?"

Lance nodded.

"Haven't met her."

"I got to know her in Libreville. She and the three fish-farming volunteers swore in a week after education volunteers did, but our training overlapped there at the end. She's really smart—got a degree in international development."

"And that makes you think of me?"

Lance laughed. "Oh, no, don't be silly. It's just that she always seems so…earnest. But in a nice way," he hastened to add when he saw my expression.

I wasn't sure I liked the idea that Lance had pegged me first and foremost as "earnest." To prove to him I could be fun and impulsive, I shouted in Fang for two more "33" beers, which made all the Fang speakers nearby crane their necks and stare at me in surprise.

An open-bed military truck rumbled up next to the market's center. Once it stopped, a dozen soldiers jumped out and began to prowl around. The reaction was instant; everyone seemed to lower their gaze and busy themselves with their wares, their purchases, rather than meet the soldiers' eyes. All except for the town *fou*, who wandered up to them and greeted them cheerily.

Every town had a *fou*, it seemed—a crazy guy, his mind gone. This one had matted dreadlocks, dusty, torn Western clothing and an uneven gait. Unlike in the U.S., the crazies seemed to be treated benevolently here. The soldiers, however, ignored him as they glanced around the marketplace before trooping into a nearby restaurant. The fou cackled and waved. Everyone else seemed to heave a collective sigh of relief and go about their business.

The serving girl brought us the two beers. "Cheers," I said to Lance, and clinked my bottle against his before taking a sip.

Lance sipped and set down his bottle. "Hey, what did you think about last night's conversation? The one about the spirit-dancer guys."

"The Gule Wamkulu?"

"Yeah."

"Very interesting."

"Sure, to watch, for entertainment. But the rest? I mean, come on. The people seriously think it's spirits dancing? Their ancestors?" Lance looked skeptical.

"I think you should never assume you can understand someone else's spiritual beliefs."

"Yes, but don't you think sometimes African spiritual beliefs are a little far out?"

"Are you religious at all?" I asked.

"Sort of. We did the church thing on Sunday as I was growing up."

"So, do you believe the Christian dogma, the miracles, the Holy Trinity, the Virgin Mary?"

"Sure."

"There you go. That's what we believe. That's what we were raised on."

Lance pondered this as he took a swig of beer.

"Yes, but Christianity is *real*. It's proven."

This amused me. "Proven?"

"I believe stuff I hear in a church. I can't say I believe a dude in a costume and mask, dancing, is animated by anything other than the dude wearing the costume."

"Gule Wamkulu!" a voice blared out from behind us.

Lance and I both jumped in surprise, and looked around.

The fou had returned. "Gule Wamkulu," he crowed. "*Ah, ntang, oui, oui, c'est vrai*! Gule Wamkulu!" He seemed to love the new phrase, even though it was Chichewa and not Fang, repeating it with increasing glee and fervor. Lance began laughing as I regarded the fou in unease.

He began to pace around. He shook his fisted hands, as if he were playing maracas. "Gule Wamkulu, eh, eh!" He strode from one end of the restaurant patio to the other, repeating his mantra. The other diners turned to regard him indulgently before losing interest. In Lance and me, though, he'd found a rapt—or trapped—audience. He strode right up to our table and leaned in toward me, closer, closer, until we were face to face and I could see the striations of his bloodshot eyes, the tiny freckles on his dark brown cheeks. His smell, a mix of urine and sickly sweet metabolizing alcohol, made me recoil, which made him lean closer.

"Back off, bud," I said in English, too rattled for French, much less my limited Fang. "You're creeping me out. Go away. Shoo!"

He laughed, delighted, as if he'd understood my words and found them charming. "*Vous voyez?*" he exclaimed. "*Eh, ntang. Oui. Vous voyez. Vous les voyez.*" He leaned even closer, and repeated the last words, in a lower, slower voice, as if to emphasize each word.

You see them.

I stared at him; it seemed I had no other choice. It felt as though he were sucking me in to his craziness, or maybe he was sane and only pretended to be crazy so that the others would ignore him. Because right then he didn't look crazy, he looked all-knowing.

Which, of course, was crazy.

"*Allez vous-en!*" The restaurant owner came to our rescue, striding over from the restaurant's interior. She made shooing motions with her hands as she approached our table, and the man gave one last cackle before dashing away from the restaurant. He disappeared into the crowd within seconds.

Lance hadn't stopped laughing. I, meanwhile, felt sick. Dizzy. I drew in a shaky breath, shut my eyes and massaged my temples, as if to keep his words from taking root in my brain.

I did not see spirits, I sternly told myself, nor did they see me. I had an overactive imagination and I was letting too much of Africa, and African superstition, seep in.

"That was hilarious," Lance said.

"That was creepy," I said in a shaky voice.

"What was?"

"His words."

"Which words?"

I shook my head. "Forget it. It's too hard to explain."

"Fiona, why are you acting spooked? The guy was certifiably bonkers. He was holding a conversation with the air when we arrived. And did you smell the booze on him? Drunk *and* bonkers. C'mon. That was really pretty funny. And when you spoke to him in English? Omigod. Priceless! I'm going to do that the next time a fou hassles me in Bitam. It was the perfect way to respond."

The creepy feeling began to dissipate. Lance was right.

Gradually my pulse returned to normal. I glanced at my watch. "It's getting late. We should see about getting a taxi-brousse back to Bitam."

"Aww, c'mon. One more beer? I'm having a ball."

I hesitated. "You're a bad influence, you know that?"

"Me? *You're* the one who woke me up early to go AWOL with you."

"That's true. And thank you, for joining me."

"You owe me," he said.

"No, I don't!"

"Let's stay for one more beer and we'll call it even," he proposed.

"Deal."

An hour later, we rose unsteadily and regarded the sagging mattress. "I've got a great idea that will give us some shade as we walk," I said.

I sensed we were a source of entertainment to the people we passed. "*Treinte-trois,* thirty-three," we bellowed to them, in case people hadn't already figured out why we were staggering and singing, a mattress balanced on our heads. Once in a taxi-brousse, an hour later, we laid the mattress on the floor of the truck and let the kids sit on it. The two goats aboard loved it. After the truck started moving, Lance pulled out a bag to reveal three "33" Export beers he'd bought at the bar. "A souvenir," he said. He turned to the others in the back. "Beer, anyone?"

He'd spoken in English, but they understood. Soon, all three beers had been pried opened—the locals knew how to open one with the lid of another, and for the final beer, a tiny Gabonese mama opened the bottle with her teeth, which Lance and I found equal parts entertaining and horrifying. Lance pulled out one of his Dixie Cup packets, with a smug, *see? I knew I'd use these* expression to me, and distributed cups all around. A dozen of us shared the beers, laughing and sipping, as Cameroon flashed by.

The sun had begun sinking when I arrived back at the mission, having retrieved my bicycle from Lance's after the mattress delivery. A quick glance at the pebbled drive and its lack of cars told me Christophe had left. Of course he had. I made my way slowly toward my house, all good spirits gone. On the far side of the grounds, I could see that the lights in Lisette's house were on.

What was I going to say to my friend? *Were* we still friends?

How good it had felt, this morning, to run. How tiring, now, as if I'd literally been running the whole time.

At the least, it had served one purpose. I didn't have to worry that the hunger to get re-involved with Christophe would return. Nor, I knew, would he ever try again. I swallowed a pang that arose within me. I'd have to stay away from Libreville, from his wrath. Bitam was my home, anyway, and the safest place for me.

I went into my house, turned on the lights, and sank into an armchair wearily.

Five minutes later, a knock sounded. I opened the door to find Lisette there. Her expression was unreadable.

"You're back," she said, stating the obvious.

"Yes." I opened my door wider and she stepped in.

"Something to drink?" I asked, feeling awkward, unsure of how to proceed.

"Do you still have some of that Earl Grey tea your sister sent you?"

"Yes."

"That would be nice."

Like most Africans, Lisette was unafraid of long stretches of silence, and didn't jump to fill them with inane chatter. She was content to sit at my kitchen table without speaking, as I stood at the stove, focusing on the tea kettle. "Did he go back to Oyem?" I asked her finally.

"Of course. Hours ago."

"How was he?"

"If you know him as well as you both have alluded, I think you know how he was."

"Angry?" I turned to face her. "But very controlled about it? Almost calm?"

She nodded.

I had to ask the question. I had to know. "Did you sleep with him?"

The look Lisette gave me, chilly and disapproving, was the most effective silencer I had ever received. Alison could have learned a lesson or two from her.

"I'm sorry," I mumbled, feeling the heat rush to my face. "That's not my business."

"Indeed it's not."

The rules were so different here. Just when I thought I'd figured them out, something like this would hit me.

I didn't truly know Lisette. I knew as much of her as she'd allowed me to know. Right then, the gulf between us, two women from two different cultures, felt enormous. She drove in this point even deeper, once we were both seated, sipping our teas.

"Did you know Christophe has two brothers?"

She'd spoken so casually, with words so unexpected and shocking, I was sure I'd heard wrong. I asked her to repeat herself.

She complied.

"But that's impossible," I stammered, after her words confirmed I hadn't misheard.

She looked amused. "Oh? How?"

"I would have known. The other volunteers would have told me. *He* would have told me."

In response, she only shrugged and took another sip of tea.

I saw this wasn't a point I could argue away. Lisette knew more than I. She was Gabonese, after all. It galled me to think that she might automatically know Christophe better.

"I've seen photos of his parents together," I argued. "His father is a man who loves his wife deeply."

She regarded me curiously. "Of course he does. This is why

Christophe won't mention his father's second family, away in the village."

"Does Christophe's mother know of them?"

Another incredulous look, as if I'd asked her whether animal over rice was a vegan dish.

"It is a man's legal right to have up to four wives, here in Gabon. When a wife can't produce children, or can only produce one, no one sees it as a crime if the man chooses to take a second wife or discreetly have a second family in the village. Children are wealth. Sons are wealth." She paused to sip her tea. "But out of respect to his wife, particularly in this situation, where Christophe's father is an important man and she comes from a good, highly placed family, it remains tucked out of view. Out of polite conversation."

"How old are they?" I asked faintly. "These brothers."

"They are young men. Nineteen and twenty-one. They are studying abroad. England, though, and not France."

"I didn't know," I whispered, almost to myself. "Why didn't Christophe tell me any of this?"

"Most likely because you don't know how to discuss African affairs. You barge in, ask questions that are too personal, not the kind another African would ask."

When I tried to protest, she held one hand up.

"I have noticed this about you. I love you, Fiona. I'm so happy you're here, at this post, as my friend. You've enriched my life and expanded my world and my worldview. When you say the wrong thing or ask the wrong question, I remind myself it is because you don't fully know our culture."

I sputtered, but no intelligible words of defense came out.

"You baffle me, Fiona," she continued. "You have before, a little, but now I'm truly stunned. To throw away such a friendship as the one Christophe has offered you? Was any sense of indignation or jealousy on your part worth that? He clearly cares for you. He loves you, even. Do you know how fortunate that makes you? And look what you did."

I rose in agitation, opened the fridge, studied its contents without seeing them, and shut the door. "Well, we are similar here." I turned and faced her. "Just as I'm discovering how I really don't know the full workings behind the Gabonese culture, you really don't know American women. Or at least ones like me, who would rather have no relationship over one that left me feeling emotionally unsettled and crappy all the time."

"You'd prefer solitude?"

"Most decidedly."

She shook her head in disbelief.

This wasn't going well. Antagonism had filled the room like the cloying stink of cigar smoke. Painfully aware that one destroyed friendship in a twenty-four-hour period was all my psyche could manage, I returned to the table and touched her hand.

"I'm sorry. I know I'm bumbling all over the place here. It's always been my downfall, since I was a kid." I forced the difficult words out. "You're right. I say the wrong thing, ask the wrong questions. I can't help it. There's such a need in me to *know*. To understand. To solve the mystery, once and for all."

Her expression softened. "Not everything is to be figured out, my friend. We do not question mystery so much here. Can you explain death, after all? Can you explain how one continent suffers as another prospers, and the fairness of that? Are we not all, in the end, on the same journey of life, trying to do right, and love our children, our families? Family, supporting them, is everything."

I thought of the contention I'd left back home. "Sometimes supporting family is hard."

"I can appreciate that," she said. "As we speak, I am angry at my sister who is raising my son in the village. But she is helping me, and in turn I am helping them by providing income."

"You have a *son*?" I stuttered.

"I do. He is six years old. I will spend two weeks with him and family at Christmas."

"You never told me!"

She only shrugged.

It all felt as disorienting as a funhouse. You'd have thought I'd gotten used to it by now.

Welcome to Africa. Again.

Chapter 19

As if in karmic retribution for my irresponsible adventures, I fell sick with a bout of stomach flu that made me miss classes on Tuesday and teach like a zombie on Wednesday. But calm soon returned to my world at the mission. The students never took advantage of the situation, and Lisette once again became her smiling, easygoing self. Neither of us mentioned Christophe. I pushed aside my hurt, jealousy and increasing remorse at what I'd done, painfully aware that I'd destroyed my relationship with Christophe, maybe irrevocably. But his life was with Mireille in Libreville anyway, and mine was here. By Saturday afternoon, when I went into town to run errands, I felt grounded and cheerful once again.

William had sent a message—this time delivered directly to the mission—that he'd be late coming to Bitam on Saturday, probably past sunset. Beers with Lance and his teaching colleagues in the market seemed a fun way for me to spend the extra time. Lance bought a plate of beef brochettes to snack on, topped with fiery piment oil. I watched in amusement as Lance took a dare, pouring even more piment oil on his last bite, afterward waving his hand frantically over his mouth, nose running, eyes leaking over its overpowering heat. As nightfall approached, I bade the group farewell, hopped on my bike and cycled through town. Only when

I was outside the town center did I notice my bicycle light wasn't working. For a moment, I debated going back to borrow Lance's flashlight. I decided no. It was late enough as it was, and after riding on the road for two and a half months, I knew every rut and pothole.

At first I was cautious about riding without a headlight, but the trip passed without incident. My concern evaporated as the mission lights appeared in the distance. When I began my descent on the final hill, I let the bike gather speed, greater and greater, until the night air blasted against my face and legs. It was so dark, I couldn't even see the road. The edgy thrill of it all made me burst into cackles of glee. How fast could I go? Why had I been so nervous about this? It was exhilarating, like flying past all I'd been afraid of. Lance and Lisette were bold and fearless like this all the time. Leap first, look later. Why shouldn't I be this way as well?

I flew down the hill and screeched with laughter, following it with an animal-like howl of triumph that seemed to reverberate through the forest.

Too late, I heard a truck, even though I couldn't see its lights. When it appeared from around the sharp bend, near the mission driveway, I discovered why: the truck had no headlights. In its place were wobbling flashlights, tied into place. I seemed to have endless time to consider my options. Stay on target and get hit. Brake and wipe out. Veer off the road at thirty miles an hour, negotiate the unfamiliar and get hurt.

I swerved. It was either that or die. As the truck rumbled past, the driver most likely never seeing me, I bumped and careened down the invisible periphery of the road until I hit something. The jolt threw me from my bike. For an instant I was airborne. Then I crashed, and everything good ended.

The ringing in my ears was terrible. I struggled up to sitting, gasping at the pain shooting from my wrist. My jaw felt much worse, as if it had been torn from its socket and was now on fire. I'd landed in a ditch. My face and arms felt wet and sticky, and the rest of my body seemed caked in dust and grime. I needed a towel. It occurred to me the mission was nearby. William would be there. He was waiting for me. I had to get to the house. I had to get to the house. It became my mantra. I groped around in the dark and struggled out of the ditch. Fighting waves of dizziness and nausea, I limped, one shaky step at a time, toward the light.

William was indeed there, standing on my porch. I heard him telling me he was glad I hadn't locked the door because this way he could have a beer while he waited. I stepped out of the shadows into the glare of the compound spotlight. The brightness of it sent knife stabs of pain ripping through my head.

William's words trailed off. I felt blackness creeping up behind me. Everything tilted at a funny angle, but instead of pitching forward like I'd expected, I felt an arm clamp around my waist. Walking became easier, almost effortless. I didn't even have to open my door. Inside, I squeezed my eyes shut against the light as William eased me onto a chair.

"Fiona? Fiona? Talk to me, sweetie. Can you hear me?"

Pain shot through my jaw when I tried to respond. Only a muted whimper came out.

"Nod if you can hear me, Fiona."

This was easier. I nodded. I felt his hands on me, touching my face. He made little tsks of disapproval and disappeared. I opened my eyes again, but now, in addition to the too-bright light, something else was bothering my vision. I put a shaking hand to my face to brush it away. I looked at my hand—it was crimson, wet with blood. Lots of blood. My blood. I began to pant, little animal sounds of terror. William, returning from the kitchen with a wet towel, hurried over.

"It's okay. It's okay." His voice sounded both soothing and stern. "Fiona, look at me." His command cut through my panic. I looked up. "You'll be all right. I think it's just a scalp wound that's making you bleed so much." His eyes locked onto mine, his so beautiful with those thick lashes, almost double-fringed. Nothing like Christophe's green eyes except in the way they drew me in, little anchors that kept me from drifting away. And William's voice, gentle and singsong— it was worth staying alert just to hear it. He continued to talk to me as he wiped my face, probed at my swelling wrist, my throbbing jaw. He told me to follow his finger with my eye, and tell him where I was. I did. I would have done anything that voice asked. I trusted its owner implicitly. Even when he reached down, slipped his hands beneath my shirt and pulled it off. He set it on the counter; it was saturated with blood and grime down the entire front. He disappeared into my bedroom and a moment later reappeared.

"Is this shirt okay?" he asked, holding up a red tee shirt with puppies on it, a gift Mom had sent that was so patently childish, I'd never once worn it. William stood there, holding it up, looking so serious. It dawned on me that I was nearly topless in front of him, wearing only a skimpy bra. This struck me as terribly funny and I began to laugh, only it hurt my jaw so bad, it became crying, which hurt just as bad. He came over and with a deft tug, pulled the shirt over me. I slid my arms through the holes, my body now trembling uncontrollably.

He squatted and gently rubbed my arms. "Can you walk to my truck? We need to get you to the hospital. You're going to need stitches, for starters."

"Adventure's not over?" I mumbled.

"Hate to say it, but I think it's just begun."

He was right. The next few hours were a haze of pain-wracked misery—the bumpy ride to the hospital; the hour wait among others far worse off than I; the horrifying examining table with bloodstains still on it from the last patient. The medic on duty, an enormous, hard-faced Gabonese woman, terrified me. She was unapologetic about the clinic's lack of anesthesia for the stitches, or painkillers for when she yanked my dislocated jaw back into place. My howls of pain, in the end, probably helped the jaw pop back quicker.

Back home, I hobbled to the bathroom and spied myself in the mirror. The whole left side of my face was swollen and scraped, my cheek and chin a bulging mess with black string poking out from the sutures. I had the beginning of a black eye. William saw my stricken expression as I turned away.

"If you think that's scary," he joked, "you should've seen what you looked like when I first saw you, blood streaming down your face." He assessed me and his smile faded. "It's late. Why don't you head off to bed, see if you can sleep?"

I nodded and shuffled off. William followed, with a bottle of aspirin and a cup of water that he set down on the nightstand. "I'll sleep on your living room floor tonight," he said. "Just call out if you need anything else."

If I needed anything else. Yes, I did. I needed to turn back the clock to a minute before I'd decided I was ready to start flying. For some of us, it simply didn't work.

My failure taunted me, all that sleepless night and the next day, after William left, and all I could do was sit in misery while my jaw throbbed and burned and my body rejected the stitches. I'd blown it, and I would pay dearly. When infection flared up the following day, rendering me feverish and Soeur Beatrice concerned, the inevitability of it all made me want to cry. Because there was only one place for me to go.

Med-evac to Libreville, where Christophe was.

Chapter 20

"Good morning, Sleeping Beauty," a voice said. I cracked open an eye and Rachel, the Peace Corps medical officer, was standing there, her curly brown hair a halo against the bright light of late morning. The room had flowered wallpaper, a chintz armchair in the corner and a lace-covered end table next to it. I had no idea where I was.

"Mmph."

Rachel laughed. "I see my assistant gave you the painkillers last night. They're dynamite, aren't they? Bet you slept well. All right, let's see the damage." As she looked over me, the events of yesterday slipped back into place. The afternoon flight to Libreville with William, the way he'd steered me through the airport, into the back seat of a taxi and finally to the comforting coolness of Rachel's living room. She'd been out, but her assistant had injected me with antibiotics and painkillers. Afterwards everything had grown softer and more unfocused. The sound of William chatting with another volunteer was the last thing I remembered.

My reverie was interrupted when Rachel prodded at my stitches. "Ow, ow," I yelped, arms flailing.

"Sorry. But to be honest, it's going to hurt even more when I rip them out. Which I'm going to have to do." She stood back, hands on her hips, and frowned at me. "God, you're a mess. Your jaw still looks funny too. Think I'll call in Dr. Gauthier to take a look at it—you can come with me to my office."

"Where's William?" I asked.

"He grabbed the morning flight back north. Don't worry," she added, misinterpreting my dismay, "there are a few more folks in town if you want company. They came back with me last night."

Wisps of a dream from the previous night floated through my head. Christophe had been in it. I'd been drowning in the ocean, crying out for him. I remembered waking, panicked, hearing the ocean behind me and the buzz of conversation beyond the bedroom door, in the living room. It had all felt so real. I could have sworn Christophe had been there, pulling me to safety, making the ocean recede. Never mind that there was no ocean in Rachel's house. "Were a group of you talking in the living room?" I asked.

"Were we too loud?"

"No, it's just that… Was Christophe there?"

"Essono Christophe? No, why?" She looked at me, puzzled.

"Never mind. I guess I was just having a weird dream."

At Rachel's office, Dr. Gauthier, a jovial French physician, pronounced the jaw traumatized but on the road to recovery. He administered some anesthesia to help the muscles relax and suggested I not yawn, sneeze, chew or open my mouth too widely for the next month. Rachel ripped out my stitches, impervious to my cries of pain, rinsed and disinfected the angry red wounds, doped me up and sent me to the back room to rest. As I huddled on a cot in the antiseptic-smelling room, more of last night's dream came back to me, in all its vivid intensity.

It had been some sort of beach party. I'd been wading in the ocean, well aware that the pointe shoes I was wearing were getting ruined by the salt water. I was alone; everyone else had congregated further up on the beach. They were laughing and talking, petting some sort of tuxedo-clad leopards that were circling the group, serving appetizers from trays balanced on their backs. At first, the ocean gently lapped at my thighs. Soon, however, bigger waves came and tugged at me, slapping my chest and face. The undertow sucked at my legs and made me stumble. I saw Christophe and decided he was very rude to let his ocean assault me like this, but he was too busy visiting with what appeared to be members of my family.

The waves grew more aggressive and I shouted for help, but no one heard me. The next wave pulled me away. I cried for Christophe before squeezing my eyes shut. When I opened them, I was in the dark, alone and scared. No one could come because they were having too much fun on the beach in the next room.

Just when I was ready to give in to the relentless seduction of the water that had followed me into the bedroom, someone did appear, calling out my name before slipping an arm around my shoulders. It was Christophe; it had to be Christophe, because no one else knew how to comfort me like this, drawing my shaking body to his and tightening his arms around me so that the waves subsided with a grumble. And even though the water had retreated, he still held me close until I stopped trembling. His hand stroked my hair. I felt his warmth, his heart thumping somewhere close to my ear. When I whispered that I was so afraid he'd left me for good, his response was to hold me even closer, tucking my sweaty body next to his through the tangled sheets, before he tenderly kissed my forehead. "I would never leave you, Fiona," he said.

Even though it had only been a dream, it had brought such comfort, leaving me with the feeling that everything would be all right. I rearranged the pillows under my head, gave a little hiccupping sigh and settled back to rest.

When I heard Christophe's voice an hour later, I knew I couldn't possibly have imagined it this time as well. "You mean she's here?" I heard him ask Rachel. Before I could gather my wits about me, he came into the room, stopping short when he saw me. The shock on his face reminded me how bad I looked.

I was not prepared for battle—it was enough of a struggle just to sit up straight. "Oh, baby," he said, coming closer, "you look awful." I tried to laugh, but it came out as a tortured hiss. He pulled over a stool and sat beside me, taking my un-bandaged hand. He looked impeccable in a white button-down shirt and pin-striped trousers. Beside him, I felt like a vagrant.

There was an awkward pause. "So," he said finally, "here we are again." I nodded, unsure of how to best address the situation. "I was worried when I heard about your med-evac." He saw my confusion. "William called me this morning before he left."

The news stunned me. William had seen how Christophe's presence had upset me the last time—why had he thrown me right back into the lion's den? "I had no idea you and William had become such good friends," I ground out.

Christophe stiffened. "He assumed, rightly so, that I might be concerned to learn you were injured."

"You found her," Rachel called out, appearing in the door with an exquisitely beautiful Gabonese woman in a beige linen suit. The two of them smiled at me.

When Christophe heard the women approach from behind, his expression changed. Several emotions seemed to flit across his face— unease, chagrin, regret—replaced a moment later by diplomatic politesse.

"Fiona," he said, "I'd like you to meet my fiancée, Mireille."

His expression had warned me; I had to give him that. I commanded myself to focus on breathing normally. Everything else seemed like too much of a challenge. The stranger took a few steps forward, extending an elegant, tapered hand. *"Enchantée,"* she said, her eyes calm, her voice like silk. I pulled my hand from Christophe's to shake hers, dredging up what dignity I could muster.

"Un plaisir," I replied, wincing when my performance smile produced a sharp pain.

"Poor Fiona," Rachel said in English, chuckling. "I don't think you're going to enjoy talking for a few days."

"Then I won't make it more difficult for you," Mireille said in flawless English, her manners as refined as her appearance.

She and Rachel headed back to Rachel's office. I didn't look up, not even to accept the apology I knew was on Christophe's expression. Instead I closed my eyes. He took my hand again, which I kept limp, passive. After a moment he gave it a squeeze and stood up. "I'll let you rest. I'll come by Rachel's house tomorrow to see how you're doing. That is," he added, his tone cooler, "if you don't plan on going anywhere."

This made me open my eyes. I met his chilly, expectant gaze. I opened my mouth to defend myself and pain shot through my jaw again. The anger left his face. "I'm sorry," he said, "I told myself I wasn't going to bring it up. We'll talk tomorrow."

I nodded and he slipped out.

The next day I felt slightly better, which wasn't saying much. Rachel's house was quiet. The volunteers who'd returned to Libreville with her had moved to the livelier case de passage. Once Rachel had left for work, only the ticking clock and the rumble of traffic outside broke the silence. I curled up on the sofa, content to read and glance periodically around the living room with its mix of American and African: batiks and Georgia O'Keefe prints on the wall and lacy curtains at the windows. I couldn't help but compare everything to Bitam. Libreville, while more cosmopolitan and wealthy, now seemed too civilized. In the homes of Rachel's neighborhood, one of the city's well-tended French expatriate enclaves, I sensed an attempt to keep Africa out and the West in.

The sisters at the Bitam mission, on the other hand, seemed to let Africa permeate their Western-ness. They still wore the white uniforms and headdresses that demarked them as European nuns, but the loose, relaxed way they strolled down the corridors in their frayed sandals attested to time spent in Africa—over twenty years for most of them. While they focused on their tasks when inside, they'd grow dreamier outside, pausing on their morning walks to angle their heads and smile in the direction of something they alone seemed to hear. Their roast chicken Sunday dinners featured Gabonese side dishes. Drums, not church bells, pounded from the mission belfry on Sunday mornings, calling them and other worshippers to service.

The serenity and odd familiarity of the Catholic environment allowed Africa to slip in the back door of my own mind as well. It coiled around my thoughts, my body, even as I slept, giving me vivid, spectacular dreams. Each morning upon waking, I'd feel subtly altered, in a way that both pleased and disconcerted me. I'd take my tea outside, acutely conscious of the colors around me, the sweet-smelling earth, the way the nubs of grass would tickle my feet. Nights were cooler in the northern part of the country, making the morning air fresh and tinged with magic.

The students picked up on the otherworldly calm too. It subdued them in the classroom, helping to maintain the discipline, which, in itself was rarely a problem. Soeur Hélène, the surveillant, would come into the classroom, bringing with her a pall of sadness that hung in the air. Her mournful blue eyes would focus on the troublemaker, her tiny frame bent under the weight of her grief that we couldn't all get along. "Richard?" she'd say in a sad voice. "Was this a good idea?" Richard would cower in a manner the Makokou surveillant could never have produced. All the bravado would fizzle out as if he were a pierced inflatable. "Let's go talk about this," Soeur Hélène would propose and they'd walk out, her hand on his shoulder, his head hanging. From behind, it looked as if they were heading off for her to console the student. On the rare occasion a student resisted this method, a gentle suggestion that they pay a visit to Mohammed, the mission mechanic, did the trick. They were clever, these sisters.

I missed them. I missed the market, Céleste's bean sandwiches, my friends. I missed everything in Bitam.

The sound of a car braking to a stop in front of Rachel's house brought me back to the present. I peeked out the window and saw Christophe getting out of his car. The contents of my stomach flip-flopped. I commanded myself to play it cool as I fumbled with the front door, finally wresting it open to let him in. He was wearing a tailored navy suit and silk tie that made him appear both professional and intimidating. This, I sensed, was part of his strategy. He greeted me with a kiss on the forehead, the only part of my face that didn't look battered, and followed me into the living room.

"I guess I'll go make us some tea," I mumbled, gesturing to the kitchen.

"You sit. I'll do it."

"I'm not an invalid." I drew myself up taller. "I don't need my jaw to make tea." But, as it turned out, I needed two strong, un-sprained wrists to carry the tray. He came into the kitchen five minutes later and took the tray as I stood there, swaying with indecision. Wordless, I followed him into the living room.

"So," I said, once we were both seated, "I guess congratulations are in order." I focused on my tea bag, watching it bob in my hot water. When Christophe didn't respond, I looked up at his puzzled face. "You and Mireille," I prompted.

My tea bag seemed to fascinate him as well. He exhaled heavily and looked up. "Please believe me when I say I never intended that meeting to happen yesterday. I had no idea we'd find you there. We happened to be in the neighborhood over our lunch break and Mireille, knowing my concern, suggested we stop by to get more information from Rachel."

"She's very beautiful. And considerate."

"Yes, she is."

I knew if the conversation continued along this vein, I was going to make an idiot of myself and start crying. Fortunately, he seemed equally reluctant to discuss his fiancée. Instead, he talked about the goings-on in Libreville, sharing what he'd learned from visits to the Peace Corps office. Henry's home had been the site of an enormous ant war that had raged for two days. The ants had rampaged through the house, covering one wall with solid black, as they forged onward, eating anything in their way. Henry hadn't been able to return for five days.

"And last week," Christophe said, "your fellow English teacher Sharon left."

"You mean permanently? Like she quit?"

He nodded. "It sounds like she was hoping the second year would get easier, but in her case, it didn't."

"Yeah, I guess not everyone gets a Bitam their second year."

"Ah, yes. Bitam."

There it was. I set down my tea. He waited for an apology as the silence lengthened.

In the end, he spoke first. "I have to say, I think what you did that next day was childish, rude and completely inappropriate." He studied me, his lips a tight, compressed line. "I thought we were seeing eye to eye the night before. I gave you the choice. I respected your decision and still you threw it back in my face."

"Do you honestly believe that was easy for me?" I protested, in spite of the pain to my jaw. "And you taunted me after I'd made my decision—don't you go denying that."

"Regardless, it doesn't change the fact that you reacted like a child, more concerned about yourself than the fact you had us all worried that Sunday." He shook his head. "You are the most difficult person I've ever met. Really, I don't know why I tried so hard to be friends with you."

His use of the past tense, as well as the way he now regarded me, eyes narrowed in contempt, frightened me into silence.

"I could have continued to help you, you know. Made your time here in Gabon a bit easier. But, forget it. Did you really think I'd let someone treat me like that and get away with it?" He let his words settle in, in all their chilling finality. I pressed my shaking legs together and told myself I wasn't going to cry.

"I'd decided, upon my return from Bitam, that was it," he continued. "I saw no merit in continuing our relationship. Only now..." He let the words trail off.

"What?" I was afraid to breathe.

"Just look at you."

I didn't need to look at myself to know what he was implying. The disdainful yet pitying expression on his face said it all.

"So I must confess, I don't know what to do." He raised and dropped his shoulders in a theatrical gesture.

Christophe may have been a player, but he wasn't an actor. If he'd stopped his performance a few lines earlier, he might have hooked me, made me cry, implore him to remain my friend. But he hadn't stopped. And now, observing his pompous demeanor as he dangled his carrot of salvation over me, I saw everything. He'd just played his trump card: his friendship, the one thing he was convinced no one could do without. But Christophe had forgotten something. I had no problem being left the hell alone. Going solo had always been easier for me than making relationships work out. Christophe was the one who stood to lose here. He needed people. He needed people to need him. I didn't anymore.

And like that, the power balance between us shifted. I could almost feel it in the air, a little rustle that eased the heaviness I'd felt ever since I first fell for him in Lambaréné.

He'd grown uneasy by my lack of response. I rose calmly, ignoring the adrenaline that surged through my bloodstream. "Let me ease the pain of your conundrum," I said.

I strolled over to the front door and opened it. "Get out."

He stood, mouth agape. "You want me to leave? *You* want *me* to leave? Fine, I'll leave. And I won't come back."

The dam holding back my hurt and resentment burst. "Get out then," I shrieked, and instantly regretted it. I clamped my hand against my throbbing jaw. "Get the fuck out of here," I said through clenched teeth.

He didn't move.

I stamped my foot like a toddler. "I mean it—leave! Get out of my life. You've caused me nothing but grief, anyway."

He stood there, a murderous rage staining his face. Neither of us spoke or moved. Finally, with great deliberation, never losing eye contact, he sat. After another moment of silence between us, he looked down at his hands and buried his head in them. I watched his shoulders begin to shake. When he looked back up, I saw that he was laughing, and yet his eyes were anguished. "Oh, Fiona," he said, sounding choked, "what am I going to do once you've gone?"

I could feel the tension drain out of my shaking body. At the same time, I wasn't about to get all soft and sentimental on him. "Beats the hell out of me," I muttered, still cupping my jaw. "Maybe go buy a dog to kick?"

"If it were anything like you, it would bite me in the leg before I had the chance."

"Before you could properly train it to heel?"

He studied me. When he spoke again, his voice was soft. "I wouldn't presume to try."

So began one of the strangest periods of my relationship with Christophe. He stopped by to visit each day during the three-hour lunch break, and returned each evening with Mireille. Rachel was home by then and the four of us ate dinner together (soup for me, to my frustration) followed by a game of cards. Mireille didn't seek explanations for Christophe's attentiveness toward me, nor offer apologies for her own presence. I couldn't help but notice how well suited she and Christophe were. She seemed to temper his personality—I found I almost liked him more when she was around to absorb some of his intensity. He didn't change his intimate behavior toward me; he still caressed my cheek and regarded me with a loving smile before sitting next to Mireille. She seemed to hold him with a loose hand, perhaps recognizing if possessiveness and jealousy crept into their relationship, it would poison her.

I knew when I was outclassed. I grudgingly warmed to her, finding I enjoyed her refined elegance, her amusing stories of years spent in boarding school and travels around the world. I watched her swivel her head to converse with everyone, her motions fluid and graceful. Her expensively coiffed tresses perfectly framed her face as her beautiful light-brown eyes lit up with animation. Her every movement was a dance.

On Friday night, Rachel announced I'd healed well enough to return to Bitam. "I can't guarantee you'll be able to eat Thanksgiving turkey in two weeks," she said, "but you'll at least have graduated to stuffing."

"Are you looking forward to returning to your post?" Mireille asked.

I thought about the sisters, my pretty house, my new friends, the lively market, the mission grounds and my late afternoon jogs. "I can't wait to get back." The wistful tone of my voice seemed to amuse everyone.

"You mean to say there's nothing in Libreville that can compete with Bitam?" Christophe asked.

"There isn't," I said, and the two women laughed. Christophe, however, didn't, and I had the oddest sense that I owed him another apology.

Or not.

Chapter 21

I didn't know bread could catch on fire. But there it was, flaming away in Carmen's oven. "Help," I squeaked, hands flapping, as she joined me in the kitchen. She grabbed the potholders that had been hiding from me and pulled out the two flaming baguettes, plunging them into the water, where they extinguished with a hiss. Afterwards we surveyed the charred, soggy results.

"Wow," she said, "I had no idea baguettes could do that."

I sagged against the counter. "Crap. So that's it for the baguettes, the manioc casserole and that disastrous corned beef stuffing. I'm running out of side dish ideas."

"Maybe that's a good thing." She laughed when I scowled at her. "Oh, cheer up. We can send William into town for more baguettes. Jenny cut up a half-dozen mangoes for a side dish and made something pretty tasty with chopped taro root, onion, oil and vinegar. That'll be plenty. And hey, your green papaya pie turned out nicely."

The pie really did look good. As per Daniel's recipe, I'd mixed boiled, mashed green papayas with condensed milk, egg and sugar. I'd added the spices sent by William's mom, tossed everything into a pie crust and baked. Now the pie was cooling, its crust and nubbed papaya surface browned to perfection. William came in and sniffed appreciatively at the buttery, cinnamon fragrance. "Wow, great job," he said when he spied the pie.

"Much better than last time I tried, huh?"

"Was that when you forgot to add the eggs?"

"No, the last time was when the oven ran out of propane midway through the cooking."

"That's right. But, you know, in spite of that, it was really pretty tasty." He turned to Carmen. "It was like a custard with the sauce baked right in."

He flashed me another smile before going to the refrigerator for two more Regabs. I watched him as he returned to the living room, handed a beer to Lance, and sat next to Jenny, Carmen's new roommate and the new community health volunteer. She was attractive, assertive, with shiny brown hair and a forthright jaw. Like William, she'd studied international development. Their conversations always seemed to revolve around lofty subjects, like comparative public policy, resource economics, or the lack of epidemiological and entomological data on patterns of malaria and habits of the mosquito vector. This one, conducted in murmuring voices with little coos of agreement and excitement from Jenny, seemed no different.

I turned back to Carmen, who was busy peeling carrots. "So…" I kept my voice casual. "Jenny and William dating?"

Carmen looked at me curiously. "Don't think so. Why?"

"Oh, I don't know. They just look…friendly."

She looked at me and a grin spread across her face. "And that would be of interest to you, would it?"

I waved her words away. "Oh please, don't even go there."

"God, are you *blushing*?"

"Look, you kept trying to tell me last year what a great guy he was. Fine, I agree with you. He really helped me out after my accident—I don't know what I would have done if he hadn't been around. As it is, I'll have these scars to take home with me."

"Let me see the one on your cheek again."

I inclined the left side of my face toward her.

"Damn, that's kind of cool," she said. "It looks like a tribal marking or something."

"It looks like a question mark."

She studied it again and began to laugh. "It does. That's hilarious."

"Yeah, just hilarious. A fitting souvenir for my Peace Corps experience."

"You always did have to do these things differently." Carrots finished, Carmen pulled a pan of turkey wings from the oven to baste.

"So, how's Daniel? Talk to him recently?"

"Yup." She smiled. "Thanksgiving Day, in fact. We finalized our plans for our Christmas rendezvous in Paris. A month from today, I'll get to see him." She finished basting the turkey wings in a happy reverie. "What about you?" she asked after she'd popped the turkey back in the oven. "Are you going to call home while you're in Oyem?"

"I don't think so. I mean, the actual holiday was two days ago. Besides, it always makes me feel more homesick, once I've hung up."

"Does your family do a big Thanksgiving dinner every year?"

"Oh, sure. A couple of relatives, the five of us, a neighbor or two—it's never less than twelve. One year it was twenty."

"Yikes. Who does the dishes after that? And the prep work before? Does your mom rent the linens like I hear other big groups do? Does she make certain foods for picky eaters, or are they screwed on Thanksgiving day?"

Carmen was forever curious about the big family dynamics she'd never experienced, and frequently plied me with questions like this. It was oddly reminiscent of Lane Chatham's fascination with my family, the way he'd been eager to meet them. I'd balked at the idea initially, but once we'd started sleeping together, I couldn't resist the temptation to show off my glossy new boyfriend. On the drive to Omaha for The Big Introduction, however, I felt so sick with nerves, I made him stop at a 7-11 for antacids. Lane laughed and told me not to worry so much, that he was sure he'd love my family. I didn't bother to tell him that was precisely what I was so nervous about.

Thanksgiving dinner in Oyem may not have looked like its counterpart on an American table, but we still managed to gorge ourselves on turkey wings, mashed plantains, carrots, Jenny's side dishes and feuille de manioc, brought from William's village to serve as a creamed spinach look-alike. My jaw was still in its early healing stages, limiting me to the softer food. Jenny dominated the conversation, brushing aside breezy discourse in favor of more substantial fodder: the way sexually transmitted chlamydia was rendering so many Gabonese women sterile; Franco-American relations in Gabon; the uneven distribution of the country's wealth. I tuned her out until I heard Christophe's name mentioned.

"He's a perfect example," Jenny was saying. "Have you seen the car he drives? And I heard his parents' house in Libreville is practically a mansion. He probably spends more on his shoes than a family of six lives on for a year. And then he buddies up to our Peace Corps community—what a hypocrite."

It was okay for me to bash Christophe, but when I heard someone else doing it, my hackles rose. "Yes, but he's really helped some of the volunteers out," I said.

Jenny dismissed my words with a sniff. "He helps the ones who kowtow to him, who can't solve their problems on their own."

Did she know of my relationship with him? I wondered if she was deliberately trying to get under my skin.

Lance unwittingly came to my rescue. "He's an okay dude," he told Jenny. "Me and Fiona and William had dinner with him in Bitam a month back. And he didn't offer *me* any help, but I guess that confirms I've got things under control in my classes. I really do think I have the touch." Pride crept into his voice. "Not to brag, but my students love me. They love my class. We have a ball. They tell me they can *relate* to me. Isn't that cool? That's all you need to do to be a success in your job here."

Carmen, William and I eyed each other in amusement. Lance would learn.

I fell into conversation with Kaia, a new volunteer in the fisheries, or fish-farming, or pisciculture program, which was a mouthful, so we just called them "the fish." Kaia seemed to be the quiet one of the first-year group, next to the oversized personalities of Jenny and Lance. She was sweetly pretty, and made you think of a young but bedraggled Cindy from *The Brady Bunch*, butter-yellow hair in cute pigtails and big, sad-looking blue eyes. When she spoke, she sounded intelligent yet humble, intensely human. I liked her right away.

I asked her how her work was going.

"A mix of success and frustration," she said. "I've got one farmer whose fish pond is doing really well, only his nephew is starting to be a problem. It used to be I would only see the nephew once in a while, but I guess he got kicked out of school in one of the other provinces and his family shipped him out here."

"Oh, gee. Lucky you."

"I know, right? He's bullying, opinionated, and thinks he knows best. He's training for the military at the same time, and that's making him cockier. I hope he ships out soon. Then I can go back to dealing with just his uncle."

"You have my sympathies." I shook my head. "I've had my share of problem students. They make life miserable for all involved. But, listen, let's keep in touch. I may be only an education volunteer, but sometimes help comes from unexpected places. Drop me a line if you'd like me to pop by to support you."

Jenny had been listening from across the table. "Don't worry, Fiona. I've got Kaia's back," she told me in that smooth, confident voice that was already grating my nerves.

I forced a smile. "Cool! It's just that, as second-year volunteers, we've sort of learned to think outside the box, find the unlikely solution to problems."

"Yes," Jenny said, "but some of us know how to behave in a way that circumvents bigger problems before they arise. Not just go out there and fan the flames."

Ouch.

A host of heated retorts rose to mind, as the others began to laugh.

Jenny waved her hands. "I'm sorry, that wasn't supposed to be an insult! It came out wrong. Fiona knows I didn't mean it that way, right?" She smiled brightly.

I gritted my teeth, which sent a stab of pain through my jaw, which kept me from speaking, which was probably a good thing.

"All right, gang," Carmen rose from her seat. "Time for some African pumpkin pie, which smells amazing. Any takers?"

Hands shot in the air.

"There," Carmen said. "That's something we can all agree on."

Back at the mission, the rest of the semester flew by. The students, for the most part, continued to behave in an exemplary fashion. Which didn't, however, mean I lacked a troublesome redoublant student. This year it was a female, a sullen teenager named Sophie.

Sophie was a village girl at heart, uncomfortable and uninterested in the classroom. Her frayed white uniform blouse always seemed rumpled, tucked out of the regulation navy skirt that bunched up around her heavy hips. Prior to the start of school, Lisette had pointed her out as three teenaged girls strutted past us at the market. The biggest girl looked to be about seventeen, her features too broad and surly to be considered pretty. As I watched, she shoved one of her friends, her expression triumphant. When she turned and saw us, the predatory look in her eyes faded only slightly as she offered a fake, bright smile to Lisette. She grabbed the hand of the friend she had pushed and the three of them scurried off, giggling.

"That one," Lisette had commented, "she is trouble. She is also one of your students."

Forewarned was forearmed. I was strict with her and her classmates, never giving them a chance to claim any power. I reserved my livelier projects for the other classes. When Sophie acted up, I immediately called in Soeur Hélène for disciplinary assistance.

During the final week before Christmas break, Sophie grew more unruly, prompting me to get more creative with discipline. She hated school, so I assigned her to return after the break had started, to help me. I had all the time in the world—I wasn't leaving Bitam for the holidays. Instead I'd work on my secondary project through the break, creating a community library on the mission grounds. Sophie was speechless with fury over the mandate. I smiled sweetly back at her and told her I'd see her at nine o'clock on the first day of break.

To my surprise, she showed up on time, grumbling and tight-lipped, but subdued without the presence of other students. We trudged over to the library building and spent the next four hours in silence, unpacking boxes of donated books and rearranging the shelves of existing books. I could feel a subtle shift in our relationship, particularly when a box I was holding ripped open from the bottom, raining paperbacks all around my feet. "Son of a bitch," I muttered in English, forgetting about professional decorum. We looked at each other, wide-eyed, and burst into laughter.

"Will you teach me that phrase in English?" she asked in French.

"No!" I protested, still laughing. "No way, José!"

Which I taught her in English.

After we shared a buttered baguette and sardine lunch and returned to work, she grew more comfortable. "Why do you not allow our class to do interesting projects, like you do in the class of my friends?" she asked.

"Why do you think?"

"Because you do not like us," she said, flashing me her hateful glare. Last year I might have protested, telling her how I longed to be everyone's friend. I still enjoyed doing fun activities with my students, but I needed them to respect me first. And I hadn't learned how to do both in Sophie's class.

"Why should I put energy into something special when you can't cooperate and behave in my classroom?" I retorted.

She scowled and fell silent, her eyes narrowed to slits. Her gaze fell to the paperback in her hand. It had a pink, sparkly cover and two laughing girls on the front. "If it were something fun," she said without looking up, "maybe I could do better."

"Something fun," I echoed.

She nodded.

I suddenly remembered last year, how I'd written my former French teacher during my early euphoric days of teaching, proposing a pen pal exchange. She'd been interested in the idea, but I'd dropped it after the students got too unruly. Was twelve months too late to start it up? Why not just send a packet of thirty letters to her, and see what came of it?

"Something like having an American pen pal?" I asked Sophie.

She looked up at me, eyes now wide with hope. The animation flooding her face made her seem actually pretty. I shook my head in mock regret. "Only it would take a lot of work. Too much work for you, probably."

"No way, José!" she said, which made me laugh.

Her curiosity had been piqued. As we finished up, she pestered me with more questions until I raised my hands in surrender. "We'll see," was all I could tell her as we left the library. She nodded and after I'd wished her a happy holiday, she trotted off cheerfully.

The other volunteers in the region began to clear out: Carmen to Paris; the first-year volunteers to Jenny and Carmen's house in Oyem; William to Henry's village for a meet-up with the other construction volunteers. Although I enjoyed the mission and Bitam enough not to feel too lonely over the prospect of Christmas alone, my heart leapt when I heard William's voice outside Lisette's door, two days before Christmas. I was inside, helping Lisette prepare for her departure au village to family. "You couldn't leave us, after all?" I heard her ask in a teasing voice as she let William in.

A moment later, he stormed past me, angry and sunburned, not even bothering with a greeting. In the kitchen, he splashed water on his face and scrubbed his oil-stained hands. Lisette and I exchanged bewildered glances. "Um, hi there," I called out.

"Hi, Fiona."

"Aren't you supposed to be on your way to Henry's village?"

He turned back toward us, mopping at his face and hands with a towel. "My truck broke down four miles down the road. I think my water pump is ruined."

"Mohammed's truck has a tow," Lisette offered. "He can bring your truck back here and look at it for you."

"Yes, I know. That's why I came here."

"What, not to wish us a Merry Christmas? I'm hurt," I said, only half-joking.

He scowled at me. "Merry Christmas."

Lisette laughed. "Off you go—I just saw Mohammed walk by."

William gulped down a glass of water, thanked her and left.

When Lisette finished her packing, we headed down to the mission garage. Mohammed and William were poking their heads under the hood of William's truck. Mohammed confirmed the water pump was indeed *foutu*, which made the whole truck, in addition to William's day, pretty much *foutu* as well. "Son of a bitch," William muttered to himself, staring at the engine after Mohammed left to make some phone calls.

"There is good news and there is bad news, Monsieur Guillaume," Mohammed said when he returned.

"What's the bad news?" William asked, sounding terse.

"There is not a water pump for your Toyota here in Bitam."

"Not in the whole town?" William asked, his voice rising. He slammed his hands down on the truck. "God," he said in English, "this *fucking* country." Mohammed and Lisette both took a tentative step back.

"The good news, Monsieur Guillaume," Mohammed said, "is that my brother can bring a water pump from Oyem."

We all smiled at William encouragingly.

"Tomorrow," Mohammed added.

William sighed.

"Afternoon," Mohammed added again.

William began to laugh. "And if you're telling me right now that it's going to be the afternoon, Mo, what time is it *really* going to be? In Gabonese time?"

Mohammed didn't seem to take offense. "Before it is dark, you will have your pump."

"By Christmas Eve. Great." William sighed, reached up and pulled down the hood of the truck, which shut with a bang. He glanced over at me and scowled. "Why do I get the feeling that somehow you're enjoying this?"

He was right. I thought fast.

"I'm sorry about your misfortune, but I'm glad you're going to be hanging around here for an extra day." I injected a note of hurt reproach into my voice. "I'll enjoy your company."

His scowl softened. "In that case, thank you. Guess we'll be celebrating Christmas Eve together."

The news planted itself in my heart and flowered.

Maybe I'd been feeling a little lonely after all.

Chapter 22

Christmas Eve midnight Mass at the Bitam mission was nothing short of theater. By eleven-thirty at night, every bench in the mission church, a dignified, airy, wooden structure, was occupied, as an overflow crowd spilled out into the humid night. Glossy palm fronds and homemade batiks decorated the walls. Candles lined the aisles, their smoke mixing with the smell of incense and cheap perfume. People continued to mill about, not the least bit shy about demanding that the bench occupants squeeze in even closer to make room. Even goats and chickens played a part in the festivities, a dozen of each penned up next to the Nativity scene.

William and I had joined the sisters at their bench off to the side of the altar. Mohammed had finished the repairs on William's truck too late in the day for him to make the trip to Henry's village. The sisters, I sensed, were thrilled about William's delay. He sat sandwiched between Soeur Beatrice and Soeur Nathalie, both of whom periodically turned to smile up at him and pat his arm.

Gabonese Christmas Mass, I soon discovered, was a far more interactive affair than the Christmas services of my youth. Everyone here sang with gusto, swayed to the music, and gave the priest their undivided attention. During the sermon, they leaned forward on their benches so as to not miss a single word. Whenever the priest followed an important point with the Fang equivalent of "know what I mean?" every head in the place nodded, followed by a murmured "uh huh," all in perfect unison. The worshippers seemed to throw themselves into listening wholeheartedly, precisely the way life threw them into living.

The offertory procession was spectacular. Sixteen women, accompanied by the music of a dozen drums and several balafons—wooden xylophone instruments—danced and sang their way down the aisle, gifts in their hands, their hips sashaying to the beat. The women, in their attire of identical dresses of scarlet, green and gold with matching headdresses, looked like tribal princesses. The drums were deafening, intoxicating. At the foot of the altar, the women lay down their treasures—a wicker basket full of collected monetary offerings, an earthen jug of wine, a giant bowl filled with bread. The offerings got creative from there: a *regime* of bananas, the cluster of thirty still clinging together upside-down; six spiny pineapples; a dozen batons de manioc; ceramic dishes filled with rice, with stew; an enormous bolt of colorful fabric. There was even a basket of Regab bottles.

Céleste from the market finished up the procession. Watching her, a surge of admiration rose in me. Like most Gabonese, she was a born dancer. She carried herself like a queen, moving with broad, sweeping, theatrical steps. As she danced, she lifted a doll over her head. It was handmade, with baton de manioc arms, a five-pound rice bag for the body, topped by a hairy coconut head. A string of colorful beads cinched the lumpy waist. Céleste whirled and swayed with it before setting it down gently atop the bananas. The whole offertory was so whimsical, so infused with joy and exhilaration that my heart contracted. Surely this was how the offertory of gifts to the newborn Jesus must have been, with the palms and animals and the locals heralding his arrival with what they could: their music and organic pageantry, their hearts and the fruits of their labors. Every member of the congregation was swept up in the moment, singing and swaying with the music. The thunderous drumbeats echoed off the walls and filled the building, resonating in my head, jarring loose something deep inside me.

Tears were running down my cheeks as I glanced out of the corner of my eye at William. He looked as calm and composed as ever. But when he furtively brushed at his cheek, I realized that he'd gotten choked up too. A rush of affection and camaraderie came over me. If he'd been sitting next to me, I would have taken his hand. Clutched it, and not let go.

After the crowds had dispersed and we'd wished the sisters a Merry Christmas, William returned with me to my house. In spite of the late hour, I was wide awake. I pulled a bottle of Courvoisier off a shelf and angled it at him. "I know you have to leave early tomorrow, but do you want to come in for a nightcap?"

He smiled. "A wee dram, perhaps."

We sat and I poured. We talked about the Mass, the offertory procession. "Watching Céleste really blew me away," I said. "I'd never before seen her as a dancer."

"She is. She leads a group of women who dance alongside a drumming circle in her neighborhood."

Something that had long puzzled me became clear. "I hear drums, most Saturday nights, around the time I go to bed. Is that the group you're talking about?"

"It is."

"Okay." I nodded. "That explains things. How, even though tonight's Mass was a Catholic ceremony, there was so much more to it. It was so very African."

"I agree. I think most of the locals harbor a parallel spirituality, both Western and African."

"Do you ever wonder what's going on in their minds, versus your own?" I asked. "I mean, there we all were, side by side in the church, having the exact same physical experience, hearing the same words from the priest, the lectors. But, come on, who are we kidding? I have no idea what they're thinking. My perception of it all gets filtered through my own experience. The American, the Midwesterner, who grew up so differently, with different beliefs, values, superstitions. How could I pretend to know what the whole service meant to the woman sitting next to me?"

There were more words, more startling thoughts, wanting to come out, but they got jammed up in my mind, so I stopped talking.

William hadn't replied. I looked up to see him studying me in the same startled way my brother or Lane Chatham always had when I spouted off like this. A wave of embarrassment came over me. I was about to apologize when William spoke.

"That's it. That's exactly it."

"Really?" I stammered.

"Our thoughts, our mindsets. They create and define our world. Five different people tonight—you, me, the sisters, Céleste, Mohammed—had independent experiences."

The door to my brain's hidden room of insight creaked open a little further. "But don't you suppose it's both?" I began, unaware of what words would follow, which usually got me into trouble. "All of us, separate, at the same time all of us were united. Two hundred individuals and, paradoxically, no individuals at all."

He stared at me. "That's quantum physics."

Which made me back off fast. "Oh. Sorry. Quantum physics isn't my department. Couldn't be further from it, in fact. That would be my brother Russell. He's an MIT graduate."

"But you nailed it, in layman's terms. Opposing ideas can both be correct. Ram Dass has a quote about that. 'Across planes of consciousness, we have to live with the paradox that opposite things can be simultaneously true.' Or something like that."

The brain door burst open.

"Oh, wow," I breathed. "That can apply to *everything*."

"I know. Crazy thought, huh?"

We both pondered this in silence.

I glanced over at him. "Hey," I said softly. "Thank you."

"For what?"

"For getting it. For engaging in a discussion over my ramblings. My ex, he would have rolled his eyes after my first words. Or even mocked me for my efforts."

"What an asshole."

"It was just who he was." I could see that about Lane now. "At the core, he was all Southern male. Rigid expectations of how things should be, how people should behave. Ballet dancers shouldn't be philosophers, ugly women could be doctors or lawyers, because there was no conflict of interest, no decision on whether to marry, have kids."

William began to laugh. "He said this? Seriously?"

"Dead serious. Want to know what he thought of gays?"

"I'm thinking not."

"Good call."

"This ex—what is his name?"

I hesitated. "Lane."

"How long were you and Lane a couple?"

Why had I brought this up? What about my vow to never mention Lane's name, much less go on about him?

"Less than four months," I admitted. "Nothing long-term in the least." I saw my chance to reroute the conversation. "Which was what you had, wasn't it?"

He nodded. "Four years. Although I'm not sure last year really counts, since we spent the twelve months apart."

"What was *her* name?" I challenged.

"Candace."

I visualized a Jenny look-alike. Attractive, confident, laughing in the California sun as she strode through the Berkeley campus, long shiny brown hair swinging, off to study something lofty. I disliked her already.

"What does she do?"

"She's finishing her last year of law school."

"Berkeley?"

"Yeah."

Great. Add high achiever and brilliant to attractive and confident.

"Are you sorry you two broke up?" I asked.

"Nope."

His decisiveness made me feel better. "Four years is a long time," I offered.

"It is. It was."

"Can I ask what happened? Or do you not want to talk about it?"

"I'm fine talking about it." William studied his empty glass.

"More?" I tipped the Courvoisier bottle.

"Sure."

I poured us both more, watching as his face creased in thought.

"We met and started dating when we were sophomores. We were both focused on our studies, so it was, in truth, a pretty uncomplicated relationship. We respected each other, made room for each other's academic obligations. Which were dense—I had my dual degree program and she'd set her sights on law school, international and comparative law. We formed a plan: I'd join the Peace Corps for two years, get field experience for my degree, while she buried herself in law school studies. After which, we'd reunite and go do heroic things to make the world a better place.

"It was The Plan. Which made everything seem uncomplicated and run like clockwork. But life isn't uncomplicated and smooth-running, is it? Pretty much the opposite in Africa. You can't live here without it changing you inside. Candace, meanwhile, still clung to The Plan, in a very objective, academic sense. Meeting in Paris felt more like a midterm check-in than a romantic rendezvous. She'd pre-scheduled everything. Every day, every hour. Even sex."

He grimaced as he took a sip of his Courvoisier.

"You're kidding," I exclaimed.

"Nope. Two hours, upon our arrival at the hotel. This included intercourse and an ensuing nap. Not to exceed two hours because there was an exhibit at the Louvre that garnered its own two-hour time slot. And if the sex only lasted ten minutes, well, that allowed more time for the nap. To be honest, I think she was more excited about the nap than the sex."

"Oh, William," I said, and began to laugh. Which might have been the wrong response—did guys see the humor associated with sex and the act, or was the discussion of sex all tied up with their pride, a thing you had to tiptoe around? But I couldn't help it. The thought of William, there in a Paris hotel, wide awake because Gabon was the same time zone as Paris, whereas Berkeley was nine hours later, pacing because Candace had fallen asleep after those first ten minutes, made me laugh with increasing hysteria.

William looked at me, shocked, as if only now registering how much he'd divulged. You could almost see that male-pride thing in him trying to decide which way to go. When he began to laugh, really laugh, head thrown back, chair tipping back, I knew he'd ditched any internal reserve over how he should speak or behave around me.

I still hadn't stopped laughing. "Hey!" he said. He lifted his foot and gave my chair a kick, which hardly did anything since I was already making the chair shake with my laughing. "All right, you had your fun with me. And I cannot believe I just told you that."

Finally our laughter subsided. "I don't mean to make fun of Candace," he said. "Really, she's an amazing person. She'll go far in life. But being together in Paris, I just got this sense of how our future might be together."

His expression grew thoughtful. "Not to say it wasn't a great itinerary she'd made. It was. Interesting exhibits, check. Great restaurants, check. Everything went to plan. She was so pleased. But, you know, in all that time, she never seemed *delighted*. Or overwhelmed. Or moved to tears over something beautiful. She… she's so neat and careful and organized, and doesn't seem to realize that being that way leaches out the good stuff as well as the bad."

He looked over at me. "That night of Lisette's party, I watched you run across the lawn in the moonlight, doing those leaps and those twirls, even though I knew you'd been so upset minutes earlier. Something in me went, 'There. That's someone who knows how to embrace life.' Both its ups and downs. Whatever is happening right in that moment. You seized that moment, wholeheartedly."

His gaze had become so intense, I couldn't look away.

"That's how life should be lived," he said.

Two Courvoisiers became three. A different energy began to fill the room, causing my face to grow warmer, my heartbeat erratic. We talked, about anything and everything. Ram Dass and the human condition. Burger King's distribution of those paper crowns and whether it perpetuated a colonialist attitude or just made you feel like a kid inside. What happened the moment you died. Whether Indiana Jones ever slept or ate in *Raiders of the Lost Ark*. Nothing was too sacred or banal. Anything to keep sharing his company.

The spell broke when I caught sight of the time. "Oh, William,"

I exclaimed, "it's after three o'clock. I am so sorry. I didn't mean to keep you so late."

"Whoops, time to go."

We both rose. My heart, already thudding, began to hammer against my chest as I walked him to the door. Once there, he paused and turned to look at me. "Your scars are healing," he said.

I nodded, no longer trusting myself to speak.

He reached over and gently traced the question mark scar on my cheekbone. As his fingers skimmed over my skin, his thumb grazed my lips, producing an electric charge that tore through me and left my knees weak. He took a step closer.

He was the perfect height for me—a few inches taller, with my face, my lips, inches from a pulsing spot on his neck. His hands fell to my hips. My hands landed on his forearms. We hovered there, in that space where you realize that although this person is your friend, this is no friendly overture.

My hands moved first, as they slid up to his shoulders. My fingers, even more daring, touched the pulsing spot on his neck before coming to rest at the nape of his neck. His lips brushed mine and everything between us seemed to instantly realign to this shocking new configuration. Pleasure shot through me. But his next kiss, more assertive, sent a bolt of pain, not pleasure, through my still-healing jaw. I stiffened and pulled back involuntarily. He stepped back as well, dropping his hands as if my hips had burned them.

"I'm sorry," I said. "It's my jaw."

"Of course," William said, but I caught a flash of something else in his eyes.

And like that, the mood changed. When I stepped closer again, he took a tandem step back.

"I don't think this is a good idea, Fi."

He was rejecting me. I couldn't believe it.

"You're right," I said quickly so he'd think it was my idea too. I continued talking, a flow of bright chitchat to cover up the terrible awkwardness that hung in the air. I thanked him for coming by, apologized again for keeping him so late and heartily wished him a Merry Christmas.

I went to the door to open it. He'd remained frozen in the same position.

"Look," he said. "It's just that I think things are a little complicated right now."

"Complicated," I repeated, a bubble of anger rising in me. "Yeah, I've heard that one before. Right after they told me they were confused."

William shook his head. "I'm referring to you."

"What do you mean?"

"Complicated for you."

I was slow to catch on to his implication.

"You're not referring to Christophe, are you?"

He nodded.

I waved my hands in protest. "No, no, that was a last-year thing, a stupid infatuation. There was a summer fling, but it all ended when I came to this post."

"I don't think so." The only other sound was the cicadas and crickets screeching outside. "You called for him that night at Rachel's house in Libreville. You cried for him. You thought I was him."

It all came back—my dream, the feverish delirium. *I was so afraid you'd left me for good,* I'd said. And then the comforting arms that had tightened around me, with the response, *I would never leave you, Fiona.* The gentle kiss on the forehead—it had been William.

I felt like I'd run into an unseen glass door. "I thought it was a dream," I whispered.

"No."

His clinical calm ruffled me. "So you're the one who kissed my forehead and told me you'd never leave me?"

Now he was the one reduced to silence, mouth working without any sound coming out. "You were awake," he said finally.

"I guess I was."

I hated where the evening had gone. We now resembled polite strangers, struggling to escape a difficult situation. I forced a hostess smile. "Anyway," I said, opening the door, "I apologize for keeping you up. I know you have a long drive today, so I'll let you get back to your room."

He still hadn't moved. "No. I don't want to leave on this bad note. Not on Christmas Eve."

I glanced at the clock. "Christmas morning, actually," I admitted.

A glimmer of a smile appeared in his eyes.

He reached out, right past me, and pushed the door. It slammed shut with a decisive *whump,* producing a thrilling, jittery moment of unknowability, where I realized I didn't have William figured out. He took a step closer to me and his hands slid around me, one over my shoulders, the other encircling my waist. He drew me in, tightly, so that we were wedged together.

I went boneless with relief, with gratitude. It felt so very good to be held close. It also gave me the chance to experience once again the way our body parts fit just right, with legs, pelvis and ribs neatly aligned. Christophe and I had never fit that way; our heights were too similar and he wasn't the hugging, stay-close-together type. How could I have mistaken the two of them?

"Merry Christmas, Fiona," William said softly, and kissed my temple with such tenderness, I almost cried.

"Thank you," I managed, without sounding too weepy or helpless (I hoped).

We disentangled. "All right," he said. "I really need to go. I'm driving away in three hours." He stepped past me, moving much faster than I, still dazed from the hug, from all I'd just learned. He reopened the door, slipped out, and only when he was safely in the yard did he pause and meet my eyes.

"Have a good Christmas break," he said.

"Thank you. Tell Henry hi for me."

"Will do."

I watched him walk away before I shut the door. I leaned against it and sagged.

What a shock, his words. What comfort, his hug.

What a mess I'd just made of our easy friendship.

Part Four
New Year

Chapter 23

"Okay, here's one for you," I told Lance. I picked up the pen pal letter from my kitchen table and read it over the screech of night insects outside my window. "'I respectly come before you today to expressing my high words of adoration to you. I wish to tell you that I love you and I am much happy to serve as your pen lover.'" We laughed and I shook my head. "I kept telling them it was pen pal, not lover."

"You were the one who told me the Gabonese were sensuous people."

"Yes, but I was referring to the adults, not the kids."

"I saw another one here." Lance leafed through my students' letters and singled one out. "'How many tongues do you have near your family? In my land we have many tongues, but I only utilize two of these.'" He looked over at me. "They're trying to say 'languages,' right?"

I nodded. "I imagine they checked the French-English dictionary in the back of their textbook and used the first listed translation for the word *langue*. But hey, that's cool—it means they looked inside their book on their own."

"Here's an even better one." He snatched up another letter. "'How many women do your father have? And boy childs? My father he holds three women and twenty childs in which that is to say seven are boy childs and four are no more of this live.'"

"Yikes. That'll certainly give the American students something to think about."

I'd struck gold with the pen pal project. Sophie and her entire class had responded enthusiastically, and, with genuine diligence, had set about writing their pen pal letters. Like that, they'd gone from my most difficult class to my best.

"Uh oh. Here's a student who's seeking a pen pal of means," Lance said. "'Please, my dear friend of the pen that I love with many hearts, send me Nike shoes in the size of eight or two pairs if it does not derange you.'" He chuckled as he set it down. "I have a neighbor who speaks English to me, and he always ends his requests with 'if it does not derange you.' Do you suppose I should tell him the English translation of *déranger* is 'bother' and not 'derange'?"

"Nah. We get the point, don't we? And besides, sometimes I do feel a little deranged here."

"No kidding." Lance clasped his hands behind his head and leaned back in his chair. "I hope these projects you're doing are worth all the extra effort you're putting in. You set up a *library* during Christmas break?"

"I did."

"Was it quiet, here at the mission?"

"Yup."

"How was New Year's Eve with the sisters?"

"More fun than you'd think. They'd baked all sorts of Belgian goodies and we drank brandy and sang songs. More than one of the sisters got tipsy. It was cute."

"Libreville was wild," he said. "I had a hangover that lasted two days."

"You do know how to party, Lance."

"It's important to be good, really good, at something. And I'm thinking I might not be the world's best English teacher after all."

I chuckled. "Yeah. Been there myself."

After Lance left for the night, I washed dishes, neatened the living room, and headed to my bedroom. There, I waited expectantly. Sure enough, shortly thereafter, drumming started in the distance. Which I now knew, courtesy of William, came from Céleste's neighborhood and their drumming group.

I'd learned to differentiate the drums. There were the deep, resonant ones, which sounded like boulders plunging into water, and smaller ones that had more of a high, percussive slapping sound, like popcorn popping. Whenever I heard the drumming, something in me would grow still, alert, like a dancer awaiting her cue. The Saturday evening after Christmas, so quiet in Bitam with the students and other teachers gone, I'd felt the urge to explore their sound up close. But halfway down the footpath to Céleste's neighborhood, my flashlight a lone beam piercing the darkness, I'd heard loud, agonized shrieks, as if a woman were being tortured. In a panic, I'd turned and sprinted back to the safety of my house.

Tonight curiosity took hold once again, especially after learning the shrieks I'd heard had come from a hyrax, a small, furry grey mammal whose nearest relative in the animal kingdom was the elephant, which made little sense, but that was Africa for you.

The pearly glow of a full moon that lit the path made a flashlight unnecessary tonight. I walked, compelled by the sound of the drums, and yet, the closer I got, the more uneasy I became. A dreamy, vertiginous feeling invaded my mind and slowed my footsteps. It came to me that this trudge through the forest was just like my malaria dream. Next, I'd come upon a group dancing and drumming around a fire, and a bent, gold-colored woman with feathered tufts, who would lead me away and push me to into an abyss.

I stopped, swallowed and told myself to get a grip. I simply had to find out what lay at the origin of those drum sounds. I crept ever closer until I could see the action, yet still remain hidden. Yes, to the drummers, four or five of them, and yes to the fire, the dancers in a large semicircle, swaying and jiggling their hips. But that was it. No bent, gold-colored woman who planned to cause me harm, nothing ominous in the least.

I chuckled out loud. Why had I'd been so anxious? This was great to watch; dance practically at my doorstep. If I wasn't able to dance this way, at least I could observe. I watched for twenty minutes, letting the music and movement fill me. Finally I crept home, feeling uplifted and a little sheepish.

It seemed William didn't come by as often as he used to, but maybe I'd just grown hypersensitive to his presence, his absence. I'd been so nervous about how we would act around each other after Christmas, but he'd shown up the day after New Year's with a chicken and a box of American condiments his mom had sent, and we let all of that distract us. He acted just as warm and friendly as always, but nothing more. I vowed to follow his lead and not bring up Christmas Eve and the kiss.

Tonight we were laughing about a family drama relayed to him in a letter. His sister Katie, a vegan activist, had put a slash through another sister's leather coat, which had all the females in the family up in arms against her.

"Katie's the one who told you if anything happened to you here, she'd come out and kill you a second time?" I asked, as I brought a bowl of peanuts to the coffee table.

He chuckled. "Yes, that's Katie. She's very principled, but, if you ask me, this is taking things a little far. Would your sister have done anything like that?"

"I'd say no. Alison is all cool and composed, although right now, she might be acting less so. My mom wrote that she was all wrapped up in her wedding planning and stressing about it."

"When's she getting married?"

"The last Saturday in March," I said.

"Oh no, you're going to miss it."

"Yeah. It's okay though. It's better this way."

The moment the words came out, I regretted them. William looked at me oddly.

"Why?"

I shrugged.

"What does that shrug mean?"

I shrugged again, searching for a way to divert the conversation back to hothead Katie.

William persisted. "Is it her fiancé? Do you not like him, or something?"

This was where I was supposed to reply, as I did when Carmen asked, that Alison's fiancé was just great. But a reckless dizziness came over me and I blurted it out.

"No, I like him fine. I especially liked him when I was dating him. Enough to lose my virginity to him."

A terrible silence followed my announcement, giving me ample time to consider the idiocy of my decision to be honest.

"Oh, Fi," William said finally.

William's voice carried a particular quality that I found so appealing, a way of demonstrating compassion and concern without overt pity. Which explained why the rest of the story tumbled out so easily.

"You see, Alison is very beautiful. A regional celebrity. And once Lane met my sister, that kind of killed it for Lane and me. Except that I was slow to catch on."

"How did you find out?" he asked.

"I caught them together. At a shopping mall, of all places." I rubbed my temples, as if that might take some of the ache out of the retelling. "I saw him first, and it stopped me in my tracks. There was such a look of infatuation in his eyes. The way I'd seen in his eyes only once toward me. The day he met me."

"And he was looking at your sister."

"He was."

"How did she react?"

"She was stunned to see me. They both were. But she recovered fast."

The memory sucked me back in. The way Alison's look of alarm had faded, replaced by that composed expression I'd come to despise in her pageant queen years. She didn't address me directly. Instead, she turned back to Lane.

"We can tell her," she said. "It's time she knew."

Nothing more needed to be said. I could read it in their body language. Not only were they involved, they were in love.

"How could you?" I said to Lane, as, to my everlasting shame, I began to cry. "We're *dating.* I can't believe you'd do this to me." My voice had grown shrill; I realized people around us were pausing to take note, listen in.

"Stop it, Fiona," Alison hissed. "You're only turning this into a more embarrassing situation. Wake up. He's been trying to break up with you for months. Have you no sense of shame?"

That Alison should turn this moment into a scolding, a dressing down.

That was it: the moment for which I'd never forgive her.

What I remembered beyond that was not conversation but images. The ice cream cone in Alison's hand. The way Lane kept furtively licking from his cone—with pleasure, at that—as Alison and I exchanged harsh words, me with tears squeezing out, knowing I looked uglier when I cried. Alison's composure. Her ice cream, at least, was in the same state as I, melting, creating a mess, dribbling down its cone onto Alison's hand. I focused on that little imperfection; it somehow helped me make my way through the rest of the terrible scene and what followed. Because, in stepping back and whirling around, away from Alison and Lane, I promptly bumped into a mom and her young child, knocking him over, as if to prove that, ballet dancer or not, I was the most graceless human being on earth right then.

There in the safety of my house, I began to cry again, helplessly, as if it had been twenty-three days and not twenty-three months since I'd caught them.

William moved his seat closer to mine, reached out and rubbed my shoulder. I sat there crying until I grew numb, depleted. William rose, pulled the jug of water from my little fridge, and poured us both a glass. I sipped it and dabbed at my eyes with the corner of my tee shirt.

"Okay, "he said. "When you're ready, I'm going to challenge you a little."

"Great," I sniffed. "Thanks. Bring it on."

"It seems your sister's betrayal was twofold, and that's one of the reasons you're having a hard time with it all. True or false?"

"True," I admitted.

"All right. Catching them together aside—because I'm right with you, that was a shitty, hurtful situation—there is the other part. Your sister chastising you for staying in a relationship you should have seen was over. True or false?"

"True."

"Say you'd been dating someone else and you'd let it go too far," he said. "And your sister saw this. Would she have been out of line to say something?"

"Truth? I think I would have still told her to fuck off."

"Yes, but it would be annoyance at a sister thing, right?"

I glared at William.

"All right," William said. "Try this. Replace your sister with Carmen, her observing and speaking up."

This was easier. "Okay, I get it, Carmen wouldn't have been shy about speaking her mind. And, yeah, you can bet she would have railed on me if I'd kept things going with Christophe."

Here William hesitated. You could almost hear the unspoken query hovering in the air.

So, it really is over with you two?

"Anyway," I said hastily, "I hear what you're saying. And you're right. One comment was coming from the big sister. The other was coming from the soon-to-be-ex-boyfriend's new love. It was just horribly unfortunate for me that the two were one in the same."

"Agreed."

I drew a shaky breath and exhaled slowly.

"So, how are things with her now? Do you write each other?"

"We do," I admitted. "Which is a pleasant surprise. I'd call it a cautious truce."

"The wedding—is it going to be the traditional kind, in the church, big family event?"

"It is."

"It's going to be hard for you, being here, so far away."

"I think you're right."

"We'll just have to create a little celebration right here, that night. We'll hunt down some good food and raise our beer bottles high together. Sound good?"

I managed a wobbly smile. "Sounds good."

"And in the meantime, I say we head down to the market, check out the night life, eat, drink and be slothful."

I smiled broader. "Sounds great."

We kept up the lively banter as we hopped into his truck, drove into town, grabbed dinner and spent the rest of the evening at the adjacent outdoor bar, getting tipsy and laughing a lot. I gave William a nudge with my shoulder as we were sitting side by side, watching the activity. "You know, I really like you, Guillaume," I shouted over the noise. "You're the greatest."

"So are you, Fi," he said, and we exchanged beery grins.

It was approaching midnight when we returned to the mission. William parked and we walked toward my house. When the path split, one direction to his guest room and the other to my house, I declined William's offer to walk me to my door. "I'm fine, I'm fine," I assured him, but just then I took a misstep and stumbled into a pothole. William caught my arm before I tipped over further.

"Honest, I'm not accident prone," I said and we both laughed.

"Sure you're fine?" William asked, still holding onto my arm. I nodded. He gave my arm a friendly squeeze, but instead of just letting go, his hand slid down my forearm. Our hands caught and held for the briefest moment before separating. The surprise contact gave me a jittery, adolescent thrill. I covered up my reaction with a wave and a breezy "good night" and marched ahead, not stopping to look back. Once in my house, I mulled over the incident. He'd just held my hand. Or had I been the one to catch his hand and latch onto it? And yet, it took two to hold hands.

I sensed it was an issue we would once again address on his next visit.

I couldn't wait.

Chapter 24

Africa, however, had plans for me beyond the exploration of an infatuation. A week after William's visit, Soeur Beatrice called me into her office to inform me that Christophe's mother had been killed. She'd been hit by a speeding car in Libreville while crossing a street. She'd died at the scene. The news made headlines in the family's native Oyem and through the Woleu Ntem province. The whole country, in fact.

I thanked Soeur Beatrice for the information, pushed through the rest of the day's teaching, went back to my house and cried. I couldn't stop thinking of the tragedy of it all, the smiling family in the photographs, the loss that Christophe, so close to his mother, must have been feeling. I scribbled out a letter, tore it up, wrote another, crumpled it, and ultimately settled on a simple note that read, "I'm thinking of you and your family. All my love, Fiona," that I slipped into the mission's outgoing mail.

Death seemed to be in the air. A week later, Lisette and I heard the frantic honk of a car horn on the main road, instantly followed by tires screeching and a terrible *bang*. Lisette's eyes widened. "Oh, that was bad," she said. We raced out of her house and headed toward the road. A hundred meters from the mission entrance, we saw that a beer truck had crumpled a taxi-brousse, most likely from the beer truck's overtaking of another car on a blind curve. The panicked passengers had spilled out and now circled the wreckage, screaming. Two of the sisters were hurrying towards the scene. In their white outfits and headdresses, they looked like angels flying to the rescue.

I'd viewed bad accidents before, but from the safety of a car window. Even then, I'd always managed to arrive at a time when everything was under control. I followed Lisette, but I wasn't prepared for the chaos, the crying people, shirts and faces splattered with blood. The women's keening shrieks sounded eerily like singing. Everything seemed unreal, as if I were simply observing a film clip on the evening news. The full force of it hit me—I bent and threw up. Lisette, who had run ahead, turned and saw me crouching on the ground. Her perplexed face softened. She walked back and held out her hand to me.

I shrank back. "I don't know what to do," I whimpered.

"Help them."

The taxi-brousse had been knocked off the road by the impact of the beer truck. The driver of the taxi still sat slumped and motionless behind the shattered windshield. Of the dozen passengers, over half were injured, staggering and weeping. Soeur Beatrice was trying to calm a well-dressed young woman who was lying on the ground, screaming in French that this couldn't be happening, that her family was waiting for her.

I followed Lisette over to an older woman who'd been thrown from the back of the taxi-brousse. She didn't look as badly injured as the others, but as Lisette and I drew closer, I saw blood trickling from the side of her mouth. Her eyes fluttered open at our approach. Her breath seemed to rise and fall in tortured gasps. Per Lisette's command, I ran to the refectoire for blankets. When I returned with them, Lisette began tucking one around the woman. I dropped to the woman's side and impulsively took her hand, which felt cold and papery. She looked up at me in confusion. Her gaze swung to Lisette and she asked something in Fang. She sounded agitated.

"*Non*," Lisette assured her. "*Elle n'est pas fantôme.*" She turned to me. "She's afraid of you. She thinks she's dying and that you are a part of the spirit world, come to take her."

"Not this again! Tell her I'm *not*. Tell her I'm human, just like her."

Lisette rose to her feet. "You tell her."

I stared at her, uncomprehending.

"Sit with her," Lisette said. "Talk to her."

"She doesn't need conversation, she needs serious medical help. We need to do something more for her. Find help."

Lisette gave me a look somewhere between pity and impatience. My next words dried up in my mouth as I realized help was not going to arrive. *We* were the help.

Lisette didn't even bother to reply. Once I'd gingerly seated myself next to the woman, she dashed off to help Soeur Beatrice with the others.

I took a deep breath and lifted the woman's surprisingly light shoulders. Sliding my legs underneath them, I rested her head on my thighs like a pillow. I took the woman's hand again and tentatively stroked her blood-flecked arm. When she tried to speak again, her body tensed, wracked with what surely must have been pain. My limited Fang vocabulary soon failed me. She didn't seem to understand my French either. And suddenly I remembered the dusty mama I'd met my first week in country, when I'd gotten lost en route to the bathroom at the checkpoint stop. She'd spoken to me in a patter of incomprehensible words, but there'd been something oddly soothing and hypnotic about it.

"Don't you worry," I crooned in English to the woman on my

lap. "I'm going to stay here, right here with you, until someone else can come who will know what to do. This is a difficult situation, but there are many of us here, so we'll figure out what the best solution will be."

She coughed, a horrible gurgling sound, and I quickly wiped away the spit and blood that came up. "You're not going to die, because I'm not going to let you. Okay? We're going to get through this together? Okay?"

She seemed to particularly like the "okay" word, giving me little nods in reply. I told her about how we'd get her up to the refectoire and how much she'd like the mission grounds, with all the pretty shrubs and the green lawn. The woman smiled through cracked lips, her breath ragged and congested. Her eyes flickered shut, although I could sense she was still listening, still responding with nods. I told her about how sometimes the egrets landed and picked at the lawn after it had just been mown and about the time the egret had flown into the refectoire, freaking us all out. The woman relaxed further, the tension leaving her shoulders. The rise and fall of her chest became less abrupt.

I found myself relaxing as well, stroking her forehead, her leathery cheek. The chaos around us seemed to fade as I looked up at the canopy of emerald trees surrounding us. I told her how different they were from the trees in suburban Omaha, and yet how much I missed seeing those trees, the colors of their leaves in autumn. When Lisette walked up five minutes later, it jolted me from my reverie. I smiled up at her. "I think she's resting better now."

Lisette glanced down at the woman and looked back at me. Instead of the approval I'd expected, her face was a portrait of pity. "Oh, *chérie*," she said, her voice soft, sad, weary.

I'd always been slow to catch on to important relationship developments. The woman had died. Her head hadn't suddenly lolled to one side, like in the movies. There'd been no final gasped words, no urgent message to pass on. She'd just slipped away, leaving absence where once was life.

I couldn't move. I couldn't speak. My mind couldn't process the razor-thin line between life and death. She'd been there and now she wasn't. It was that simple.

Three people died in the accident. Four others were seriously injured, delivered by Mohammed to Bitam's little hospital. Afterward, Soeur Beatrice thanked Lisette and me for our help. I had trouble responding. My lips felt numb, my heart frozen.

Over the next few days I continued to stumble around in a daze, unable to wrap my mind around the concept of life's fragility. Lisette struggled to understand my traumatized reaction over the death of the woman who'd died on my lap. "She lived a full life," she said. "It was a tragedy, yes, but tragedies like this happen every day. Even in your country."

When I saw Christophe's glossy Mercedes pull up on the mission's front drive late Friday afternoon, something in me thought, *Yes, of course.* As if he and I had planned it this way.

I walked up to where he'd parked and was speaking with Soeur Beatrice. She offered him her condolences and he flashed her a smile of thanks. Even in his grief, I noted, he was still beautiful, still charismatic. But once it was just the two of us, the charisma seemed to fizzle out of him.

We found a private spot on the grounds, sat and talked. He thanked me for the note, brought me up to date on the events of the past few weeks—the chaos following the terrible news; the whirlwind of events and ceremonies in Libreville and more recently in Oyem. He spoke quietly, pausing only to gaze around as if in surprise that he was here.

As the sun began its descent, we went to my house. "Would you like to go into town for dinner, or stop by Lisette's?" I asked. When he shook his head, I found myself feeling relieved. I didn't want to have to guard my behavior to fit Lisette's expectations of how and why I should grieve the deaths of these women I didn't even know. Christophe knew me—he would understand. Just as I understood him.

I told him about the accident at the mission, over dinner and a bottle of wine he'd brought, and then asked more about his mother. He seemed reticent at times—I recognized I was probably violating Gabonese taboos about discussing the deceased, but he answered each question.

I made us coffees, but the caffeine had no effect on him. Soon his eyes began to droop.

"Look at you," I said. "You're so tired. Please don't tell me you were considering driving back to Oyem tonight."

He gave a melancholic shrug.

"Stay here at the mission," I urged. "Tomorrow, too. This is a healing place; it will do you a world of good."

He looked like he was fighting to stay awake even as he spoke. "I think you're right."

"Good. Do you have a bag, anything for overnight?"

"In my car."

"You go get it while I arrange for a guest room with the sisters. Make yourself at home while I'm gone."

I made the proper arrangements and returned to the house ten minutes later. Inside, however, I stopped short. Christophe had indeed made himself at home. His bag was by the bedroom door. His shoes and shirt lay on the floor, leading, like a trail of bread crumbs, to my room, where I found his belt, his trousers.

All the way to my bed, where he lay, bare back exposed, the sheets covering his lower half.

Oh, God.

What had I gotten myself into?

I needn't have worried. He'd already fallen into a deep sleep.

I'd never had the opportunity to study him like this before. Even during our Cap Estérias getaway, he'd been awake before me, fallen asleep after me. He looked so young. Like the boy he'd once been. The one whose mother had been his best friend.

This beautiful, privileged man, whom, it seemed, had everything, and yet, emotionally, had just lost his childhood everything.

I stood there, tears spilling out, sniffing.

He stirred. "Come here," he murmured, eyes shut. "I need you."

I wasn't sure if he was dreaming of his mother, talking in his sleep, or what. It certainly wasn't something I'd come to expect from the awake Christophe.

"Fiona."

This jolted me out of my reverie. His eyes were half-open.

"Come here. I need you."

He held out his arms. I approached, still unsure as to whether he was awake or dreaming. I cautiously slipped in alongside him in my clothes. I was wearing a gauzy skirt that annoyingly rode right up to my thighs. To my relief, my legs made contact with fabric as well as bare skin. He'd kept on his underwear, at least. Once I was there next to him, he went for the comfort-seeking position, head on my shoulder, arms looping around my waist, under my back, tugging me closer as though I were one of those oversized body pillows.

He said nothing. A few seconds later, his even, deep breathing told me he was asleep.

I'd felt a lot of ways toward Christophe, but this was the first time it had been maternal. The first time I myself had ever felt maternal. Hearing the soft, shuddering sigh he made in his sleep, the universally recognized "everything will be all right" sound, gave me such a powerful sense of purpose.

I hadn't been able to save the dying woman. I hadn't been able to save Christophe from his devastating loss. But I could give a living being the comfort of another living being. Goosebumps crept over my skin and for a moment I felt as though I weren't the comforter so much as a conduit. I could almost feel it pumping through me like a pulse. It felt so mystical, so unprecedented, I could only lie there, tears slipping down my face, hoping my ragged gulps of breath didn't wake Christophe, whose presence, coupled with that other, nameless presence, seemed unutterably precious just then.

All of life did. Africa picked off people with chilling randomness. But here were the two of us, alive and breathing.

Precious stuff, indeed.

Chapter 25

The woman who'd died in my arms after the taxi-brousse accident had not died after all, it appeared. She was in my front yard and she was talking to Christophe. Since it was Saturday morning, she'd brought a dozen fresh eggs to the sisters like she always had. Apparently death didn't change the commission.

In the background, the approaching rattle of William's pickup truck signified his imminent arrival. A few minutes later his voice joined theirs in conversation. William knew the dead woman, too. And the dead woman knew not only William but Christophe's father.

"You resemble him," she told Christophe.

"So I am told," Christophe said. "It is an honor."

"Are you returning to Oyem today?" she asked him.

"I haven't decided."

"My community wishes to invite you and your friends to our drum circle this night. We would like to honor your mother and celebrate her passing."

"Thank you. I accept. We will attend and I'll stay another night."

"This is good to hear. I will inform the others."

The dead woman bade him and William farewell and left for the place dead people here went to, because this was not the U.S., where dead people went away for good once they'd died. Christophe and William headed toward the forest, which had a door, which sounded very much like my door. Its opening and ensuing slam woke me with a start.

I heard William's and Christophe's voices in my living room.

In shock, I sprang out of bed, looking around in bleary-eyed confusion.

William murmured a question I couldn't hear.

"I think she's still sleeping," Christophe replied.

"No, I'm not," I called out, hastily changing out of my wrinkled skirt and top. I caught sight of my disarrayed hair in the mirror over my chest of drawers and winced, pinning it into a sloppy bun.

The two were in the kitchen area, chatting. I came out of the bedroom, calling out a cheery "good morning." Christophe's bag was blocking my bedroom door; I stopped to move it.

"So you *are* up," William called out. He caught sight of what I was doing.

Christophe's bag. My bedroom.

Our eyes met. "Good morning," he said in a strained voice.

It's not what you're thinking! I wanted to cry out, but all words had dried up in my mouth.

Too late anyway. He'd turned away abruptly. I felt sick.

Christophe, meanwhile, looked relaxed and cheerful. "Did we wake you?" he asked from his spot by the stove, where he'd set the tea kettle to boil.

"No." I tried to mirror his tone. "I heard you two talking with someone."

"Yes. The woman who sells eggs. What was her name?" Christophe asked William.

"Céleste."

The dream-but-not made more sense now. "Yes, Céleste," I said.

"And she invited you to one of their ceremonies tonight."

William looked at me in surprise.

Christophe seemed amused. "I see you've learned Fang," he remarked.

"Only bits," I replied. "Why?"

"What else did Céleste say to me?"

"Something about how you resemble your father. Céleste and her community wanting to honor your mother's passing with a ceremony, your Oyem plans. Or something. I don't know, I heard it in my sleep."

"They were speaking in Fang," William said.

I gaped at him and Christophe both. "Really?"

They both nodded.

I raised my hands and shoulders helplessly. "That's the subconscious mind for you, I guess." My head started to pound. Too much stimulus and thinking for so early in my day.

The tea kettle began to whine.

"Coffee?" Christophe asked me, holding up a third mug.

"Yes. Thank you."

William wouldn't look at me. Upon my return from a trip to the bathroom to brush my teeth and splash water on my face, he focused on everything but me—readying the Nescafé instant coffee and canned milk as Christophe took the boiling water off the heat. He'd cut the baguette Christophe had gone out to buy in town, and set butter, strawberry preserves and peanut butter on the table. I studied his tense face in mounting despair. He, for his part, looked particularly good. His hair had been getting lighter in the sun and the contours of his face had changed, thinner in the cheeks, adding prominence to his jaw, which, at this moment, looked clenched. I wanted to reach over and touch him, but I knew a *back off* signal when I saw one.

A knock at the door seemed to make him inordinately happy. He went to open the door before I could react, and greeted the arriving Lisette like a long-lost friend.

"Come in, come in!" he told her. "Join us for breakfast."

Lisette proved a great help in diffusing the curious tensions in the room, as we ate and sipped our coffees. She flirted and bantered with both men, teasing William into a good mood. William told her about the group's invitation to the night's ceremony.

"Wonderful," she said. "Why don't we start the evening with a dinner at my place before we head over? I'll invite Moussa and Bintou, as well."

William and Christophe looked at each other and nodded.

"Excellent," Christophe said. "And that leaves us plenty of time free right now." He turned to William. "Should we go to this site you were talking about?"

William's glance flickered over me and returned to Christophe. "But you came here to spend time with Fiona."

"Oh, we'll have all evening together." He turned my way. "Right?"

"Right!" I tried to sound as bubbly and relaxed as everyone else, inside reeling in dismay. No nourishing time with William today. Or Christophe. None.

"Good." Christophe and William exchanged looks and smiled.

"Should we make an early start of it?" William asked.

"I'm ready," Christophe said, rising from the table. He glanced around the room. "I just need to put my bag in my guest room." As he went over to retrieve it, I tried one last time to catch William's gaze, which he ignored by staring at his coffee cup. Lisette, taking in all the dynamics with a bemused expression, caught my eye with a *men... what can you do?* look.

Once William and Christophe departed, I let my frustration spill out. "He thinks I slept with Christophe," I fumed to Lisette. "Not just slept with him but *slept* with him. Did you see the way he was ignoring me?"

Lisette took a sip of her coffee. "William is intelligent," she said, which didn't help much because misunderstandings and hurt pride had nothing to do with intelligence.

"And Christophe, he ignored me too." I rose and gathered the various jars on the table, clinking them together in my agitation. "It was like I wasn't in the room. And here I'd felt so... *relevant* last night, being there for Christophe. Like I'd been a real comfort."

"You should feel honored, Fiona," Lisette said gently. "A man can pay a woman no higher compliment than to turn to her for comfort at the time of his mother's death. But today, he needs only Guillaume."

"William, oh boy. Did you see his face?" I asked. "Did you?"

"I did." She eyed me, this time in sympathy. "Best that you are apart today."

At the ceremony, Christophe spoke Fang with the locals. This time, listening, I understood nothing. Although I knew it was part of Christophe's heritage, it shocked me, as did seeing him in traditional African attire. Both seemed to change the way he acted, making him seem more down to earth, his body more integrated in the communication process. That said, the superior quality of the shirt and trousers ensemble—the rich, almost velvety cotton; the intricate, multicolored design; the two-inch borders embroidered with golden thread—still made him stand out like royalty.

It felt strange to be a participant in the ceremony instead of watching from the shadows. It was still early. A dozen people prepared, moving plank benches into place along the periphery of a giant semicircle, in the middle of which they'd built a four-foot tower of kindling for the bonfire. A half-dozen drummers gathered off to the side, setting up their places as they chatted and arranged their drums.

Céleste came to greet our group, and sized me up. "So, this time you participate, yes?"

I gaped at her in surprise. I'd always assumed I was well hidden while spying. "I like to watch," I said, wincing at the absurdity of the reply, how it didn't begin to address the issue. But Céleste only nodded and invited us to sit in the place of honor, where a half-dozen chairs had been set up amid the benches. Moussa and Bintou, the Malian husband and wife who taught sciences at the mission, had joined our group, and the six of us took our seats.

Everyone came by to greet Christophe and ceremoniously clasp his hands. Young girls brought us palm wine in ancient-looking clay bowls. The drummers began to pound out a tentative rhythm on their drums, as a few women joined them with shakes of gourd rattles. Céleste sang out a call-and-response in Fang with her six dancers. But it was only a practice run, and the sounds soon tapered off. Our bowls of palm wine were topped off. Lisette rose to speak with Céleste, and I moved a seat closer to Christophe and William, who were engrossed in conversation.

"...shouldn't try so hard to understand animism," Christophe was saying. "Or any of the local religions or traditional beliefs, for that matter. It only serves to complicate the Westerner's expatriate experience. Like your colleague, Joshua," he added. "He's gotten too involved in bwiti."

"You mean he went through an initiation?" William asked, and Christophe nodded.

Taking a near-lethal dose of iboga in the process. I drew in a sharp breath. "Whoa, that was risky. Does Chuck know?"

"I'm inclined to say no," Christophe said. He shook his head. "I can't understand why you Americans do things like this. You have everything—good families, college educations, employment opportunities. Why do you have to go searching for trouble like this?"

"It's not *trouble*," I retorted. "It's getting to know our host culture."

"There are things about African culture that will defy a Westerner's attempts to understand it," Christophe said. "Digging deeper invariably results in problems."

Even though William had maintained his chilliness toward me, we were still on the same page here. "It doesn't mean we aren't compelled to try," he argued. "We value curiosity, learning, thinking outside the box. Some of us are restless, curious. Questions rise up and we seek out answers."

The drummers recommenced, which ended the conversation. William looked like he could have happily argued politics and religion with Christophe all evening, or discussed the merits of palm wine, or village life, or African clothing. Anything besides looking at me. Swallowing my hurt, I returned to my own seat by Bintou and Moussa.

The entertainment began in earnest. The drummers quickly developed a full-sounding rhythm, irresistible to listen to, mesmerizing to watch. Céleste and her women rose and began to dance. Initially it was the kind of dancing I'd seen from my protected spot: a subtle movement originating from the hips, knees bent to support side-to-side stepping. But soon it grew more complex, the women engaging their entire bodies, arms flung in tandem, heads flung back, feet a brisk, moving pattern. Energy flowed from the women, from their core. Admiration swelled within me. Not only did the women dance with great proficiency, it was in perfect unison. It came, I sensed, not from rehearsing so much as having the same deeply ingrained intention. Their blissed-out expressions told me they weren't trying to perform so much as allow this force to flow from within them. I'd never felt so envious of their African-ness, the unquestioned ability to dance so beautifully, so organically. As I watched them, my own muscles tensed, quads and abdominals straining, vicariously engaged in what I was watching.

That was all I wanted to do: watch. But during a break that followed, Céleste came over with two of her dancers and invited Bintou, Lisette and me to join them. Bintou and Lisette rose with ready smiles.

Dismay washed over me. I did ballet. Not this.

"You, too," Céleste said to me, and the other two dancers nodded. I didn't move. I couldn't.

"Fiona," Lisette said. "We dance now."

"I can't dance that way," I said to her through gritted teeth.

"Then you can dance your own charming American way."

As if.

"Please. Come with us to dance," one of Céleste's dancers encouraged.

Seeking a like-minded ally, I turned to William. "Guillaume, tell them it's not that easy for a white person to just get up there and dance. During a time of mourning, to boot."

William looked decidedly unsympathetic. "You're a dancer, Fiona. I think your argument falls short. And here in Gabon, dance *is* a part of mourning."

"Fiona." Céleste had never addressed me by my first name before, and it made it harder to avoid her piercing gaze. "It is time that you dance. The guest of honor has requested it."

I turned to Christophe, shocked. His expression was unreadable.

"You told Céleste to come over here and persuade me?" I asked him. "Which is to say, insist on it?"

"Yes."

"*Why?*" I protested.

"You need to dance again," Christophe said.

"Stop acting up, Fiona," Lisette hissed. "You're drawing attention."

I glared at her and Christophe both. "Fine. I am beyond uncomfortable here," I told Christophe. "But I'll do this for you, and in honor of your mother."

He studied me. "Thank you. And believe it or not, I'm doing this for you."

"Oh, right," I spat.

"We dance now?" Célèste asked me.

It would appear I had no choice. I rose. "Yes. We dance now."

I trailed behind all the women, feeling cold in spite of the humid warmth. The crackling bonfire up close seemed more ominous than festive. Sparks shot upward before disappearing. One spark flew out toward me, a warning of sorts. I wanted to run the other way, down the path and to the safety of my house. Instead I followed the dancing women's movements, their hips, the bend of their knees, the pattern their feet made.

Of course I stumbled, which brought the expected laughter from the other women. But it was good-natured laughing, more supportive than judgmental. In many ways, it was like my early ballet classes, watching April move and wanting so much to move that way, that everything in me grew quiet and focused, intent on discovering where the movement originated, getting it wrong over and over, if need be, in pursuit of getting it right.

So I got it wrong, and observed, got it wrong, and observed. I modified my own movements, made them smaller, more economical. I became intensely curious, determined to learn, relentless in my pursuit of kinetic discovery. At some point I realized Lisette and Bintou had returned to their seats. It didn't matter. The music kept going.

Which meant the dancer kept dancing.

Chapter 26

In March, the pen pals replied. I brought the enormous box with me into the classroom the following day and the students crowded around my desk. "Sit down," I called out over the hubbub, "or we don't open the box." The students shot back to their seats.

I ripped into the box. Food came out first: a bag of tortilla chips, two sacks of miniature Snickers bars, licorice, hard candy and chewing gum. The students squirmed in their seats, frantic with excitement. When I passed the food out, they tore into the candy bars, stuffing them into their mouths. The tortilla chips were eaten more tentatively, but nothing American could be bad, in their minds. They crunched the unfamiliar triangles, testing the nacho cheese flavor before pronouncing it acceptable.

Then came the gifts. Thirty wildly decorated pencils, thirty ballpoint pens featuring *Scooby Doo* cartoon characters. Pads of flowered paper, spiral notebooks, stickers of puppies, kittens and clowns. When I held up several Hot Wheels cars, the boys leapt out of their seats and hurried forward. I had to shoo them back down. The girls reacted the same when I pulled out tiny bottles of cheap perfume and fruit-scented lotion. And still I pulled out more: balloons, magic markers, comic books. The students were slack-jawed at the sight of the treasures from their new friends.

"It is true then, Miss Fiona," Mathieu, one of Céleste's sons, exclaimed. "All Americans are very, very rich."

"No, no," I protested, "these things cost very little in the U.S.—anyone could afford them." This, of course, only impressed them further.

The enclosed letters, one for each student, provided further cross-cultural education. The American students' questions were as entertaining as my students' had been. "What is it like to live in the jungle? Are you always sweaty?" Or, "I have a pet rat named Herb. Do you have a pet?"

"Miss Fiona," Sophie asked, her voice tentative, "what is 'pet' word meaning, please?" All eyes were on me, eager for the response, as almost every American student seemed to have mentioned a pet as a member of the family.

Pets, aside from stray dogs that hung around neighborhoods, did not exist in provincial Gabon. The Fang were known to eat cat. My translation of *"animal familier"* didn't seem to help my students. "Please, Miss Fiona," another student tried, "how does one say 'rat' in French?"

"Le rat."

Her face reflected her confusion. "A *rat* is a member of her family?"

"What's your favorite food?" also puzzled my students. My explanation of the cultural importance of McDonalds and Hostess snack foods, Pizza Hut and hot dogs ("No, they aren't really made of dog") fell short. The students nodded their heads politely, straining to understand.

Equally foreign to them was the concept of listing off one's assets. "I've got a ten-speed bike." "My dad owns a Porsche." "My best friend has a swimming pool in his backyard." The American students described themselves and their lives through their material belongings. That, I realized with a jolt, was how we Americans defined ourselves.

But there was one great perk to the materialism of the American students. Sophie had received an extra gift attached to her letter—a small jewelry box. Inside was an exquisite gold comb, with tiny iridescent butterflies affixed at the top. When I'd sent off the original letters, I'd attached a note to Sophie's scrawled attempt. "Please give her someone special," I'd written to my former teacher. Apparently Sophie had acquired not only a special pen pal, but a generous one as well. Sophie pulled the gold comb out of its box and stared at it fearfully. She looked up at me and frowned.

"This is mine?" she asked, her voice tense. I nodded. Her eyes narrowed at me in mistrust, but when I remained silent, she gave me a curt nod and looked back down. She stroked the butterflies gently with the tips of her fingers. The students sitting around her noticed Sophie's prize and clustered around her desk, clamoring to see. When Sophie pushed the comb into her hair, all the girls cried out in admiration. A smile broke through Sophie's broad, somber face. Seeing the way her eyes shone, I felt tears rise in the back of my throat. If I'd accomplished nothing else right during my two years here, I told myself, I'd done this.

It had been a good day for personal mail, as well: two letters. The first was a blue international aerogramme from my ballet buddy April in New York. We'd been exchanging letters ever since last year when Alison gave her my address. This one was short, two paragraphs dashed off in April's scribbled handwriting that made me smile, visualizing her between rehearsals, or killing time in her dressing room before a performance, sharing what was so glamorous to me and probably seemed everyday to her. Changes might be forthcoming in her world, she shared, which made her nervous, but she had me as a role model as someone who'd flourished through big changes. Reading this, I chuckled. Oh, if April only knew how close I'd come to failing, time and time again.

The second letter came from Kaia, the fish volunteer posted south of Oyem.

Hey, I have a favor to ask. Can you come to my village some weekend for a visit? I could use your support in standing strong against my farmer's troublemaking nephew. Maybe a Friday arrival and a Saturday morning visit to my farmer's pond?

Thanks, and I hope to see you in the next month or two!

I smiled. Finally, my chance to help someone, the way Christophe had helped me last year. I walked right over to my desk and pulled out pen and paper.

Hi Kaia,

Yes, I am more than happy to help you! Maybe a few weeks from now? Send me your preferred date and we'll make it happen.

Hang in there, and see you soon!
Fiona

Chapter 27

March was the month William stopped visiting. It was also the height of the rainy season with daily downpours, searing heat, choking humidity, and mud that clogged the roads, my shoes and bicycle wheels. As I trudged back to the mission following my attempts to mail a box, my thoughts returned to William and how much I missed him. The first two weekends after his and Christophe's visit I'd listened with hope for the distinct rattle of his truck, to no avail. The third weekend, I'd put in a day of work into my library project, certain that he'd swing by the mission if he came to Bitam.

No William. I'd swallowed my crushing disappointment and comforted myself with the knowledge that I'd see him the Saturday of Alison's wedding. He'd promised, and William never forgot his promises.

I shifted the unwieldy box in my arms, took a misstep and went skating across a patch of mud. As I struggled with windmilling arms to keep myself upright, the box from the pen pals to the U.S. sailed from my hands and landed with a plop in a puddle. I didn't know whether to laugh or cry. I hadn't been able to mail it because I'd filled out the wrong form—twice, according to two different clerks. By the time I'd had the right form and the right clerk and waited my turn for the third time, the director, whose signature was required, had left for the day. I'd invested two hours of my time and patience with nothing to show for it. It seemed par for the course these days.

But I could handle it all, because I had dance again.

Christophe had been right, in the end. When Céleste had seen me return to the drum circle the following Saturday night, she'd chuckled and nodded. She'd likely had me pegged all along.

I found myself rediscovering little dance secrets, such as the way I could use the other dancers' movements to assist me in mine. No step was too hard because I simply mirrored the others, sucking up the energy they'd tapped into. They were amazed a white woman could move like them. I myself was surprised at how easy, how vital, it turned out to be.

It was my double life. During the week, I played the role of demure teacher and diligent Peace Corps volunteer. I'd put time into my library project, visit the market with Lisette or Lance and retire at a reasonable hour. Then, late Saturday night, I'd hear the drums. I'd head down the path and feel something in me leap with excitement, as if I were running off to meet a lover. Once among the others, I'd fall into the groove that gave me the energy to continue on and on.

One night, the ceremony had special visitors. Four women strode to the center, attired in traditional costumes, chalky white slashes painted on their faces, and began to dance. Their practiced moves, more forceful and energetic than those of the local women, told me they were professionals at this kind of dancing. The last woman, however, was in a category of her own, a prima ballerina of tribal dancing. She was huge, solid like a mountain, her hair braided in tiny tresses that poked out in all directions. She had protruding cheekbones and a wide mouth that drew focus to her face. Her eyes were dramatically outlined with black liner. But it was the fierce light shining from them and the authority in her movements that made me take a respectful step back.

Her name, Céleste informed me, was Marie-Belle, and she'd trained for eight years as a priestess in Ghana. The family of the deceased had paid for her and her acolytes to join them here this evening. The four of them had spent the past twelve hours fasting and meditating, to assist them in their communication. I didn't ask Céleste with whom they'd be communicating. I wasn't sure I wanted to know.

Just watching Marie-Belle dance made my skin prickle at the nape of my neck. She had a formidable presence I couldn't quite decipher. She'd smile and nod periodically to herself, as if in agreement with an invisible guide, before launching into another sweeping movement. She was like a cyclone, commanding everyone's attention, sucking up the energy around her only to fling it back out to the spectators.

It brought back the memory of William's description of the Gule Wamkulu and I knew, beyond doubt, that this woman had accessed the same energy from the same place. She was not dancing; she was being danced.

Her acolytes, during their turn in the center, began to slow down, moving to a rhythm that seemed to be in their minds alone. One dancer stopped in her tracks and sank to a supine position, where her body undulated on the earth like it was water. Another lifted one arm and waved it back and forth over her head, gazing up at it, mesmerized. A third tilted her head back and began to spin in circles, a dozen rotations, which gave the ballet dancer in me vertigo.

What unnerved me about it all was not so much their movements as much as the body language that told me in no uncertain terms these women had gone Somewhere Else. Where, I wondered? Where, precisely, was Somewhere Else? And what did it feel like to dance away consciousness, to transcend realms?

I decided, with a shiver of unease, that it wasn't something I needed to know.

On the day of Alison's wedding, I couldn't stop thinking about her—
the classic beauty of her face and the way she could make a room light
up with her smile. I envisioned the rustle of her satin wedding dress,
the flushed glow on Mom's face, the way Dad was sure to get misty-
eyed today. If I'd been there, I would have too.

My almost-twin, only eleven months older, this sister I'd been so
close to as a little girl, whether we'd had interests in common or not.
She was getting married and I wasn't there. It was the biggest day of
her life and I'd be absent, because I'd nursed a grudge that I valued
over the big picture.

I swallowed my sorrow, the overwhelming regret for how everything
had turned out between us, and set to work cleaning the house and
grading homework. I coached myself to not think about the wedding or
the fact that William hadn't shown up. I finally gave up, hopped on my
bike and wheeled through the mud into town, where I hunted down
Lance. Together we wandered over to the market. After we'd bought a
few items and visited with vendors, we adjourned to a bar for Regab.

Lance's classes, predictably, had grown rife with discipline
problems. I shared a few stories of last year, and soon we were
engaged in a laughing, beery, "top *this* one" exchange.

"There you are," a familiar voice called out. I looked up and saw
William walking toward us. Relief coursed through me. William had
kept his promise after all. No matter what kind of games we were
playing here, my friend had come through. I smiled at him as he
joined us. He sat and signaled for a beer.

I wanted to know why he'd stayed away. At the same time, I was
afraid of what consequences the truth might bring. "Wow," I said,
keeping my voice light, "I haven't seen you in a long time."

"It *has* been a long time, hasn't it?" He smiled up at the server
who'd brought his Regab over. He took a gulp, then sat back with a
sigh. "Rough week."

The Regab, however, soon revitalized him. We chatted about recent goings-on until he glanced at his watch. "So, I take it Jenny hasn't shown up yet?"

I frowned. "Why would Jenny be here?"

"She's coming through the area."

Lance and I looked at each other, perplexed, before turning back to William. "What do you know about it?" I asked, uneasy.

"She's visiting me for a few days. She wanted time away, so I invited her to my village."

The Regab leapt around in my stomach. "And that's why you came here today?" My voice came out shrill and accusing.

William smiled at me with a determined brightness. "Yes, one of the reasons." He noticed my expression and his voice grew gentle. "She's struggling. I think she's going through the 'this isn't what I thought it would be like' phase. Remember that? I just wanted to try and help out. When I was in Oyem a few weekends ago, I told her to visit any time. I got a message this week and we agreed to meet here."

He'd gone to Oyem on a weekend and not stopped in Bitam along the way. Or maybe he *had* stopped in Bitam but had avoided the mission. Which was to say, me.

Lance and William continued talking, unaware of my dismay. Surely William hadn't forgotten about the wedding, I told myself. All I had to do was offer a little prompt.

Unfathomably, I didn't.

Jenny showed up an hour minutes later, as afternoon thunderheads piled up in the sky. She waved, her assertive, confident smile and American voice drawing attention as she strode over to us. "Hi! Sorry I'm so late!"

"No problem," William assured her. "Want a beer, or are you ready to go?"

"I'm ready when you are!"

William gestured to his empty bottle. "I'm ready."

Was he deliberately trying to snub me?

"But... wait!" I cried.

"Yes?" he asked me. "Was there something you wanted from me?"

Oh, very much a snub. And painful confirmation that, one, he hadn't remembered about the wedding, and that, two, even William could let people down. I wouldn't have thought it.

"No," I told him. "Sorry."

The four of us rose and left the bar. Lance and Jenny began acting goofy together, humming the theme music to *The Brady Bunch*, trying to change the words to fit the Peace Corps experience. I trailed behind, wheeling my bike, as we passed through the market alleys that reeked of urine and rotting fish guts and the other smells I was usually too cheerful to notice. Jenny and Lance stopped to peruse a crate of pirated music cassettes on sale in a stall. When the merchant gestured to two big boxes behind him full of new inventory, Jenny gave a little coo of pleasure.

"Ooh, I've been looking for a chance just like this. Do we have time, William?"

"Sure we do." William paused and looked around for me. When he saw me, something in his expression seemed to soften. "I need to pick up a truck part from Mohammed at the mission. Do you want a ride there? We can throw your bike in the back."

A tiny bit of the familiar, beloved warmth had returned to his voice.

I thought fast. "Sure. In fact, if we want to move right now, you can get the part while Jenny and Lance finish up here. So once she's ready to go, you'll have done your errand."

"Great idea." He turned to Jenny. "Why don't you and Lance take your time here? Fiona and I are going to make a run to the mission. I'll swing back here and pick you up once I'm done."

Jenny hesitated and cast me a flickered glance. "Well… okay."

"Be back soon," William promised.

William and I walked side by side as I wheeled my bike. With each step, my heart lightened. Okay, so I wouldn't get an evening with William. But I could have a few minutes. It would clear the air. It would give me a chance to argue my case.

Because I could feel what was starting to happen. Jenny had plans to claim him. I could read her intention loud and clear. I couldn't afford to have a misunderstanding hinder my own chances with him.

The accumulated storm clouds issued ominous rumbles as William and I approached his truck. William looked up. "Uh oh. We'll want to make tracks before this storm hits."

"Wait!" we heard behind us. I looked over and saw Jenny running toward us.

"I changed my mind," she called out. "William, I don't want you to have to go back and forth on my account. How selfish of me! I'll just go with you now."

She stood there, smiling in that controlling way of hers.

Oh, so clever in the way she'd phrased it. She and I, if not William, understood that her "selfish" and "noble" behavior were the other way around. I could only smile back at her as my toes curled up against the base of my sandals.

"Sure, okay," William said.

As I paused to dislodge a too-big chunk of mud from my bicycle wheel, she scampered over to the door on the truck's passenger side before me. She stood there, hand already gripping the door handle, and I saw that she would not allow me to even sit by William.

There would be no ten minutes of heartfelt communication. Jenny would see to it that William and I were never alone.

I was too discouraged and low to compete with her today. I

stopped in my tracks, twenty feet from William's truck. He looked back at me curiously.

"I'm sorry, I just realized something I forgot," I lied. "Go on ahead without me."

"But it's going to rain on you. We can wait while you take care of your business."

"No. Really. Just *go*."

I hadn't meant for my reply to sound so harsh. Jenny tried unsuccessfully to hide her gloat.

"Just go, Guillaume," I said in a less hostile voice. I didn't wait for his answer. Instead I turned my bicycle around abruptly and walked back toward the market.

Of course the rain came down in torrents on my own return to the mission, soaking me in seconds. Mud clung to the tires and I dismounted, walking my bike in the rain. Eventually it subsided. By the time I made it back to the mission, soggy and bereft, it was almost dark, but the rain had stopped. And William and Jenny were long gone.

Grading tests was a shitty way to spend the evening when, right then, seven time zones away, my sister was getting married. The grounds were silent as I worked. But just before I went to bed, I heard the drums start up. My lone escape.

I took it.

Chapter 28

We didn't need Marie-Belle and her acolytes tonight to make the dancing feel electric. I'd come alive; I was all but on fire. My legs, hips and arms felt unstoppable. My sandals slapped the dust as my skirt, faded after nearly two years, flapped against my knees. I'd freed my hair from its clasp and it spilled out in profusion like a lion's mane. Sweat beaded my brow, my back, little trickles rolling down my spine. Energy poured out of me, filling the space.

I could feel Céleste and the other women responding to it. They didn't seem to notice it was induced by agitation that buzzed around in my thoughts like flies near a carcass. I might have lost William. I'd missed the most important day of my sister's life. The Gabonese were still going to tragically die no matter what I did. The thoughts made me want to crumple and sob. Instead I danced. When Céleste and the other dancers stopped for a break, I kept going, ignoring my protesting muscles and growing fatigue.

Thirty minutes more. An hour.

I began to feel better. Lighter. More lightheaded, yet, paradoxically, more energized. It was as if the energy from Marie-Belle and her acolytes had remained here, in the dirt of the dance circle, lying in wait for the right person to step in and assume the role of dance priestess. No, I hadn't had seven years of training in Ghana.

But I'd devoted over a decade to the art and craft of dance. I'd lived in Africa for twenty-two months and, after all, I was the white woman with spirit eyes. I let Marie-Belle's spectral presence fill my mind and guide me, my body following obediently.

Time ceased its relevancy. I kept going. So did the drums. I began to think of one particular drummer as *my* drummer—an aging man with a shock of fuzzy hair and alert eyes. His hands moved so fast, they were a blur. I found, however, when I moved in synchrony to his hands, my steps became effortless. It was as if I'd been lifted off my feet, marionette-style, and all I had to do was give into the experience. The drum had a curious counter-rhythm, a high, popping sound. I could pick up every nuance of the music, could even feel the drummer's hand slapping the drum, and hear the taut skin's reply. The drummer looked up at one point and smiled at me, an expression of fiery glee. We exchanged grins, a conspiracy between two performers who understood that once you got inside the music, anything was possible.

A dizziness came over me, as if the borders of my world had grown fuzzy, and yet in another way, things had never seemed in sharper focus. I could feel every sensitivity receptor turned on high, straining to pick up information. I tried to translate what the drum was saying, but it made me too dizzy, as were the turns I began doing. Not elegant pirouette or fouetté turns from ballet days. These turns were performed looking up, with arms flung out randomly, feet pattering in their own little circle of dirt.

How far can you go? The rules in ballet were simple. You focused on a fixed point on the wall to avoid getting too dizzy during turns. If you failed to do so, the dizziness would overtake you and at some point you'd fall, maybe even pass out.

Or would you? What happened at that moment when you lost control? Was there a divide? Could you suspend that moment between conscious and unconscious? Would being in that place give you answers?

The other drums seemed to be coming from all around me now—even inside me as I continued to spin, with the little pop-pop drum leading the way, always right in front of me, urging me on. Nausea arose. I needed to stop and throw up, but the drums told me no, so I kept going, focusing on that one sound, coming from my drummer guide. Things grew blurrier and blurrier until the night scene around me became a great, long tunnel of blur, screaming past me in a rush. I knew that I dared not stop, not even look around, because then I would surely be cast off into the great abyss that existed outside the tunnel. I clung to the pop-pop beat until the world upended and I spilled onto it, the cool, crumbly earth catching me.

The drums gave a few final pop-pops before stopping. Then everything grew still and dark.

Sunday morning. Or afternoon. Who knew? Who cared? Only the sound of persistent knocking pulled me from my fog of sleep.

I opened one eye. My bedroom was bright with late morning sun.

"Fiona?" I heard William call out. "You home?"

What was William doing back in town?

I stumbled out of bed, pulled on a pair of shorts and shuffled to the door. I opened it, squinting at the bright light. William stood there, alone.

"Hi," he said.

"Hi," I managed back.

"What's up?" he asked.

Fog still clogged my brain. I couldn't bring up what had transpired last night, because I still wasn't sure what had happened. Beyond the drums, the dizziness, the tunnel, had been something that hurt my head to even try to ponder it. I remember the way my head rang, pounded, like it had after my bicycle accident, and that I'd been so unutterably drained in ways that had nothing to do with physical fatigue. I remember the other women helping me walk once I'd risen, treating me gently, with reverence and respect. Even a little fear. It had seemed to take everything in me, the acting skills of a performer, to affect a casual demeanor.

No one had asked me to explain. Which was a good thing. There would have been no coherent way to explain what had happened. Not then, not now.

Maybe not ever.

"Are you going to invite me in?" William asked.

I stood there dumbly. "Why are you here?"

"I screwed up. Fi, I'm so sorry."

If he was going to tell me, with all that regret in his eyes, that he and Jenny had become intimate last night, and that he was here to apologize for leading me on, I was going to crumple on the spot.

"It was your sister's wedding. I promised you I'd make the night special for you."

Relief made me even more lightheaded than I'd been.

"It's fine," I said, opening the door wider for him to pass. "It was my problem, not yours. And it's over, so no big deal."

"Yes, it is a big deal." He sounded angry. "I was going to help you celebrate it and I screwed up."

"It's okay, Guillaume."

"No, it's not."

We stood there, face to face, inside my house. I knew I must have looked terrible, but I couldn't summon enough artifice to fake it.

"Want some coffee?" I asked. I looked at the clock. It was past ten o'clock. "Wait. Jenny's visiting you. Where is she?"

"She's still in the village. That was what she wanted, the village vibe. I told her I needed to come see you and she assured me she could fend for herself there."

"I'm sure she's right. She's an excellent fender."

Which came out wrong and made her sound like a car part, but my brain was still only firing on one cylinder.

What happened last night?

It scared me that I didn't know the answer.

"A cup of coffee would be great," William said. "Why don't I make it while you get dressed." He gestured to my stretched, skimpy, nearly transparent nightshirt.

Whoops.

"Good idea. Thank you."

We carried our hot drinks outside and took seats on a bench in a nearby grove. In silence, we sipped our coffees.

"Thanks," I said a few minutes later. "This is good."

"You're welcome."

"And thank you for coming by. You didn't have to do that." I spoke carefully, afraid that the weirdness circling my head might still slip out and make me seem stranger than people already thought me. They'd all looked scared of me last night. Reverential though, too. Like I'd been to the spirit world and back. Then again, maybe I had.

"It's a nice day today," he commented, looking around at the dewy freshness of the grove.

"Sure," I replied without glancing around.

"What did you do last night?" he asked. "I thought you said something about grading papers."

"I went dancing."

"What, like in town, with… your fellow teachers?"

Fellow male teachers, the hesitation meant. I almost smiled.

"No, no. I was hardly in the mood for that."

He grimaced. "No thanks to me and my obliviousness."

"I told you, it's okay, Guillaume. It's past."

"So, where did you dance?"

"Céleste's neighborhood."

"Where the ceremony for Christophe took place?"

I nodded.

"Well, that's interesting." He studied me over his steaming mug. "They could hardly get you to dance the last time."

"Christophe had been right. It was time for me to start dancing again." I sipped my coffee. "I don't know what was keeping me from it. My pride? Fear of failure?"

"So, it was good to dance last night?"

"Not really." The reply came out, uncensored.

"What do you mean?"

"Oh… nothing." I took a too-big gulp of coffee and felt it burn the topside of my mouth.

William didn't reply. Nor did he seem interested in changing the subject. I gave an irritated wave in his direction.

"Fi. Talk to me."

"Look," I began. "I'm not trying to be difficult here. But it was weird, last night. Dancing until… I don't know. I honestly can't explain it. It hurts my head to even think about it."

What happened last night?

Joshua. With all his involvement in bwiti, he'd get it. The weird, spiritual-meets-scary world that the Peace Corps certainly hadn't trained me for, nor would be willing to discuss. I'd see Joshua in a few weeks' time when the education volunteers met for their annual conference. Followed by a meeting for all the second-year volunteers to reunite and discuss COS—close of service—its issues and details. Because, unfathomable as it seemed right then, this would all come to an end in a few months' time.

"Put down your coffee cup."

William's words startled me out of my thoughts.

"What?" I looked at him, uncomprehending.

"Your coffee cup." He'd shifted, straddling the bench. "Set it down." Sighing in mock-exasperation, he took the cup from my hand, set it on the ground, and pulled me back toward him. Before I could protest over being hauled around, he began to massage my tight shoulders. "Oh, wow. You're tight," he said.

"My shoulder muscles have been in knots for days," I admitted. Weeks, in truth. Months.

"That's something I know how to fix."

The massage dissolved my tension. The fog in my brain, the brooding thoughts, miraculously dissolved as well. William's hands were a marvel. His fingers found and kneaded the knots below my shoulder blades, the tightness of my back, the spots where I hadn't even realized I'd been tensing. I relaxed deeper, taking fuller note of our surroundings. He was right; it was a nice morning, still cool from the earlier mist, fragrant with damp earth. I studied the adjacent morning glories and neatly tended euphorbia shrubs with their brilliant, showy red flowers. Next to us huddled the delicate, orchid-like flowers of the butterfly bush. It was so beautiful here. Sometimes I forgot that.

When William was done massaging my shoulders and back, he folded his arms around me, sandwiching me within them. It felt so safe and comforting and perfect, I didn't want to breathe. In silence, he rested his chin against my shoulder. A minute later, I gave one of those post-crying hiccuppy shudders. I tried to joke about it.

"Can we stay like this for, oh, another hour or so?" When he laughed, I could feel the vibration. A moment later, he pulled his arms back and gave my shoulders one last squeeze.

"I'm making it up to you," he said. "When we're in Libreville for the COS conference."

I swiveled around to face him and we smiled at each other. The old William had returned. I wanted to hurl myself back into his arms and tell him how much I missed him, how ungrounded and emotional I'd been feeling lately. But the best thing was that I realized I didn't have to say any of it right then. We had time.

"I'm going to visit Kaia in her village next weekend," I offered shyly. "I told her I'd be backup support for a sticky situation she's trying to solve."

"Good for you. Good for Kaia, too. The first-year volunteers can use our help."

My foot hit something with a thunk and I looked down at my upended coffee cup.

"Whoops," we said at the same time, which made us laugh.

"My fault," William said. "I put the cup there. Let me go make you another."

"Will you stick around for a second cup too?" I asked. "Or do you not want to keep Jenny waiting?"

What a big girl I was, saying her name, acknowledging her presence in William's village, his house (please, God, not his bed) so calmly. In reward, he smiled.

"A second cup of coffee with you would be great."

We rose and wandered back toward my house. I looked around in wonderment, as if aware of the beauty for the first time.

"You're right," I told him. "It *is* a nice day."

The kind of day that made you think, no matter how everything otherwise felt, that maybe things would turn out all right after all.

Chapter 29

"Another pancake?" Kaia asked, gesturing to the frying pan on her propane stove.

I looked up from my plate, where all my attention had been riveted over the past five minutes. "There's more? Omigosh, yes, I'll take another."

She brought over the pan and slid the fluffy, golden pancake onto my plate. "These are just amazing," I told her. "They're like what you'd find in a nice restaurant."

"Aww, thanks." She flashed me a shy smile. "I think it's the yogurt I use in place of fresh milk or buttermilk. Since there *is* no fresh milk or buttermilk."

I poured the syrup she'd created using thinned strawberry preserves and butter (canned wasn't too bad, in the end), necessary since pancake syrup didn't exist in Gabon. Atop it I heaped a dollop of her homemade yogurt, as firm and luscious as whipped cream. Last came a sprinkling of toasted chopped nuts that carried a hint of both savory and sweet.

"Lance told me you were the culinary queen of the province," I said between bites. "Now I understand why."

"Breakfast food is my forte. Dinners, not so much."

"Dang. I'd have come to your village earlier for weekend brunch, had I known."

She laughed. "You're not the first person to tell me that. Which makes up for the fact that accommodations here leave something to be desired."

It was such an anomaly, this crappy house of hers, more rustic than even Henry or William's homes, and the buttery, delicious smell wafting from the stove. The main room's mud-and-wattle walls had oversized cracks through which morning light filtered through. Kaia, however, was pragmatic about it all.

"It brings more light into this room by day, which is nice for a living room. The bedroom, where the cracks have been patched, is dark by day. But I prefer that for its privacy."

"My house in the Ogooué Ivindo was horrible," I told her. "Nothing to complain about next to this, mind you. But I kept having break-ins. Once they broke in while I was asleep in my bed. I don't think I had a single good night's sleep in that house after that."

Kaia cocked her head. "I didn't know that about you. For some reason I thought you were posted in Oyem your first year and transferred to Bitam after that."

"Nope. I lived in Makokou."

A curious expression crossed her face, as though she'd bit into something sour that she'd thought would be sweet. "I thought a volunteer named Keisha was the English teacher in Makokou."

"Both of us were. She taught at the mission collège and I taught at the lycée."

"Which of you had a student named Calixte?"

"I did." The mention of his name sent a ripple of anxiety through me. "Why?"

"Because he's my farmer Albert's nephew. The problem kid."

Of all the shitty coincidences.

"Oh, God," I breathed. "He was a problem for me too. In a big way."

We stared at each other in dismay. My mind scrambled to reconfigure all the variables. "How did you know he'd been a student in Makokou?" I asked.

"Because the first day I met him, he asked me, sort of furtively, whether I knew the Peace Corps woman who'd taught English in Makokou last year. Two volunteers named Keisha and Rich had COS'd the day our group arrived in country. I'd heard they'd taught in Makokou. It didn't cross my mind there were more of you teaching there. Calixte didn't mention you by name, and once I explained no, the English teacher went back to the U.S., he seemed satisfied. Even relieved. We didn't talk about it again."

"He hasn't posed any risk to your safety in any way, has he? Or made you feel uncomfortable?"

"No." She looked puzzled. "Why do you ask?"

"We just had some, I don't know, bad vibes between us."

Kaia looked worried. "This isn't a deal breaker for you, is it? You'll still come with me?"

"Of course I will!" I pushed away my own unease. I was no newbie teacher. I was approaching the final lap of a two-year assignment and I'd never felt more on top of things. "I'll be fine," I assured her. "We'll both be fine."

The problem, she explained as we cleaned up after breakfast, was that Calixte had been trying to strong-arm his uncle, her farmer Albert, saying the fish were big enough, and that they should harvest. The rural Gabonese tended to harvest the fish early, whisk the inferior end result off to market or smoke them dry and sell those—the stacks of smelly, desiccated fish one saw at every market in the country. These were tossed into sauces to add flavor and substance to a sauce devoid of other protein or meat. But they held little meat, little nutrition. A fat, mature grilled tilapia, however, could feed and nourish a family of four. There were risks to delaying a harvest, however: greater losses if the bigger fish became sick and died, the pond corrupted, or the fish stolen.

"It's hard for us to sell the big picture when so few guarantees exist." Kaia washed the last plate and set it on the draining rack. "I get it. Life is so risky here, by nature. Low risk, the tried-and-true, an inferior product that provides sustenance—they prefer this. 'Good enough' is what they aim for. Winning them over to the Peace Corps' method is hard."

I finished drying the plates. "Do you think your farmer would follow your advice if Calixte weren't pressuring him?"

"I do. He has a progressive streak that's great to see. The good news is that Calixte is only there temporarily. He'll be gone in a matter of weeks, once he finishes his military training. But these are crucial weeks. If I can get Albert to not cave in this month, we'll be set. I keep telling him the results will be *so* worth it."

"All right. Sounds like our goal is clear. Ignore the kid and support your farmer."

"Easier said than done."

"Well, today Calixte is outnumbered."

We drove to her farmer's fish pond on Kaia's motorcycle. Kaia cut the engine and in the newfound silence I could hear the high whine of millions of insects that charged toward us. They dove for our ears, our mouths, the corners of our eyes, as I slapped them away frantically. Kaia grinned and offered me a spare rolled bandanna, the human equivalent of a horse's tail.

Ahead of us lay the pond, surrounded by open, scrubby land. Two men stood, examining the pond's contents. Correction: one man and one teenager. Calixte.

The pancakes leapt around in my stomach.

He's still just a kid, I reminded myself. He had no power over me. None.

Kaia called out a greeting to Albert. He and Calixte turned at the sound of her voice.

The entertainment was mine, this time, as I watched Calixte react to my presence. He froze in confusion, as if questioning whether his eyes were seeing double Kaias. But Kaia and I bore little resemblance to each other beyond being young white American women. It sank in finally. Surprisingly, no predatory pleasure replaced the shock on his face. In spite of the fact that Calixte belonged here and I didn't, he seemed distinctly uneasy. Then he seemed to switch gears and act as though he didn't know me.

Kaia introduced me to Albert, a mild-mannered Gabonese man in his early forties who had intelligent eyes and a friendly smile. "*Un plaisir,*" he said, shaking my hand.

Calixte had to shake hands with me too. In Gabon, it would be seen as unspeakably rude to not greet a visitor in this way. He avoided meeting my eye. "*Un plaisir,*" he muttered, extending his hand.

Hardly a pleasure, I thought wryly. "Hello, Calixte," I said in English in my schoolteacher voice as we shook hands.

He squirmed uncomfortably, just like a schoolboy. "Hello, Miss Fiona."

His uncle cast him a startled look. Calixte ignored him.

"Fiona is my Peace Corps sister," Kaia told Albert in French. "She lives in Bitam. She's an English teacher there."

Albert couldn't seem to figure out my presence, nor Calixte's behavior.

"...But I taught last year at the lycée in Makokou," I added in French.

Albert's expression cleared. "Ah, so this is how you and my nephew know each other."

"Yes." I beamed at him.

"*Bien, bien!*" Albert looked delighted, his gaze bouncing from me to Calixte, back to me.

"Shall we look?" Kaia gestured to the pond. "I'm eager to see how the tilapia have grown."

"They're doing well." Albert sounded proud.

We congregated along the periphery of the pond. Beneath the water, I could see the tilapia swimming, periodically creating little bubbles as they nipped at the leaves and manioc bits Albert had fed them.

"Ooh, they're a nice size!" Kaia exclaimed. "This is wonderful."

"Yes," Albert said, but hesitated. He seemed to be waiting for Calixte to speak next. A pause rose between them that grew awkward. Kaia and I exchanged puzzled looks.

Albert glanced pointedly at Calixte, whose gaze remained fixed on the fish. Finally Albert spoke again. "My nephew's opinion is that the fish are big enough, and that we should harvest at this time."

I decided to plunge in. "Monsieur Albert, Kaia has explained to me the benefits of a few more weeks' growth. It's a very sound plan with proven success. Kaia's way, the Peace Corps' way, will work for you." Inspiration struck. "This is why the Minister of Tourism's son, Essono Christophe, is a strong supporter of all the Peace Corps volunteers and their programs. He is a close friend of mine. He was a great source of help to me last spring." I let an edge creep into my voice, a warning of sorts to Calixte. "He would not hesitate to help Kaia, in support of this fish-farming method."

"The Minister of Tourism is a son of the Woleu Ntem." Albert's voice was hushed in respect.

"Indeed yes," I said. "Essono Christophe, too, is a son of the Woleu Ntem."

"Very good." Albert turned to Calixte. "This is a strong endorsement."

Calixte scowled. "Fine," he muttered to Albert. "We do not harvest this week. This meeting is finished."

Kaia and I exchanged perplexed glances—was Calixte going to give up so easily? And why was he acting so cowed by my presence? Something didn't seem right. Then again, it was making my job easier. "I can come back next week, too," I added slyly. A lie; I'd be in Libreville. But it had the desired effect on Calixte, who shook his head vehemently.

"We do not need to work with two American females," Calixte said to Albert. He angled his head my way. "She can leave today and not return."

Albert studied his nephew in confusion. "But… last year," he said to Calixte in a low voice. "Are you not—?"

"Silence!" Calixte cut off Albert's words. He looked as if he wanted to hit his uncle. "Last year is last year," he thundered. "We will not discuss it."

This was getting more and more perplexing.

Kaia cleared her throat awkwardly. "All right. It sounds as if we are all in agreement that you'll wait a few more weeks before harvesting. Yes?"

"Yes." Calixte spoke for his uncle and himself both. "Which means we are finished here."

He excused himself, brusquely shaking our hands in farewell. He didn't meet my eyes, which was fine by me. Albert walked Kaia and me back to her motorcycle. He apologized for Calixte's rudeness and the abruptness of the meeting.

"It's not a problem," Kaia assured Albert. "Fiona and I have another farmer to visit this morning anyway. We'll spend more time together next week, you and I."

"Excellent." Albert slowed his footsteps. "And yet, I don't know why he was so abrupt," he said as if to himself.

"I'm grateful he now supports our idea to wait," Kaia said. "What changed his mind?"

"I don't know," Albert said. "Perhaps it is the presence of your Peace Corps sister." He gestured to me and pride made me rise a bit taller.

Kaia smiled at me warmly. "Thank you, Fiona."

"Of course, I have heard of you," Albert told me. "The boy has talked of you. How he was your favored student."

"Ah. Is that right?" I replied, wondering if it had been my translation of his French that delivered such incorrect information. But it was hard to find any ambiguity in "*le plus favorisé.*" "I'm surprised he mentioned myself or my class."

"He speaks of nothing *but* that time with you," Albert said. "I understand your closeness."

I felt like we were talking about two different situations.

"My closeness? With…Calixte?"

"Why, yes."

"I think you've been misinformed. We were not close."

Albert looked puzzled. "Then why did you come here today?"

"To support Kaia and her projects." I hesitated. "Perhaps you should share with me what your nephew is saying," I told Albert.

Albert glanced in the direction Calixte had gone, but he'd disappeared from view.

"The boy told me about your relationship. Your dangerous home, and how he…protected you by night. How the administration at the lycée in Makokou treated him unfairly, because of their jealousy, and found a way to kick him out once you were gone."

I stared at Albert in gape-mouthed shock. He thought Calixte and I had been lovers, that he'd slept in my bed at night. I felt ill.

"Monsieur Albert, I am afraid you have been misled. This is not the story. Not in the least. Regretfully, I had to kick your nephew out of my class, numerous times, by the end of last year. It was a difficult teaching assignment. When a fellow Peace Corps English teacher, posted in Bitam, had to leave, I was allowed to take over his post. Yes, my house in Makokou had been dangerous. I lived there alone and had troubles. I live with the nuns at the mission, now. It is a much safer place for me."

He considered this and nodded. "That is much better for a female," he said. "A woman, all alone. It is not good!"

"You're right," I said, eager to keep the peace, remembering too late Kaia's own situation.

Albert's expression grew serious. "He did not protect you, my nephew?"

I shook my head. "Not in any way."

A sorrowful look crossed Albert's face. "My nephew has lied to me. This troubles me."

Had I said too much? A frisson of uneasiness rippled through me.

"You are a good man, Albert," Kaia said in a soft but confident voice. "A smart worker with great intelligence and wisdom. If Calixte learns to follow your example, he will be fine."

When Albert smiled at her and nodded, I felt better.

At Kaia's motorcycle, he shook our hands gravely.

"Goodbye," he said to me. "Thank you for your information."

"Goodbye," I replied. "I wish you the best of luck with your fine fish pond." *And your lying, manipulative nephew,* I wanted to add, but of course I didn't.

Sunday, Kaia drove me to Mitzic, a nearby town, where we snagged a soon-to-depart northbound Regab truck ride for me. While the driver finished his lunch, we sat and drank orange sodas and watched the activity taking place in the town square. We mulled over yesterday's meeting with Albert and Calixte.

"That was creepy, huh, the story he'd told his uncle about me?" I said.

"Seriously creepy."

"No wonder Calixte was anxious for the meeting to end fast and get me out of there. So I wouldn't share the truth. Omigod, what Albert must have thought of me, that I'd been letting his nephew sleep in my bed at night." I shivered in disgust at the thought.

"Honestly? He didn't seem fazed by the thought," Kaia said. "Ironically, our presence as single women alone in this culture strikes him, and other Gabonese, as more scandalous."

"I'm so sorry I let it segue into that 'women shouldn't live alone here' attitude. That didn't help you."

"It's okay. I've heard it before. It's something a female volunteer in this program has to get used to." She picked up her soda bottle and studied it. "I have to say, though, it can get lonely, alienating, being a lone female here."

"You fish volunteers have it tougher in that way. I can't think of any posts where fisheries volunteers are coupled up. Same thing with the community health volunteers. Jenny in Oyem with Carmen is pretty unusual. Although there used to be a pair of volunteers right here in Mitzic."

"So I heard," Kaia said. "A married couple. One did fisheries, one did health. I suppose that makes it easier to pair them up."

"They left last summer before I could meet them, but Carmen mentioned they had a nice little house."

"I've seen it. It's adorable. It's still under contract to the Peace Corps. There's talk that they'll put another couple here next year. Jenny and I are already jealous."

"You know, you and Jenny," I mused. "This would be a midway point for the two of you and your territories."

"That would be fun, to move here, to share the house with her."

Kaia sounded wistful. "But that's dreaming."

"I switched posts," I reminded her. "Go ahead and dream."

The Regab truck driver headed out of the restaurant and glanced around for me. I waved and he gestured to his truck. Kaia and I rose and made our way over there.

"Thanks again, for everything," Kaia said.

"No problem. And thank *you* for two fantastic breakfasts." I gave her a fierce hug. "Hang in there. The first year is tough."

"You're off to Libreville next weekend?"

"Yep. Education conference, followed by the COS conference."

"Have fun," she said.

I thought of William. I thought of the luxury hotel the Peace Corps would put us up in for the three nights of the COS conference. I could feel a grin spreading over my face.

"I have a hunch I will."

Chapter 30

"Why do I get the feeling I've been kidnapped?" Joshua asked. He and I had just claimed a table in a Libreville bar, a French expatriate hangout, which meant it had real walls, real tables instead of wooden picnic benches or wobbling plastic tables. Customers, all well-dressed Europeans, occupied a few of the tables, sipping Pernod or chilled white wine. Jazz music, not African, whispered from speakers. Beer—Heineken only—was five times the price of Regab, which was the best way to guarantee no Peace Corps volunteers would show up. "What is this all about?" he demanded.

It was indeed a kidnapping of sorts. We'd just finished our education conference, with two days to relax and kill before the start of the second conference. I'd bribed him to come out with me for a beer without letting on where we were going. I didn't want to scare him away. When the taxi we'd taken deposited us in this unfamiliar French neighborhood, he'd grown puzzled.

"I wanted a place where we could talk without looking over our shoulders," I told him.

"Why?" He looked suspicious.

"Because I wanted to talk. And volunteers are nosy."

"All right, talk away."

I scrutinized him as he shifted in his cushioned chair, trying to get comfortable. He was still slim and pale, but he'd grown his brown hair long, keeping it back in a ponytail. He was wearing loose, colorful West African clothing. It suited him. "So," I said, "been to any bwiti ceremonies lately?"

He grew still. "What's that supposed to mean?"

"It's supposed to mean, have you been to any bwiti ceremonies lately?"

He paused, then seemed to drop his guard. "What did you hear?"

"That you got initiated."

"Who'd you hear it from?"

"Christophe. The grapevine."

"Not Peace Corps admins?" he asked.

"I'm inclined to think if they knew, you'd know it."

"Good point."

"So?" I prodded. "Anything you'd care to elaborate on?"

"Like what?"

"Maybe the way you took a near-fatal dose of iboga and hovered on the cusp of where life meets death, and what it was like?"

"I can't talk about my initiation, if that was your intention in bringing me here."

"It wasn't, but out of curiosity, why can't you talk about it?"

"You take a sacred vow when you get initiated. I can only discuss the experience, and my journey, with other bwitists."

It was more than a little freaky to hear him talk in this way, see the wariness in his brown eyes as if I were the enemy.

"Fine," I said. "I didn't come here to grill you about your experience. In truth, I was hoping you could help me translate my own experience."

"Why? What's going on?"

I gnawed on my lip before plunging in. "I'm in a weird place, Joshua."

"Weird, like what?"

I shook my head. "It's not something I can easily explain."

"Try me."

I'd caught his interest. "All right. You knew I used to dance, back in the States?"

He nodded.

"So, I've been dancing a lot lately, at ceremonies. African stuff. I've picked up on the movements by watching the others. About a month back, a woman, a trained priestess, gave this incredible performance. I could tell she'd danced herself into a trance, and it made me just burn with curiosity. Two weeks ago, I was feeling really agitated and I just poured it into my dance. And then, well, it was like I danced myself somewhere else."

"Wow."

I raised my eyes to see him regarding me with new respect.

A server approached with our Heinekens and two chilled glasses. I waited until he'd poured our beers, lit the candle between us and departed before I spoke again.

"Something in me was frantic to go somewhere else. Or something was calling me to do it. The drums, maybe? They affected me so much, it was as if the sound went inside me and altered my blood chemistry."

Joshua said nothing.

"So I danced beyond my dizziness, my consciousness. I think I fell to the ground. I think they helped me up and over to a bench. But I might have been talking through it all."

I traced a design on the condensation forming on my beer glass. "They told me I was speaking Fang. *Conversing* in Fang."

"Wow." Joshua leaned forward. "I didn't know you spoke fluent Fang."

"I don't. I know a smattering of phrases and that's it. But Céleste told me it sounded like I was just one of them."

"Holy shit."

"I know." I regarded my swirly design gloomily. "I'm pretty freaked out over it all."

The memory of it sent a visceral tug of fear through me. It was still too close. I'd gotten a reprieve with my trip to Kaia's village, but the issue wasn't going to go away on its own. Céleste wouldn't let it.

"Do you suppose they felt as though spirits were communicating through you?" he asked.

"I don't know. I think so."

"Whoa." He sat back. "Impressive."

Memories came rushing back—the screaming blur, the sense that I was hovering at the border of some realm, trying to break through to what lay just beyond. And I had. Something more had happened, something that now eluded my conscious mind.

"What if I really did go somewhere else? In my mind?"

"Would that be such an awful thing?" he asked me. "Truth be told, it's very Western to process all phenomenon through our rational minds alone, quantify everything with scientific reports and documents and FDA approval and such. You know, our ancestors, and pretty much all the ancient, indigenous tribes, *did* this kind of thing. Partaking in nature, ritual, ingesting local herbs, shrubs, to allow them to enter a different realm, a different consciousness. You can bet the Gabonese aren't fazed by dancing oneself into a trance. Probably what freaked them out was seeing you do it so effortlessly. You're so…white."

A bark of laughter burst out of me, in spite of the seriousness of our conversation. "Do you know, people have been commenting on my pale eyes since my arrival here," I said. "They say I have 'spirit eyes.' And the day Céleste met me, my first day in Bitam, this white bird, an egret, flew into the sisters' dining area and walked right up to me. You should have seen her expression. It was as if she'd seen a ghost." I laughed at the memory, but Joshua didn't laugh with me.

"Oh, boy. She's got you pegged for big stuff, doesn't she? How did you leave things with her and the group?"

"She wants me to do it again."

"I can imagine she does."

"But for the next time, she wants me to prepare. Fast for the day, meditate in the ceremonial hut, and before the ceremony, ingest something that promotes 'my journey.' Those were her words. Like iboga but not, she said."

The silence that greeted this made the whole idea seem all the more preposterous.

"Let me ask you this," Joshua said. "If you tried to pursue that feeling again, what would be the motivating factor?"

I mulled over his words. "Okay, I have to admit it. There's this hunger, a dancer's need to see how far I can go with a physical experience. I'm obsessed with the notion."

"Do you want to connect with spirits that might be trying to communicate through you?"

"God, no! That sounds preposterous. I'm Catholic-born and bred. And very, very white, inside and out. I just don't believe in that kind of thing. In fact, it feels kind of goofy to be discussing the possibility."

Anger started to build in his eyes.

"Can you honestly say that two years here hasn't changed you?" he asked. "Opened your mind to unforeseen, inexplicable things? Experiences that have blown you away, that leave your thinking forever changed? And if you're going to tell me you're unchanged, and try to crack a little joke about this instead, well, I don't know what we're doing here, and I'm done."

He half-rose in his seat, as if he couldn't get away from me fast enough.

"Joshua, stop!" I laid a hand on his. My heart had begun pounding faster, as if his agitation had been contagious. "Okay, fine. You're right. Something in me *has* changed. A lot. In fact, thinking of it now, weird shit has been happening to me all along." The woman who'd appeared and disappeared the day I got lost in the brush. The spirit eyes business. The lame woman in Henry's village on New Year's Eve with her prophecy.

You dance. That is how they will know you. And they will join you.

Had she actually said that?

She had.

I told Joshua about the woman and her words. My voice shook. Thinking about it made my head pound horribly. There'd been something more, too. Protection, maybe? Which made no sense. Surely I'd misheard. Maybe projection. That sounded appropriately psychological and spectral.

Joshua looked happy again, nodding in satisfaction, as if he'd just won a high-stakes bet.

I drew a deep, shaky breath. "Oh, man. It's not done with me yet, is it?"

"I don't think it is."

"Oh, jeez. Oh, shit." But even as I spoke, I could feel excitement building in me.

Joshua noticed that, too.

"I need to issue a very important caveat, though." His expression grew solemn. "You should be aware of this. In the middle of my initiation, where they were forcing more and more iboga down me, with my body rejecting it, I asked myself if it was all worth dying for. Because that was where I was sure it was heading. I literally thought I was going to die. I told them I wanted to stop, and they only chuckled and kept force-feeding me the iboga."

"Joshua, that was so risky! It could have killed you."

He ignored the reprimand. His eyes burned into mine. "They knew what they were doing. And so will your people. But there's a good chance that, combined with the hallucinogens, you will think you're dying. That's where the most powerful spirit communication takes place, at the cusp of living and dying. *That* might be their goal for you. So if you decide to do it, make sure it feels like a quest you'd risk your life for."

My insides contracted. I could hardly breathe.

"I scared you," he said.

"You did."

"Good. You needed to hear it. Because this is no game, what they do. Nor is it a circus trick. It's as real, as serious, as life itself."

Silently we watched the candle flame flicker and bob merrily between us.

"Do you have any regrets?" I asked.

"None."

"It's changed you."

He nodded. "For life. For the better."

"What's it going to be like to leave in a few months' time?"

"I'm not ready to leave. In fact, I put in a request earlier today. I want to extend to a third year."

That brought us right back to reality, to Libreville. "Are you serious?" I exclaimed.

"I am."

"Joshua. What's your family back home going to say?"

"They're not my priority. My family here, the people at my post, the bwiti community—they're the ones I'm thinking of."

I studied him. "Should we be concerned about you?" I asked.

"Define 'we'."

"Peace Corps. Chuck and Rachel."

"No."

"Okay, Carmen and me."

He hesitated. "Nah." He smiled at me in a way that made me see the old Joshua. "But thanks for caring."

"Thanks for coming here with me. It's been… illuminating."

He laughed. "Doesn't that describe it all?"

On the taxi ride back to the case de passage, the spooky, mystical energy between us began to dissipate. Being in Libreville itself was like waking up from a fretful dream. Everything here, from the blaring traffic to the bustling crowds and myriad shops, seemed lively, cosmopolitan and cheerfully abrasive. My spirits grew bright. When I thought of the fact that I would see William in two days' time, they grew even brighter.

The COS conference: three nights in a luxury ocean-front hotel; private beach and swimming pool; air-conditioning and soft beds; hot running water, bathtubs and French soaps.

And William.

"I have just one thing to say to you," said Chuck on Sunday night, at the opening session of our conference. An image flashed onto the projection screen in front of us: our original group of twenty-six trainees at the airport in Paris almost two years ago, minutes before boarding the flight to Africa. The eleven of us who remained howled with laughter. We all looked clean, neat and ridiculously wholesome, except for Carmen, with her spikey hair and black-rimmed eyes.

"Look," I cried. "It's Robert! I haven't thought about him in ages!"

"Look at *you*, Fiona!" Carmen gasped, laughing, and I was shocked at how aloof I looked, standing slightly apart from the group. My hair was slicked back into a tight bun; I'd forgotten how much I used to do that, an emotional shield of defense in a non-ballet world.

"And you, too, William!" Carmen couldn't stop laughing. "Omigod, you look so grim."

She was right. William had posed on the opposite end of the group, starched white shirt buttoned high, looking pained, like a high school principal forced to pose with the unruly students he'd just disciplined.

I looked over at him now, sitting between Henry and Buzz. Had I really not thought of him as seriously attractive before? He was wearing a white button-down shirt, the same one in the photo, in fact, minus the starch. His face was tanned, his thick golden hair tamed back, his physique more buff and toned from physical labor, and he'd never looked better. I watched as he laughed at a comment Henry murmured into his ear. His face lit up with animation, eyes bright, smile broad.

He glanced my way and caught me staring. A hot blush rose to my cheeks and I ducked my head to inspect the patterned carpet.

It had been like this since I'd first spied him three hours earlier. I'd taken ridiculous care with how I looked, blowing half a month's living allowance on a silky ivory trouser and top ensemble, very Paris-meets-Africa. I'd put on makeup for the first time in months: petal-soft French foundation, coral lipstick, liner for my pale eyes and brows. I'd dried and styled my hair with a blow drier. William's stunned expression when he encountered me had made me think I'd overdone it. But he'd smiled and hugged me in the same way he always had. Since then, we'd remained apart, like kids at a middle school dance, hovering by our same-sex friends' side as we eyed each other from across the room. It was both absurd and adorable.

The night's session was brief, mostly an overview of what Chuck and two other administrators and a few returned Peace Corps volunteers would share with us about COS procedures and facts. It was hard to concentrate, with so much new stimulus swirling around us. Chuck's words, however, sank in.

"You're here to learn how to leave. You're here to recognize what's important in your life in Gabon, at your posts, and make the most of your remaining time. Because you don't want to put off doing something important that, once you get home, you'll regret not having done. Don't go thinking you have all the time in the world. You don't."

I thought of William, across the room. Right then, I wanted to be next to him with a desperation that cut my breath short. I wanted to feel his arms slide around me and hold me close. In such a short space of time, he'd become so important to me. He was warm, intelligent, funny, passionate, principled. He was everything I wanted. And unless I stopped dancing around the issue, avoiding any chance of rejection from him, I was going to lose him. Not just during this conference or here in Gabon, but for life. He'd move on and I'd return to Omaha, alone. The thought appalled me.

How ironic: play it too safe, and you lose. Big.

Time to leap into the abyss of the unknown.

After the evening's session had ended, all eleven of us trooped down to the hotel's elegant lobby. The far corner held a bar and lounge area, with floor-to-ceiling glass windows that overlooked the lit swimming pool and behind it, the darkened Atlantic Ocean. But the European luxury, with its potted palms, framed artwork, Persian rugs atop polished floors, seemed all wrong for our cheerfully boisterous group. Outside the hotel, two blocks away, we found an outdoor bar with plastic tables and chairs, loud music and cheap Regab, and commandeered half the place.

Everyone claimed a seat. When Joshua took the spot next to Carmen, I hesitated. William looked at me, smiled and patted the seat next to him.

Elated, I sat.

After Henry had regaled the group with his story about the army-ant invasion that had powered right through his living room in October, leaving him homeless for a week, William angled himself my way.

"That's a new outfit," he said.

"It is," I agreed.

His eyes traveled slowly down the length of it and back to my face.

"It looks very good."

"Thank you." I managed to sound calm, matter-of-fact.

"I keep meaning to ask. How's your jaw these days?"

Here, too, I kept my expression neutral, even though I wanted to laugh. There wasn't a chance I was going to have any poorly timed issues about my jaw this time and ruin everything. "Good as new," I told him.

"Glad to hear." He reached over for his beer but set the bottle back down before even taking a sip. "So… talk to Christophe lately?"

This time I couldn't not laugh. "Christophe who?" I nudged his thigh with mine.

He grinned. "I think you are laughing at me."

"I am."

He reached over and gave my thigh a mock-reproving squeeze. His hand lingered for just a moment before he removed it. The gesture, the physical contact, stole my breath.

"And meanwhile," he said with great dignity, "I am simply setting up my social calendar, and we'd talked, earlier, about a group dinner."

"My apologies."

"Thank you. So, have you spoken to our friend?"

"I have."

"And in conversation with Mr. Essono, did you two arrange dinner for the four of us?"

"I did. We are scheduled to dine with him and Mireille on Tuesday night."

"Are you looking forward to it?"

"Frankly I'm pretty caught up in what's going on right here to give it much thought."

He smiled at me, gave my thigh another soft, lingering squeeze, and everything inside me turned to butter.

"William," Carmen called out. "What's this I hear about you being roommate-less?"

We looked up to see Henry and Carmen grinning at us. "Poor guy, all alone in that big room," Henry said. "Dude, should we all show up and turn the room into party central, so you won't be lonely?"

"I think that's what they made double bolts for," William told him. "Or to protect against."

"Your own room. Oh boy," Carmen said, and began to chuckle to herself.

A discussion arose over what everyone thought of our luxury accommodations and whether Henry should try and fake out the administrators, pretending that he'd gone native. "How about I tell them my girlfriend at my post is pregnant, due any time, and I've decided to stay in Gabon to be with them?" Henry proposed.

"That's been done already," someone else pointed out. "Twice."

"Two wives?" Henry asked. "Both pregnant. That been done?"

"I think you're good to go, there."

William stretched and made a great show of looking at his watch. "I think I'll call it a night," he said. "Anyone else ready to head back?"

"You know, good idea." I sprang right up, ignoring my largely untouched beer. "Want to be fresh for tomorrow's sessions!"

Two others, a married couple, joined us as well, which helped make it seem less obvious that I was intent on following William. I avoided looking at Carmen, who was doing her best to catch my attention so she could leer at me.

On the walk back, I inhaled all the stimulus—the city nighttime activity, the warm breeze, the sound of music from different venues, the tang of the ocean in the air, the romance of a tropical night. I welcomed the chatter of the married couple, for whom it was just another night. The four of us made our way into the lobby, where they wished William and me a good night. Alone with him, I grew tongue-tied. My heart began to pound faster.

William, too, seemed nervous. "Henry and I stopped by an artisans' yard on our way into Libreville today," he said. "I bought some really nice looking masks."

"Oh, really? That sounds great," I stammered. "I'm looking for something like that to send home to family. Should I… Can I… come check them out?"

"Sure!"

"Like.. right now?" My heart was banging in my chest like a loose shutter in a storm.

"Definitely," he said.

"Great!"

Whew.

As we walked down the hall, we both began to relax. "We bought other things, too," William said. "I'll have to pull out my wooden serpent to show you."

"Oh, now that's one I haven't heard before," I commented dryly before I could judge its appropriateness.

William stopped, frozen, and I wanted to kick myself. Then comprehension—and a blush—flooded his face as he began to laugh. He reached out and gave me an affectionate swat on the ass. "Bad girl. Bad, bad girl," he said, shaking his head. "What are we going to do with you?"

I had a hunch he'd come up with something. I certainly hoped so.

Chapter 31

William's new masks, chalky white and rimmed in black, really were beautiful. Their large elongated faces, facial markings and abstract features demarked them as authentic Fang masks, the same kind that played such an influential role in twentieth-century modern art. William was ruffling through his duffel bag in search of his wooden serpent when the power flickered and went out. In the sudden darkness, we both paused and began to laugh. "Yep, luxury hotel or not, we're still in Africa," William said.

"I can't see you. Where are you?"

"Here."

"Where's here?" I groped around with my hands until I found him. "Is that you?"

"No."

I laughed. "It sure feels like you." My hands slid up the familiar route of his arms to his shoulders. My cheek brushed his, and that was all it took. His lips found my half-open mouth. A little animal sound of relief and pleasure escaped from the back of my throat.

Several sensations raided my mind at once—the pleasurable shock of our hip-to-hip contact; the tang of beer lingering in his mouth; the lusciousness of the way he kissed. My arms twined around his neck, fingers digging into the soft pile of his hair. His hands glided over my silky trousers, my backside and waist until I felt so breathless and lightheaded, I sensed my legs might not be able to support me much longer.

With a clicking sound, the lights came back on.

We both blinked, disconcerted, aware that this was the moment to either pull back and make a joke, or continue to scale the wall that separated friend from lover.

He pulled back.

"Guillaume," I whispered, holding on to him this time. In truth, clinging.

He reached down with one hand and pried off a sandal. Straightening, he flung it like a Frisbee toward the light switch adjacent to the door. The rotating sandal clipped the switch and instantly cut the overhead light, returning us to semi-darkness. As I began laughing, he reached for me. "Where were we?" he murmured. Without waiting for a reply, his mouth covered mine again.

Wall scaled.

As he kissed me, he nudged me back toward the bed until it pressed against the back of my trembling legs. I fell back onto the mattress and he followed suit.

I'd dreamed of feeling his weight on me ever since that Christmas Eve kiss. I'd spent sleepless nights wondering what would have happened if things had gone differently that night. But even that wouldn't have been as perfect as this. There was something about waiting three and a half months for an experience to make you relish every bit of it. Which, apparently, included not rushing things. William was different from the others I'd been with; there would be nothing hasty or furtive here. Instead, his hand slid down my legs and back up in a way that communicated an equal sense of longing and hunger, but patience, too. Calculated deliberation. It drove me crazy. It was so much fun.

A few minutes later he paused to prop himself up on his elbows. I reached up and began unbuttoning his shirt with shaking fingers. When the last few buttons resisted, I ripped the shirt open. A button flew and hit the lamp with a ping, making us both laugh. My silky top followed William's shirt to the wayside. My bra.

"William?" I whispered ten minutes later.

"Yeah?" he whispered back.

"I think my new slacks are getting wrinkled."

He rose to his elbows again and peered down at them. "We can't let that happen."

"It would be a crime."

With a deft tug, he liberated the silk trousers and placed them with great care on the unused side of the bed. Neither of us commented when they slid off the bed and onto the floor a moment later. We were too busy liberating William's jeans and getting right back to the business of discovering each other's bodies.

Mine. He's mine.

I felt this more than thought it. The non-thought continued, making me deliciously, recklessly uninhibited, as my hands moved down his back, the smooth curve of his ass, greedily claiming anything I could reach. My legs curled around his and clung, like an octopus in a primal mating ritual. His hand edged down, past the barriers of my silk panties, touching me where I'd grown swollen and slippery. I gasped, an *oh!* of pleasure that seemed to galvanize him.

We had a game going on. Gentle followed by animal. Followed by slow, stretchy movements, like ballet, except that you didn't use your mouth in ballet. He loved contorting my limbs and I loved draping myself over him for maximum skin contact. He was like a master choreographer, intuiting where the slow adagio movement fit in, and when to ramp things up. His timing was impeccable; he waited until I was seconds from orgasm (number three) before slipping inside me. I'd thought climaxing at the same time was something that only happened in movies and romance novels. Nope. As I felt something in me spiral out of control, William clutched me and gasped out my name, shudders shaking his body. He didn't let go for a long time afterward. Neither did I.

Hours later, following round three, I slipped away to use the bathroom. Upon my return I stopped to study William, visible in the moonlight filtering through the windows. He was lying in bed, watching me from under heavy-lidded eyes. "Why are you smiling?" he asked.

I took a few running steps and leapt back into bed. He gave a big *whoof* as I thudded against him. "Because I'm very happy." I burrowed beneath the sheets to make contact with his skin. "Because it's been a good second year, but I think I like the ending the most."

"Oh, but it hasn't ended yet," he said, sliding his arms around me.

"You mean it gets better?"

His arms tightened. "Stick with me and we'll find out together."

"Okay."

I slung my leg over his thighs and rooted around on his chest for the best place to rest my head. When I found that position where we interlocked perfectly, it seemed to complete some sort of magic circle of security. Sleepiness hit me like an anvil and all became quiet and unutterably safe.

Until, at some later point, it became not so safe.

It was my bwiti initiation, though I didn't remember agreeing to one. They were feeding me iboga and had been for a long time. I knew, without looking, that they'd streaked white paint on my forehead, just like the slashes of white paint that bisected their own dark faces.

More iboga. One brought over an entire branch while another grabbed hold of my injured jaw. "No," I cried, but the minute I opened my mouth to speak, they got it in.

Villagers had filled the hotel room. I looked around at them and the world spun. The tunnel reappeared, even though I wasn't dancing. This time I stepped into it and let it take me to that other place.

Somewhere Else.

All around me, landscape I'd never seen before. A plateau punctuated by sparse, brambly bushes and pale green lighting, like Omaha skies just before a tornado. A very old place, its edges eroded and stripped of all moisture. More like the moon than earth. It was so foreign, it scared me.

I squeezed my eyes shut. When I opened them again, I was in a less foreign place. A Catholic church. A cathedral.

The interior was breathtaking. Above me, a buttressed ceiling soared stories high. A long line of priests, robed in snowy white and gold vestments, had lined up behind a casket. The interior was dim, but from on high, stained glass windows cast beams of colored light down the massive grey stone walls. One priest carried incense, its brass cage dangling from a pendulous chain, swirls of the smoke rising. A pipe organ swelled out an opening hymn and the procession began. The movement jostled me and I realized I was the person in the casket. The iboga dose had failed, been too much, and I'd died. I could see through the lid, and see everyone's somber faces. I wanted to call out, but I couldn't speak because I was dead, and that was it. Finished, *c'est fini*, forever and ever, and what would my family say when they learned I'd died? My parents, Russell, Alison. The cry of anguish when Alison found out, which I'd heard, because when you're dead you can see and hear everything, everywhere. You are The Ancestors now. I saw the way Ally sank to her knees and gave an unearthly howl, before screaming, "Fi! No! Please no!" It pierced me so deep, hurt so much to see, which meant I wasn't dead, because to hurt this bad meant you were still alive.

I struggled against the coffin lid, crying out that I wanted my family, I needed to be alive for them, that this was all wrong. No one heard me.

"No!" I tried to scream again. "Noooo!"

"Fi. *Fiona.* I'm here. You're safe."

My eyes flew open to find William, hunched protectively over me. We were in his bed and I was alive.

My heart was slamming against my chest. I clutched at him, stunned to realize it had only been a dream. It had seemed so real. Even now, the scenario clung to me, terrible in its inference and intensity. I was panting, as if I'd been running.

William went and fetched me water. I gulped it down, and gradually the dream and its hold started to recede. "I feel so stupid," I mumbled. "I'm sorry I woke you."

He ignored the apology. "Do you want to tell me about it?"

I drew a steadying breath and shared what I could remember.

"Ally thought I'd died. It was terrible, watching her take the news." It was as if I'd actually seen Alison wail in grief, and it had been so pure, so feral, it was agony. Her grief had been mine. No surprise; we were sisters, almost twins. Grudges changed none of that. I began to cry again, helpless against the onslaught.

William held my hand until I calmed down and was able to tell him the rest of the dream, the bizarre landscape, the bwiti ceremony-but-not.

"Whoa, that's insane," William said once I'd finished. "Did you take your Aralen last night or something?"

In spite of the heaviness that still hung over me, I laughed. "No."

"I guess it's something else you're trying to process, subconsciously."

Of course it was. Family aside, it was Céleste's request to me.

I fell abruptly silent, a silence that stretched out.

"What is it?" William asked.

I hesitated a moment longer, dreading even thinking about it. "It's something to do with Céleste's dance circle. Something I need to figure out on my own. I'm sorry, that's all I can say right now."

I could tell William didn't like this, but he seemed to understand. "When you're ready, know that I'm here for you," he said.

A deep sense of gratitude welled up in me. "Thank you," I said, and took his hand. The warmth of it, the way his hand instinctively curled around mine, strong and warm, made me feel dizzy with happiness.

Sometimes when taking big, big risks, you won big.

This was big.

I learned a lot at the conference over the next few days. I learned how my hand could stay within the confines of William's for an hour and never cramp; how it was possible to appear engrossed in what the speaker was saying, while William's hand wandered under my shirt, caressing my back. I learned that standing too close to him in the hallway and grazing my lips against his neck produced a frozen, deer-in-the-headlights look in his eye; that I only needed a few hours of sleep each night; and that quiet, serious William had a passionate, insatiable side that drove me wild.

A few informative bits sank in, about reverse culture shock, tips on job-hunting, and final close-of-service procedures, but it took Carmen to jolt me back to full awareness. After lunch break on day two, she and Joshua strolled back into the meeting room together, dressed in identical African outfits, red and gold-patterned drawstring pants with matching tunic tops. Carmen had slicked her hair back and tucked it into a ponytail. They looked like twins.

Joshua took in my shocked expression and smiled. "She liked my other outfit so much, we went to the market and hunted down these," he explained.

As Joshua began telling another volunteer how to find the shop, I studied Carmen. "That's a man's outfit," I told her.

"I know." She grinned. "I like it."

"What are they going to say back home?"

"Who cares? And as it turns out, I'm staying."

"You mean here in Libreville after the conference ends?"

"No. As in, I'm staying in Gabon a third year."

"Carmen!" I cried. "Since when?"

"Since Chuck and I talked yesterday. I've been invited to serve as next year's volunteer leader for education."

"When were you going to tell me?!"

"Maybe I've been trying to get your attention and you've been a tiny bit preoccupied?"

"Okay, fine. But… What about Daniel?"

Carmen grimaced. "Gotta make that call today. It's over between us."

"Carmen! What the hell?!"

"It's just gotten too hard." Suddenly she looked weary. "We're living in two very different worlds and it's made us snipe at each other. Really kind of dislike each other. And there's no rewind button to press, to go back to that first year when our experiences were equal. I will always have my second year in Africa and he will always have his med-evac. Frankly, the decision to stay a third year was easier because it solves the 'what comes next' with us."

Carmen had been considering this for some time, I realized. And looking at her, I could tell she'd made the right choice. Her eyes were lit from within, like earlier days, anticipating new adventures, new responsibilities.

"Oh, Carmencita. I, I…" Words failed me. I'd miss her. Daniel would miss her. But she knew how to be true to herself. "I love you so much." My voice broke. "Please let's be friends forever."

Carmen reached over and gave me a fierce hug. "Always and forever, Africa sister."

The final evening, William and I were in his hotel room, preparing for our dinner out with Christophe and Mireille. I'd pretty much moved in; we agreed the time together was too short to be voluntarily separated. Our easy conversation drifted from one subject to the next as he shaved and I slathered myself with lotion, post-shower. The assessment of Carmen's new outfit led to shopping, which led to the topic of buying items to bring back to post. He needed chocolate bars, he told me. Jenny had used the last of his Libreville chocolate to make chocolate chip cookies, baked in his little propane oven. His workers hadn't known what to make of them at first. None of them had ever tasted a warm chocolate chip cookie before.

I smiled at the image. "This was the last trip she took to your place?"

"The one before that, actually."

"Ah." I tried not to feel jealous.

"On this last trip, she made them muffins. But she promised them she'd make more of the chocolate chip cookies the next time she came out. I am on strict orders to bring back not two bars of chocolate but six."

"Jenny's become a frequent visitor there, hasn't she?" I kept my voice light.

"She has." He rinsed off the last of the shaving cream and dried his face with a towel.

My confidence failed me. Insecurity slammed into my stomach like a fist.

William noticed. "She's in a bit of a bind, Fi." He reached out and caressed my hand. "That post isn't working out for her. It's too city-based. She's miserable. If visiting a village makes her feel less so, I want to offer that option to her."

I had focused my gaze on the little bottles of hotel amenities. I looked back up to find William watching me, his smile gone.

"You'll just have to trust me," he said. "The same way your eyes have asked me to trust you in the past."

I raised my hands in a surrender gesture. "All right, I'll trust you. Provided you answer me one question honestly."

"Okay."

"All this. Us, I mean. Are you going to tell me it's … complicated?"

He studied me and for one terrible instant, I thought he was going to tell me yes and that would be the end of my bubble of security. If this turned into a Lane or Christophe situation again after the way I'd thrown myself in so wholly, something flowering within me would crumble, disappear and never resurface.

William smiled, a look of such affection and tenderness, I felt my throat grow tight.

"No, Fi." He reached out, pulled me over and wrapped his arms around me. "No. It's never been less complicated."

"I'm glad." My voice cracked. And after that, nothing else, and no one else, mattered. Not even keeping Christophe and Mireille waiting at the restaurant a bit longer while we revisited the bed.

Priorities, after all.

At the restaurant, Christophe noticed immediately. He spied my hand, clasped in William's, and sized me up as the maître d' led us to the table where he and Mireille had already been seated. My cheeks grew hot. I'd felt oddly reluctant about seeing him tonight; I hadn't realized until now that I'd be nervous. He rose to greet us, expression unreadable as he planted a soft kiss on both my cheeks, French style. I exchanged kisses with Mireille; she, too, had noticed, but her reaction was easier to decipher. She was smiling. Broadly.

The four of us settled in our seats. I reached under the tablecloth, found William's hand and clutched it. The maître d' made an elaborate speech, promising gustatory delights and ensuring us he was at our beck and call for our smallest needs. He departed, nodding to two waiters who'd hovered behind him. "You two are our guests tonight," Christophe said as the waiters hurried forward, one bearing champagne, the other a quartet of champagne flutes.

"You're too kind," William said. "All the ways you've helped myself and Fiona. Dinner's on us. It's the least we could do."

"No, no." Christophe gave an expansive wave of his hand. "They know me here. They won't even bring a bill to the table."

"Which is why I made arrangements earlier," William said.

Christophe seemed startled, then privately annoyed. "Well. Aren't you the tricky one?"

Talk ceased as the waiters arranged the glasses, popped open the champagne and poured. Christophe smiled across the table at William, who smiled back at him. I met Mireille's eyes. She looked amused. It was like a game of cards, all of us holding winning hands. Christophe, curiously, didn't seem to realize that he, too, was holding one.

I felt a flash of sympathy for him. This was not the script he'd planned and rehearsed.

Too bad.

William draped one arm over my shoulders as the other hand dropped to my lap. "We were on time after all," he murmured into my ear.

"I'm glad I didn't make us late," I murmured back, and met his eyes, which reminded me of the way I'd met his eyes forty-five minutes earlier, seconds before I'd climaxed. His fingers, caressing my bare shoulder, made me forget where we were and who we were with.

"I hate to interrupt you two." Christophe's wry tone cut through our pheromone fog. "It's just that I'd like to propose a toast."

Mireille smothered a chuckle as William and I straightened, and William and Christophe smiled at each other in that same phony brightness.

I caught on finally. In the animal world, such an exchange between two males might have entailed bright plumage waving threateningly, or two pairs of antlers coming together with a crash. But here, in this elegant venue, William had made his point in his own tasteful way.

Christophe lifted his glass. "To good friends," he said.

"To good friends," we all echoed, as we clinked our glasses together and drank.

Christophe rebounded, of course. The four of us chatted, placed our dinner orders, and the mood grew relaxed. When William and Mireille fell into conversation about Peace Corps-built schools within the country, Christophe turned to me.

"How are classes?" he asked.

"Much, much better than last year, thanks."

"Not such trouble with problem students there at the mission, I'd imagine."

"True. But do you want to hear something crazy? I recently encountered my former problem student, the one you had to help me with last year. One of the fish volunteers in our province, Kaia, needed a little backup support. I went and came face to face with him. Boy, was he shocked. We both were."

"Was he rude to you, or menacing?"

"Never less so. He was nervous around me, in fact. Turns out he'd made up some story to his uncle, Kaia's farmer, that he'd been one of my preferred students and not a problem student in the least. And that we'd had…relations, outside the classroom." I grimaced in distaste. "You can bet I set the record straight."

"How did the uncle react?"

"He was a good guy about it. He listened, and didn't try to contradict anything. It was very civil. He seemed quite disappointed that his nephew should do such a thing. I imagine Calixte caught an earful that evening."

Christophe frowned. "The boy's pride is likely hurt now. Watch your back."

I waved away the warning. "No need. I live far from the problem. Besides, what high school dropout wants to interact with a former teacher? My presence clearly flustered him."

Christophe didn't look convinced.

"Don't worry," I told him. "I understand the way it works here now."

He shook his head. "You might think you're fully seasoned, that nothing more can faze you. To that, I'll say, you don't know Africa yet. You likely will never know Africa. How the Gabonese are, beneath the surface. What we truly value and what we deem unacceptable."

I could feel something in me resist what he was saying. He noticed; his chin took on the stubborn tilt that had always preceded our arguments. It was so similar to the way we'd started, nearly two years earlier, that I could only laugh. "So it began, so it ends," I said.

His expression relaxed and he began to chuckle. "I don't think we've come to the end, Miss Garvey." He glanced over at William and gave a grudging nod. "I'm happy for the both of you."

"Thank you."

"Mireille just sent the two of you wedding invitations."

"Date?"

"June tenth. You're still in country, correct?"

"We are."

He drew a slow breath, a heavy exhale. "And so a new chapter begins. For all of us."

"I'll drink to that." I nudged William and he and Mireille both looked over.

"A toast." I lifted my glass. "To new beginnings."

Everyone lifted their glasses.

"To new beginnings."

Chapter 32

The classroom felt different the morning of my return to teaching, as if twelve weeks, not twelve days had passed since I'd left. September's veneer of order and cleanliness had faded to expose dingy blackboards and scuffed walls. The students' sagging, frayed uniforms mirrored their half-hearted energy. By ten o'clock, my spirits were faltering. Then I thought about William, about us, and the buoyant mood returned. Life was good. Very good.

The best thing about returning to the classroom on a Thursday was that in a day, the teaching week would be finished. William and I had agreed to put two and a half solid days into our jobs before connecting again, on Saturday afternoon. With renewed zeal I planned lessons for the final six weeks of class, and on Friday afternoon I cheerfully toiled at my community library project. At four o'clock I called it quits and grabbed a ride into town with Mohammed, who was picking up a truck part.

I was in a ridiculously good mood as I crunched down the footpath from the market to Lance's neighborhood. I saw beautiful colors I normally overlooked: scarlet trumpet flowers, golden dirt framed by jade forest, pillows of snowy clouds punctuating the afternoon sky. I inhaled the tannic air and sang out greetings to everyone I passed. Even the presence of Jenny, answering my knock at Lance's front door, didn't bother me.

She didn't seem particularly happy to see me, but she smiled politely and let me in. The living room was in its usual fraternity house disarray, the smell of popcorn covering up the dirty-socks odor. "Oh, hi Fiona," Lance called out, poking his head out of the kitchen. "Have a seat." He came out a moment later, bearing a ceramic bowl of popcorn.

I dropped onto the couch, the vinyl cool against my damp skin. A deep *baaaa*, sounding like an old man clearing his throat, was followed by obscene snorts and a higher pitched reply. Instead of my usual sigh of disapproval, I laughed.

"When are you going to cut the grass by your house instead of letting those goats eat it?" I asked Lance.

"I like having them around—they make me feel less lonely."

"This house is a magnet for green mambas and gaboon vipers with that high grass so close, you know," I warned as I reached for the popcorn.

"Yes, but this way the goats visit me."

As if to back up Lance's point, the older goat bleated and belched. Lanced beamed at me.

"That's Scratchy Pierre—he likes me too, can you tell?" He grabbed a fistful of popcorn, rose and threw it out the window. Immediately, we heard the patter of hoofs, thuds and bleats as two goats fought for the unexpected bounty.

I turned to Jenny. "So what's up?"

"They aren't replacing Carmen. They don't want teachers in the big cities. Then why me?" she asked. "Why am I living there and not in a smaller town?"

I sat back and listened with an open mind. She wasn't competition. And like William said, no first-year volunteer had it easy around this time of the year.

"You know," I said, "there's this house in Mitzic, that borders Kaia's territory. I told Kaia you two should talk to Libreville about nabbing the house for yourselves, before they consider putting a married couple there in September. That's an ideal town and post for a community health volunteer."

She eyed me suspiciously. "That would be making trouble."

"Seems to me it would be avoiding trouble. If your current setup isn't working, it isn't working."

A determined glint came into her eye. "I'll make it work."

I shrugged. "Well, hang in there. Let me know if I can help in some other way."

"Thanks," she said, still wary.

I turned to Lance. "How was your week?" I asked.

"Kinda sucked." He grinned at me. "But it's over. So that's good."

"Anyone for a beer in the marketplace? My treat," I said.

"Wow, someone's in a good mood," Lance said.

"It's the reward for surviving nearly two years of teaching. The end is in sight."

We went to the market for beers. Darkness fell. Jenny was spending the night at Lance's place, so we ate dinner together, plates of meat and rice, with a second beer.

"Okay, I'm off," I said to them shortly after seven o'clock. "I need my rest." Because William would be over the next night, and we might not get much sleep. At the thought, my high spirits flew higher.

As I approached the taxi-brousse station, the buses still operating to and from Oyem and the Cameroon border, a group of military men seemed to have created a stir. They'd been in the marketplace for a while, I could tell. Some of them were walking unevenly, the lurch of the drunk. This was Friday night revelry for them, and not work, fortunate for us. And yet, a menacing feeling seemed to surround them as they prowled the area, splitting into smaller groups to go drink more, eat food, or simply harass people passing.

The older military men seemed to have made a game of hazing the younger ones, still in training. I peered closer and saw, with an icy prickle, that one of them was Calixte.

I stopped in my tracks, did an abrupt ninety-degree turn, and continued on, getting out of the area before he noticed me. Once at the head of the footpath that led to the mission, I breathed easier.

I became aware of footsteps behind me as I walked. Trying to appear casual, I glanced over my shoulder. A trio of young military guys walked several paces behind me.

I walked on. My heart began to hammer against my ribs. My knees felt trembly. I increased my pace and maintained focus on the path before me, the beam of the flashlight guiding my way.

The footsteps grew closer.

"Hello, Miss Fiona," a familiar voice sang out in a sly, singsong way that made my blood run cold. "Why do you hurry? Have you found yourself a man to protect you?"

I stopped and forced myself to turn around calmly. "Ondo Calixte. What is it that you want?" I made my voice ring out, so that I sounded impatient, aggrieved, and not scared.

The uniform made him look older, all the more terrifying. By the way the three of them preened, I sensed they'd just been given their uniforms, and they were out to test their new power. Their puffed-up chests told me they were succeeding. And liking the feeling.

"Your papers, please," one of them, shorter than the others, said to me.

Were they friggin' kidding? A little sound of disgust escaped my lips, that they did not take kindly to.

"You will do as we say," the second one, tall and spindly, intoned, but since he was clearly still in his teens, he was less scary.

"I do not have my 'papers,'" I snapped. "I am walking back to my home after taking a trip into town. I am on a walking path. One tends not to need one's 'papers' when one is engaged in a daily routine."

The tall, spindly boy hesitated. Even though I'd spoken in clear French, I got the sense he didn't understand all my words. Then again, training for the military didn't require an extensive academic background or lexicon. Stand. Sit. At attention. Fire. Cease. At ease. Shut up. Attack.

Thumpa, thumpa, thump went my heart.

"You do not understand that we are in charge here," Calixte said, and I had to admit that he, unlike his two compatriots, had the ability to look and sound menacing.

"I understand that you're a boy, playing at being a man." I tried to sound bored, unafraid.

He scowled at me, radiating pure contempt.

"You, who spoke poorly of me to my uncle. What kind of woman are you? You are not married. You have no husband. No children. Something is wrong with you and that's why you left your family, your country, and are here, hiding behind your teacher's job. Our women would find shame in all this. But you?" He sized me up. "You act as though we should be respecting *you*."

He took a step closer. I took a step back. It was like some creepy tango.

"I'm done here," I said, and whirled around to continue walking. But he grabbed my arm. Instinctively, I shook it off, and he grabbed it again. Gripped it.

"Fuck off, you little shit," I shouted at him, shaking it free with considerable effort on my part. "Get the hell out of my way."

Calixte grabbed me again, and this time he tugged me off the footpath, into the brambly area before the forest took over. I could see the way his chest was heaving, and that he, too, had lost the cool he'd planned on keeping. "Let me go!" I shrieked, my fear growing.

He ignored my words and with a grip that felt like iron, dragged me deeper in the brush. His comrades were standing on the path still, dumbly, disbelieving. Violence had filled the air; you could feel it, along with a sense that rationality had flown from the equation, replaced by animal instincts and behavior.

I could feel the way Calixte, holding onto me, was trembling with the adrenaline of it all. His eyes were wide with intoxication, not just booze but the power he knew he had. He was aroused by my fear. Sexually aroused.

The other two were alarmed, now. "*Allons nous,*" the tall, spindly boy kept repeating with increasing urgency. "Let's go. This is too much."

"Ondo, you're not thinking," the short one said. "She's not worth it."

"Go, then. Get out of here. I have something to settle with her."

"Ondo! It's not worth it," the taller boy insisted.

"*Vas-t'en!*" he roared. *Piss off.* And he must have held some power over them too, because they skittered away.

Seeing them depart, my terror doubled. Tripled. The short one, who'd seemed to still have a trace of the good boy in him, cast me a look of apology over his shoulder. Pity, even. When he disappeared from sight I felt lightheaded with panic and despair.

No one was going to save me.

Who knew how Calixte had thought this would unfold—unfathomably, my compliance?—but he hadn't expected me to put up such a fight. Panic flashed in his eyes, and I could almost see the plan change in his head. He couldn't just force himself on me, and have that be that, Miss Fiona bested once and for all.

That had been the plan, I realized. Somewhere in his twisted brain, he'd thought he could have his way with me and see it as payback. Or somehow see it as his due. How long had this been his fantasy? Since my visit to Kaia's post? Since I'd gotten him kicked out of my class last year? Or maybe since the moment he met me in Makokou and I mistakenly assumed he was a man and I'd smiled at him, almost invited him inside, only to reject him thereafter.

"Get your hands off of me, you creepy fuck!" I screamed.

He didn't understand the English, but he understood the insult, and it seemed to fuel him. He slapped me across the face. It burned like fire.

Things had gone hideously out of control. He'd pushed me up against a tree, mostly out of view from the path. I could feel his calloused hands tearing at my blouse, reaching my bare skin, his beery breath hot on my face, the horror of his fingers running up my leg from beneath my skirt. I screamed for help and he slapped my face again, hard. I detected the presence of someone on the path, who paused, stepped our way and squinted into the shadows, before hurrying away. No one approached any further. No one would confront a man in military attire; it would only put their own safety and security at risk.

He pressed his upper body against mine, hard, pinning me into place. I heard the musical sound of a belt buckle being undone, the unmistakable *zzzzz* of a zipper. I saw the glint of a knife in his other hand, as he used his elbow to pin down my shoulders, his forearm across my neck, prepped to cut off my air supply the next time I made noise.

Oh, God, I screamed inside. *He's going to rape me. Then he's going to kill me.*

I knew it, the way an animal knew it was going to die. The way the dying woman in the roadside accident had known. That had been

338

why she'd relaxed in my arms. She'd given up.

Done. Over. The casket dream I'd had in Libreville now seemed chillingly prophetic. I was going to die. Peace Corps Gabon was going to have to call my family and tell them the news. Ally would hear it, fall to her knees and scream in agony. *Fi, no! Please, no!*

Calixte shoved his pants down, groping to pull out his member. He'd hauled up my skirt; I could feel his fist bumping against the soft skin of my inner thighs, and something in me gave up, went dead.

You will think you're dying. That's where the most powerful spirit communication takes place, at the cusp of living and dying.

Joshua's words.

And the woman from Henry's village. *They will come to you. Protect you.*

Right before a tornado comes, it gets very still. The sky turns green and there's something akin to a giant intake of breath, a tremendous drop of air pressure. Then you feel everything around you change. Fast.

It was the tunnel in reverse, a blurry, fiery thing that shrieked through me, awakened me, powered me. It didn't just carry me, it allowed me to fight back with the power of a half-dozen strong women. Angry, strong women.

At first it was nonverbal, simply a force that allowed me to effortlessly shove him away. Next came the voice. The words. In Fang. I didn't even think in English first, translating to French, then Fang. It just came out. But it was the howls, mixed with the words, that made the hesitating Calixte grow anxious, then rattled, then rigid with terror.

His fly was open, his pants down around his hips. The sight made something in me explode with wrath. I straightened and gave his shoulders another vicious shove, because I could. He stumbled back. I stepped closer to him because fear no longer factored into the equation. It did, however, for him.

The louder I shouted, the more his eyes widened in fear. Finally he turned and began to run away. Rage and that otherworldly thing fueled me. I began to chase him. And no one was quite as fleet-footed as a lifelong dancer who was under the protection—possession?—of spirits. How slow and ungainly Calixte seemed. He didn't help matters by looking over his shoulder constantly while running.

I could have kept running forever. I'd never felt such power.

The path led right back into the town and the marketplace. One would have thought he'd prefer to slip away unnoticed. Instead, the pursuit took us into the heart of the town, where I saw people were stepping out of bars and restaurants, alerted by my continued shrieks. Calixte was crying out, now, too.

My hair was down, the ponytail clasp torn out in the struggle and abandoned in the dirt. A cut lip from where he'd slapped me had filled my mouth with the metallic taste of blood. My blouse was torn and askew. And still I ran.

Céleste stepped out. The minute I saw her, the thing powering me evaporated. She ran toward me, crying out, asking what had happened. I slowed to a stop and wordlessly pointed to Calixte, who'd found his compatriots and, unfathomably, was clinging to them, weeping.

"Fiona!" another familiar female voice cried. "What's going on?"

Jenny appeared, running toward me.

I was safe.

The nightmare might have ended, but it was impossible to shake the sense that I was still dreaming. A gentle fog cushioned everything I said or did. I heard myself speak, agree that yes, I'd like to sit down. No, I didn't need to go to the hospital, I told Lance and Jenny, what I needed was just to sit down. I felt the hardness of the chair beneath me as I sat, the cloistered protection of an indoor environment, a tiny bar with posters of the president, the Pope, and Gabonese soccer stars taped to the walls. The Pope waved at me from across the wall. I watched as Lisette, Moussa and Benoît joined us, stricken and concerned. Jenny took the seat next to me. I heard the buzz of voices all around me, Lance's strident voice, Jenny's lower, soothing one telling me to take it slow, that I was safe. She was a marvel. She'd slung one arm around my shaking shoulder, and she held my hand, which I gripped back. Quite the shift from our relationship just a few hours ago. Lance seemed to be part of the personality reversal game, too, now as serious as William, demanding that we file a report with the gendarmes, that the attacker be brought to justice. He'd attacked *a Peace Corps volunteer,* Lance kept repeating, voice hushed with disbelief. Not just an average local but an American woman who'd devoted two years of her life to helping the Gabonese. It was beyond reproach.

In that dreamy space, I had the ability to see it all—Lance's outrage, his Westerner's sense of justice that bordered on entitlement; the way his Gabonese friends reacted uneasily, because they liked Lance when he was the funny guy, the clown. They didn't know what to make of the Lance who was shouting and glaring accusingly at everyone around him, as if the attack had been partially their fault. I didn't have the energy to tell Lance that this was not going to flesh out in the righteous way he was visualizing, the perpetrator brought to justice, everything cleanly exposed, bad guy punished, innocent victim looked after. Africa was not so cut-and-dried, black-and-white. Peace Corps volunteers, young women like myself, had been murdered in their attempts to pursue American-style justice over lesser issues than this. The thought that I'd come so close to joining their ranks made me shake even more.

Jenny, still holding my hand, asked me gently about the attack. I provided what details I could muster, leaving out the spirit presence. "He lives in the Woleu Ntem?" she asked. "This turned out to be the one Kaia was talking about at Thanksgiving, whose uncle is her farmer?"

"Yes," I said, and she looked at me, appalled.

"He's evil," I said. "He has darkness inside him."

A wave of heat and nausea rolled over me. "Oyem isn't safe for you," I told Jenny. The words came out in a voice colder and harsher than my own.

"You will *not* live in Oyem once Carmen is gone. Peace Corps will *not* post another solo female volunteer in that city. There's evil lurking there. Kaia will *not* stay alone in that village. The two of you will take that house in Mitzic and be safer."

Jenny blinked, twice. "Fiona. You can't know this."

I couldn't explain to her how I knew. I couldn't explain anything, even to myself.

"Yes, I can," I said. "I know what needs to happen. I'll make it happen."

Ten minutes later, Céleste pushed her way through the group to our table. Lance rose. She met his expectant gaze and told him no, the attacker hadn't been arrested. Instead, she told us, Calixte was "seeking sanctuary." He claimed to have been attacked and chased; he had everyone in the marketplace as witness to the latter. They were not declaring me the culprit, so to speak. Spirits were. Vengeful spirits. According to Céleste's report, Calixte was still crying, shaken, begging for protection from my spirit wrath.

Lance was apoplectic. "I've never heard such bullshit in my life!" he burst out in English. "This is a crime! He's making any excuse he can to avoid prosecution!"

"My friend," Benoît said, "please try to understand this situation from an African's point of view."

Lisette chimed in and the three of them began to heatedly discuss the issue. Céleste, meanwhile, stepped closer to me. The fog was still thick in my brain, something she alone seemed to be able to pierce. No surprise. She spoke the same non-language of those who'd gone a little too far over the edge into the other realm. I watched her eyes move over my face, size up my scratched-up condition.

"You have taken a journey," she said in Fang.

"*Eh*," I replied, that curious Gabonese one-word assent, accompanied by a little chin nod.

"They came to protect you."

"They did."

Céleste considered this for a long moment.

"Normally one must dance first," she said in Fang. "Meditate. Fast for the day."

Joshua's words returned to mind. "I thought I was going to die," I told her. "I was sure. This is why they came. Because Joshua told me that's where the most powerful spirit communication takes place. At that place where life meets death."

She didn't ask who Joshua was. Likely she knew, in the way she seemed to know things. "*Eh*," she said, and nodded to herself several times more.

Jenny, her arm still around me, released my hand and a moment later I felt the cottony softness of a wad of Kleenex. Only then did I realize I was crying. I studied the wad in fascination. It was so neat and clean and white and Western. I hadn't realized you could find these in Africa. Trust Jenny and her resourcefulness. "Thank you," I said to her in English.

She smiled and gave my shoulders a tighter squeeze. "We're here for you," she said, and planted a soft kiss on my cheek.

Her kindness, the warmth of her gestures, broke down something in me. Or maybe it was the opposite. Something broken, beginning to repair. The fog retreated a bit. So did the memory of what I'd just told Céleste. In Fang, at that. I think. It was like the time I sustained a concussion during a dress rehearsal for *Nutcracker*. I'd slipped on an artificial snowflake in "Land of Snow" and fell, hitting my head with a terrible thud, rendering everything hazy and disorienting for the next several hours. It was a scary feeling, not recognizing your own thoughts, not having access to the usual order residing in your brain. Here I was, right now. I knew that I'd been attacked. I understood this fuzziness was a form of being in shock. I knew something paranormal had happened out there. The rest was still fuzz. All I could do, in the end, was ride it all out.

One last event made the fog clear. Céleste had left and returned, this time with a military man, the sergeant in charge of Calixte's group. He was sending his men back home to Oyem. Taking Calixte with them.

"He should be thrown in jail here," Lance raged. "Or at least detained."

"The boy is so contrite," the sergeant said. "So shaken. He will not bother her again."

"That is *not* enough," Lance said.

I met Celeste's eyes and made a decision. She gave me a little *go ahead* nod.

"Fine, you can take him," I said to the blandly smiling (who knew they could smile?) sergeant. Ignoring Lance's squawk of protest, I rose, gave my disheveled hair a shake, enhancing its wildness, and walked right up to the sergeant. We met at the same height, which I could tell disconcerted him. I also didn't display the correct fearful deference toward a man of uniform. Which didn't particularly concern me right then either.

"You tell your *boy*"—I emphasized the plebian status—"that it's not only me he has to fear, but my American sisters. From here on out. If he bothers them in *any way*, now, or a month, or a year from now, tell him I will know. Never mind that I'll have returned to America. I will know."

My gaze had latched onto him. He looked helpless, and more than a little terrified. "I will know," I repeated. "And I will come back and find him. And you."

Had it been wrong of me? I wondered, thirty minutes later, as Lisette, Moussa and I made our way out of the marketplace. To so terrify the sergeant, and, in turn, my attacker, alluding to vengeance I couldn't possibly implement? And yet, I hadn't chosen the words. They'd just come out of me.

"*Regardez, elle est là.*" I could hear the electrified spectators murmur to each other as we passed. "*C'est la blanche mystique.*"

The mystical white woman. What power my strangeness had bought me.

Africa took, and Africa gave.

What the hell. This, I'd take.

Chapter 33

They say you can really tell a person's character by the way he or she behaves in a crisis. Not that I needed any further confirmation that William was a person of extraordinary character and merit, the kind of guy you hang on to for life.

His arrival, late that evening, stunned both myself and Lisette, who'd come back to my house with me, unsure of leaving me alone. I clutched at him, afraid it was a dream, that he'd poof away. His shirt felt scratchy and smelled smoky. I took those as good signs. Apparitions didn't have an odor.

William seemed relaxed, at ease, which calmed me as well. He'd gotten the news an hour earlier when a taxi-brousse had rumbled to a stop in his village, he reported to Lisette and myself. The driver, who'd passed through Bitam, had shared the story that had the marketplace all abuzz, that *la blanche, l'américaine,* the one with the spirit eyes, had such powerful juju that she'd not only scared off her attacker, but had flown after him in a fury.

"That's me," I tried to joke. "Strange Fiona, making even the villain run off in fear." Neither William nor Lisette cracked a smile. I looked at them both and promptly burst into tears, which went to show that maybe I wasn't as calm as I'd thought.

William's arms came around me and held me close. "I'll leave you two," I heard Lisette tell him, and then it was just the two of us as I cried and stopped, cried and stopped. William didn't try to cheer me up, distract me, psychoanalyze me, or anything. He just held me over the next few hours and let it all roar through me.

Amazingly, once I fell asleep, it was the deep, untroubled sleep of a child. I woke to sunlight, utterly disoriented. I heard William in the kitchen, taking a whistling tea kettle off the stove. When I shuffled into the room, he smiled at me.

"What time is it?" I croaked.

"Ten o'clock."

He made me coffee and I settled, still in a daze, at the kitchen table. "I'm off to make a call to Libreville," he said. "Soeur Beatrice said I could use her office phone. You'll be okay?"

"Of course. I'll make us some French toast while you do that."

"No, no. Just relax, Fi."

I was fine, I told myself firmly, and once he left, I set to work on the French toast, proving to both of us that I was capable of anything. When he returned, I smiled broadly at him from my spot at the stove. He looked skeptical, but smiled back.

"You were able to make your phone call?" I asked.

"I was. I got a hold of Rachel. She says this is serious stuff and they want you coming in."

"No. I don't need to."

This produced a wry smile. "Rachel said she thought you'd say that. She told me to tell you that Plan B would then be in effect. You are now a 'volunteer of concern,' and you should expect a visit from a Peace Corps Gabon administrator within two weeks' time. And she wants you to call her tomorrow, once I've left."

"Fine. But it's not going to change anything." Or maybe it would. Because here was what we would discuss too: getting Jenny out of

Oyem. Getting that Mitzic house for Jenny and Kaia for their second year. I would insist. No matter how crazy the idea sounded by day, I knew a mandate from the Great Beyond when I heard it.

I frowned at the slices of French toast, sizzling despondently in the pan. Even though I'd given them well beyond the three minutes per side that Kaia's recipe stated, they still looked pale and soggy. "I don't understand why this recipe isn't working," I fretted. "Kaia made it seem so easy."

"I told you to relax and not to bother."

"I want to keep busy."

"Maybe circumstances have you still feeling a little... distracted?" William sounded amused.

"I'm not distracted in the least."

"Is that right?"

"Yes."

"Okay, maybe in the next batch, though, you'll want to use those eggs you set out."

He gestured and I spied a trio of eggs sitting next to the canned milk and opened packet of vanilla sugar.

"Oh," I said in a less confident voice. "Those."

"But hey, you might have come up with a new recipe—fried milk baguettes. We'll give 'em a try. In the meantime, why don't you let me take over? Have a seat, sip your coffee. Relax." He pried the spatula from my hand and nudged me gently toward the table.

He cracked the eggs into my French toast mixture, stirred it up and sliced more bread, while I sat at the table and sipped my coffee. "I need to call Christophe, too, at a more reasonable hour," he said.

I set my cup down abruptly. "Oh, William, don't. He's just going to freak out. Calixte is scared shitless of me now. Honestly, I've got this one covered."

William flipped the slices of French toast before speaking. "I understand what you're saying, Fi. I know Christophe pretty well, too. But I'm doing this for him, not you. Actually, I'm doing it for me. Because, I have to be honest. I'm freaked out here. The woman he and I both love was attacked."

It sank in that he'd just told me he loved me. We both seemed to realize this at the same time. But instead of turning red and chuckling ruefully with a "whoops, how'd that slip out?" he turned down the stove heat, sat down next to me and took my hands.

"I love you," he said, his beautiful blue-green eyes serious and fixed on mine. "And, fine, I'm supposed to play it cool and not say that, literally the same week we became intimate. But, see, that wasn't just 'having sex' for me. It wasn't 'a Libreville thing.' That last night together, it was, literally, making love. And three nights later, someone tried to steal it all from us when you were attacked. Assaulted. Nearly raped. You could have been killed. So, see, I'm pretty freaked out. Frankly, I want to get in my truck, go find the kid and rough him up pretty bad. I don't know if you can appreciate how a male in this situation might feel. Christophe will. I need him more than you do, right now."

I stared at him, stunned. "I love you," I said in a choked voice. "For everything."

Not nearly as eloquent as his speech. But never had five words meant more. And judging by the way William held me tightly and kissed my forehead, he understood.

He released me with a gentle squeeze. "All right, I've said my bit. Now I want something from you."

The determined glint in his eye made me uneasy. "Yes?"

"Something happened last night that you're not telling me. What's more, I want to know if this is in any way related to what's been troubling you lately. Since the weekend I forgot your sister's wedding. And don't tell me 'nothing.' I know better."

He was right. It was time.

I took a deep breath and shared everything I'd been holding back. The dance trance; the prophetic words of the woman at Henry's village last year. Céleste's interest in seeing how far I could go. The ease at which I'd ultimately fought off Calixte, making me believe there'd been some paranormal power involved.

William listened to it all without reaction or judgment. He'd returned to the French toast and once I finished, he drew in a deep breath. We both did. "Fi. Damn," he said as he set the cooked slices of French toast onto the platter.

He joined me at the table, and we ate calmly as though it were any other Saturday. "You know, this milk-and-sugar one is pretty interesting," William said, which made me laugh.

"So, I heard that Céleste was there last night, through it all," he added.

"Yes."

"How did you leave things with her?"

"I'll go tonight to her neighborhood. There will be another drum circle. Will you go with me?"

"Of course I will. And what do you suppose you'll tell her?" His voice sounded casual, but I saw the way his hand clutched his fork.

"That I'm done."

"No more dancing?"

"Oh, I'll still dance. I'll always dance. But that's all I'm looking for. A little African dancing and nothing more. No trances, no connection with a world beyond this one."

He hesitated before speaking again. "You remember what Chuck said at the COS conference? Not to go home wishing you'd done that last thing at your post?"

"Yes, I remember."

"… and?"

"I don't need to. I don't want to. Not after what happened last night. And Céleste knows that. I won't even have to say a thing to her—she just always somehow knows."

"You sound pretty sure of your decision."

"I am."

"Okay," he said, and the relief on his face was evident.

I set my fork down. "Guillaume?"

"Yeah?"

"I'm ready to go home."

He reached over and took my hand. "Me too."

"Guillaume?"

"Hmm?"

"How do you leave Africa? How do you get on a plane and just fly out of here, knowing you'll never come back?" I had trouble completing the sentence. I loved the mission like a second home. I would never see it again, after this.

"Maybe, deep inside, you don't ever completely leave. Or maybe it's that Africa never completely leaves you."

"I think you're right."

William speared the last piece of French toast. "There's an active African dance community in Berkeley. Every week, just a few blocks from where I used to live, they'd hold a class at the local community center. Wednesday evenings, for ninety minutes, rain or shine. They've been doing it for over a decade. You could hear the drums from a block away. It's what made me put on my Peace Corps application that I wanted to be posted in Africa."

"Will you go back to that area?" I asked him.

"I think I want to." He spread jam on the French toast slice. "It had a very intercultural vibe. I can't imagine going back to a place where I'm only around mainstream America. I don't think that will ever be my thing again."

"I get it. I don't see myself ever settling down and staying in

Omaha, or anywhere in Nebraska. As much as I can't wait to see my family and spend some time at home. Which is a weird feeling."

"Agreed. That's why my plan is to spend a few weeks back home first." He paused, set down his knife, and took a big breath. "All right, I'm going to come out and propose it. What the hell, I fast-tracked telling you I loved you." He turned to face me. "Come out with me to California when I move out there. Check the area out. If you like it as much as I think you will, stay. Stay with me."

"Are you serious?" I stammered.

"Dead serious."

I drew in a shaky breath and realized that, not only could it work, but it would be wonderful. Perfect. Meant to happen. That my friend April had just sent me her own news, made William's suggestion seem nothing short of prophetic.

"You're not going to believe the letter I got two days ago," I told William. "Wait. You have to see it to believe it." I scrambled up, strode over to the desk, grabbed the letter and brought it to William. I leaned over his shoulder, rereading as he read aloud.

Hi Fiona,

It's all still hush-hush, but I just had to tell someone! I'm taking a leap of faith and making a huge change. Leaving New York and the ABT to move to San Francisco. One of the former principals here, Anders, a friend and a mentor to me, is taking over directorship of the West Coast Ballet Theatre, and he asked me to join him there. As a principal! My lifelong dream come true! Promise me you'll come visit, once you're back home? It's so beautiful, you'll love it.

Love and hugs,
April

William began laughing so hard he couldn't stop. "Did you time this on purpose?" he demanded.

"I just got it Thursday!" I was laughing too. I felt giddy beyond words.

He reached up and around for me and pulled me onto his lap. "Fiona Garvey," he murmured against my neck, "you are the most unprecedented, fascinating, amazing woman I've ever met. I can't wait to see what happens to you next."

"You'll be the first to know," I assured him.

He kissed me. Not the gentle, reassuring kisses of last night, but the lush, inviting kisses of our nights at the hotel, complete with hungry, roving hands that made all my thoughts fall away. The kitchen chair we were sharing wasn't quite as comfortable as William's hotel bed, but this was here, we were together, we'd made plans to stay together, and it all felt like a dream come true.

The things life handed you when you took that scary leap into the unknown.

THE END

Acknowledgements

Ghosts helped me write this story. I don't know how to thank them. Literally. More on them later. For now, heartfelt thanks to the living beings who helped me craft and refine this story. To Anne Hawkins and John Dalton, thank you for your early faith in my ability to tell a good story. In the novel's 2002 incarnation, thank you readers Sarah Marion, Grace Harstad, Kathleen Hermes, Sarah Liesching (my very first reader, hungrily devouring the pages, sometimes within minutes of completion), Donna Zimmerman, Evelyn Liesching, MarySue Hermes, Amanda Mahon, Sue Novikoff and fellow returned Peace Corps Volunteers Adrienne Pierce and Elizabeth Letts. Speaking of RPCVs, thank you for your friendship and shared memories from Gabon, 1985 to 1987, Demitris Voudouris, Sheri Soderberg Cioroslan, Chris Van Dyke, Nancy Hartmann Marosi and Jill Bouma, among others. Later Gabon RPCV friends include fellow writer Bonnie Lee Black and writer-editor Darci Meijer. I so appreciated your support and interest as I kept inching forward with my writing. Gabon RPCV Tom LeBlanc, your article and musings about bwiti and its initiations were mesmerizing—thank you. For reaching out to share information about Kader Rassoul, I am deeply indebted to RPCVs Jenny Hamilton and Suzi Bouveron. The same debt of gratitude goes out to Joel Holzman and Stacy Jupiter, for information about bwiti and Karen Phillips.

Some stories, like cheeses, are best left to age in the cellar for a good long spell. This was one such story. In the manuscript's second incarnation, fifteen years later, my thanks go out to fellow writers Kelly Mustian, Anne Clermont, Karen Dionne, Kristina Riggle, editors Sandra Kring and Lauren Baratz-Logsted. Thank you, James T. Egan and Bookfly Design, for another brilliant job on cover art. Armfuls of thanks to my husband Peter and son Jonathan. It's not easy to live with a creative writer, particularly one writing about complex, mystical Africa, and my gratitude to you both is as enormous as my love, which is to say, seriously enormous.

And now, about those ghosts.

In late 1992 I learned Kader Rassoul, a much-loved Peace Corps Gabon administrator, had died from injuries sustained in a vehicle accident on Gabon's notoriously poor roads. He was wonderful, a superior who managed to be a friend, to so many. Although saddened by the news, it wouldn't hit me with full force until 2002 when, inexplicably, the inner mandate to write a novel set in Africa consumed me, resulting in a surreal ten-week marathon as I wrote and wrote and wept (never knowing *why*) and completed the first draft. Kader and his too-early death were on my mind constantly. Through my attempts to connect with those who knew Peace Corps Gabon and what might have happened to Kader, I also learned about the 1998 murder of Karen Phillips, a 37-year-old Peace Corps Volunteer, who was found dead the morning of December 17th, in Oyem, in the weeds, a hundred yards from her home. The horrifying details, the murky, unknowable nature of what had transpired, stunned me. Curiously, it was only in my 2017 revision that the shattering, irreversible implications sank into me and altered my story. No, this isn't Karen's story, not in the least. Likewise, Kader shows up nowhere in the story. But I felt their presence behind me, within me, as I wrote, and I see their presence in the finished product. And now I better understand, in ways I couldn't possibly fathom as a befuddled 22-year-old Midwesterner, the Africans' firm belief that the dead do not fully leave this world.

Creative writing itself is a mystical process. Not everything that arises makes sense, or is meant to be understood. (Pretty much like living in Africa.) With this in mind, I allowed my 2017 draft's culminating point to veer in an unexpected direction from its 2005 "completed" state. I was, in truth, reluctant to go where it was nudging me. It was a dark place, troubling, intensely uncomfortable to write. But a presence, the whisper of a female voice inside my head, said, *It needs to be this. Please. Do this for me.*

So I did. Which is why this book is dedicated in particular to Karen, whose murder in a foreign country dealt her and her family the rawest deal imaginable, something that breaks my heart into tiny pieces every time I ponder it. Karen would have liked my story's revised conclusion. She would have nodded, smiled, and said, "Yes. There. Now I feel more at peace."

More Books by Terez Mertes Rose

Off Balance, Book 1 of the Ballet Theatre Chronicles
http://amzn.com/B00WB224IQ

Alice thinks she's accepted the loss of her ballet career, injury having forced her to trade in pointe shoes onstage for spreadsheets upstairs. That is, until the day Alice's boss asks her to befriend Lana, a pretty new company member he's got his eye on. Lana represents all Alice has lost, not just as a ballet dancer, but as a motherless daughter. It's pain she's kept hidden, even from herself, as every good ballet dancer knows to do.

Lana, lonely and unmoored, desperately needs some help, and her mother, back home, vows eternal support. But when Lana begins to profit from Alice's advice and help, her mother's constant attention curdles into something more sinister.

Together, both women must embark on a journey of painful rediscoveries, not just about career opportunities won and lost, but the mothers they thought they knew.

OFF BALANCE takes the reader beyond the glitter of the stage to expose the sweat and struggle, amid the mandate to sustain the illusion at all cost.

Outside the Limelight, Book 2 of the Ballet Theatre Chronicles
https://amzn.com/B01M0NIIX0/

A Kirkus Indie Books of the Month Selection and a Kirkus Indie Top 100 Books of 2017

Ballet star Dena Lindgren's dream career is knocked off its axis when a puzzling onstage fall results in a crushing diagnosis: a brain tumor. Looming surgery and its long recovery period prompt the company's artistic director, Anders Gunst, to shift his attention to an overshadowed company dancer: Dena's older sister, Rebecca, with whom Anders once shared a special relationship.

Under the heady glow of Anders' attention, Rebecca thrives, even as her recuperating sister, hobbled and unnoticed, languishes on the sidelines of a world that demands beauty and perfection. Rebecca ultimately faces a painful choice: play by the artistic director's rules and profit, or take shocking action to help her sister.

Exposing the glamorous onstage world of professional ballet, as well as its shadowed wings and dark underbelly, OUTSIDE THE LIMELIGHT examines loyalty, beauty, artistic passion, and asks what might be worth losing in order to help the ones you love.

Praise for *Outside the Limelight*

"A lovely and engaging tale of sibling rivalry in the high-stakes dance world."

— *Kirkus Reviews* (Starred review)

"Balanchine said dance is music made visible; Terez Mertes Rose's *Outside the Limelight* is dance made readable. She reveals both the beauty of ballet and its pain in a compelling, deftly written novel that unfolds like a series of perfectly executed chaîné turns. Not to be missed!"

– Tasha Alexander, NYT bestselling author of *A Terrible Beauty*

"*Outside the Limelight* sweeps us backstage, through the wings, past the dressing rooms, and into the lives of its dancers, where we see them up close, flawed and beautiful."

– Adrienne Sharp, bestselling author of The True Memoirs of Little K and White Swan, Black Swan

"From the theater's spotlights and shadows comes a nuanced drama of pain and beauty without one false note. I didn't want it to end!"

– Kathryn Craft, award-winning author of *The Art of Falling* and *The Far End of Happy*

"Readers will relish this fresh, enlightened insider's look at two talented dancer sisters beset by professional rivalry & bound by love. This glowing novel is full of heart. Enchanting."

– Sari Wilson, author of *Girl Through Glass*

Praise for *Off Balance*

"A refreshing and gritty story about friendships, dreams, and life. The reason why this story works on so many levels is the author's ability to create characters that ring true. Terez Mertes Rose delves deep into her characters' back story to show how they really are: human and flawed. While her characters are off balance, Rose has balanced her novel perfectly."

— Self-Publishing Review, 5 Stars

"Terez Mertes Rose writes with an urgency that keeps us reading long past our bedtimes."

— Dance Advantage

"Any readers who have ever grappled to find the courage to strengthen or to soften, to embrace a dream or to let go of one, will find themselves rooting for the two willful, yet wounded, protagonists in Terez Mertes Rose's edgy debut, *Off Balance*. I loved this exquisitely written, fast-paced novel from the first page to the last."

— Sandra Kring, bestselling author of *The Book of Bright Ideas*

"A realistic and gripping account of the grittier side of ballet."

— Grier Cooper, former professional ballet dancer and author of *Wish* and *Hope*

Forthcoming in late 2020

**_Ballet Orphans_, Book 3 of the Ballet Theatre Chronicles
(a prequel)**

About the Author

Terez Mertes Rose (who also publishes as Terez Rose) is a former Peace Corps Volunteer and ballet dancer whose work has appeared in the *Crab Orchard Review*, *Women Who Eat* (Seal Press), *A Woman's Europe* (Travelers' Tales), the *Philadelphia Inquirer* and the *San Jose Mercury News*. She is the author of *Off Balance* and *Outside the Limelight*, Books 1 and 2 of the Ballet Theatre Chronicles (Classical Girl Press, 2015, 2016). She reviews dance performances for Bachtrack.com and blogs about ballet and classical music at The Classical Girl (www.theclassicalgirl.com). She makes her home in the Santa Cruz Mountains with her husband and son, where she is at work on a Ballet Theatre Chronicles prequel (which additionally connects *A Dancer's Guide to Africa* to the series).

Proof